THE GREAT DUCK MISUNDERSTANDING

and Other Stories

THE GREAT DUCK MISUNDERSTANDING

and Other Stories

The Very Best of American Fishing & Hunting Humor

Compiled by
BRIAN R. PETERSON

WILLOW CREEK PRESS

Published by Willow Creek Press,
P.O. Box 147, Minocqua, Wisconsin 54548

Editor: Andrea K. Donner
Design: Amy Kolberg

A Note on the Type
The text of this book is set in Palatino, named after Salvatore Palatino, who commissioned the typeface. Linotype and Stereotype jointly designed this type in response to the need for a typeface available in both digital and hot metal composition, and copyright theft in Germany, Canada, and other Low Countries. The roman is based on an engraving by Lord Fount Leroy, and the italic on the curves of George Garamond's Italian wife, Rosa. The type was first used in a privately printed edition of the Nordic epic, *The Song of Sven Stoolsoftnerson*. We hope you like it.

Library of Congress Cataloging-in-Publication Data

The great duck misunderstanding & other stories : the very best of
   American fishing & hunting humor / compiled by Brian R. Peterson.
      p. cm.
   ISBN 1-57223-983-2 (softcover : alk. paper)
   1. Fishing stories, American.   2. Hunting stories, American.
   3. Humorous stories, American.   I. Peterson, B. R.   II. Title: Great
   duck misunderstanding and other stories.
   PS648.F57G74 2005
   813'.0108357- -dc22
                                                    2005020435

Printed in the United States

For Nicole

Daughter Extraordinaire

Acknowledgements

The final selection of material may cause a midnight move into a witless protection program, and, if so, I'd like to take the informal advisors to this collection with me. They are serious, literate advocates of humor: Arthur DeLaurier, John Quaintance, George Reiger, John Orrelle, Ted Leeson, and Nancy Anisfield. Thanks to Tom Petrie, Publisher, and Andrea Donner, Managing Editor, of Willow Creek Press for their original interest in such nonsense and continuing patience and good cheer. Thanks to Katie McKalip of the Outdoor Writers Association of America for sounding a call for submissions and identifying an under-represented group, women writing funny and well about the outdoors. And a special tip of a spray-painted orange Filson® cap for the fine work and any hour access of my feral-hog/hunting boot busting pal and editor, Sal Glynn. The book would be much less complete if it wasn't for the due diligence of a number of publisher's permissions staff. Their quiet research and attention to detail are critical to any anthology. Of course, the truly brave are those contributors who decided, with great generosity, to display their wares in this ersatz collection. Each deserves a life of leisure or, if that's unlikely, at least someone to rub their feet at night.

Table of Contents

Introduction

Humor is serious business and it is no less serious when taken afield. Those who have spent any time in a good hunting or fishing camp know that humor is an integral part of their time away from home. What else can you do but laugh at how the elements, the fates, and the strong mind/weak body batter us? Where else can you really shed that urban veneer to laugh without purpose? Humor is applied in the camp, along a river, and in a duck blind much like a poultice. All members of the sporting society participate, from practical jokes on the most junior to gentle ribbing of the most senior. The humor can be very edgy but has its limits—whatever you do, you don't want to interfere with the possible success of a party member. Unless he's your brother-in-law. And your marriage was falling apart anyway.

Fishing stories are mixed with the hunting tales in these pages. Much too often, opposing camps form even in the same general recreation and it's time we learned and laughed about and with our field brethren. Insiders and practitioners you can trust have told most of these stories.

In a perfect world, a number of early funny folks would have reported from the sporting field: Odgen Nash, S. J. Perelman, and the Marx Brothers (although Groucho did a decent riff on elephant hunting). They were from an era when car ads talked about game being carried in the station wagon. James Thurber did come through and his story, "The Wood Duck," is included. The early cartoonists, especially those contributing to the *New Yorker*, did great takes on hunting and fishing, sometimes from the animal's point of view but with great aforethought.

The problem today is that most humor is about politics (national, sexual, racial, and religious). To further politicize hunting or even fishing makes both sides real cranky, especially since it has been observed that humor is now more rant than wit. But I would buy a front row seat to a Dennis Miller rant at a Bassmaster® weigh-in, and travel anywhere to watch Eddy Izzard announce an international fly-fishing competition. And I'd take George Carlin on a wild boar hunt. He would soon run short of the top seven words he couldn't say on television.

Humorists, especially those who write about hunting and fishing, have had relatively few outlets for their stuff, but this is generally true for all publishing. E.B. White early noted, "The world likes humor, but it treats it patronizingly. It decorates its serious artists with laurel, and its wags with brussels sprouts. It feels that if a thing is funny it can be presumed to be something less than great, because if it were truly great it would be wholly serious." The larger sporting magazines like *Field & Stream, Outdoor Life,* and *Sports Afield* (and the earlier *True* and *Argosy*) have long supported the humor arts, yet over the years, frustrated funny guys have had to turn to self-publishing. Selections from some of the best small run, privately financed books are within.

The collection includes some favorites of the best known practitioners and I've done my best to include the lesser known (no fault of theirs) sports. Some are introduced with great enthusiasm, while others need little introduction. Read the excerpts and then buy books by these funny people, and tell your local library to buy their books as well. They need the encouragement (money). My own taste in humor runs toward the spicy and some material may not seem appropriate to traditionalists and children under the age of two. I've included outdoor humor from unlikely sources and ask that the piece not be judged the piece by its author. For example, one writer may like to fish but not hunt deer or even like deer-hunters but if they write funny about the former, that piece is most likely included. One or two may be cranks of the highest order. If they write funny, they are included.

I must confess to an initial reluctance to wading through an enormous quantity of fly-fishing material. I'd never start a story about fly-fishing early in the day, especially while sitting and never in the prone position for fear of falling asleep, especially if the story was stimulated by a mid-life or wife crisis. Early in my search, fly-fishing humor seemed a most infrequent hatch. Nelson Bryant once described the emphasis of fly-fishing for trout as being on the ritual rather than the kill. As any humorist worth his or her salt knows, mindless ritual is a target-rich environment. A good humor editor also knows there is a built-in conflict between sincerely dispensed information and comic misinformation. While a good fly-fishing writer may be of good humor, the desire to teach can so easily flip-flop to preach by even the most experienced hand. But I was wrong. By all modern humor standards, there are quite a number of very funny fly-fishing stories and some of the best of those are included in this collection. In fact, funny stories about fly-fishing seemed easier to find than those about bait casting.

Writing humor is hard work. Anyone in the bleacher seats knows that the clowns are the circus and rodeo's hardest workers. Humor is best slow cooked and the hardest beat must be in newsprint. Its particularly hard to be witty and wise every week. Even top guns like Dave Barry have to hide for a while. Often the best you can hope for in your morning newspaper is good-natured ribbing and folksy anecdotal set pieces. Magazine writers have it a little easier (certainly in their word rate) and accompanying illustrations expand the copy.

Truly great humorous sport writing has a long history in our country, and skilled practitioners are being rediscovered. For example, writing in an early *Harper's Magazine,* Charles Einstein built a convincing case for what he called the "Red Smith Irregulars." In the article, Einstein points out that first and foremost, Red Smith (a sports writer for the *New York Herald*) was "commandingly literate." As an avid bass and trout fisherman, he could with deceptive ease throw off a definition of a black bass as a "derby-wearing, cigar-smoking fish to whom a hook in the mouth is no worse than a bad cold." Smith's description of a rainbow appearing during a bone-fishing expedition, "The colors were tastefully overdone, like a loan company calendar," elicited Einstein's and my "wow!" Several of Smith's best fillets are wrapped within, as are other members of the Fourth Estate. The best humor writers are typically very good writers first.

"Me n' Joe" stories have been a traditional format for outdoor writers but who could not enjoy the sophisticated character set pieces in Galen Winter stories about "The Major" and Corey Ford's shenanigans in his "Lower Forty Shooting, Angling and Inside Straight Club." Masters of this humor format are national treasures and are included. In this anthology, however, a reader will quickly learn that wackos need not be invented for humorous purposes. They are more likely to be your neighbors.

There is a special space reserved in these pages for humorists that didn't and don't write for a specific audience. Or, it seems, for profit. Satirist Tom Lehrer wrote political humor for himself, unlike the sycophants inside the Washington D.C. belt-line. Shel Silverstein certainly couldn't have been described as a needy public figure and he took no prisoners when talking about fishing. John Lurie, actor and jazz musician's pseudo-fishing show, *Fishing with John,* is perhaps the most unnecessary or most necessary fishing video ever. Lurie takes his special guests to some of the most dangerous and exotic places on earth. The ice-fishing segment with William Defoe at the northernmost point of Maine is the funniest sketch about that winter numbness. There certainly should be more room for such nonsense, more Edward Lear-like nonsense in outdoor humor

Because of the retrospective nature of parts of this collection, some worthy material could not be reprinted. Presses and authors disappear, and permissions from estates, relatives, and other no-goods were sometimes impossible to secure. Keith C. Russell's *The Duck-Huntingest Gentlemen: A Collection of Waterfowling Stories by Keith C. Russell and Friends* is worth the search: in particular the stories "Nolo Contendere" by Ferdinand J. Hruby, MD and "Smokin' 'Em" by Oakley V. Andrews. I re-discovered Frank Gannon's terrific wit too late to include a short piece titled "Duck!" in Vanna Karenina. Mea culpa to others I may have missed. Jerry Clower's hunting stories are not available for reprint. One of his best, "The Coon-Hunting Story," can be heard on his earlier tapes and in a book titled *Stories From Home.* Several of my most favorite Gene Hill's stories were also not available for reprint but "To Your Health" and "Why Not?" lighten his melancholic *A Hunter's Fireside Book.* An early lampoon of outdoor magazines could not be located, nor a video of Jonathan Winters imitating a large mouth bass. Gary Larson cartoons can only be reproduced in educational tracts. Everyone has their own favorite Larson cartoon, like the deer with a "bummer" bulls-eye birthmark on its chest and a deer hiding behind a tree from one of Larson's hunting bumpkins thinking, "He's trying to shoot me all right. Do I know this guy? I've got to think!" Only a few very good cartoons are included, as the intent was to find the funniest narratives. If this book were to be published in full color, Bill Buckley's entire new book, *Misery Loves Company: Waterfowling and the Relentless Pursuit of Self-Abuse,* would have been sewn in as it captures in great photographs the agony and ecstasy of duck and goose shooting.

Some authors are neglected. For example, Mark Twain's "The Hunting of the Cow" was passed on, not because it didn't display Twain's characteristic edge, but the take on Teddy Roosevelt's famous Louisiana bear hunt just didn't read funny. Readers will also not be burdened with dialect humor, which is probably best heard than read. Humor about foxhunting or African dangerous game is extremely scarce. The British pursued foxhunting and foxhunters in *Punch*-style editorial cartoons and the very best safari stories are only heard in hotel hospitality suites and in the bush. Stephen Budiansky does, however, do a bang-up job on describing modern foxhunting ("essentially an inner struggle against dashed hopes") in "Tallyho and Tribulation" (*The Atlantic,* September, 2000). Dangerous game and any humor related to the pursuit are both intrinsically high-risk. Safari and trophy room humor most often appeared in cartoon form, notably with the great John Fowler safari cartoons in early *Playboy* magazines.

Other subjects are neglected simply because an extended funny story about squirrel, pheasant, and rabbit hunting couldn't easily be found. If there is a funny story about spearing suckers and getting caught by the game warden with northerns in your hip boots or of pushing the fat butt of a gray squirrel into his hidey-hole as an act of mercy, please advise. If there is a funny story about flushing a pheasant with your nose while on a low crawl to a bustling duck decoy spread, or fiddling with a new variable scope, mistaking a spike buck for a doe, I haven't read it. Or wrote it.

Ed Zern formally reviewed ninety years of humor in *Field & Stream* in their July 1985 issue and his generous overview concluded with the thought that sometimes, "the outdoors is a laughing matter." He and other earlier outdoor humor greats created an appetite for the work of an extraordinary group of rascals writing with great wit about our favorite field sports.

This anthology was assembled with the hope of mining a tradition of good humor for my own amusement, then my hunting and fishing pals. My intention to include a responsible, representative sampling was originally as pure as the driven snow. However, once the tavern closed, all bets were off.

Brian R. Peterson

The Naming of Sawbuck Point

Steven Mulak

We leaned into the wind as we walked back across the sand flat. It seemed no matter how we twisted around and ducked our faces behind our hat visors, there was no escaping the sting of the blowing sand in the January wind. Finally, John stopped and unslung the load of eiders from his shoulder and pulled the hood of his parka over his head. He tightened the drawstring until there was only a tiny opening around his eyes. I followed suit. It was when we started off again that we first noticed the car parked next to my brother's old Blazer far ahead of us, and the person standing next to it watching us through binoculars.

Earlier, the trip out to the beach had gone much easier. In the pre-dawn darkness the wind had been at our backs, and all that we carried then were our shotguns and a box of shells in each pocket of our parkas. Without all our usual duck hunting equipment, John's dog probably thought we were out for an early jaunt along the beach. I should say here that one of the attractions waterfowling holds for me is all the nifty paraphernalia connected with the sport; camouflaged boats and decoys and blinds and canvas bags full of "stuff," all of it of the heavy-duty kind, guaranteed never to let you down. I like it all. But it's refreshing, too, to go pass-shooting every so often where none of the above is necessary: Just hunker down and blast away and have a ball—and bring plenty of shells.

Flocks of eiders followed the surf line around our point in order to get into the shallow bay beyond. They have a disinclination to fly over land, so their flight paths are fairly predictable where a sand spit or breakwater juts out from the shoreline. We didn't need a blind, just a place to blend into the beachscape. Ice floes can make a perfect hiding place, but the morning's wind and tide had combined to completely clear the beach. There were a few pieces of eroded salt marsh on the point, looking like great hunks of sod. They put us farther from the water's edge than we would have liked to be, but we crouched behind them and waited. Unlike hunting blacks and other "civilized" ducks, there is a certain prehistoric aspect to eider shooting, founded in the not-remote possibility that we might be the first humans ever seen by these ducks. It must be something like what all waterfowling was like a century or more ago.

Some flights stayed farther out at sea, but most cut the corner sharply and passed right in front of us, just a few feet above the breakers as they fought the wind. It was easy to pick out the strikingly black-and-white drakes from the drab hens and V-neck-marked immatures, but much tougher to hit them in the conditions of high wind and maximum range. They're far from wary, but they do have something of a collective instinct that will cause a flock to ease away from the beach if we were up and moving around at their approach. Deliberate and in cadence, their formations paraded by. When we'd spill one of the big birds, the others in the flock wouldn't flare or hardly miss a wingbeat. Rather, like the 18th century soldiers they so reminded me of, they would simply close ranks and push onward. Fife and drum music would not have been out of place.

Despite the cold, despite the wind, despite the blowing sand that quickly turned our automatics into single-shot guns that complained "Clean me!" in a gritty voice each time the action was worked, despite my needing more than two boxes of shells to take seven ducks, despite my having to put up with my brother singing snatches of "Sylvia's Mother" all morning long—despite all that, I managed to have a wonderful time. There is something rare and spectacular about duck shooting on a clear day, and the sky was the sort of cold blue that goes all the way to the horizon. The morning was full of visual images and Technicolor memories of big ducks and long distances and full choke words like "wallop" and "magnum." On one shot, I dropped a drake in the surf that was down but not out. When John's dog went after him the duck dove into an oncoming breaker and I could see the duck swimming inside the rising curve of the transparent wave. The birds were plentiful: Enough so that the serious fun that waterfolwing usually is with its long waits between too few shots turned into the whoop-'n'-holler sort of fun normally associated with catching pumpkinseeds and plinking rats at the dump. Eider are big, durable ducks, and in the wind even our tightly-choked loads of fours didn't always kill them outright and we had to chase several. We limited out before ten.

At this point I should say something about the table qualities of eiders: They are nonexistent. Eiders are the ducks they were talking about when they made up the "cook 'em with a brick" joke. Once we tried preparing them as dog food, but all we got was a dirty look from John's retriever. But if you'd like to try them, send me your address. I warn you, though, there'll be no backing out: Once I've got your name, you've got my eiders.

Who's that?" I had to raise my voice to be heard in the wind. John squinted a fast look at the person who had parked next to his rusted-out Blazer and shook his head. We plodded on toward the foot of the beach road, walking the Neanderthal-like walk of wader-wearers everywhere. In spite of the recent popularity of camouflage clothes and all things outdoor, we hardly looked like a page out of a fashion magazine: Our parkas were tattered and bleached out from one too many seasons on the salt marshes; our guns looked the way once-lovely guns always do after spending a few hours near salt water; our noses were running, and even John's dog was fighting off a late-season case of the mange.

As we approached the parking area, it became clear that the person who had been watching us was a middle-aged woman, and that she was very unhappy about something: Her frown radiated anger from 100 yards away. As if in juxtaposition to our appearance, she was nattily dressed in an expensive-looking trench coat with a matched set of Icelandic wool accessories. And, conspicuous by its absence, was the duck blood, sand, and feathers we both wore. Even her Saab seemed to make John's old duck hunting car seem all the more dilapidated. We stepped across the wire cable at the road's end and she came forward and lit into John: "You men are a disgrace! I've been watching you. There is no useful purpose in killing eider ducks. I should turn you both in! I even saw that one…" She pointed to me but I didn't look… "kill a duck that the dog retrieved by slamming its head on his gun butt. You're disgraceful—both of you! Eiders are peaceful ducks…"

She pronounced "eider" with a long "e," but other than that she was right: My shooting *had* been disgraceful! And maybe I should be reported: If the guys at the skeet club ever found out how lousy I'd shot, they'd ban me to the trap range forever. We were in every way legitimate: in season, within the limits, legally licensed, sufficiently stamped, properly plugged, earnest, square and forthright—even if we didn't look it. But hunters everywhere are on the defensive when they encounter someone like the Binocular Lady. I muttered a little prayer of thanks that she had cornered John and not me and snuck around and opened the tailgate of the old Blazer through the broken rear window. I piled both shoulder loads of ducks into the back. Right on the top, one of the eiders had his tongue protruding from his beak at a right angle, almost in a cartoon imitation of a duck that was down for the count, and another looked like we'd bludgeoned him to death. I closed the tailgate quickly.

Understand that my older brother is the sort of fellow who is so quiet that at times he seems to be killing time, waiting for something else to happen. I'm usually the one who asks permission to hunt or talks with game wardens or makes inquiries. He owns a restaurant, and should get used to dealing with people. At least, that's what I told myself as I cowered in the car, not daring to glance at the abusive scene playing outside the side window.

Right around the time I was beginning to seriously contemplate driving off by myself, John got in. He turned the ignition key (he leaves the keys in the Blazer, hoping someone will steal the old heap) and slid a ten dollar bill behind the overhead visor. He spoke without looking at me. "Don't say a word. Just look straight ahead." I didn't and I did. We drove off.

A quarter of a mile down the road John took a corner and pulled to the curb. "Listen to this…" He turned to me and the expression on his face contained the boyish delight I recalled from long ago—a look reminiscent of a time when little boys shared great secret plots and jokes together. He nearly giggled. "We'll have to give this sawbuck to DU, but you should have seen the look on that woman's face! Did you see it? It was great!"

I held up my hand. "What's going on? I don't know what you're talking about."

"This…" He held out the ten dollar bill. "That woman gave it to me—I mean GAVE it to me, for Chrissake!" He laughed out loud.

"Why?"

"Why? Because she thought we were poor or on relief or something. She said, 'I wish it could be more.' Why weren't you watching? It was beautiful!"

I was certain I had missed something in the conversation. "Wait a minute. The last I head, she was calling you a 'wanton murderer,' for God's sake. Now, I'm aware we both look like ragamuffins, but it's a big jump from being a murderer to being somebody a do-gooder gives money to. What the hell did you say to her?"

"I said…" He paused for effect, trying to look smug, but ruined it when he started giggling. "I said, 'Honestly, Lady, me and my retarded brother there only shoot enough to feed our family.'"

"In this fog they could be right on top of us and we'd never know it."

*Self-described as "the most humorless guy you'll ever want to know,"
author Ray Coppinger's small book,* Fishing Dogs, *is a tight, classy, yet
relatively unknown bit of humor. Coppinger is a retired yet still serious
scholar who, during a family vacation when he was left home to his own
devices, penned a just right romp on dogs as fishing companions. The
book's subtitle,* A Guide to the History, Talents, and Training of the
Baildale, the Flounderhounder, the Angler Dog, and Sundry Other
Breeds of Aquatic Dogs, *is an indication of great things to come, including nicely understated illustrations by Peter Pinardi. My hard-to-pick-a-
favorite fishing dog is the bow plunk dog.*

Bowplunk Dogs

Ray Coppinger

One of the more famous American ballast dogs is the bowplunk dog
known as the Maine bow dog. This breed was originally recognized by Mr. Barnaby Porter of Damariscotta, Maine. With his kind
permission, his breed standard is printed here for the first time, though
I'm sure such a fine description has probably been printed in other
places for the first time too.

Observations on the Maine Bow Dog
by Barnaby Porter
*It's time the Maine coon cat was put in its place. It has been highly
overrated as a breed all these years, and I'm not so sure anyone has a true
and accurate idea of just what makes a coon cat a coon cat anyhow. It's an
appellation that has come to have about as much meaning as "colonial
farmhouse." Rather common-looking balls of fluff are what they are.*

*Of much more convincing pedigree is a hardy and noble breed of dog,
heretofore not made much of because of its humble beginnings and conspicuous absence from the show ring. This is the magnificent Maine Bow Dog,
his name deriving from his deeply ingrained habit of standing, proud and
brave, on the bow of his master's boat as it plies the lively waters along the
Maine coast.*

There is nothing quite so moving as the sight of such a dog holding his station, ears flying and a big smile on his face, as his sturdy vessel bounds over the sparking whitecaps, his profile emblazoned on the horizon.

The points of conformation in the Bow Dog breed are far from strict. The dog's size, color and general appearance have nothing to do with it. Even pom pom tails are allowed. Good claws are the only mandatory physical attribute. It's mostly a matter of character and carriage. The animal must have superb footing and balance, and most important, he must display the eagerness and bravery of the true Bow Dog. A passion for boats and the water is essential, for the dog must be willing and able to maintain the classic stance, chin up and chest out, in even gale force winds.

Individual Bow Dogs may vary greatly in style, but their dedication to duty must be unquestionable. One I know, named "Wontese," who looks something like a Springer Spaniel, is such a glutton for cold and punishing duty that his uncontrolled but enthusiastic chattering has become legendary. Another, named "Duke," wears a sou'wester. Remarkable, these dogs.

Being in the Working Dog class, Bow Dogs are permitted the occasional slipup to be expected in the real world conditions under which they must perform. Mine, an almost flawless specimen, was most embarrassed one day when he broke stance for a brief moment to take a flea break. There was a blustery chop on the sea, and in a flash, he slipped ingloriously over the side, his gleaming claws raking the bow as he disappeared from sight. A valuable dog like that, I had to come around and fish him out of the waves. I hoisted his drenched bulk back aboard, and without so much as a thought about shaking off, he leaped up forward to where he belonged, brave and proud, ears flying.

That's a Maine Bow Dog if I've ever seen one. It made me proud to be his master.

Mr. Porter obviously knows his dogs, and he does a good job of reporting on the courage and nobility of this breed, which stands in the bows of fishing boats and looks good no matter what—even though there is great variability in the way they look. (This is lucky, however, because there is a similar variability in the looks of Maine fishing boats and even greater variability in the looks of Maine fishermen. Matching bow dog to boat should not be the problem it is with the baildales.) Mr. Porter seems unaware that his dog belongs to a functional breed classically known as the ballast dog, and though he does realize that the

FISHERMAN WITHOUT BOWPLUNK DOG

FISHERMAN WITH BOWPLUNK DOG

breed is highly functional, he misses the connection between the dog's function and its "conspicuous absence from the show ring," since it is not registered with any kennel club in the world, so far as I know.

The purpose of a ballast dog standing in the bow (the front, or pointy end of the boat) is to hold it down in the water while you paddle or steer from the stern. (The reason it is called the "stern" is because it is a very serious part of the boat, being where you hang the outboard motor, and steer from.) Trolling (named after the character who fished under bridges when you were a kid) also takes place in the stern. Really good bow dogs have an innate sense of "trim." As the speed of the boat increases, the dog leans farther and farther forward, keeping the boat "trimmed," or relatively even in the water.

Mr. Porter was on the right track when he listed the problem areas in Maine bow dogs. He correctly points out that they should be agile, as well as able to concentrate for long periods of time and avoid fleeting distractions. This means a good Maine bow dog really ought not fall overboard. Natural selection would have taken care of this problem years ago, if only fishermen would just keep going and tend to business instead of forgiving a fallen dog. But the dog is half of a closely-bonded team, and that attachment is rarely ruptured just because one member of the party made a mistake. Very few fishermen have the sheer Darwinian courage not to turn back in an attempt to rescue a fallen bow wow, and this prevailing softheartedness has been a large factor in the dog's morphology: a successful bow dog has a hefty scruff.

Hunting Camp Cook

Baxter Black

Fall is hunting season. Airports from Bozeman to San Antonio are filled with men in camouflage suits carrying gun cases out of Baggage Claim. They are here to stalk the fleeting deer and the wily elk. And, they bring with them millions in revenue, part of which winds up in the pockets of outfitters and guides.

Good hunting camps do much to attract hunters, often year after year. Some camps are elaborate, others Spartan, but all boast a good cook.

Hank's brother Dan ran a guide service in the Big Hole. He enjoyed much repeat business due, according to other outfitters, to his reputation of having the most entertaining camp in western Montana.

The star of the Big Hole Wilderness Experience and Wildlife Procurement Extravaganza was Big Eddie, a puppy-hearted pit bull/Power Wagon cross. At six foot six, 280 with a full beard, he took up a lot of room in a two-man tent. He was officially the camp cook.

There was a natural hot spring near the camp. Dan had tapped this resource by installing an eight-foot stock tank in the spring, thus creating the only hot tub on the mountain. One twilight, a member of the hunting party came in dog tired. He swung up the trail to the hot tub, anticipating a good soak before supper.

Unbeknownst to him, Big Eddie was basking in a little hot water therapy. As the hunter stumbled into the clearing, Big Eddie rose to his full height, shedding water like a three-hundred-pound buffalo robe, and covered himself in surprise! The frightened hunter wheeled, and ran into camp screaming there was a grizzly bear in the hot tub!

On another occasion, Big Eddie had stayed in camp during the day to watch the sourdough rise. From his tent that morning, he spotted a nice cow elk ease into a clearing near camp. Eddie grabbed his gun, chambered a shell, and stepped through the flaps. His dangling suspenders caught on the upright and jerked him over backwards. A shot rang out! The propane tank exploded! The supply tent caught on fire, disintegrating a pack train full of expensive, down-filled, waterproof, brand-name, guaranteed, color-coordinated, Davy Crockett-recommended, eco-approved, nothing-under-three-hundred-dollar stuff. Not to mention a couple of Weatherby rifles.

But despite his frequent Boone and Crockett screwups, Eddie had a way about him that reminded the visiting hunters that they were in the presence of a primitive force.

Eddie served stew one night. The whiner of the group stirred it with a spoon and then griped, "I don't like carrots." Big Eddie bent over the petulant hunter. He took the plaintiff's fork and picked the carrots out of his bowl one at a time, and ate them.

"There," he said.

Comatose
God of Fishing

John Louis Anderson

No sport has attracted the following among Scandinavian/ Americans that fishing has, and for good practical and theological reasons. First, all other sports require a lot of talking, running, or throwing things. Second, that state which other cultures and religions call nirvana—the condition of being at complete oneness with one's environment—is achieved by the Scandinavian only while fishing. Only fishing offers the perfect transcendental state: absolute silence (for lack of anything interesting to talk about), absolute motionless-ness (rivaled only by rigor mortis) and a total intellectual and sensory deprivation (broken only by mosquitoes).

Buford's Hawg Posse

Russell Thornberry

Buford Zurcges (pronounced "Zurks") had hog problems. His Texas Hill Country ranch, which was primarily an angora-goat-raising operation, was being overrun with wild hogs (pronounced "hawgs" in Texas). These feral hogs were a cross between the Russian boars that were imported into Texas in the early 1900s, and free-roaming domestic hogs. They were a problem to goat ranchers because they had developed a liking for goat flesh, and they were eating goats like it was going out of style.

Buford ran about ten thousand head of angoras, and since the hogs had moved in he was losing as many as six goats a night to them. He had tried everything to get rid of the hogs, but it was a losing battle.

They were totally nocturnal, so he couldn't find them in the daylight. He tried hunting them at night, but the hogs got wise in a hurry; as soon as they heard Buford's truck, they'd retreat into the thick brush and hide until he was gone again. He even tried hunting them at night with dogs, but on his first attempt the hogs killed three of his four hounds.

Once Buford found where the hogs had dug a crossing under his fence so he set a dynamite trap for them. He managed to blow one hog into a swine mist and destroy a great length of expensive fence. It seems that he also vaporized several goats with the explosion, making the dynamite approach something less than practical.

He tried live-trapping the hogs, baiting them with corn, but he caught only a couple of shoats that had not yet developed a taste for goat. Later he tried baiting his trap with a live kid, but all he caught was the kid's mother. Buford was at the end of his rope and desperate for a solution to his hog problem.

Buford ran into some of his neighbors at the coffee shop in town and told them about his hog problems. They were naturally sympathetic, since they were also losing goats to the all-consuming hogs. As the ranchers pondered their plight, Buford hit on a new idea.

"What about a posse?" he asked. "We could gather up all the hounds we got left and meet at my place. Then we could saddle up and foller the dogs on horseback, right in broad daylight. Then when the hounds get on a hawg, we'd be right there handy. We can pack our side irons and blow them hawgs away, once and fer all!"

The idea struck a chord with the ranchers. It was the best idea they'd heard yet. Not only was it a good idea; it appealed to the wild western cowboy that still lived within each of their hearts. It was going to be a real, "sho-nuff," Texas-style hawg hunt. There in the coffee shop, on that sunny April morning, the first "Hawg Posse" in Texas history was formed. In fact, it appeared that it was the first of its kind anywhere.

The following morning the trucks and horse trailers rolled into Buford's yard. There were a total of seven men in the posse, and between them they had eleven "hawg dogs," which ranged from redbones to blue ticks, along with some unidentifiable breeds that looked like they'd be more at home behind a high fence at the local junkyard. As the posse saddled their horses, the dogs worked out their social order with the usual tail sniffing and growling. A couple of times they broke into full-scale frenzied dog fights, but they were quickly subdued by the pointed toes of cowboy boots. At last the posse was ready. The men were sitting high in their saddles, with six-guns strapped to their hips. Except for the pack of dogs ahead of them, they looked for all the world like the James Gang heading out for a train robbery.

The posse left the yard in single file and turned west down the dirt road that headed toward the pasture where Buford had been suffering the greatest losses. The dogs ran ahead of the posse, with their noses to the ground, baying and yelping as they ran. A broad grin broke out across Buford's face. He knew he was holding a winning hand this time. The hogs were in for a big surprise.

A half mile later, the lead dog let out a mournful bay and left the road, heading south. The rest of the dogs immediately followed his lead. Their baying and yelping suddenly reached a fever pitch, and the chase was on.

"They're onna fresh track!" Buford yelled above the chorus of hounds. "Let's go get 'im!"

The cowboys spurred their horses into high gear and the race was on. The posse broke out of rank and spread out across the maze of narrow, meandering goat trails that wound through the mesquite brush.

Somewhere up ahead, above the wailing hounds, came the squealing screech of a big boar hog. The hounds were in an absolute frenzy. The riders steered their steeds toward the sounds.

As Buford broke into an opening at full gallop, he saw one of the redbone hounds lying lifeless beside the trail. It was split from one end to another. The boar had gutted the poor dog with one slash of his tushes. Buford reined his prize quarter horse to a halt and examined the pitiful hound. The poor critter was gasping his last, so in an act of mercy Buford pulled his .44 from his holster and ended the dog's agony.

In a matter of seconds Buford, with his horse Ginger, was back in the chase. It was a scene to behold: horses and riders thundering through the mesquite in a huge cloud of dust. They were closing in on the hounds, while the high-pitched screaming of the hog was clearly audible above the ruckus of the dogs.

Buster Creighten was in the lead and was the first to catch a glimpse of the hog. "Whoooeee!" Buster cried, waving his six-shooter above his head. "That's the biggest hawg I ever saw... betcha he'll go five hunnerd pounds!"

"There he goes!" howled Jimmy Bradshaw, above the roar of his .45. "Dang it," he groaned, "I shot one of muh own dogs!"

As the posse was closing in on the hog, Buford realized that the hog was heading straight for a page-wire fence. He figured the hog had a crossing dug somewhere under the fence and was going to try to dive through it to escape the posse.

"Oh, no ya don't!" Buford mumbled to himself, as he spurred Ginger on, and headed for the fence, as hard as he could go. He was flanking the rest of the posse, which was following the hounds.

Buford broke out of the brush onto the fire lane that paralleled the fence at the exact same second the hog appeared. He reined Ginger hard to the left, galloping headlong toward the hog. Buford was awestruck at the size of the boar. "No wonder I'm losing so many goats," he thought. "A hog that big could eat two or three goats a night, all by himself."

The hog saw Buford coming, and turned south, running as hard as he could down the fire lane. He was headed for his fence crossing alright, but with Buford and his horse bearing down on him, there was no time to slow down. The hog was getting winded. Buford could see him slowing down. There was only a hundred yards left between Buford and the hog. Behind him, Buford heard the other riders and the dogs. The distance quickly dwindled as the big mare's hooves pounded in rhythmic thunder down the fire lane. Ginger was flying; her gait so smooth that she seemed to float above the ground. Buford was leaning ahead in the saddle like a professional jockey.

Letting go of the reins with his right hand, Buford pulled his .44 caliber six-shooter out of its holster. There was a particular rhythm that he could feel. As Ginger flew past the left side of the weary hog, Buford would swing the pistol down and shoot without ever slowing down. That way Ginger could maintain her smooth floating gait, and aiming would not be hindered by having to hang on.

With the fence forming a barricade to his right and the horse closing tight to his left, the big hog, unused to marathon running, was in trouble. He tried to pick up speed, but there was nothing left in reserve. He had good speed for short bursts, but he was not designed to outrun quarter horses over the long haul. The ground was trembling as Ginger came thundering down on him.

Buford pulled the hammer back on the pistol and extended it downward to his right, in line with the hog. It would be over in a second. The speeding quarter horse dissolved the remaining distance. Fifteen yards… ten yards… eight… five.

Through gritted teeth, Buford said, "You can kiss yer goat-eatin' carcass good-bye," and he drew aim at the faltering hog.

The hog was finished and he knew it. He couldn't run another step. In a mad, desperate, last-ditch bid for survival, the hog bolted hard to his left, in front of the oncoming horse and rider.

Buford already had a bead on the hog when it suddenly cut to the left in front of him. His trigger finger was committed and there was no turning back. He swung the pistol to the left, following the hog, and fired, all in one fluid movement, hitting Ginger squarely between the ears. The thundering of her hooves suddenly ceased, and for a brief second Buford and Ginger were literally sailing ahead through space, propelled by the horse's great speed. However, as gravity got involved, Ginger and Buford's sailing was transformed into a thunderball collision of man, horse, and dry Texas dirt. It was a terrifying sight. Through the dust cloud the other riders could see the whirlwind of arms, legs, saddle and hooves, as Buford and Ginger seemed to meld into one huge rolling mass.

When the dust settled, the rest of the posse stood in a circle around Buford's mangled body. "Ya reckon he's dead?" Buster inquired dryly.

"Dang sure oughta be," said Bernie Stubbs, as he respectfully removed his hat. "That's the worstest dang horse wreck I ever seen!"

Eventually the posse noticed that Buford was still breathing, so they took him to the hospital. His injuries, while multiple and serious, were not fatal. More injured was Buford's pride. After all, he had earned the dubious distinction of being the only man ever to have shot his own prize quarter horse out from under himself while at a full gallop.

The posse never assembled again, and as for Buford's hog problems, he's still got 'em. But since the hawg posse incident, Buford has mellowed toward many things in life, not excluding hogs.

"Yer just natcherly gonna lose some goats if yer a goat rancher," he'll tell you. "Ain't nothin' much ya can do about it either. Guess them hawgs gotta make a livin' too."

A Good Mountain Pony

Russell Thornberry

As I painfully recall the horses of my hunting past, I can identify each one by some part of my body that no longer functions the way it did before. I should also explain that I'm no featherweight. Throughout my adult life I have consistently tipped the scales at over two hundred pounds. The subsequent discrimination is all too apparent at the corral gates. I can walk up to an outfitter's corral and, from a hundred head of horses, instantly point to the animal that will be mine. He's the one that pulled the Budweiser Wagon for thirty years before graduating to mountain trails. Mountain trails is another term for purgatory, where he'll plod out the remainder of his life before going on to fill hundreds of wonderful cans of Dr. Ballard's premium dog food.

He will stand a head taller than any horse in the corral, and his feet will fit snugly into a size XXL pie plate. His eyes will generally be two different colors and usually, they'll drift around in his head, totally independent of one another. According to the outfitter, this unique characteristic enables him to keep one eye on the rider and the other on the trail. My opinion is that it's the product of numerous slaps across the forehead with a two-by-four.

My horse will have no knees! He'll somehow hump up and down the mountains without bending his legs at all. His bone-jarring gait comes in three speeds: slow, slower, and dead still. And the rider has no control over which speed the horse will choose or when he will choose it.

Two things terrify such a horse: being first in line and being last in line. He cannot stand the pressure of leading, because he has no idea of where he's going, and yet he also lives in fear of being the last one there! His fears subside when he's somewhere in the middle of the procession. Such a horse will follow the horse in front of him right to his death, but don't ask him for any act of creative independence.

Reins are essentially useless as a steering mechanism on a mountain pony. I have reefed back on the reins so hard that my steed's head was upside down and backwards, staring me right in the eyes, while I was still in the saddle, and it had no apparent effect on his chosen speed or direction. I'm convinced that reins are attached only so the rider will have something to do with his hands while riding.

And then there are the names. Spunky names like Clyde, Fred, Jake and Toad. Happy names like Widowmaker, Snake and Stomper. Encouraging names like Pokey, Gimp and Buckets. But names really mean very little, since every hunter renames his steed shortly after the hunt begins. Those names are inevitably more suited to the horse's true personality or lack thereof: Brain Damage, Dim Bulb, Dr. Ballard, Bear Bait, and others too precious to mention.

I once rode a magnum-size gelding who answered to nothing, so I called him Safeway. The name was derived from the fact that he never stopped eating. He was always full of groceries. Safeway's favorite dish was bushes. On one occasion I tied him to a ten-foot willow while I stalked a caribou. When I returned he had eaten the entire willow, including the roots, and was in the process of swallowing his halter, which I suppose he thought was part of the bush. When Safeway stopped at a stream to drink, he would top it off with a mouthful of rocks.

He was brainlessly happy most of the time, but when it came to crossing a marsh or muskeg his otherwise docile personality was transformed into that of a raging maniac. As soon as Safeway heard the splashing of the horses ahead of him entering a muskeg, I could feel him turn to solid steel between my knees. He became so tense and rigid that he could barely walk. As soon as he felt the spongy ground beneath his feet he lunged ahead with all his might, paying no attention whatsoever to where his feet landed. His driving and lunging invariably sank him to his ears in the bog. His eyes would roll back in terror and his huge feet flew like a treadmill, throwing half-acre pieces of muskeg in every direction. The harder he fought, the further he sank until, eventually, the only sign of him was the muffled sound of his blowing and farting somewhere down there in the oozing quagmire. With all the riders and trail hands hauling on the halter and screaming and cursing in unison, Safeway would eventually emerge, covered in slime and gasping his last. As soon as his feet hit solid ground he'd stop and eat a bush or two and carry on again as if nothing had happened. This routine would sometimes take place four or five times a day. I learned to eject myself from the saddle at the first sign of an upcoming muskeg.

I had the unique pleasure of riding another mountain pony named Friendly. I was immediately suspicious of his name but he was a handsome horse. Both eyes were the same color and his feet were not oversized, so I gratefully accepted Friendly as my transportation for the hunt. He was a pleasure to ride and he handled like a dream. He picked his way carefully through muskegs and was as sure-footed as a mountain goat. Eventually I gained such confidence in Friendly that I'd actually doze off and leave the driving to him. It was during one of those brief naps that I learned of Friendly's single flaw. While I was nodding off, I was suddenly thrown to the ground with a bone-jarring crash. I looked around in stunned surprise to see Friendly lying on the ground beside me, shaking his head in a daze. It appeared that my sure-footed steed had run into a tree.

The wrangler who was riding in the lead looked back over his shoulder at us, sprawled there on the ground, and said, "You'll have to keep an eye on Friendly. He falls asleep walkin'. He'll run right into trees or walk over cliffs. Just keep an eye on him."

"Thanks loads for the information," I retorted.

For the rest of the trip I talked constantly to Friendly. When no one was looking I even shared my coffee with him, in hopes that it would keep him awake. I told him stories and sometimes even sang to him, especially on narrow mountainside trails. The rest of the trip went well. A couple of years later, when booking another trip with the same outfitter, I asked how Friendly was getting along. Sadly I learned that Friendly was no more. He was sleepwalking on a railroad track, apparently in a very deep sleep, when a train ran over him. Thankfully, no one was riding him at the time.

The official publications of state fish and game departments are an occasional source of outdoor humor. For 23 years, Harold Umber was the editor of North Dakota Outdoors *until he retired in early 2002 and, in one particularly nice piece of "geezer" humor, he wrote a list that older sportsmen could understand and appreciate.*

You Know You're An Old Guy

Harold Umber

YOU KNOW YOU'RE AN OLD GUY

1. When you clear the condensation off your glasses and you can't see any better than when they were steamed.
2. When your eyes water and you aren't facing the wind.
3. When you tell yourself you'd rather mow the lawn than go hunting on opening day.
4. When the cranes are in and you stayed in town to watch the parade.
5. When the most vivid sound you hear while hunting is your feet hitting the ground.
6. When everyone you meet calls you sir.
7. When you lose more shells than you shot.
8. When the only persons you can find to hunt with are the other old guys.
9. When someone asks you how road hunting has been and you are not insulted.
10. When the young son you faithfully trained as your hunting partner hunts with some other guy's son that he faithfully trained as his hunting partner.
11. When the old guy you are hunting with yells, there is a grouse flying over your head and your response is... what?
12. When mallards come into your decoys, your partner shoots three times and you don't even wake up.
13. When you forgot to reload after your last miss and blame your gun.
14. When the gravel road that takes you to your hunting grounds is marked 80th Street North.
15. When your wife wants you to go hunting.

16. When your response to questions is, "I feel strongly both ways."
17. When the shotgun and rifle you hunt with aren't made anymore.
18. When the only duck you shoot all day has teeth and you're happy about it.
19. When the last outdoor magazine you subscribed to lapsed in 1955.
20. If you argue that the steel fishing rod you use is more sensitive than this modern graphite stuff.
21. When your friends tell your hunting stories better than you do.
22. When both you and your dog have gray hair.
23. When the suspenders on your hunting pants are always twisted in the back.
24. If you remember when Garrison Diversion was not a political issue.
25. When the ownership of land you used to hunt was owned by the present owner's father.
26. If your thermos has a glass liner.
27. If all your hunting photos are black and white.
28. If your duck decoys are made of reeds.
29. If your medication takes up as much room in your lunch box as your sandwiches.
30. When you start wearing your long underwear beginning on Labor Day.
31. If your first shotgun was a new Model 97 Winchester.
32. If you turn down your hearing aid so your nap is not disturbed by your partner blowing his duck call.
33. If your duck boat and decoys are made of wood.
34. If your friends in the cemetery outnumber your friends at the high school reunion.
35. If you remember when duck stamps cost a dollar.
36. If you remember when there was no such thing as a 3-inch magnum.
37. If you refer to the U.S. Fish & Wildlife as the Bureau of Biological Survey.
38. When the only four-wheel drive vehicles in the country were surplus World War II army jeeps.
39. If your hunting boots come up to your knees and are made of genuine leather.
40. If the last time you went deer hunting you brought your license from the hardware store and you didn't have to wear florescent orange.

P.S. Harold says that one of the best things about retirement is "you can hunt on a Tuesday, Wednesday and Thursday and Friday if needed."

Brave Hunter, Stout Woodcock

P.J. O'Rourke

Some of the best bird covers are old garbage dumps. The word *cover,* used in the sense of hunting ground, is a variant of *covert,* although there is nothing M.I.-6-ish or Mossad-like about game birds as far as I can tell. Birds do not go to the dump because they're thinking that's the last place I'd look for creatures of natural beauty and untamed grace. Nor do they need to. Given my faculties as a sportsman and the skills of the dogs with which I hunt, birds could hide in the foyers of bed-and-breakfasts, in bowls of wax fruit.

Birds go to the dump because—I hate to break this to Friends of the Earth—animals have no aesthetics. Eels congregate in the sludge on the bottom of New York Harbor. Trout bite on feather, fur and tinsel dry flies as ugly as Barbie clothes. To a raccoon, a trash can is Paris in May. Rabbits desert the most elaborate nature refuges to visit your ill-planned and unweeded vegetable garden. Wild geese adore golf courses, even the unfashionable public kind.

Considering animal taste, I'm not sure I want to know why birds are attracted to dumps. And considering my own taste—gin slings, madras pants, Ed McBain novels, Petula Clark LPs—I'm not sure I want to know why I'm attracted to bird hunting. But I will try to make sense of the matter.

I've been shooting in New Brunswick, Canada, for a decade. Usually 8 or 10 of us make an outing in the fall. We are an ordinary lot, halfway through life's actuarial leach field and pretty well-fixed. We're not likely to be tapped for a Benetton ad.

Some of us are avid hunters and deadly shots, and some of us have a gun that doesn't fit and needs a different choke and the safety keeps sticking. I was using the wrong size shot and too light a load. I'm beginning to get arthritis in my shoulder. I have a new bifocal prescription. My boots hurt. The sun got in my eyes.

This is not one of those men-go-off-in-the-woods hunting trips full of drink, flatulence and lewd Hillary Clinton jokes. For one thing, some of us aren't men. A couple of us aren't even Republicans. We pack neckties, sport coats, skirts and makeup (although I don't think anyone wears all four). There is little of the Cro-Magnon in this crowd. Though there *is* something about three bottles of wine apiece with dinner and six-egg breakfasts… Did somebody step on a carp? And you've heard about Hillary whispering to Bill, "Give me 10 inches and hurt me!" So he made love to her twice and played golf with Newt Gingrich.

Our New Brunswick sojourn is not a wilderness adventure either. We're no Patagonia-clad apostles of deep ecology out getting our faces rubbed in Mother Nature's leg hairs. And we're too old to need a 30-mile hike, a wet bedroll and a dinner of trail mix and puddle water to make us think life is authentic. If we'd wanted to push human endurance to its limits and face the awesome challenges of the natural elements in their uncivilized state, we could have stayed home with the kids.

No. We spend the first half of the shoot in the deep woods but at a good lodge with an excellent chef. The chef not only cooks six-egg breakfasts and Bordeaux-absorbent dinners but also packs delightful lunches for us; for example, moose sandwiches, which are much better—also smaller—than they sound.

For the second half of the shoot, we drive to the Bay of Fundy and stay at a handsome inn where the sensible innkeepers bring out the old bedspreads and second-string towels so there will be no need to apologize for the mess left by gun cleaning, dog brushing and male-pattern baldness. The innkeepers also let us into their kitchen to cook what we've killed. Some of us may not be brilliant shotgunners, but we are all serious game cooks, even though I'm not used to cooking on a commercial gas range, and shouldn't there be some kind of government standards concerning brandy flammability?

The Bird: Rapture With a Scolopax Minor

What we are hunting in New Brunswick is mainly woodcock, *Scolopax minor,* a chunky, neckless, blunt-winged, mulch-colored bird with a real long beak and a body the size, shape and heft of a prize beefsteak tomato. Rereading that sentence, I see I have failed to capture in prose the full measure of the woodcock's physical attractiveness. Probably because it looks like a knee-walking shorebird in urgent need of Jenny

Craig. It does have lovely eyes. And a wonderful personality, too, for all I know. Anyway, the woodcock is, in fact, a cousin of the sandpiper and the snipe but makes its home on less-expensive real estate.

Woodcock live in the alder patches that occupy, in horizon-knocking profusion, the numberless stream beds and vast marsh bottoms of New Brunswick's flat, damp topography. The alder is a pulpwood shrub whose branches grow in muddled sprays like bad flower arrangements. Hunting in young alder thickets is like walking through something with a consistency between Jell-O and high hurdles. Old alder thickets, which grow as high as 12 feet, present grim, decaying vaults of face-grabbing, hat-snatching limb tangles. But the alder thickets where the woodcock roost are, like us, in their middle years. And these have all the bad features of alders young and old, plus a greasy mud footing and foliage that, even in late fall, is as dense as salad.

Once such a mess of alders has been entered, it becomes impossible to tell the time of day or where you are supposed to be going or whence you came, and the only thing you know about your direction is it's not the one the dog's headed in. Every now and then you come upon a dump. The overturned cars and abandoned refrigerators are, at least, landmarks. And if you've been in the alders long enough, they're a positive delight to the eye. The old woodsman's adage about being lost is "always go uphill." This is a problem in New Brunswick, which doesn't have much in the way of uphills; indeed, the entire province seems to sit on a downhill slope. Anyway, based on my own experience, the only thing going uphill when you're lost does is give you a terrific view of places you've never seen before.

The woodcock are in the alders because the soil there is full of earthworms, which is what the woodcock eat. The flavor of all birds is notably influenced by diet. A Canada goose shot in a field of corn is a treat. A Canada goose shot on the fourth green and filled with fertilizer and lawn chemicals is disgusting. Fish-eating ducks taste like fish that have been eaten by ducks. Woodcock are delicious. This raises the worrying thought that we really should be hunting and frying night crawlers. They are certainly easier to find and kill. But worm-digging gear is not going to look stylish in an Orvis catalog.

The Dog: Intelligent, yet French

You need a dog to hunt woodcock. Most pointing dogs can be trained to do it, but the breed of choice is the Brittany, a knee-high orange-and-white canine about as long as he is tall with no tail worth the mention and looking like an English springer spaniel with a better barber and a marathon-running hobby. Brittanys were bred in the eponymous province of France about 150 years ago specifically for woodcock hunting. They have a character that is both remote and excitable—yappy and grave at the same time, something like a John Simon theater review. Brittanys are very intelligent, whatever that means. Does a very intelligent dog have a good and logical explanation for humping your leg?

What a Brittany has, in fact, is an intense, irrational, foolish, almost human desire to hunt woodcock. He possesses several techniques. He can run into the alder cover and flush a bird that is much too far away. *Flushing* is what a hunter calls it when a dog scares a bird silly and makes it fly. It will then fly in any direction that your gun isn't pointed. This as opposed to *pointing,* which is when a dog scares a bird even sillier and makes it sit down. The Brittany can also run into the alder cover and point a bird that is much too far away. When a Brittany points, he goes absolutely rigid and still (and does so in a way that makes him look like he's about to hike a dog football or moon a dog sorority house rather than in that paw up, tail out, King Tut tomb-painting posture that dogs have on place mats from the Ralph Lauren Home Collection). The Brittany wears a bell around his neck. The idea is to keep track of the dog in the woods by following the noise of the bell. Then, when the dog goes on point, the bell will stop ringing and you're suppose to head directly toward... You understand the problem. Brittanys may be intelligent, but the people who thought up the bell were, to put it bluntly, French.

The Brittany can also do what he's supposed to do and hunt right in front of you—"working close," as it's known—in which case he'll walk over the top of the woodcock, leaving you to flush it yourself by almost stepping on the thing, whereupon it will fly straight in your face with an effect as nightmarish as a remake of Hitchcock's *The Birds* starring Michael Jackson and Lisa Marie.

The Shot: It's Not the Bird That Has to Worry

When everything goes exactly right, which is none of the time, the Brittany will go on point someplace where I can see him do it. I'll "walk up" the woodcock, which will take flight at an obliging distance. The woodcock has powerful breast muscles and is capable of almost vertical ascent. It will rise above the alders, beating its wings so fast that its feathers make a loud whistling sound. Then, in a motion called "towering," the bird will pause for a moment before flying away. This is when I take my shot. And, assuming that the alders haven't jammed my hat down over my eyes or knocked the gun out of my hand and assuming that I remembered to load my gun in the first place and that I haven't stepped on the dog while walking up the bird and gotten myself bitten on the ankle, then—if my hand is steady and my aim is true and nothing blocks the way—I'll miss.

I regard it as armed shopping, a tame pursuit when you think about it. Going to the grocery store is what's bloodthirsty. Consider all of those Perdue oven stuffers you've bought for dinner over the years. How many of them had any chance at all? You mighty nimrod, you. Every one you stalked, you killed. Whereas for me, there's hardly a bird that comes before the barrels of my gun that doesn't get away free. Nay, better than free: The bird receives an education about what those orange and hairy—and pink and winded and pudgy—things are doing in the woods. I am a university for birds.

Birds of course do get shot on these trips, even if not by my gun. And the dog is actually as important to finding dead birds as he is to missing live ones. Woodcock possess almost perfect camouflage, and, while difficult to see when living, they—for some reason—disappear completely into the leaf mold once they've been killed. It is hard to imagine what Darwinian benefit there is to an invisible corpse. Though there may be one. If the thing that eats you can't find you when you're ready to be eaten, maybe that gourmand will give up on the whole enterprise. It's a modification of the oyster defense mechanism, which is to look incredibly snotlike at mealtime. In fact, there are a number of interesting evolutionary questions about woodcock. How'd they lose the beach-front condo? Why would anyone migrate to New Brunswick? And how come they eat worms? Is it a bet or something? According to Guy de la Valdene's authoritative text on the woodcock, *Making Game* (Clark City Press), *Scolopax minor* has lived in North America since the middle Pleistocene, for a million and a half years. But there were no earthworms on this continent until the seventeenth century. They were introduced in potted plants from Europe and Asia. Before 1600, were the woodcock sending out for Chinese?

That dogs are able to find birds, alive or dead, is not surprising. Dogs more or less "see" the world through their olfactory sense. (Therefore, what I look like to a dog after a long day in the alders is something I won't dwell on.) Woodcock—to judge by our dogs' behavior—must smell to a Brittany like coffee in the morning or Arpège at night. The surprising thing, rather, is that hunting dogs don't leap on the live birds or gobble the dead ones. The whole point of breeding bird dogs is to come up with a pooch who—contrary to every imaginable predatory instinct—doesn't catch his prey. He lets you, with your shotgun, do it for him. (Or not. It is a fact known only to bad shots that dogs smirk.) Suppose you sit a six-year-old boy on the end of a dock with a fishing pole and every time the bobber goes under, you grab the rod and land the fish. Suppose you get the child to put up with this all day—and not only that but like it.

And pointing is only half of what dog breeders have accomplished. The dog also retrieves. Imagine you found a Guess? jeans model in your front yard, naked, covered in baby oil and intensely interested in affection. And suppose you carefully picked her up, being sure not to hug her too tightly or return any intimate caresses, and delivered her to your next-door neighbor, the guy who's had your Skilsaw since last February and always lets his crab grass go to seed.

The Prize: A Bird in the Pan…

I have no idea what dogs get out of hunting. And once I started to think about that, I realized I don't have much of an idea what people get out of hunting, either.

Partly it's a social thing. All of us on the trip are good friends, and it's nice to be off together in a place for which our bosses and offices can never quite figure out the area code. ("Where was that you said you were going? New Orleans? New Guinea? New Jersey?") But we could go to each other's houses and turn off the phones and run through the shrubbery in our old clothes, if we wanted.

There's nature appreciation. But, although New Brunswick has some appealing coastal vistas and some handsome salmon rivers, the province is not a scenic wonder, and the land we hunt is no prettier than the average Ohio cornfield. Still, we do appreciate it. There's something about being out in nature with a purpose—even if that purpose is only to torment dogs and scare feathered creatures—that makes you pay more attention to the outside world. A hike is such a pointless thing, no matter how wonderful the view. When you hunt, you have to keep a careful eye on weather, terrain, foliage and dangerous animals such as me if I happen to be in the cover with you, swinging my gun around in every direction trying to get the safety to release. There's even a religious aspect to a detailed examination of the outdoors. The universe, on close inspection, seems hardly to have been an accident. Or, if it is an accident, it's certainly a complexly ordered one—as if you dropped mushrooms, ham, truffles, raw eggs, melted butter and a hot skillet on the kitchen floor and wound up with an omelet. That said, the alder patches are something God created on Monday, after a week-end toot.

Hunting also produces a good, solid sense of false accomplishment. After a long day of bird getaways and gun bungles, of yelling at dogs and yourself, you really think you've done something. You don't get this feeling from any other recreation. Probably it's a throwback to the million years or so that man spent thumbing through the large stone pages of the Paleolithic L.L. Bean catalog. The cave paintings of Lascaux, after all, depict bison hunts, not tennis matches.

The fact that my friends and I don't have to hunt to get food may actually be our reason for hunting. Fun can be defined as "anything you don't have to do." Or is that right? You have to eat. And eating is the one sensible thing that we do on this trip.

Woodcock is almost fatless and can be cooked as rare as steak without a chicken tartar effect. Woodcock has a slightly liverish flavor, but it is liver to make a Neoplatonist of you. This is the cosmic ideal of liver, liver in the mind of God or, anyway, in the mind of Mom— liver that tastes like your mom thought you should think it tasted.

The only real meat on a woodcock is the breast. When cleaning a woodcock, you can split the breast skin with you thumbs and pull the muscle off the carcass. Take this, cut it in half and roll the halves around in a hot frying pan in good olive oil with a little salt and pepper and maybe a dash of Worcestershire sauce and a sprinkle of rosemary, and you've got... something nobody else in the house will touch. It's ugly as a sea slug and smells like tripe, but it tastes superb. We use the drumsticks as hors d'oeuvres, a kind of snob's answer to buffalo wings. Really serious woodcock cooks sauté the "trail," the intestines, and serve them on toast. We're not that serious.

We have meals of high savored woodcock, served with steaming heaps of fiddlehead ferns picked from the nearby woods and bowls of piping New Brunswick potatoes, small as golf balls and sweet as pies, plus rolls and buns and scones and jiggling plates of wild foxberry jelly and pots, tubs and buckets of strong drink and desserts beyond telling besides.

Here at last is something I really *am* good at. I can tuck in with the best of them. And I get better at it every year. I have the let-out pant seats to prove it.

When dinner is over, we yaw and waddle away from the table and back to our rooms for one more drink or three or five and to make some truly inventive excuses for our shooting—"I was thinking about my ex-wife and I pulled the trigger too soon"—and to tell each other various bits of highly improbable avian lore. Then we are up again at dawn to hunt the other fine item of prey that New Brunswick offers—duck.

The Proud Tradition: Man, War and Duck

One of our guides on these trips, Robert, is an expert on ducks. He can call ducks, shoot ducks, make duck decoys, name from memory every kind of duck found in North America and give each kind its Latin moniker. Robert can tell you everything you want to know about ducks except why anyone would ever go hunt them.

The idea of duck hunting is to get up about the time that people who are having fun in their lives are going to bed and get dressed in dirty flannels, itchy thermal underwear, muddy hip boots, clammy rain ponchos and various other layers of insulation and waterproofing, then clamber, trudge, wade, stumble and drag yourself miles into a swamp while carrying coolers, shell boxes, lunch buckets, flashlights, hand warmers, Buck knives, camp stoves, toilet paper, a couple of dogs and 40 or 50 imitation ducks, then sit in a wet hole concealed by brush cuttings and pine boughs until it's dark again and you can go home. Meanwhile, the weather will be either incredibly good, in which case the ducks will be flying in the clear sky thousands of feet above you, or incredibly bad, in which case the ducks will be landing right in front of you, but you won't be able to see them. Not that any actual ducks are required for this activity, and often none are sighted. Sometimes it's worse when they are. The terrible thing about duck hunting is that everyone you're with can see you shoot and see what you're shooting at, and it is almost impossible to come up with a credible excuse for blasting a decoy in half.

A couple of years ago, I was in Bosnia covering the war there for *Rolling Stone.* And I was hunkered down in a muddy trench, behind a pile of shrubbery and tree branches, watching tiny Serbs attack in the distance. "This seems familiar," I thought. It was indeed the very image of duck hunting (although, for some reason, this time the ducks had the guns).

And sure enough, one month later to the day I was hunkered down in a muddy trench behind a pile of shrubbery and tree branches with Robert and my pals. It was pissing down rain. I'd forgotten my pocket flask. Somebody had left the sandwiches in the bottom of the canoe and they'd turned into bread-and-mayonnaise soup. The glass liner had broken inside the coffee thermos. Everybody was out of cigarettes. And the dog had rolled in something awful. Of ducks, there were none. Not even any bottom-feeding coot, the recipe for which is:

PLANKED COOT
Arrange bird on a one-inch-thick kiln-dried oak plank.
Roast in oven for two hours at 350 degrees.
Baste every 20 minutes with a red wine, olive oil, vinegar
   and garlic clove marinade.
Throw the coot away and eat the plank.

It is only natural that war and hunting are of a kidney. Hunting has been intimately connected with warfare since the beginning of civilization. And before the beginning of civilization there probably wasn't a difference. The traditional leisure activity of archers and lancers and knights and such, when not killing people, was to kill other things.

We don't need hunting in the modern world. It makes the wilderness so primitive. It upsets actresses and undergraduates. And, anyway, we can easily bag a cheeseburger out the window of our car. But we do need war. At least I assume we do—to judge by the amount of it that's going on in the world at any given moment. And it's my theory that the entire purpose of the annual hunting trip is to make war look, comparatively speaking, like fun.

First published in *Men's Journal*, November 1994.

A Cover Story

Outdoor magazines routinely use humor between covers but rarely, so very rarely, on the front cover. Reynold Brown was one of the best artists able to communicate great sporting humor on the cover of a national magazine; not just once but three times in the mid-1950s, all for Outdoor Life. *A March, 1952, cover featured the Brown family doctor testing a rod in a sporting goods store. The two included here are "Big Game Taxidermy" from the December, 1952, issue (below) with Reynold's high school art teacher, Lester Bonar, holding the rabbit and Mrs. Brown's brother Pete, behind the counter. "Tall Fish Story" (page 46) covered the March, 1954 issue with a neighbor, Al Sugden, starring as the model for the final cover.*

The most famous song that takes aim at bad hunters was, of course, written by Tom Lehrer, considered by many to be our most famous living satirical song-writer. The creator of such classics as "The Vatican Rag" and "Poisoning Pigeons in the Park" could be counted on to shoot from the lip.

The Hunting Song

Tom Lehrer

I always will remember
'Twas a year ago November,
I went out to hunt some deer
On a morning bright and clear.
I went and shot the maximum
    the game laws would allow,
Two game wardens, seven
    hunters, and a cow.

I was in no mood to trifle,
I took down my trusty rifle
And went to stalk my prey.
What a haul I made that day.
I tied them to my fender, and I
    drove them home somehow,
Two game wardens, seven
    hunters, and a cow.

The law was very firm, it
Took away my permit,
The worst punishment I ever
    endured.
It turned out there was a reason,
Cows were out of season,
And one of the hunters wasn't
    insured.

People ask me how I do it,
And I say "there's nothing to it,
You just stand there looking cute,
And when something moves, you
    shoot!"
And there's ten stuffed heads in
    my trophy room right now,
Two game wardens, seven
    hunters, and a pure-bred
    Guernsey cow.

*Editors note: A cleverly illustrated version of this song appeared in the October, 1957 issue of *Mad Magazine*.

Channel Fishing

George Reiger

When our son was young, my wife and I had no television. We wanted our boy to become a reader, not a viewer. Our plan was largely successful, except for one baby-sitter who not only had a set, but believed her viewing was vital to keep "Little House on the Prairie" in syndication.

When we finally bought a TV, the antenna on our coastal-Virginia roof could only pick up two networks clearly and two public broadcasting stations fuzzily. That was okay, since I mainly watched local weather forecasts to determine when it'd be safe for me to run offshore in my 17-foot Whaler.

Then I began doing some documentaries for public television on decoy carving and angling history. After our accountant told me I was doing enough TV work to qualify for a deductible upgrade on our reception, I acquired a satellite system.

What a revelation! One channel selling junk jewelry 24 hours a day; another featuring "celebrities" no one over 30 has ever heard of; still others devoted to politically correct cartoons, silly games and over-seasoned food. But then I also found channels for the likes of me, featuring classic movies, science, history, wildlife, travel and—especially—fishing. Yet because I have some familiarity with these subjects, I soon noticed that the medium's appetite for moving images always takes precedence over accuracy, thoughtful dialogue, and even—occasionally—ethical behavior.

One wet and windy morning, I recorded snippets of conversation from all the angling shows I could find on several different channels and then blended them into a single make-believe outing. Every cliché that follows was spoken during one or more shows. Only their sequence has been rearranged. Henceforth, any viewer who loses the audio portion of a fishing show can use this as a guide to find out what the anglers are saying.

So long as they're fishing, but not catching: "Does it get any better than this?"—"The answer to a prayer."—"I wonder what the poor people are doing."—"I feel sorry for people who never see stuff like this."—"Sweet stuff." — "What a place!"—"Amazing!"—"Absolutely amazing!"—"I can't believe it."—"You better believe it."—"I'm speechless."—"I'm ready."—"Let's do it."

Finally, a fish appears: "You see him?"—"I see him!"—"I don't see him!"—"He's right there!"—"Where?"—"You got him?"—"I got him!"—"He's on!"—"He's off."—"I've still got him!"—"He's ripping it!"—"He's one mad fish!"—"Man, he's mad!"—"What a monster!"—"Stay out of there, you bad boy!"—"Oh, he's a good boy!"—"He's sure a good one."—"We having fun yet?"—"I got him wore out."—"He's taking line!"—"Bonefish never quit!"—"Cobia don't know the meaning of the word quit."—"Bluefish are no quitters."—"Come on fish!"—"These fish sure love to fight."

As the battle draws to a close, the dialogue changes tone, depending on whether the angler is fishing with a fly rod versus baitcasting, spinning or trolling gear. A fishing-show host may be proficient with all kinds of tackle, but he acts more polite with a fly rod in his hands: "What a beauty!"—"That's a dandy!"—"Nice fish!"—"They're all nice."—"Congratulations!"—"I learned from a master."—"Perfect eating size, but we'll let this one go."—"That was great!"—"Let's find another."—"That works for me."

In the following scenario, several anglers continue fishing after they've already landed a limit. In the original shows, the action involved lingcod, cobia and striped bass. In the striper show, previously boated fish were kept "alive" in coolers full of sea water while other fish were landed. If one of those stripers was larger than a captive fish, the previously caught fish was thrown back, and the freshly caught striper dropped in its place. In the case of the lingcod and cobia, the extra-limit fish were "lip-gaffed" and brought aboard for a "photo-op" before being dropped back over the side:

"What you got there, boy?"—"Look at the size of him!"—"Look at the size of that mouth!"—"Mine's bigger than yours."—"My fish could eat yours for breakfast!"—"He's not that small!"—"He's bait!"—"Put a hook in him and catch a real fish!"—"He swallowed the hook."—"He sure wanted that bait."—"Think you can get the hook back?"—"I don't see it."—"He's bleeding."—"That's not so bad."—"We got to keep him."—"We can't."—"Just cut the leader."—"We should keep him."—"The hook will rust out."—"The fish will be no worse for wear."—

"There he goes!"—"See, he's fine."—"Wash [or watch] that blood."—"Give me a high-five!"

Regardless of what species are caught—or how they're caught—all trips end with the same sentiments with which they began: "Unbelievable!"—"One of the most unique experiences of my life."—"Really unique!"—"How could it be any better than this?"—"It couldn't be any better."—"I wonder what the poor folks are doing?"

Some outings wrap up with a back-at-the-lodge interview with the resort manager. This was my favorite: "You lived here all your life?"—"Yep."—"I bet you've see a lot of changes."—"Yep."—"I bet you've seen things a person like me could never imagine."—"Yep."

While channel surfing, I discovered an angling series apparently inspired by The Man Show's "Girls Jumping on Trampolines." It features three young ladies who'll never fish anywhere they might have to wear more than a bikini. I feel sorry for two of the girls, who seem more genuinely interested in fish and fishing than the "man-handler" who travels with them. (What does that guy do?!) The girls squeal, and wiggle and jiggle, whenever a fish is hooked. The two not in the fighting chair lean over the lass who is to give her words of encouragement and the camera an eyeful. (I didn't take any notes while watching this show, but I did clean my glasses during commercial breaks.)

Well, I see by The Weather Channel there's a storm brewing off Japan, which won't affect the East Coast for at least three weeks. Sounds like a good time for another once-in-a-lifetime, really unique experience on the tuna grounds in my (now) 19-foot Whaler.

How could it get any better than this?

#6

Nancy Anisfield

The day my husband shot me was crisp, with 25-degree temperatures and high, thin December clouds that still let in enough sunlight to make the snow bright. We'd just been liberated from the civilized suburban state where my family had gathered for the holidays. Craving Vermont air and some non-politically-correct sport, we headed out with our German wirehair pointer for a late day grouse hunt, hoping to bear witness to a few of his notably ungraceful points.

Working up the south field, we saw plenty of tracks in the 4-5 inches of fresh snow. Sure enough, near the back tree line, Scrub snapped to a halt, poised on top of a ledge outcropping below which clustered three nasty old apple trees and a thick patch of buckthorn. I circled behind him to the left. Terry pushed out in front of the cover below us.

It was unlikely that I'd get a shot, being behind the trees and above the logical, more open flight path at the bottom of the ledge. I moved forward, the bird flushed and Terry fired.

In that fraction of a second you can't actually remember as the passage of time, I heard a "click" and felt a sting on my chin.

"I've been hit by a ricochet," I yelled.

"What?"

"I've been hit by a ricochet!"

"You've been what?" he called back, now analyzing the bird's flight trajectory, his gun mount, his swing, the tension on his trigger, what he ate for lunch and all the variables needed to confirm that indeed, he missed.

"Ricochet. Yeah, whatever," I mumbled, knowing instantly I wasn't going to get much attention as long as I was still standing, hadn't dropped my Franchi in a lake or discovered that the missing evolutionary link was actually a Draahthar.

So I grabbed a handful of snow and pressed it to my chin. My plan was for the trickle of blood to spread through the snow, giving the impression that at least a quarter of my face had been pulverized. Still no sympathy.

"Lemme see," he asked, with one eyeball scanning the tree line where the bird had gone.

"No big deal," I replied in my best passive-aggressive voice, knowing full well it wasn't any big deal but thinking that the mere fact of having a shotgun pellet in my face ought to be worth something in the long run.

Realizing I was about to begin a dramatic enactment guaranteed to beat Sarah Bernhardt on her best day and realizing that he'd be the only one in the audience, Terry gave Scrub a whistle and agreed to head home where I could more appropriately examine the damage.

Just 50 yards from the ledge, however, Scrub locked again into one of his magnificent corkscrew points—elbows out and head swiveled around far enough to audition for *The Exorcist*. Probably figuring Terry wouldn't dare draw blood a second time that afternoon, the foolhardy grouse soared straight out and became dinner. At least the trip wasn't for naught.

Back at the house, we reviewed the episode to make sure there was nothing unsafe in our positions or gun handling. I couldn't find any pellet in the small hole in my chin although the area was a bit swollen. Then came the best part.

The telephone. Never underestimate the sheer pleasure a man can get from calling his buddies and saying, "Guess what? I shot my wife." He called his hunting pals; he called his long-distance friends. He called his business contacts; he called his acquaintances. By the time he started working his way through the greater Burlington area phonebook, I started to dream of making similar calls, knowing full well no jury would find me guilty, even though it wouldn't be just a ricochet that I'd be reporting.

Follow-up: The pellet traveled an inch or so down under my chin. It's still there. There's also a perfect #6 shot-sized hole in the checkering on my Franchi which means either there were two stray pellets or the one in my chin hit the gun first. I had that gun refinished over the summer, but left explicit instructions that the hole was not to be repaired. I may get some sympathy yet.

Epstein's Conversion

Charles Gaines

We finally left the dock at Cozumel at 9:00 A.M. and were tossing around in the strait a thousand yards off the coast of Yucatan by ten. There was not a single trout angler in sight, and that was just fine with Epstein.

In fact, there wasn't any kind of fisherman in sight, though this was May and the middle of the annual sailfish run. A thirty-knot wind was blowing, there were eight-to-ten-foot seas running in the strait, and nobody but José wanted any part of it. All those fifty-foot Strikers and Merritts and Hatterases sitting back there at the dock like a meeting of the board of directors of the Bass Weejun Company, and every one of their captains with something else to do today but fish. Including the guy Epstein and I had chartered: Emilio.

"Ees too windy. Maybe mañana," he had said, and gone back to cleaning the already spotless cabin of the fifty-two-foot Egg Harbor he captained. It belonged to a man from Pennsylvania—a trout angler, Epstein was sure, who had instructed Emilio never to go fishing when the wind was blowing.

I had reminded Emilio that we had to leave *mañana,* and also that neither Epstein nor I had yet caught a sailfish on a fly rod. That was what we had come down here to do, but for the past two days we had let Emilio and the wind keep us from trying, and had settled for catching sail after sail on twenty-pound trolling tackle. Today was our last chance.

"Good-bye," Emilio had said to that, and closed the cabin door.

More seriously, it was fishing's last chance with Epstein. Epstein had given up fishing. Until this week he hadn't touched a rod since a July afternoon almost two years before, when a long simmering hatred for what he called "trout anglers" had finally boiled over.

We had been fishing emergers on a snobbish little brook in

Vermont, the guest of George Talbot, a man I knew who was always talking about "riseforms" and his latest reading of Dame Juliana, but was otherwise, to my mind, okay. Not to Epstein's mind, however. He and Talbot had developed a strong antipathy for each other over the course of the two days we fished together, and I was much relieved at the end of the second day when it appeared that Epstein and I were going to get back to New Hampshire without any outright unpleasantness between the two of them.

Talbot and I had been taking down our rods, talking peacefully beside his car in the warm dusk with a bottle of Beam on the hood between us, when Epstein came splashing out of the brook, his forefinger through the bleeding gills of a large brown trout.

"Look at this," he shouted to me. "Do you believe this fish came out of this piss-ant little stream?" He tossed the trout at our feet, where it pitched feebly a couple of times in the dust. Talbot looked at the fish, then up at me, his face pale.

"Do you intend to kill this lovely fish?" he asked Epstein without looking at him.

"You bet, pal," said Epstein happily. "Kill it and eat it."

"I'm sorry, but I have to ask that you let me measure it first."

"Be my guest," said Epstein proudly.

Slipping to his knees, Talbot pulled a retractable tape from his vest, straightened the fish, and measured it. "She's not legal," he said. "We'll have to release her."

"What are you talking about?" Epstein demanded. "The limit is eight inches. That fish has to be over fifteen."

"Eighteen exactly," said Talbot. He was quickly constructing a little stretcher out of twigs. "I think she'll be okay if we can just get her back to the water without *touching* her anymore." He looked up at me, ignoring Epstein. "We have a regulation here that we kill only fish between eight and sixteen inches. Or, of course, anything over twenty inches..."

"*What?*" thundered Epstein.

"Of course, *most* of us haven't killed a fish of any size in years." Talbot slid the trout gently on the stretcher he had made and stood up carefully. "I think she'll be all right, don't you?" he asked me.

"Well," I said, "it's bleeding from the gills."

"Let me get this straight," said Epstein. We were both following Talbot as he cat-walked toward the stream, holding the trout stretcher gingerly aloft. "That fish is two inches too long to be legal, and it's also two inches too *short* to be legal? Is that right?"

" 'Legal' isn't exactly the right word. It's just the way we all agree to do things here on the Passacowadee."

I hadn't liked the sound of Epstein's voice, so I said, "Look here, Talbot, I really *don't* think that fish is going to live…."

Epstein interrupted me by suddenly hopping in front of Talbot and snatching the trout off the stretcher. "The way I see it," he said, looking from Talbot to me and back again, his eyes glittering, "we've got two classic trout-angler problems here. Number one"—he held up the fish by its tail—"is this fucker going to live or not. And number two, he's two inches too long for those of us here on the Passacowadee."

Talbot nodded without taking his eyes off his patient. He wanted the brown back and reached out. He was too late, though, because just then Epstein stuck the trout's entire head into his mouth and bit down. Holding the tail with both hands, he gnawed away furiously at the trout, snorting and huffing like a grizzly and spitting out trout blood and pieces of flesh, until finally he had chewed off the head—which he spat on the ground at the feet of the pale and hypnotized Talbot. Epstein grinned wolfishly. In his last civilized utterance of any kind to a trout angler, he said in a deceptively benign voice, "You see how easy it is to solve problems if we just put our heads together?"

Of course it was not everyone who fishes for trout who drove Epstein to give up the primary passion of his life, but only that percentage (growing daily, he believed) who qualified in his mind as trout *anglers.* Epstein's trout angler had rules to govern every pleasure, and that was what Epstein most despised about him. But he also hated the fellow's stuffiness and academic bent, his pipe and tweed hats, how vulnerable he looked in waders, his sheepish enthusiasm for following other trout anglers, his womanish sentimentality, the prissy way he ate and drank, his physical cautiousness, and his obsession with minutiae: little flies, little rules, little tools hung all over his vest, the invention of little tactical problems to make trout fishing seem harder than it is.

In the last year or so before he quit fishing, Epstein had begun to see trout anglers behind every bush and tree. In West Yellowstone and Ennis, in Oregon and Idaho, in Labrador and Ireland—everywhere he went they were waiting for him, pursing their lips over some local rule, wading cautiously in shallow water with the help of a staff, making flaccid little casts, spooking fish they never saw, lighting their pipes, and talking sentimentally. Talbot was just a merciful last straw. When pushed, Epstein would acknowledge that Talbot was not the most egregious trout angler he had ever met, just the last; and he would even express some regret at having thrown Talbot bodily into the Sundown Pool of the Passacowadee.

But however good or bad his motives, Epstein had sworn off all fishing that day in Vermont—and not fishing began to ruin his life. His marriage and his medical practice fell into shambles. He began to drink too much, and he developed an unnerving habit of picking fights with anyone wearing a uniform.

I happen to enjoy the company of people who are actively engaged in wrecking their lives over something they like or don't like, so long as they are not members of my immediate family; but one night at a party, Epstein's wife took me aside and asked me for help. She looked up at me with her great, dark eyes and asked me to "do something." We rarely saw the Epsteins socially, and I was moved. So I talked him into coming down to Cozumel with me. He had never done any salt-water fishing, and I was sure he would take to it. For the first few days, though, he found Emilio's pussyfooting delicacy about the weather and the cleanliness of his boat to be just other forms of trout angling. Fishing, it appeared, was about to lose Epstein permanently. And then we walked down the dock and met José.

José was sitting in a rusty lawn chair in the stern of a dumpy, homemade-looking thirty-foot boat called the *Gloria*. He knew no English, and Epstein and I little Spanish, but we worked out the essential details in a matter of minutes. Epstein and I were given to understand this clearly: We had found a skinny, barefooted Indian with a potbelly who didn't give a rat's ass how much wind was blowing.

The *Gloria* didn't have sonar or teak decks or a shower. Neither did she have a few more necessary accouterments to sport fishing—such as outriggers, a mate, or bait. But she did have an ice chest full of Dos Equis, and Epstein and I found a nice blue-skirted lure which we rigged without a hook on one of José's decrepit fifty-pound trolling outfits. As soon as we hit the straits, José turned upsea, cut the *Gloria* back to trolling speed, put on a Jimmy Buffett tape, and—holding a beer in one hand and spinning the wheel with the other, laughing and singing and hopping around to keep his balance like a potbellied parrot—he commenced to go fishing.

At first, Epstein and I couldn't stand up in the cockpit. But when we could, we let the lure out, and sailfish started jumping all over it. Everywhere we looked beyond the transom there were sailfish—herds of them, lit up and running over each other to get the lure. I gave Epstein the fifty-pound outfit and lurched toward the cabin for my fly rod.

"They're trying to eat the goddamn thing," Epstein shouted after me. All either of us knew about fly fishing for billfish was what we had read.

I staggered back into the cockpit holding the fly rod. "Just don't let them cut it off—it's the only lure we've got." Epstein was crouched at the transom, his legs locked under it, whipping the boat rod up and down and making the blue lure, thirty yards back, leap and plunge. Through the waves we could see sailfish diving and jumping all around it. I tried false-casting and couldn't because of the wind, so I dropped the big red-and-white-streamer into the prop wash and let the boat's momentum carry it back about fifteen yards.

"I'd better go tell José what to do," said Epstein. "Here." He shoved the boat rod over to me. "I'll tell him to throw the boat out of gear when I shout."

"How are you going to tell him that?"

"Small, small problem, amigo," said Epstein. "Size of a trout angler's dick."

While he was gone, the boat quartered into a particularly big sea, yawed, and crashed into the next trough. Behind me I heard glass shatter and Epstein curse; then he was beside me again at the transom, grabbing back the boat rod.

"José is all set. I'm going to bring this fucker in."

I pulled the tip of the fly rod up into the wind to my right as far as I could without lifting the streamer off the water. Then I stripped some line off the reel and onto the deck and hoped I could make one good cast. Epstein was reeling fast, and the blue lure skipped toward us, hounded by sailfish. When the lure was about fifty feet away and still coming, Epstein said, "You ready?"

I nodded.

"José!" Epstein yelled, and just as the boat went out of gear, he yanked the rod up and backward over his head, lifting the lure off the waves and catapulting it toward us. Confused, the sails milled forty feet off the transom. I lifted the fly rod's tip another inch or two and pushed it hard forward. The streamer picked up, caught the wind, and rode it out perfectly to the sailfish, pulling loose line off the deck. When it slapped down, I started stripping it back in foot-long jerks. The streamer hadn't traveled a yard before a sailfish charged in a quick, silver furrow of water and ate it. I let go of the underside of the transom with my knees, reared back to hit the fish, and slipped. Epstein caught me and held me upright. "Hit him again," he said, and I did, three times, and we watched the backing pour off the reel.

"Why is there blood all over the deck?" I asked Epstein.

"A window broke in the cabin, and I cut my leg on it."

"Isn't that an awful lot of blood?"

He was still holding me upright against the transom while I played the fish, and I could feel blood running down the backs of my legs.

"It's okay. Just don't lose that baby! Can you *believe this shit?*" Epstein whooped. The sail was tail-walking a hundred yards back, its lean, violet body snapping like a flag in the wind. "We have wasted our whole fucking *lives* fishing mudholes for guppies. I have just been made *whole,* goddammit...." He added after a moment, "I have to puke now." His voice was still so delighted I thought he was kidding. He wasn't. Without letting me go, he turned his head and threw up violently on his shoulder and the deck. When he was finished, he coughed a couple of times and spat. "Deep-sea fishing!" he shouted hoarsely into my ear. "To hell with women and work!"

With Epstein holding me upright and with José handling the boat beautifully, I had the sail tired and circling just off the stern in eight minutes. When the fish moved under the boat, I yelled for José to go forward. Taking me to mean the fish was ready, I guess, he threw the boat into neutral and popped back into the cockpit like a jumping bean, gloved for billing the fish, thrilled to death with everything that was going on—even, it appeared, the unexplained blood and vomit all over his deck.

"Go *forward,*" I yelled to him and pointed to the fly line running directly under the stern, which at that moment stopped and refused to budge. The fish had run the line around the prop.

"Shit," Epstein said and let me go.

"Aiyeee!" said José. He popped back into the cabin, reemerging in seconds in a mask and fins and, before Epstein or I could figure out what he was doing, he jumped overboard into the heaving sea.

Epstein and I looked at each other, then overboard. It was not a place anyone would have wanted to be. Between the fish and the fly line was a foot of fifteen-pound leader tippet. Though we didn't say it, neither Epstein nor I believed that the tippet had not already parted, either on contact with the prop or at the fish's first surge. But within seconds, the line came unstuck, and I felt it to be, miraculously, still connected to the fish.

Epstein pulled José back into the boat, and José got the engine going, and the boat turned upwind. Then he came into the cockpit and grabbed the sailfish by its bill. He pulled the fish half over the transom, and Epstein started clubbing its electric-blue head with a Coke bottle.

"Stop it," I said to him. "That's my fish, and I want to release it." Even before I had finished the sentence, I was sorry I had spoken it.

Epstein paused with his hand raised and looked at me. His face was set with a fierce new assurance, and his eyes had the same non-committal savagery in them that you often see in animals' eyes.

"The hell it is," he said quietly. Then he clubbed the fish again with the bottle, and José let it slide dead onto the deck.

Both of them straightened up and grinned at me. Epstein had tied his tee shirt around his thigh, which had finally stopped bleeding. In real life he is a doctor, but he doesn't look like one. He is also an ex-college football player and wrestler, an enthusiastic fist fighter and sky-diver—a big, trouble- and pain-addicted man. Later, back in Cozumel, not trusting Mexican clinics, he would disinfect and sew up his wound himself. It took thirty-five stitches to close the cut, and then we went out and drank a world of Cuervo Gold and said very little to each other.

One thing Epstein did say, late that night, was that he had found his religion. He said that very loudly at about three in the morning while staring unsteadily at a stuffed blue marlin hanging in the lobby of our hotel. And I suppose I believed him. I have not seen Epstein since that moment, but occasionally I hear about him and his fishing. A captain I know wrote me recently that he and Epstein took a Striker, a Morton's salt box full of cocaine, and two hookers down to Chile this past winter to look for swordfish, but spent all their time shooting sharks and getting laid in the tuna tower.

I have learned that very little in life is simple, even fishing. But there for a moment or two in the cockpit of the *Gloria*, standing astride his sailfish, shirtless and hairy, new-looking and sweating, and caked with dried blood and puke, Epstein was, I believe, simply a happy man. After he had grinned at me for a long time, he picked José up and hugged him. Then he sat the little Indian carefully back down on the deck.

"Muchas gracias," Epstein told him.

José ran up to the wheel, cracked a *cerveza,* turned up the Buffett, and winked at us over the stained shambles of his boat. He put the throttle in the corner, and the *Gloria* heaved forward. "More fish now, sí?" he shouted.

Epstein squinted approvingly at him, as if trying to calculate just how many trout anglers the little fellow was worth.

A Ditch Runs Through It

Martin Meckal

I should have known it would be crowded that Memorial Day. Common sense should have told me that a river with pools named "Convention Center," "The Mall," and "Sea of Humanity" would get pressure. Nevertheless, I was unprepared for my first look at Vermont's famous Au Beaverware.

Eleven Thousand frantic anglers were wading, scrambling like seals on the rocks, and elbowing one another along the banks for as far as I could see. The collective motion of their waving rods resembled a limitless wheatfield brushed by the wind. The air reverberated with the piercing hiss of a thousand false casts and the crackle of shearing tippets as inept anglers popped off flies by the hundreds. A station wagon with massive speakers on its roof cruised the road next to the river, blasting the mob with its message of bargain prices at Mad Mike's Mile of Muddlers, the world's largest fly shop, located in downtown Arlington.

I watched in disbelief as a canoe flotilla of a size unrivaled since the height of the fur trade drifted out of control through the flailing gauntlet. A wave of profanity surged through the angling horde. Each craft trailed a massive web of fly lines, backing, and landing nets, while its occupants, staring wildly through a cocoon of feathers, floss, and fish hooks, desperately thrashed the surface to a foam. Rafts of lucky hats rotated slowly in the back eddies. It was a nightmare.

Despondent, I climbed back in the car, ripped my trout decal off the dash, and vowed I would never fish a crowded stream again.

For the next two years, I methodically studied satellite photos of New England and discovered 7.6 million miles of virgin waters just waiting for the adventurous angler. It's in ditches. That's right, pal, in ditches that are teeming with minnows, a gamefish that, gram for gram, rivals any tarpon. (That is, of course, with appropriate tackle.)

Using the skills I had gained as an H-O train modeler, I built myself a splendid medium-action minnow rod of Tonkin cane that I obtained from select swizzle sticks. Waxed, heavy-duty thread made a perfect .01-weight fly line, and I fashioned the knotted leaders and tippets from baby hair.

To save weight, I built the reel (and a spare spool for a sinking line) from titanium. The adjustable drag is so smooth that I can slow down those heart-stopping 3-foot runs that get into the backing and make the reel scream (well, squeak, anyway).

I ordered a lot of custom-made No. 48 hooks, which are ideal for my favorite dry fly pattern—the Ultra-Light Cahill. Believe me, nothing compares with the thrill of a 2-inch minnow shattering the surface when he hits one of them and then tailwalks for a foot and half.

Sure, it was a nuisance fitting ball bearings in the reel or tying blood knots in the little leaders, and yes, you still have to learn how to double haul if you want to reach the other side of the ditch. But there are no crowds, and it only costs $1.75 to get your trophy mounted. And whether it's a trout, a tarpon, a bass, or a minnow, your heart sinks just as far when the fish throws the hook. I only hope no one makes a movie about it.

Mental Health Deflates in Winnebago Sturgeon Shack

Dick Ellis

Saturday, February 14, A Sturgeon Spearer's Diary.

4:30 a.m.: Opening morning. Heading north on Highway 45 toward Winnebago with just the stars as my companions. Mentally sharp. Ready. Enthusiastic. I haven't seen a sturgeon in eight years of sturgeon spearing. Today's the day.

6:30 a.m.: Met my guide, Bill Jenkins in Pipe, Wisconsin, on the east side of Winnebago. Every year I give Bill $50.00. He lets me stare down into a hole. Show me a better bargain.

6:45 a.m.: Jim Sullivan of Jefferson gives me a ride out to my one-man shack far out on the ice of Winnebago. Jim's been spearing for a decade, with hundreds of hours staring into the water. He thinks he saw one nine years ago. I'm in the presence of greatness.

7 a.m.: All settled in now, in my six foot by eight foot shack. The trap door in the floor has been lifted back and I can sit on this folding chair and stare down at a refrigerator sized hole. Above the hole hanging down from a nail is a heavy, iron, five-pronged spear, with a rope attached poised to drop when the monster appears. The gas heater has been lit by my guide. It will soon be toasty warm in here

7:15 a.m.: Fire's out. It's freezing.

7:20 a.m.: It's quiet now, and black. I can see about 12 feet down into the swirling green hues of Winnebago and if I tilt this notebook just right, I can scribble by that hue almost legibly. At about eight feet my guide has suspended my decoy, a two-foot long white piece of plastic pipe. What a stupid fish to rise to a piece of PVC pipe I think as I stare down at a piece of PVC pipe. Unexplained, brief flashback to my beautiful wife, Lori, in a warm bed that I left on a Saturday morning so I could drive up here alone and sit in a cold shack and stare at this pipe. Yep, that's a stupid fish all right.

8:30 a.m.: Well, at least it's warm now. It's been 90 minutes and Mr. Big no doubt is just a minute or two from arriving underneath the ice. I'm still mentally sharp.

8:32 a.m.: A bubble just came all the way up. I watched it.

8:33 a.m.: Nuther one.

8:35 a.m.: John Jenkins, Bill's son and veteran spearer, just showed up. He has many sturgeon under his belt. He wants this reporter to get one too. I don't know why but year after year after year after year John wears the same look of pity around me. He gives me his secret weapon decoy. It's a… and please keep this quiet so everyone's not utilizing it… a plastic pail. I thank John profusely as the pail is lowered to hang next to the white pipe. John tells me that Paul Wargowski is on his first sturgeon hunt, his shack just 100 yards from mine. Old Paul (who's actually only about 30) flipped back the lid this morning and there was a 58-inch sturgeon. Just three minutes into his first season, and his tag is filled. I tell John to congratulate good old Paul Wargowski of Whitewater for me. Although I don't know him.

8:36 a.m.: John just left. I don't like Paul Wargowski of Whitewater.

8:37 a.m.: I'm humble, a little emotional as John leaves the shack. I mean, how many guys give you a pail? I make a note to give John a can, or maybe even a bottle some day.

8:46 a.m.: Well no wonder it's a secret weapon. I stare down and the pail is going round and round, twirlly, twirlly, twiirrlllly in the green hues. The pipe just sits there like a lazy pipe. Pull your weight, man, I yell. No reaction.

9:45 a.m.: Twirrlly, twiiirrrllyyy, twwwwiiirrrllly. Still mentally sharp. But I think there may be someone in here.

9:48 a.m.: He's here all right. Somewhere in the dark. Lurking. I'll act unalarmed.

10:30 a.m.: If I stand on my tip-toes, I can just barely squash my hair on the ceiling.

11 a.m.: Discussing things with myself for an hour now. Made unsettling self-discovery. I'm pretty boring. Not good. This shatters my whole self-image. Little wonder I never had a date in high school.

11:30 a.m.: Tried playing 100 questions about my life. Only missed seven. Self-esteem rising again.

11:37 a.m.: Just checked my notes. 27 pages of "all work and no play makes Dick a dull boy." What does that mean? That guy in the shack is messing with me.

11:45 a.m.: It is indeed toasty warm in here. I'm down to my T-shirt, sweating. There's a fly climbing up the wall. Yea, right. In February. In Wisconsin. Like that's not a "plant." Now I know someone is in here, watching, watching, watching me. Watching me to see if I kill the fly. To see if I'm sane. I saw *Psycho*. Norman Bates. Dressed in his Mother's clothes. He wouldn't kill the fly either. He knew "they" were watching, too. I'll wait this thing out. I will not touch that fly.

11:55 a.m.: It's a bit hot. Should have worn Lori's skirt. That short, black leather number.

NOON: Just smashed the fly with the spear. I knew they were watching. A siren just went off.

12:30 p.m.: Bill Jenkins is here. Spearing's over for the day. Bill wants to know why I look so flushed. He pries my fingers off the spear handle. "Dick... Dick... Are you all right?" I hear his distant voice. "Am I all right?" I hear my answer. "Am I all right? I will be just as soon as you sign me up for next year."

Prairie-Dog Hunting

Joe Bob Briggs

I'll be danged if Bush didn't ban all the AK-47 Kalashnikov semi-automatic assault rifles right in the middle of hunting season, and it stopped an order of forty-five I had come in from Bangkok, and now I'm gonna have to cancel all my hunting trips this year. Usually, around mid-April, thirty or forty of us go out to West Texas and hunt prairie dogs with AK-47s. Last year we bagged about forty-three thousand of the little suckers, but we won't get anywhere near that using conventional weapons. And I'll tell you one goldurn thing, Mr. Bush—if somebody gets hurt out there this year, his blood is on *your* hands.

The truth of the matter is, you *need* an AK-47 these days, or at least an M-1, if you're gonna compete with the modern prairie dog. Three years ago—I'll never forget this—my buddy Vince Gabbert went ahead of us to recon a ridge on our flank, and as soon as he stuck his head up over the crest, a unit of about thirty prairie dogs flung themselves at his face. Fortunately, he was able to squeeze off seven hundred rounds and pretty much turn the pd's into little salad-bar croutons, but he was a shaken man when he worked his way back to base camp.

I want you to think about that, Mr. Bush. You say these weapons aren't needed for sporting. I want you to think about what would have happened to Vince if he hadn't had the needed firepower that day. Would he have a face? Would a .22 have done the same job?

I think not.

With each passing year, the prairie dog turns into a wiser and more dangerous adversary. Sure, in the beginning all they did was burrow little holes in dirt piles. But last season we stumbled onto a village of prairie dogs that was surrounded by triple-strand barbed wire, booby-trapped with slingshot mines. Of course, it was prairie-dog-sized barbed wire, so we were able to step on it and remove the obstacle. But my point is that we have an entrenched and resistant enemy with no interest in Western-style democracy. I don't know if you've ever seen your best friend get a mesquite thorn directly in the cheek from a pd "slinger." But I'll tell you this. Once you see it, you'll never again hesitate to pour twelve hundred rounds of lead into the little furry cheeks of a resisting rodent.

Let me tell you how bad it's gotten. Two years ago, just outside of Whiteflat in Motley County, four of us were ambushed by prairie-dog mortar fire that, as near as we could tell, was being launched from a copse of elm trees. We hit the dirt, covered our heads, and slowly worked our way toward the trees, dragging our bodies along with our elbows. But when we got close, suddenly the firing stopped. There was nothing but silence, for better than fifteen minutes. Then Sam Wilkins, covering our left flank, spotted a single prairie dog. He had moved just beyond the tree line, into the open space in front of us. He stared straight ahead, then slowly, like he was in a trance, he began to dance. It was a weird, mesmerizing dance. If you've ever seen a belly dancer in a Tunisian restaurant—that kind of dance. He had a tiny flute with him. The flute couldn't have been any bigger than a little girl's fingernail. He began to play Ukrainian folk melodies, dancing all the while. None of us said a word. Then Sam Wilkins, without warning, screamed, "He's just shimmied for the last time!" and he squeezed off a terrifying barrage. The dancing, flute-playing prairie dog disintegrated, vanished, blown into a thousand pieces. But Sam had given away our position. Within fifteen minutes all three of my friends were dead. I only managed to survive by rolling down an embankment, abandoning my backpack, and traveling only by night for three days.

I know what happened now.

The prairie dogs were directly underneath us all that time—thousands of them, waiting for us to make one wrong noise. The dancing prairie dog gave his life so that the others might live.

This is not like any enemy man has ever faced.

And they say we don't *need* AK-47s to hunt with.

Trout

Franz Lidz

I live on a wooded Chester County hillside overlooking the gurgling waters of White Clay Creek, about an hour's drive from Philadelphia. But on Opening Day, I can't get out of my driveway. It's not that raptorlike Philadelphia Phillies fans have swooped down on me. The pickups stacked up in my driveway—and for miles along the narrow road leading to civilization—are left by crazed fishermen. At six A.M. on the trout season's traditional Saturday opener, the White Clay banks are clumped with anglers eyeing clumps of stocked trout. At seven A.M., those anglers are as tightly packed as sardines, which are not stocked.

This year I figured, as long as I can't drive, I might as well cast. For verisimilitude, I ask my neighbor Lindsey Flexner to come along. He actually knows how to fish. "First, you'll need a fishing license," he advises. And so, the day before the home opener, I drive to DiFilippo's General Store on the edge of Kennett Square, a drowsy little hamlet that bills itself as the "Mushroom Capital of the World." That may be true, but it is also the world's apostrophe capital. One three-block stretch of State Street boasts Sam's Sub Shop, Kirk's Martial Arts, Samantha's Café, Torelli's Men's Shop, My Sister's Shoes, Harrington's Coffee Company, Stephen's Menswear, Burton's Barber Shop, Rebecca Cooper's Consignment Boutique, Marston's Furniture, Clifford's Hair Fashions, Fran Keller's Eatery, B. B. Wolf's Restaurant, Kim's Nails, and Johnson's Catering. DiFilippo's, which is across the street from Fleming's Used Cars and catty-corner to Russ's Transmissions and Andy's Autotech, has a cryptic sign out front that reads:

HEY DADDY-O!
MONEY ORDERS—KEYS
STOP WE MAY HAV IT

Hey Daddy-O! I've always imagined that DiFilippo's interior was decked out like some Rat Pack bachelor pad, and that DiFilippo himself was a Vegas hipster who spoke in the finger-snapping lingo favored by Dino, Sammy, and Frankie: "Absopositively!" and "How's your clyde, Clyde?"

But the elderly fellow hunched over the register is more dinosaur than lounge lizard. I ask if he's DiFilippo. "Yep," says Leonard DiFilippo. I ask if the store is DiFilippo's or DiFilippos'. "Singular, " he says. "Used to be plural, but my brother up and quit."

I tell him I want to buy a fishing license. "Trout?" he asks.

"Bingo, dingo!" I say enthusiastically.

The ancient hepcat coolly ignores the remark. As he completes the paperwork, I ask where to get gear. He points eastward and says: "Pete's."

At Pete's Outdoors (tucked between Rubinstein's Office Products and Granny Smith's Deli), I stock up on poles and nets and hooks and sinkers and hip boots. Then I drive home and await Opening Day.

Lindsey and his seven-year-old son, Dylan, show up the next morning at six. My ten-year-old daughter, Daisy, is already dressed and outside, clomping around in her hip boots. We bushwhack through the pickups to the Landenberg United Methodist Church; where the sign out front reads: TIME IS JUST A STREAM I GO A-FISHIN' IN. A mechanic from Dave's Auto Service serves us a pancake and sausage "fisherman's breakfast." Daisy wraps her sausages in a paper napkin. "In case we run out of bait," she explains.

Bait we buy across the road at the Landenberg Store, which everybody calls Rosemary's. The sign by the door says: BAD DAY AT THE CREEK? WE HAVE FRESH TROUT FOR SALE. "You'll have no problem landing a trout," says the proprietor, Rosemary Bauer. "It's as easy as fishing in a toilet out there." An indelicate phrase, that.

In the last darkness before dawn, we join the swelling school of fly fishermen standing shoulder to shoulder in camouflage fatigues. They all seem to have festooned their hats with scores of dry flies as though at any moment they might dunk their heads into the current to land a three-pounder. "This has about as much to do with real trout fishing as putt-putt does with real golf," mutters Lindsey. "These aren't even real trout—they're hatchery dogs who've been raised on puppy chow."

Lugging a box of tackle and two plastic Baggies filled with worms, we immoderately compleat anglers climb through brambles of wild rose to the clear shallows. The camouflaged guy to our left yanks trout after trout out of the water. "It's all in the cast," he tells Daisy. She sails a nightcrawler along the edges of a granite outcropping, where most of the creek's trout population supposedly lurks. Then she slowly cranks the wiggler back in short, lively spurts. Daisy repeats this for forty minutes or so before asking: "When are we supposed to catch the fish?"

Dylan has already given up. He's in the middle of the creek, building a dam. "Look, I'm a beaver," he says, splashing a twig into the water. Lindsey, irritation mounting, tells him to be a quiet beaver. "Trout get scared off by a bunch of noise," he says. "They may be hatchery dogs, but they're still fish."

Lindsey casts earthworms for two hours before switching to Power Bait, a Play-Doh-like substance the color of ballpark mustard. The side of the container warns: "Not for Human or Pet Consumption."

"If it's not fit for humans or pets," I say, "then why feed it to the trout we're supposed to eat?"

"Just chew around the bait," Lindsey advises. He Play-Dohs a hook and says, "When fish are real finicky, you want something subtle." Around ten-thirty he subtly drops a hook into some weeds. A rainbow strikes, and Lindsey nets all seven inches of it. It flops on the bank, much to the dismay of Dylan. "I hate to see animals suffer," he says, and promptly grabs a log and bashes the fish's head in.

"Dylan," I say. "Remind me never to stub my toe around you."

Five minutes later my fiberglass rod bends as a fish struggles against my line. This one is only a chub, maybe two inches long. Three, fully extended. "It counts more," consoles Lindsey. "It's a native." I keep casting—mealworms, waxworms, church sausages. Yet my perserverance goes unrewarded: Over the next two hours I snag lots of fishermen's lines, but no fish.

Bad day at the creek, so we shuffle down to Rosemary's to buy a fresh trout. The third-grader at the door proudly displays his string of six big rainbows. Lindsey holds his tiny fish aloft. "Nice catch," says Rosemary. "Whose is it, Daisy's or Dylan's?"

Like I say, it's a very possessive place.

Sexfried Fishslab

Ted Nugent

Sex is the first word that comes to mind when trying to describe my annual Nuge Tribe Gonzo Lake bluegill fishfry. It's that damn good. Hot, juicy, firm, undulating, a little greasy. Absolutely deeeeelicious! And a damn riot to catch. This feast for the soul runs from early April, just after full thaw when the small front lake begins to warm, through the entire month of July, sometimes into September. It's the only time of year I actually hate rock 'n' roll because it is summertime, and the livin' aint so eazy in between hunting season when I am driven to rockout and tour like a maniac, scaring whitefolk with my over-souled R&B guitarspeak. Damn! But in amongst the throttling sonic bombast spiritual carnage across the hinterland, I do make it a point to get home a few times each week during this fish slamming orgy to clean massive quantities of 'gills, crappie, and hogass bass from our wonderfully productive private lakes at our family home hunting camps.

My kids never learned to fish; they simply wet lines and haul in gargantuan Slabbage from the depths. With ultralite tackle and a slithering of nitecrawlers, itsa cinch. It's too eazy. They're spoiled rotten. Me too.

Any size fish will do. I understand there is a size limit on bass, but call me Rosa Parks with a hook, cuz the smaller the slab, the sweeter the meat. I defy.

Fresh is everything. Catch em, slice em, fry em, and eat em as fast as ya possibly can. We limit our mess haul based on how much we plan to devour at the next sitting and how many we are willing to filet. Did I mention that I am the FiletMaster? I am the FiletMaster. With a foaming bucket of thirty or forty writhing fishies, I run my Accusharp blade sharpener over my small Outdoor Edge filet knife, and all I can say is "stand back." With an assembly line of dedicated scalers at my side, deftly supervised by ScaleMaster Rocco Winchester, ya best don full-face goggles and body armor, for the shit will be flying hither and yon, to and fro, like shrapnel of luv!

With a still squirming scaled gill, head right and down in my left hand, I bonk the nekkid little turd in the head with the handle of my knife to calm em down a bit (Simmer down, smasha!) Then with cool, smooth, precise single-strokes of the narrow blade, I affectionately carve 99 percent of the ultra-yummy flesh from the skeleton, headfirst to the tailfin, following the ribline so close as to shave bone, then I turn the fish over and do the other side the same way. The precious flesh is washed clean in a bucket of clean water, then placed directly into a bowl of icewater. It takes us approximately thirty seconds per fish. All remains go back into the earth as garden mulch or coonbait. And the circle shall not go unbroken. Sing it!

We make the effort to filet even the smallest of fish, even as small as four and five inches. The smaller ones really are better tasting. We waste nothin'. On private lakes, and usually public waterways as well, it is important to remove as many fish each year as possible (to a point, of course) so as to relieve the lake from overpopulation and its result-ant abuse and habitat destruction. Without adequate harvest, fish will stunt and disease and wastefully die off. Even the teeniest tiniest fish are kept and tossed onto the shore for vermin, turtles, and birds to eat. I like balance. Itsa beautiful thang.

Then the festivities begin.

Rabbit Track Soup

The perfect recipe! 0 grams fat, 0 grams sodium,
0 grams cholesterol, 0 calories.

24 sets of prime Upper Peninsula rabbit tracks imbedded
in at least 3 inches of fresh snow.

Using a large, flat shovel, carefully remove top two inches of
snow containing rabbit tracks and place in a well-scrubbed bucket.
Make sure the snow is white (not yellow) and free of small, dark,
round objects or other debris. Place the snow in a 6-quart soup kettle
and heat on medium high to the desired temperature. Serve in dark
bowls for contrast with the snowy white soup. May be garnished
with a pinch of north wind.

Best-Dressed

Sam Venable

November 14, 1982

Checklist for opening of deer season:

- ✔ Rifle and ammo.
- ✔ Sleeping bag and tent.
- ✔ Coffee pot, sardines, beer, chocolate bars, Twinkies.
- ✔ Blaze orange jacket and hat.
- ✔ Playing cards.
- ✔ Knife.
- ✔ Licenses, stamps, permits.
- ✔ El-cheapo camouflage rainsuit.

Wait, now! What's with the camo suit? Are showers expected?

It doesn't matter, responds Billy Jacobs. If it rains, you get wet. The rainsuit stays in the trunk of your car. You use it to keep things clean.

Perhaps I should explain.

Billy is a transplanted Georgian. He likes to hunt deer. And he's pretty good at it. (Who else do you know who could talk a new wife into spending the honeymoon on his 'n her tree stands during archery season? I point this out so you will know this fellow has some smarts; he didn't come over on the first load of pumpkins.)

A couple of years ago, Billy drove to Catoosa in his brand new car.

"I was always proud of that car," he recalled. "I even used to wax it before I'd go to the woods."

Billy killed a fat spike buck that day. He field-dressed the animal, dragged it to the car, and started to load up for the trip to the checking station.

"Man, I didn't want to put that thing in the trunk," he said. "It was so bloody, I knew it'd mess my car up. I was standing there, trying to think what to do when I spotted the rainsuit.

"It was one of those ol' cheap, plastic things. I figured I'd never wear it, so I just decided to wrap the deer up in it."

Jacobs wrestled with the suit and carcass to no avail. Then his mental lightbulb flickered.

"I got to figurin' that the deer wasn't much smaller than a human," he noted. "So I just slipped the pants on him.

"They fit so well, I buttoned the coat on, too. Even got the little hat that came with the suit and mashed it down on his horns. He looked pretty good."

Billy was on a roll now. No way he was gonna conceal his decorated deer underneath the trunk lid.

"I just sat him straight up in the trunk and drove to the checking station."

By the time Jacobs arrived, he had attracted quite a procession. When he pulled to a stop, "fellers came pourin' out of their tents.

"This one ol' boy, he came up and looked at the deer for the longest time. Then he asked me—real serious, now, no jokin'—if the deer was wearin' that suit when I shot him."

Billy didn't have the heart to tell him any different.

Nattering Nabobs of Negativism

Sam Venable

March 25, 1984

Wild turkey season opens next weekend. That means countless hundreds of otherwise normal people will be walking around the woods, dressed like trees and making noises like barred owls and nubile hen turkeys.

This cult of madness is the fastest-growing hunting sport I have ever witnessed, bar none. What began a few years ago as a quiet spring outing for old men in bib overalls has mushroomed into a megabucks business for wildlife agencies, gun makers, resort operators and equipment suppliers alike.

Since many of you will be making your maiden hunt for this grand and wily fowl, permit me to offer a word of advice. I shall not bore you with my thoughts about calling, camouflage, woodsmanship or what shell to use. Mainly because I am dumber than a stump.

But I am a decided expert in one area: developing proper mental attitude. So lissen close, children. I ain't gonna say this but oncst:

To maintain even a smigden of sanity, forget everything you ever read or heard about the power of positive thinking.

Instead, admit defeat before you step out of the car. Realize you are in pursuit of a feathered ghost. Face up to the fact that wild turkeys are extinct and have been for decades, and that the pictures of successful hunters you see in newspapers and outdoor magazines each spring are, in truth, retouched tintypes from the 1890s.

That way, when you hike back to the car at noon—without a bird, as usual—you won't be gripped by those terrible pangs of failure.

I hunted turkeys a number of years before I ever killed one. Each time I'd get a gobbler going and would slip close and set up and start calling. I'd try to remember everything my mentors had told me.

I was eager. I was ready. I was positive. I did everything by the book.

I always failed.

Then early one morning, I ran in the general direction of a gobbling tom—slipping and sliding with each step, naturally—and plopped myself down with all the enthusiasm of a man preparing for a root canal.

I will call to this turkey, I told myself; such is expected of a turkey hunter. But the hateful thing, yodeling somewhere on yon side of the hollow, will either: (a) run the other way, (b) stop in his tracks and not move until sunset, (c) vanish like the fog, (d) maybe slip within 100 yards and see me when I blink my eyes and not stop flying 'til he hits the Carolina line. Or if, through some fluke of avian genetics, he does come strutting within range, I will miss him clean.

Five minutes and $1\frac{7}{8}$ ounces of No. 4s later, I headed for the truck with 20 pounds of turkey slung over my right shoulder.

It has happened that way ever since.

When I stay sharp, alert, cunning and wise to the ways of turkeys—the sort of moxie Vince Lombardi would have preached had he been a turkey hunter—I suffer inglorious defeat.

When I am mentally whupped, ready to give in, and wondering what I am doing in these God-forsaken woods in the first place, I am knotting a kill tag to the bird's legs in short order.

Dale Carnegie and Dr. Norman Vincent Peale and all those other positive thinkers might be fine fellows. But they don't know beans about hunting turkeys.

The Great Duck Misunderstanding

Russell Chatham

Two drake mallards are limp on the kitchen counter. These large birds, just down from Canada, were ambushed near a marsh in southwestern Montana about four in the afternoon one still, bitter, cold December day. Regrettably, there was a third, not now present.

The slough had been stalked over several rises and through a stand of cottonwoods. There I stopped to warm my hands and admire the elegant thirty-year-old pigeon-grade Winchester Model 12 I'd just acquired, in a trade for a large painting of the Big Sur hills washed in summer light. An odd juxtaposition of places, moods, objects.

When the ducks broke from cover, jumping almost straight up and squawking, they fanned out. The first one went down cleanly. The second and third, nearly out of range, were cripples that coasted into a flat swampy field covered with a foot of snow. I found number one right away, mounted in a snowdrift exactly as he'd hit it. The others were nowhere to be seen. I began to crisscross, finally stepping on one which somehow burst up into my arms.

The third mallard died beneath the snow, becoming one of those pointless killings thoughtful hunters recall with sadness. Or maybe he tunneled his way out of Park County into another possibility with only a little lead in his foot, though it's doubtful he ever lived to hear Spanish being spoken in the towns beneath him.

Back in the kitchen the transition is being made from wild animal to something to eat. I am going to treat my new girlfriend to one of those special culinary experiences doors are locked for. She comes in unexpectedly early, while the birds are still being plucked. When she sees them she does her version of Eddie Cantor trying to blow up a truck tube, and runs into the bathroom. I lose heart and consider serving her cat shit while I have roast duck. But I already knew most people get it wrong.

My father was a sensitive man whose spirit had been utterly broken early on, and he replaced it with a shroud of ennui which effectively kept life at arm's length. His systematic self-denial only faltered when there were ducks for dinner. Duck was the only food to which he ever really warmed, and in his defense of the quality of duck as dinner, he forbade the serving of it to guests or children, neither of whom could be trusted to appreciate it. I even think the failure of his marriage was largely due to the fact his wife "didn't think ducks were that good."

It must be an inherited characteristic. When I catch trout I normally turn them loose afterward. And even when I take one home knowing it will be delicious, I'm still far more interested in catching the fish than eating it. The same with grouse, certainly a delectable bird. And so it goes with bass, salmon, pheasant. But when I see a duck, even one of those on the city-park pond that takes bread crumbs out of the palms of old ladies, the desire to kill and eat is nearly Satanic.

All game birds are exquisite on the table, but there are certain fanatics for whom nothing does the job quite so perfectly as a prime wild duck. Those on the inside often argue darkly over which species is most superb. Easterners defend the black duck; westerners, the sprig or pintail, midwesterners, the mallard. Everywhere, the tiny teal is spoken of in hushed tones. In the South, the real connoisseur will hear of nothing but the sublime wood duck.

But most people get it wrong, and so you learn not to talk about it. Raving about how you like to eat duck might bring invitations to dinner from hunters who have freezers full of them. Many of these hunters will be baffled by such enthusiasm because they themselves would "rather have a T-bone." You'll find out why when dinner is served. The missus will have stuffed the ducks with bread crumbs and baked them in a 325 degree oven for three hours, creating in the process a classic *je ne sais quoi*. Served thus, with some dried-out peas, mashed potatoes and a cup of coffee, a date with an icebox full of wet hair would be preferable.

The best way to bail out the evening, aside from very heavy drinking, is to convince the hosts the bird was delicious, and hope they'll give away the rest of the ducks from their freezer. Later they will make fun of you as a screwball, but you will have skated off with the raw material for many quasi-orgasmic moments.

I am sitting with my friend Joe in his living room overlooking San Francisco Bay. I know Joe shares and understands my love affair with the wild duck. We talk of duck hunting and duck eating.

"Let's go next door," he says. "My new neighbor is a duck-eating fanatic."

Next door it is clear that Hal, his new neighbor, doesn't trust me any more than I trust him. I am sure he uses too cool an oven, over-cooks the birds, and makes a disgusting sauce, if any. He no doubt believes I dredge the birds in flour, chicken-fry the living piss out of them, and dish them up with boiled potatoes.

"How do you fix them?" I ask cautiously.

"Roast them in a hot oven."

"How hot?"

"Five hundred degrees for about twenty minutes."

"Jesus, that's right! Use sauce?"

"Yep." Hal knows he has an audience now and stops to causally refill his glass.

"Wine sauce?"

"Wine, Worcestershire, lemon."

We fall onto the couch excitedly. His sauce is perfect, that is to say, exactly like mine. He coats the birds generously with butter and salt. He uses a very hot oven. Cooks them fast. Likes them rare. With wild rice. Wine sauce. French bread. And good wine.

Joes is giggling absurdly. He gets a shotgun out of the gun rack and tracks imaginary birds with it across the living room. Hal and I get down to some serious duck talk. By serious, I mean we are going to do it. Have a duck dinner together.

The problem is that duck season has been closed for eight weeks. A Long Island duckling or any other market duck is as much like a wild duck as a twelve-pound self-basting turkey is like a mourning dove. We could use frozen birds left over from the season and trust that they've been treated properly. Hal admits having two sprig. Joe has three teal. This little piggy has none.

Trade, that's it, trade somebody something for one. How about a nice fresh striped bass for a mallard or two? My brother still has ducks in his freezer and yes, he says he would like to have a bass.

I know a place to catch one and the following evening I'm fly casting into the teeth of a spring gale, waiting for the first feeders. The first one comes almost to the boat before the hook pulls loose. With an easy flip of its tail I see a plump mallard glide out of sight into the murky waters of the bay. The wind gets stronger and my chances of not hooking another fish are steadily improving.

Surprisingly, a bass surfaces near shore, and in a quick backhand maneuver I cover him and he's on. This duck puts up a good fight but is no match for the ferocity with which I haul him over the transom and make him mine.

When you consider the great cuisines of the world, notably those of the Orient and France, many of the finer dishes are made with duck. In a sense, duck is to chicken what pork is to veal. It has extraordinary texture and flavor.

Because of their fine qualities, ducks have been domesticated for centuries. In France the two most commonly raised for the table are Rouen duck and the smaller Nantes duck. There are several other varieties, including a crossbreed used especially for foie gras. The Rouen duck is unique partly because of the way it is killed. In order to be sure the bird loses absolutely no blood, it is smothered. Because of this the blood remains distributed in the meat, giving it a reddish brown color and a special flavor which is highly valued. These ducks are eaten the day they are killed to avoid a possible build up of toxins.

Wild ducks are found in the Orient, but there, too, the birds were long ago domesticated and thoroughly incorporated into the cuisine. For instance, in the north, ducks are sometimes inflated with air so that the skin lifts away from the flesh to become very crispy, creating the famous Peking duck. In the south, ducks are often filled with seasoned liquids, then roasted to create Cantonese duck. The Chinese roast, simmer, braise, smoke, steam and deep-fry ducks. The results are universally sublime: the aforementioned Peking duck, roast-honey duck, chestnut-braised duck, red-simmered duck, eight-jewel duck, white-simmered duck, Nanking duck, duck steamed with tangerines, steamed deep-fried pressed duck, stir-fried duck, tea-smoked duck, and hundreds of variations on these recipes.

The French have their famous *caneton à l'orange* and variations thereof, duckling mousse, duckling with cherries, olives, turnips, sauerkraut or peas, and the remarkable *gallantine de caneton*. But perhaps the duck's finest moment in classic French cuisine arrives in the form of *caneton Rouennais en salmis à la presse*, described by the redoubtable Paul Bocuse as Rouen duck from the Hôtel de la Couronne, and of which he says, "…it is the best one can imagine." Essentially, this is a roasted duck, carved in the standard French manner, served with a sauce made in part of the reduced juices pressed from the bird's carcass. This dish is guaranteed to make you forget all about the farmer advancing across his barnyard, pillow in hand.

All of this exotic and sophisticated cookery notwithstanding, a wild duck remains a wild duck. The reason why domestic and wild birds are so unlike one another is very simple. Domestic ducks walk slowly around the barnyard, and are generously fed so their meat lacks density and becomes laden with fat. In the United States, the ducks which best demonstrate this are the Long Island ducklings available in markets. Wild waterfowl are all migratory. They travel thousands of miles at high speed. It is said that the reason ducks and geese fly in a "V" formation is that the strongest bird leads and the others follow in his slipstream. When he tires, one of the birds which has been traveling toward the rear moves up to take his place. These waterfowl suggest the vast scope of seasonal mysteries through a tremendous display of grace and nobility.

The heart is the only other muscle which must sustain longer and more even activity than the breast of the wild duck or goose. For this reason, the breasts of these birds are very large, rich with life-giving blood, and extremely dense, the birds themselves being almost entirely without fat. Wild goose, incidentally, is also totally unlike its domestic counterpart. No other table bird has as much fat as a barnyard goose. Wild goose, like wild duck, has none. Therefore if you follow a recipe for domestic goose while trying to cook a wild one, you'll ruin it.

As with other dark-meated birds and animals—sage hens, doves, antelope and deer for instance—very precise cooking is essential. Oven temperature should never fall below 450 degrees and cooking time is short. Mere minutes too long and these meats will be dried out and ruined. All game, especially wild duck, should be cooked rare. If you don't like it you should stick to gruel or corned beef hash. A friend recently pointed out that waitresses in the sleaziest diner in America always ask how you want your steak cooked. You might say in this case it's a toss up who is more ignorant, the fry cook or the customer. In a truly fine restaurant, never is the diner asked how he would like something cooked. That is the chef's job.

In Europe, game is available in most good restaurants. Chefs there have centuries of experience to inform them and they never get it wrong. In America, it is unlawful to sell game of any kind and so it remains the hunter's reward alone. Here, the chef who must get it right is you.

I call Joe. "Got some ducks. When can we do it?"

"How about this Thursday night? That'll give us time to think about it for a few days, you know, *to get ready.* I'll call Hal because he'll want to leave work early that day."

On Wednesday I am in San Francisco looking around some of the galleries when I run into a woman I'd met almost a year earlier. We were at a party and she had taken me home. She was a musician and in her apartment a cello leaned against the Steinway. I had thought of Casals passionately instructing a young female student to "hold it like it was your husband." Was I going to be her cello?

She was so fully ripe a woman, with such an important frame, that there was nothing to do but whatever she might ask. She came right to the point, telling me to get undressed and wait for her in bed. In that zone of half-consciousness we all recognize as the result of too many drugs I began to wonder if she was crazy and if so was she also dangerous. I heard voices coming from the bathroom. Perhaps, I thought, she is talking to herself before slashing her wrists, or worse, planning to bring razor blades to bed. When I peeked through the door she was naked and had a green parrot on her shoulder and they were talking. When it got light she had woven me into a cocoon of sexual heat that stupefied me for weeks.

Now, a year and half-dozen fruitless phone calls later, we are sitting having a cappucino and her voice is deeper than I remember, her hair darker red. When we are about to part she says simply, "Be at my apartment at nine tomorrow night. Ciao."

"Joe listen, there's this woman… well, what I was wondering was could we possibly do the duck thing on Friday night."

"Are you kidding? You're kidding, aren't you? Hal would short circuit. The ducks are thawed! We've been *getting ready.*"

"But I… you're right. What am I saying? I'll be there."

On Thursday I make an ingredients run. You can't trust anyone else to do this. First stop is the Sonoma Bakery on the town square in Sonoma to purchase the San Francisco Bay area's finest loaf. The French salesgirl drops the magnificent two-pounder into the bag and it hits bottom with a sound like hands clapping.

Next stop is Petrini's in Greenbrae, one of the great supermarkets on earth. I buy two-dozen fresh bluepoints, large perfect avocados, two grapefruit, fresh lemons, parsley, shallots, garlic, unsalted butter, Worcestershire, red currants, red-currant jelly, a dry red wine for the sauce, and at the deli counter, a good brie.

In Sausalito I find two bottles of Echézeaux and Pommard, old, heavy, aromatic reds that seem just the thing to go with the duck. And a bottle of Cordon Bleu brandy. I have a handful of dry bay leaves from a tree near my mother's house, and from the Ramy Seed Co. in Minnesota, a pound-and-a-half of extra-long-grain wild rice.

When Joe and I get to Hal's his lady is putting on her coat. "I don't want to know anything about this," she says, backing out the door. Hal explains that she saw it before and was appalled. His ducks are sitting on the sideboard. From his wine rack he has taken two bottles of Châteauneuf-du-Pape and they are standing open. I open my bottles and we begin to examine the ducks, counting wounds, guessing ages, noting the peculiarities of each species. We have a mallard, two sprig, three teal, and two wigeon.

We dress up the bluepoints with a dash a Tabasco and lemon juice. They are light and fresh, perfect with a bottle of Fumé Blanc which just happened to be in Hal's refrigerator. The bay outside the window looks like modern art, shiny and pinkish in the afterglow of a smooth spring day. Two canvasbacks swim by and I undress them in my mind.

The beginning of our sauce is the end result of a previous meal. A stock was made by simmering duck carcasses with vegetables, and was then frozen. Now it will be heated and reduced. We drop in a couple of the bay leaves.

"What the hell do you think you're doing, Hal?"

"I'm going to stuff the ducks with this onion."

"I knew it. Joe, he's going to ruin the goddamn ducks."

"Trust me. I stuff them loosely. Little salt and pepper. Little onion. Little butter. Splash of sherry."

"Okay. But make mine extra loose. And for God's sake, when you put them in the oven don't let the ducks touch one another."

We bring the wild rice to a boil twice, rinsing it each time. The trick is to cook it more by soaking in hot water than by actual simmering. Brought to a boil for the third time, in chicken stock rather than plain water, it is removed from the heat and left to stand. I make a small salad of avocado slices and grapefruit sections, finishing it with a vinaigrette dressing.

We turn the oven up to 500 degrees. Before roasting, the ducks must be completely and heavily covered with butter softened to room temperature. The birds are then salted and put on a low rack set on a shallow roasting pan.

Timing will be crucial, so it pays not to drink too much until the birds are cooked, carved and served. The three big ducks go in first, followed seven minutes later by the wigeon. Six minutes later the three teal go in, and ten minutes after that all the ducks are done. When the ducks come out of the oven, Hal and I carve them carefully into two halves, disjointing the wings and legs from both the carcasses and the breast meat. These are set on a warm platter.

Meanwhile, Joe has added to the stock a dash of Worcestershire, a bit of finely-chopped shallot, and several squeezes of lemon juice. The stock is boiled rapidly for some minutes to develop its flavor and also reduce it a bit further. Finally it is strained into a skillet, brought to a fast simmer, and the carved duck placed skin side up in it to take the blood-rare edge away from the carved face. We are careful not to leave the birds in this stock more than about ten seconds. Hal has a wonderful kitchen utensil not much in demand around the suburbs these days: a duck press. The halves of duck are placed on a covered, heated platter, ready to be served. The carcasses are then pressed to extract every bit of juice, which is then added to the reduced stock. We add some pre-soaked currants, and the sauce is done. Finally, the French bread is toasted under the broiler, rubbed with a garlic clove, and liberally buttered. We are ready to eat.

Before long, rice and sauce cover the table. Lemon wedges lie scattered about. French bread is torn loose. Each bite of rare, juicy meat is a new thrill, wild duck being something like a cross between filet mignon and fresh deer heart, only with more flavor than either.

Our wine glasses become increasingly grease-smeared as we pick up each carcass and suck it down to bare bone and gristle. We carelessly gulp the fancy vintages. Our shirt fronts are ruined. Juice and blood run from elbows onto knees and the floor. The room is blurred. We belch, fart, laugh and groan.

As the carnage winds down I think about my date and wonder if it's too late, but the face of the clock refuses to come into focus. I find a mirror and what I see reflected there can only be described as soiled.

I grab a glass of cognac and flop into a lounge chair out on the deck. The salt air feels good and as I gaze vacantly into the middle distance, nearly comatose, I wish without much conviction that her tits were in my eyes.

Hairy Gertz and the Forty-Seven Crappies

Jean Shepherd

ife, when you're a Male kid, is what the Grownups are doing. The
Adult world seems to be some kind of secret society that has its
own passwords, handclasps, and countersigns. The thing is to get In.
But there's this invisible, impenetrable wall between you and all the
great, unimaginably swinging things that they seem to be involved in.
Occasionally mutterings of exotic secrets and incredible pleasures fil-
ter through. And so you bang against it, throw rocks at it, try to climb
over it, burrow under it; but there it is. Impenetrable. Enigmatic.

Girls somehow seem to be already involved, as though from birth
they've got the Word. Lolita has no Male counterpart. It does no good
to protest and pretend otherwise. The fact is inescapable. A male kid is
really a *kid*. A female kid is a *girl*. Some guys give up early in life, sur-
render completely before the impassable transparent wall, and remain
little kids forever. They are called "Fags," or "Homosexuals," if you are
in polite society.

The rest of us have to claw our way into Life as best we can, never
knowing when we'll be Admitted. It happens to each of us in different
ways—and once it does, there's no turning back.

It happened to me at the age of twelve in Northern Indiana—a
remarkably barren terrain resembling in some ways the surface of the
moon, encrusted with steel mills, oil refineries, and honky-tonk bars.
There was plenty of natural motivation for Total Escape. Some kids got
hung up on kite flying, others on pool playing. I became the greatest
vicarious angler in the history of the Western world.

I say vicarious because there just wasn't any actual fishing to be
done around where I lived. So I would stand for hours in front of the
goldfish tank at Woolworth's, landing fantails in my mind, after incredible struggles. I read *Field & Stream*, *Outdoor Life* and *Sports Afield* the
way other kids read *G-8 And His Battle Aces*. I would break out in a

cold sweat reading about these guys portaging to Alaska and landing rare salmon; and about guys climbing the High Sierras to do battle with the wily golden trout; and mortal combat with the steelheads. I'd read about craggy, sinewy sportsmen who discover untouched bass lakes where they have to beat off the pickerel with an oar, and the saber-toothed, raging smallmouths chase them ashore and right up into the woods

After reading one of these fantasies I would walk around in a daze for hours, feeling the cork pistol grip of my imaginary trusty six-foot, split-bamboo bait-casting rod in my right hand and hearing the high-pitched scream of my Pflueger Supreme reel straining to hold a seventeen-pound Great Northern in check.

I became known around town as "the-kid-who-is-the-nut-on-fishing," even went to the extent of learning how to tie flies, although I'd never been fly casting in my life. I read books on the subject. And in my bedroom, while the other kids are making balsa models of Curtiss Robins, I am busy tying Silver Doctors, Royal Coachmen, and Black Gnats. They were terrible. I would try out one in the bathtub to see whether it made a ripple that might frighten off the wily rainbow.

"Glonk!"

Down to the bottom like a rock, my floating dry fly would go. Fishing was part of the mysterious and unattainable Adult world. I wanted In.

My Old Man was In, though he was what you might call a once-in-a-while-fisherman-and-beer-party-goer; they are the same thing in the shadow of the blast furnaces. (I knew even then that there are people who Fish and there are people who Go Fishing; they're two entirely different creatures.) My Old Man did not drive 1500 miles to the Atlantic shore with 3000 pounds of Abercrombie & Fitch fishing tackle to angle for stripers. He was the kind who would Go Fishing maybe once a month during the summer when it was too hot to Go Bowling and all of the guys down at the office would get The Itch. To them, fishing was a way of drinking a lot of beer and yelling. And getting away from the women. To me, it was a sacred thing. To *fish*.

He and these guys from the office would get together and go down to one of the lakes a few miles from where we lived—but never to Lake Michigan, which wasn't far away. I don't know why; I guess it was too big and awesome. In any case, nobody ever really thought of fishing in it. At least nobody in my father's mob. They went mostly to a mudhole known as Cedar Lake.

I will have to describe to you what a lake in the summer in Northern Indiana is like. To begin with, heat, in Indiana, is something else again. It descends like a 300-pound fat lady onto a picnic bench in the middle of July. It can literally be sliced into chunks and stored away in the basement to use in winter; on cold days you just bring it out and turn it on. Indiana heat is not a meteorological phenomenon—it is a solid element, something you can grab by the handles. Almost every day in the summer the whole town is just shimmering in front of you. You'd look across the street and skinny people would be all fat and wiggly like in the fun-house mirrors at Coney Island. The asphalt in the streets would bubble and hiss like a pot of steaming Ralston.

That kind of heat and sun produces mirages. All it takes is good flat country, a nutty sun, and insane heat and, by George, you're looking at Cleveland 200 miles away. I remember many times standing out in center field on an incinerating day in mid-August, the prairie stretching out endlessly in all directions, and way out past the swamp would be this kind of tenuous, shadowy, cloud-like thing shimmering just above the horizon. It would be the Chicago skyline, upside down, just hanging there in the sky. And after a while it would gradually disappear.

So, naturally, fishing is different in Indiana. The muddy lakes, about May, when the sun starts beating down on them, would begin to simmer and bubble quietly around the edges. These lakes are not fed by springs or streams. I don't know what feeds them. Maybe seepage. Nothing but weeds and truck axles on the bottom; flat, low, muddy banks, surrounded by cottonwood trees, cattails, smelly marshes, and old dumps. Archetypal dumps. Dumps gravitate to Indiana lakes like flies to a hog killing. Way down at the end where the water is shallow and soupy are the old cars and the ashes, busted refrigerators, oil drums, old corsets, and God knows what else.

At the other end of the lake is the Roller Rink. There's *always* a Roller Rink. You can hear that old electric organ going, playing "Heartaches," and you can hear the sound of the roller skates:

"Shhhhhh… sssshhhhhhhhh… ssssssshhhhhhhhhhhhhhhh…."

And the fistfights breaking out. The Roller Rink Nut in heat. The Roller Rink Nut was an earlier incarnation of the Drive-In Movie Nut. He was the kind who was very big with stainless steel diners, motels, horror movies, and frozen egg rolls. A close cousin to the Motorcycle

Clod, he went ape for chicks with purple eyelids. You know the crowd. Crewcuts, low foreheads, rumbles, hollering, belching, drinking beer, roller skating on one foot, wearing black satin jackets with SOUTH SIDE A.C. lettered in white on the back around a white-winged roller-skated foot. The kind that hangs the stuff in the back windows of their '53 Mercuries; a huge pair of foam-rubber dice, a skull and crossbones, hula-hula dolls, and football players—Pro, of course, with heads that bob up and down. The guys with ball fringe around the windows of their cars, with phony Venetian blinds in the back, and big white rubber mudguards hanging down, with red reflectors. Or they'll take some old heap and line it with plastic imitation mink fur, pad the steering wheel with leopard skin and ostrich feathers until it weighs seventeen pounds and is as fat as a salami. A TV set, a bar, and a folding Castro bed are in the trunk, automatically operated and all lined with tasteful Sears Roebuck ermine. You know the crew—a true American product. We turn them out like Campbell's Pork & Beans.

This is the system of aesthetics that brought the Roller Rink to Cedar Lake, Indiana, when I was a kid.

About 150 yards from the Roller Rink was the Cedar Lake Evening In Paris Dance Hall. Festering and steamy and thronged with yeasty refugees from the Roller Rink. These are the guys who can't skate. But they can do other things. They're down there jostling back and forth in 400-per-cent humidity to the incomparable sounds of an Indiana dancehall band. Twelve non-Union cretinous musicians—Mickey Iseley's Moonlight Serenaders—blowing "Red Sails In the Sunset" on Montgomery Ward altos. The lighting is a tasteful combination of naked light bulbs, red and blue crepe paper, and orange cellophane gels.

In between the Roller Rink and the Dance Hall are seventeen small shacks known as Beer Halls. And surrounding this tiny oasis of civilization, this bastion of bonhomie, is a gigantic sea of total darkness, absolute pitch-black Stygian darkness, around this tiny island of totally decadent, bucolic American merriment. The roller skates are hissing, the beer bottles are crashing, the chicks are squealing, Mickey's reed men are quavering, and Life is full.

And in the middle of the lake, several yards away, are over 17,000 fishermen, in wooden rowboats rented at a buck and a half an hour. It is 2 A.M. The temperature is 175, with humidity to match. And the smell of decayed toads, the dumps at the far end of the lake, and an occasional *soupçon* of Standard Oil, whose refinery is a couple of miles away, is enough to put hair on the back of a mud turtle. Seventeen thousand guys clumped together in the middle, fishing for the known sixty-four crappies in that lake.

Crappies are a special breed of Midwestern fish, created by God for the express purpose of surviving in waters that would kill a bubonic-plague bacillus. They have never been known to fight, or even faintly struggle. I guess when you're a crappie, you figure it's no use anyway. One thing is as bad as another. They're just down there in the soup. No one quite knows what they eat, if anything, but everybody's fishing for them. At two o'clock in the morning.

Each boat contains a minimum of nine guys and fourteen cases of beer. And once in a while, in the darkness, is heard the sound of a guy falling over backward into the slime:

SSSSGLUNK!

"Oh! Ah! Help, help!" A piteous cry in the darkness. Another voice:

"Hey, for God's sake, Charlie's fallen in again! Grab the oar!"

And then it slowly dies down. Charlie is hauled out of the goo and is lying on the bottom of the boat, urping up dead lizards and Atlas Prager. Peace reigns again.

The water in these lakes is not the water you know about. It is composed of roughly ten per cent waste glop spewed out by Shell, Sinclair, Phillips, and the Grasselli Chemical Corporation; twelve per cent used detergent; thirty-five per cent thick gruel composed of decayed garter snakes, deceased toads, fermenting crappies, and a strange, unidentifiable liquid that holds it all together. No one is quite sure *what* that is, because everybody is afraid to admit what it really is. They don't want to look at it too closely.

So this mélange lays there under the sun, and about August it is slowly simmering like a rich mulligatawny stew. At two in the morning you can hear the water next to the boat in the darkness:

"Gluuummp… Bluuuummmp."

Big bubbles of some unclassified gas come up from the bottom and burst. The natives, in their superstitious way, believe that it is highly inflammable. They take no chances.

The saddest thing of all is that on these lakes there are usually about nineteen summer cottages to the square foot, each equipped with a large motorboat. The sound of a 40-horsepower Chris-Craft going through a sea of number-ten oil has to be heard to be believed.

RRRRRRRAAAAAAAAAHHHHHHHHHWWWWWWWWWWRRRRRRRRRR!

The prow is sort of parting the stuff, slowly stirring it into a sluggish, viscous wake.

Natives actually *swim* in this water. Of course, it is impossible to swim near the shore, because the shore is one great big sea of mud that goes all the way down to the core of the earth. There are stories of whole towns being swallowed up and stored in the middle of the earth. So the native rows out to the middle of the lake and hurls himself off the back seat of his rowboat.

"GLURP!"

It is impossible to sink in this water. The specific gravity and surface tension make the Great Salt Lake seem dangerous for swimming. You don't sink. You just bounce a little and float there. You literally have to hit your head on the surface of these lakes to get under a few inches. Once you do, you come up streaming mosquito eggs and dead toads—an Indiana specialty—and all sorts of fantastic things which are the offshoot of various exotic merriments which occur outside the Roller Rink.

The bottom of the lake is composed of a thick incrustation of old beer cans. The beer cans are at least a thousand feet thick in certain places.

And so 17,000 fishermen gather in one knot, because it is rumored that here is where The Deep Hole is. All Indiana lakes have a Deep Hole, into which, as the myth goes, the fish retire to sulk in the hot weather. Which is always.

Every month or so an announcement would be made by my Old Man, usually on a Friday night, after work.

"I'm getting up early tomorrow morning. I'm going fishing."

Getting up early and going fishing with Hairy Gertz and the crowd meant getting out of the house about three o'clock in the afternoon, roughly. Gertz was a key member of the party. He owned the Coleman lamp. It was part of the folklore that if you had a bright lantern in your boat the fish could not resist it. The idea was to hold the lantern out over the water and the fish would have to come over to see what was going on. Of course, when the fish arrived, there would be your irresistible worm, and that would be it.

Well, these Coleman lamps may not have drawn fish, but they worked great on mosquitoes. One of the more yeasty experiences in Life is to occupy a tiny rented rowboat with eight other guys, knee-deep in beer cans, with a blinding Coleman lamp hanging out of the boat, at 2 A.M., with the lamp hissing like Fu Manchu about to strike and every mosquito in the Western Hemisphere descending on you in the middle of Cedar Lake.

ZZZZZZZZZZZZZZZZZZZZZTTTTTTTTTTTT

They *love* Coleman lamps. In the light they shed the mosquitoes swarm like rain. And in the darkness all around there'd be other lights in other boats, and once in a while a face would float above one. Everyone is coated with an inch and a half of something called citronella, reputedly a mosquito repellent but actually a sort of mosquito salad dressing.

The water is absolutely flat. There has not been a breath of air since April. It is now August. The surface is one flat sheet of old used oil laying in the darkness, with the sounds of the Roller Rink floating out over it, mingling with the angry drone of the mosquitoes and muffled swearing from the other boats. A fistfight breaks out at the Evening In Paris. The sound of sirens can be heard faintly in the Indiana blackness. It gets louder and then fades away. Tiny orange lights bob over the dance floor.

"Raaahhhhhd sails in the sawwwwnnnnsehhhht...."

It's the drummer who sings. He figures some day Ted Weems will be driving by, and hear him, and...

"...haaaahhhhhhwwww brightlyyyy they shinneee..."

There is nothing like a band vocalist in a rotten, struggling Mickey band. When you've heard him over 2000 yards of soupy, oily water, filtered through fourteen billion feeding mosquitoes in the August heat, he is particularly juicy and ripe. He is overloading the ten-watt Allied Radio Knight amplifier by at least 400 per cent, the gain turned all the way up, his chrome-plated bullet-shaped crystal mike on the edge of feedback.

"Raaahhhhhd sails in the sawwwwnnnnsehhhht...."

It is the sound of the American night. And to a twelve-year-old kid it is exciting beyond belief.

Then my Old Man, out of the blue, says to me:

"You know, if you're gonna come along, you got to clean the fish."

Gonna come along! My God! I wanted to go fishing more than anything else in the world, and my Old Man wanted to drink beer more than anything else in the world, and so did Gertz and the gang, and more than even *that*, they wanted to get away from all the women.

They wanted to get out on the lake and tell dirty stories and drink beer and get eaten by mosquitoes; just sit out there and sweat and be Men. They wanted to get away from work, the car payments, the lawn, the mill, and everything else.

And so here I am, in the dark, in a rowboat with The Men. I am half-blind with sleepiness. I am used to going to bed at nine-thirty or ten o'clock, and here it is two, three o'clock in the morning. I'm squatting in the back end of the boat, with 87,000,000 mosquitoes swarming over me, but I am *fishing!* I am out of my skull with fantastic excitement, hanging onto my pole.

In those days, in Indiana, they fished with gigantic cane poles. They knew not from Spinning. A cane pole is a long bamboo pole that's maybe twelve or fifteen feet in length; it weighs a ton, and tied to the end of it is about thirty feet of thick green line, roughly half the weight of the average clothesline, three big lead sinkers, a couple of crappie hooks, and a bobber.

One of Sport's most exciting moments is when 7 Indiana fishermen in the same boat simultaneously and without consulting one another decide to pull their lines out of the water and recast. In total darkness. First the pole, rising like a huge whip:

"Whooooooooooooooop!"

Then the lines, whirling overhead:

"Wheeeeeeeeeeeeeoooooooooooo!

And then:

"OH! FOR CHRISSAKE! WHAT THE HELL?"

Clunk! CLONK!

Sound of cane poles banging together, and lead weights landing in the boat. And such brilliant swearing as you have never heard. Yelling, hollering, with somebody always getting a hook stuck in the back of his ear. And, of course, all in complete darkness, the Coleman lamp at the other end of the rowboat barely penetrating the darkness in a circle of three or four feet.

"Hey, for God's sake, Gertz, will ya tell me when you're gonna pull your pole up!? Oh, Jesus Christ, look at this mess!"

There is nothing worse than trying to untangle seven cane poles, 200 feet of soggy green line, just as they are starting to hit in the other boats. Sound carries over water:

"Shhhhh! I got a bite!"

The fishermen with the tangled lines become frenzied. Fingernails are torn, hooks dig deeper into thumbs, and kids huddle terrified out of range in the darkness.

You have been sitting for twenty hours, and nothing. A bobber just barely visible in the dark water is one of the most beautiful sights known to man. It's not doing anything, but there's always the feeling that at any instant it might. It just lays out there in the darkness. A luminous bobber, a beautiful thing, with a long, thin quill and a tiny red-and-white float, with just the suggestion of a line reaching into the black water. These are special bobbers for *very* tiny fish.

I have been watching my bobber so hard and so long in the darkness that I am almost hypnotized. I have not had a bite—ever—but the excitement of being there is enough for me, a kind of delirious joy that has nothing to do with sex or any of the more obvious pleasures. To this day, when I hear some guy singing in that special drummer's voice, it comes over me. It's two o'clock in the morning again. I'm a kid. I'm tired. I'm excited. I'm having the time of my life.

And at the other end of the lake:

"Raaahhhhhd sails in the sawwwwwnnnnsehhhht...."

The Roller Rink drones on, and the mosquitoes are humming. The Coleman lamp sputters, and we're all sitting together in our little boat.

Not really together, since I am a kid, and they are Men, but at least I'm there. Gertz is stewed to the ears. He is down at the other end. He has this fantastic collection of rotten stories, and early in the evening my Old Man keeps saying:

"There's a kid with us, you know."

But by two in the morning all of them have had enough so that it doesn't matter. They're telling stories, and I don't care. I'm just sitting there, clinging to my cane pole when, by God, I get a nibble!

I don't believe it. The bobber straightens up, jiggles, dips, and comes to rest in the gloom. I whisper:

"I got a bite!"

The storytellers look up from their beer cans in the darkness.

"What...? Hey, whazzat?"

"Shhhhh! Be quiet!"

We sit in silence, everybody watching his bobber through the haze of insects. The drummer is singing in the distance. We hang suspended for long minutes. Then suddenly all the bobbers dipped and went under. The crappies are hitting!

You never saw anything like it! We are pulling up fish as fast as we can get them off the hooks. Crappies are flying into the boat, one after the other, and hopping around on the bottom in the darkness, amid the empty beer cans. Within twenty minutes we have landed forty-seven fish. We are knee-deep in crappies. The jackpot!

Well, the Old Man just goes wild. They are all yelling and screaming and pulling the fish in—while the other boats around us are being skunked. The fish have come out of their hole or whatever it is that they are in at the bottom of the lake, the beer cans and the old tires, and have decided to eat.

You can hear the rest of the boats pulling up anchors and rowing over, frantically. They are thumping against us. There's a big, solid phalanx of wooden boats around us. You could walk from one boat to the other for miles around. And still they are skunked. We are catching the fish!

By 3 A.M. they've finally stopped biting, and an hour later we are back on land. I'm falling asleep in the rear seat between Gertz and Zudock. We're driving home in the dawn, and the men are hollering, drinking, throwing beer cans out on the road, and having a great time.

We are back at the house, and my father says to me as we are coming out of the garage with Gertz and the rest of them:

"And now Ralph's gonna clean the fish. Let's go in the house and have something to eat. Clean 'em on the back porch, will ya, kid?"

In the house they go. The lights go on in the kitchen; they sit down and start eating sandwiches and making coffee. And I am out on the back porch with forty-seven live, flopping crappies.

They are well named. Fish that are taken out of muddy, rotten, lousy, stinking lakes are muddy, rotten, lousy, stinking fish. It is as simple as that. And they are made out of some kind of hard rubber.

I get my Scout knife and go to work. Fifteen minutes and twenty-one crappies later I am sick over the side of the porch. But I do not stop. It is part of Fishing.

By now, nine neighborhood cats and a raccoon have joined me on the porch, and we are all working together. The August heat, now that we are away from the lake, is even hotter. The uproar in the kitchen is getting louder and louder. There is nothing like a motley collection of Indiana office workers who have just successfully defeated Nature and have brought home the kill. Like cave men of old, they celebrate around the campfire with song and drink. And belching.

I have now finished the last crappie and am wrapping the clean fish in the editorial page of the *Chicago Tribune*. It has a very tough paper that doesn't leak. Especially the editorial page.

The Old Man hollers out:

"How you doing? Come in and have a Nehi."

I enter the kitchen, blinded by that big yellow light bulb, weighted down with a load of five-and-a-half-inch crappies, covered with fish scales and blood, and smelling like the far end of Cedar Lake. There are worms under my fingernails from baiting hooks all night, and I am feeling at least nine feet tall. I spread the fish out on the sink—and old Hairy Gertz says:

"My God! Look at those *speckled beauties!*" An expression he had picked up from *Outdoor Life*.

The Old Man hands me a two-pound liverwurst sandwich and a bottle of Nehi orange. Gertz is now rolling strongly, as are the other eight file clerks, all smelly, and mosquito-bitten, eyes red-rimmed from the Coleman lamp, covered with worms and with the drippings of at least fifteen beers apiece. Gertz hollers:

"Ya know, lookin' at them fish reminds me of a story." He is about to uncork his cruddiest joke of the night. They all lean forward over the white enamel kitchen table with the chipped edges, over the salami and the beer bottles, the rye bread and the mustard. Gertz digs deep into his vast file of obscenity.

"One time there was this Hungarian bartender, and ya know, he had a cross-eyed daughter and a bowlegged dachshund. And this. . . .."

At first I am holding back, since I am a kid. The Old Man says:

"Hold it down, Gertz. You'll wake up the wife and she'll raise hell."

He is referring to My Mother.

Gertz lowers his voice and they all scrunch their chairs forward amid a great cloud of cigar smoke. There is only one thing to do. I scrunch forward, too, and stick my head into the huddle, right next to the Old Man, into the circle of leering, snickering, fishy-smelling faces. Of course, I do not even remotely comprehend the gist of the story. But I know that it is rotten to the core.

Gertz belts out the punch line; the crowd bellows and beats on the table. They begin uncapping more Blatz.

Secretly, suddenly, and for the first time, I realize that I am In. The Eskimo pies and Nehi oranges are all behind me, and a whole new world is stretching out endlessly and wildly in all directions before me. I have gotten The Signal!

Suddenly my mother is in the doorway in her Chinese-red chenille bathrobe. Ten minutes later I am in the sack, and out in the kitchen Gertz is telling another one. The bottles are rattling, and the file clerks are hunched around the fire celebrating their primal victory over The Elements.

Somewhere off in the dark the Monon Louisville Limited wails as it snakes through the Gibson Hump on its way to the outside world. The giant Indiana moths, at least five pounds apiece, are banging against the window screens next to my bed. The cats are fighting in the backyard over crappie heads, and fish scales are itching in my hair as I joyfully, ecstatically slide off into the great world beyond.

© John Troy

"Anybody can get hooked in a tree; you can tell
the real pros by how they get loose."

Honey, He Shrunk My Head!

John Meacham

As soon as Talbot Taylor answered the telephone, he knew he would get his deer that day, and he knew it would be a buck. A big buck. A huge buck. A MONSTROUS buck. A buck whose rack would easily surpass the 140 points needed to qualify for the Illinois Big Buck Recognition Program, and probably the 170 required for the Boone & Crockett record book.

Talbot knew that the buck he would get that day would probably be so big that he would never have to hunt another one. It was in the bag. Or rather, it was in the shop. The phone call was from taxidermist Robbie "Mountain Man" Horner, who told Talbot that his trophy was finished and ready for him to pick up.

"Pick up!" Talbot said. "Are you kidding! As much as I'm paying you, I expect delivery, and I expect it right now!"

Talbot couldn't help chuckling as he slammed down the receiver. He'd been eagerly awaiting this day for nearly three months. Now that his moment of triumph was just minutes away, he knew it would be even more satisfying than he had dreamed.

"When he gets here, I'll have to find some little flaw to complain about," he thought, even though he had seen enough of Horner's work to know that the man was truly an artist. "Maybe I'll even demand a discount. Boy, that would really twist the knife in his gut!"

Yes, and Talbot would do it, too, because hurting Horner was the only reason Talbot had hunted this deer, and the only reason he had taken it to Horner to have it mounted. The man had been his bitterest rival since their high school days, when Horner was the quarterback of the football team, and Talbot played flute in the band. When Horner hit home runs and pitched no-hitters for the baseball team, and Talbot carried the bats and balls. When Horner was captain of the basketball team, and Talbot warmed the bench. When Horner could get a date with any girl he wanted, and Talbot spent Saturday nights with the boys.

"But he cares more about deer hunting than he did all of that put together, so this buck of mine should just about get me even," Talbot thought. He was so excited that he paced the floor as he listened for Horner to drive up the lane. When he finally arrived, Talbot waited until he was on the front steps before telling him to go around to the back.

Horner was carrying the head under a white cloth. Talbot met him at the door and took his own sweet time inviting him in, even though it wasn't exactly sunny and warm on that February day.

"Well, Horner, you certainly took your time with this job," Talbot said. "I suppose you put it off as long as you could, and I can't say that I blame you."

"I didn't take my time, Talbot," Horner replied. "In fact, since this was yours and I knew it was your first deer, I did it ahead of a couple others that came in earlier. You wouldn't believe how busy I've been. I still have bass to mount from last summer."

"Oh, come on, Horner! Don't try to hand me that line of bunk! It broke your heart to mount this deer, and you know it!"

"Why should it have done that, Talbot?"

"You just don't give up, do you!" Talbot said. "You could be man enough to admit that I've whipped you, but since you won't, I'll spell it out for you. I saw your picture in the *Kickapoo County Smoke Signal* with that record buck you shot in 1995, and I made up my mind to get a bigger one in 1996. I'd never hunted deer or anything else in my life, but I did some homework and found out that Pike County has been one of the best places in the whole country for big bucks over the past few years, so I booked a hunt with George Metcalf on the White Oak Reserve up there. He guided me every step of the way. I outfitted myself with the best equipment money can buy, I was in exactly the right place at exactly the right time on opening morning, and you've seen the result for yourself."

"Yes, I've seen it, and it's a nice little deer, Talbot, but…"

"Little deer! Little! Why, this deer is half again as big as yours!"

"THIS DEER!"

"Of course, this deer!" Talbot said. "Which deer do you think we're talking about? This deer right here!"

Talbot whipped the cover off the head Horner had set on the

kitchen table and gasped. His jawbone bounced off his big toe as he realized he'd been had.

"Horner, where's my buck?"

"What are you talking about, Talbot? This is it."

"Oh, no, it isn't! My deer was a 12-pointer, and this is a six! My deer had a two-foot spread, and this one is barely half that! My deer's rack was thick and heavy! This one's looks like it's made of toothpicks! You're trying to pull a switch on me, and you're not going to get away with it!"

"Switch! I wouldn't do a thing like that, Talbot. It would cost me my reputation. I'd lose my business. What reason would I have to switch your deer head?"

"Oh, you had plenty of reason, buddy! You're just carrying on with a long tradition of putting me down!" Talbot said, and listed his grievances, one by one.

"I couldn't help any of that, Talbot," Horner said. "I was just bigger than you."

"Yes, and you didn't mind rubbing it in, either! You were the one who started calling me 'Too Tall' Taylor!"

"Yeah, that was me, all right," Horner admitted. "But I just did that to be ornery, because you were so short back then that you had to stand on a stool to comb your hair. I don't reckon you have to worry much about that now, though, Talbot. You don't have a whole lot of hair left to comb. Anyway, 'Too Tall' wasn't near as bad as what they used to call your granddaddy. I heard they called him 'Tall Butt.'"

"You just leave my grandfather out of this, Horner! I'll have you know that I'm very proud of my grandfather, and I'm honored that I was named after him!"

Talbot's full name was Talbot Buttram Taylor, II. Like many another man, Talbot, Sr. had made a fortune in the stock market during the Roaring Twenties. The difference was that he had seen the crash coming and unloaded before it arrived. Flush with cash, he had bought thousands of acres of Southern Illinois land at rock bottom prices during the Depression. Talbot, II's father, Tadd L. Taylor, sold most of this to the coal companies, adding so much to the family's fortune that young Talbot, as an only child, could indulge his every whim without a second thought.

"All right, Talbot, I'll let your grandfather rest in peace," Horner said. "But while we're talking about our high school days, I guess we ought to talk about Beth."

"What about her!" Talbot said.

"Why, don't you remember? I went steady with Beth Lee Hamm our senior year, and all that you other guys could do was watch and wish."

"That's right, but I'm the one who married her," Talbot reminded Horner—as if he had to remind him.

"Yeah, you're the one who married her—while I was off in Vietnam, fighting for Uncle Sam. But I've never held that against you, Talbot."

"Maybe not, but let's get back to the present here," Talbot said. "If you didn't switch my head on purpose, you must have done it by accident."

"No, I didn't. I put a metal tag in your deer's ear when you brought it in. I put a metal tag on the hide when I caped it out and I put another one on the bag I put it in. That's your deer, Talbot. You were just so excited when you shot it that you let your imagination run away with you, and it's been growing in your mind ever since."

"My imagination didn't run away with me, and neither did anything else, Horner, and I can prove it!" Talbot said. "I just remembered that Beth took a picture of me with my trophy before I took it to you, and pictures don't lie. Now, how do you like that!"

"I like it just fine, because it will prove that I'm right," Horner answered calmly.

Which it did. Talbot called to Beth, who was in the living room, and she brought him the photo. To Talbot's amazement, there he was with the same little deer that Horner claimed was his.

Of course, there could be only one explanation. Beth and Horner were in this together, and had somehow faked the photograph. They had undoubtedly destroyed the negative, too. And there could be only one reason why. They had rekindled their old flame and were lovers again. His wife and his lifelong enemy were having an affair behind his back, and had planned this trick just to make a fool of him.

Talbot said nothing, but silently vowed never to rest until he had taken his revenge. But first, he had to get them off their guard.

"I guess you were right, after all, Robbie," he said, extending his hand. "It looks like you're still the champ, and I'm still the chump."

"That's OK, Talbot. Forget it. And I wish you'd forget this rivalry nonsense, too. As far as I'm concerned, that's all in the past. Well, I have to get back to the shop. What time should I pick you up tonight, Beth?"

"Seven o'clock will be fine, Robbie," Beth told him. "What are you looking so shocked about, Talbot? You know all about this. It's our class's 25th anniversary, and we're having our reunion at the Valentine Ball tonight. We're supposed to go with the person we went with back in 1972, and Robbie and I were the King and Queen of Hearts. Don't you remember?"

Talbot remembered, all right! How could he ever forget! That was the night Beth had "worn" the dress that scandalized the school board and inspired him to write what had become the unofficial class song, "O little Gown of Beth Lee Hamm."

Talbot wondered whether she'd try to squeeze into it again tonight. He had no doubt that she could, if she wanted to, because his wife's figure was no more and no less awesome now than it had been back then. She had stayed in shape. At that moment, however, he didn't really care what she wore or didn't wear to the dance, because he had just had a brainstorm, and Beth and Horner's "date" would fit right in with his plan.

Horner returned at the appointed hour, and Talbot told them he had some business to take care of and would join them at the dance later. As soon as they had gone, he loaded his electric drill and his coarsest grinding wheel into his car, drove to Horner's taxidermy shop, climbed in through a window and up on a chair and reduced Horner's trophy to a button buck. When he had finished, those record antlers were nothing but splinters and dust.

Back on the road, Talbot debated whether to go to the high school, or home. If he went to the ball, it was entirely possible that Horner and Beth would humiliate him again, in front of all their old friends. But if he went home, he would be handing his wife to Horner without a fight.

Talbot turned toward the school, but as soon as he stepped through the door, he knew he'd made a big mistake. Two of Horner's old football teammates grabbed him by the shoulders. Talbot recognized them as an offensive lineman and a defensive tackle.

"The Mountain Man wants to see you, and he wants to see you now!" the lineman said. The two bruisers practically carried him into the gym, where Horner and Beth were seated on their thrones under the south basket.

"How could he have found out what I just did so soon?" Talbot wondered. He looked frantically for an exit, but they were all blocked by ex-linebackers. Horner rose from his seat and stepped to the microphone.

"I have an announcement to make," he said. "When the committee met to plan this celebration, they decided it would be appropriate to hold a new election for the royal couple. They counted the ballots yesterday and the winners, by a landslide, are Talbot and Beth Taylor. Congratulations, Too Tall! Everybody tells me it was Beth's campaigning that put you over the top. I know that's why I voted for you.

"Now, before I hand over my crown and you and your lovely lady lead us in the traditional first dance, there's just one more thing I have to say," Horner continued. "Talbot, your classmates—especially the men—want you to know how much they admire you for being able to keep your wife as happy as you obviously have for all these years. So, in recognition of your new title as the 'Horniest' Man in the Class of 1972, I hereby present you with this trophy. I'm sure you'll recognize it."

As the same two football players who had escorted him in brought him his head—or rather, his trophy buck's head—on a silver platter, all Talbot could think about was how beautiful Beth looked in—well, mostly in—her famous frock, and how much he was going to miss her when he was gone.

"Beth and I have been planning this practical joke ever since you brought this deer to my shop," Horner told him. "We really had you going for awhile this afternoon, didn't we, Talbot!"

Talbot didn't answer. He was too busy watching his life flash in front of his face.

The Cows Are Trying to Drown Me

Rich Tosches

I t was on a warm October day in 1979 that I found a stretch of the North Platte River that was bordered by farmland, the flowing water sparkling in the autumn sun, the kind of water that seems to be begging to be fly-fished by a moron. Recalling bumper stickers I had seen, I had my kid beat up your honor-student kid. Oops. Wrong bumper sticker. The one I mean says ASK FIRST!—and so I tracked down the landowner and asked permission to fish on his property.

He gave his approval and then added these words: "Be careful of the cows."

Be careful of the cows?

First of all, I couldn't see any cows. I had seen two white-tailed deer off in the distance as I walked along a road near his ranchland, and I wondered now if the amiable fellow thought they were cows. This is what can happen to you when you spend endless hours sitting on a horse in the hot sun, worrying about all the things ranchers worry about—mostly why your three sons insist on living in your house despite the fact that they are in their forties, and one of them calls himself "Hoss" and eats so goddamn much that your cook, Hop Sing, has tried to poison him, and the fact they never seem to have any girlfriends, which makes you wonder if maybe all three of them are gay!

Sorry.

Second, I wondered just how careful you have to be with cows when you're armed with nothing more than a five-weight St. Croix fly rod and a boxful of dry flies? I mean, even if you accidentally hook one, I'm sure the 6X tippet would break before the cow got into your backing—unless you were using Rio-brand leader material with superb abrasion resistance plus high knot and tensile strength.

I bet that will get me a big fat sponsor contract! I can see the new advertisement series now, featuring me saying: "Use Rio leaders and tippet. It can stop a cow!"

Anyway, I thanked the man and headed downstream and found a spectacular looking pool at the tail of some riffles. I sat on the bank for a few moments and saw heads popping up, heads of big rainbows slurping Tricos. I tied on my favorite, a parachute Trico, which is like a regular Trico except just as it hits the water a man leaps from an airplane, pulls the rip cord, and lands safely on the tiny fly.

No, a parachute has a tuft of hair that you can actually see from more than twelve inches away, making it the ideal fly for those few people who cannot see a fly the size of a pinhead floating thirty feet away with the sun in their eyes—the losers.

On my fifth or sixth cast, the fly made a nice drag-free float and a trout sucked it in and we battled then under the warm fall sun, a sixteen inch rainbow eventually sliding onto a gravel bar at my feet. I released the fish and caught four more in the next half hour, a thrill that made me lean my head back, gaze at the deep blue sky, and say out loud, "Mooooo!"

Turns out that wasn't me. It was a cow that had, along with perhads twenty-five of her friends, snuck up behind me in that stealthy, leopardlike way that cows have. I turned and admired the cows—huge creatures with brown hair covering their entire bodies, enormously large asses, and big eyes and eyelashes—and I thought, "I wonder what my high-school prom date is doing these days?"

The cows kept inching closer to the river, looking—and here I use the old expression—"thirsty as cows." I moved a few feet downstream, but three of the cows moved, too, and cut me off. Then a few stepped down off the upstream bank and held their ground as the main attack force of cows lurched off the bank toward me.

There comes a time in a man's life when he's forced to ponder the meaning of life. This generally comes after about eight beers, and sometime around midnight we settle on this: "Thank the Good Lord Jesus Christ that I am not married to Martha Stewart!"

I had not had any beers on this fine day in the wild lands of Wyoming, but I pondered the meaning of life anyway and came up with this: I am about to die a bizarre death that will involve cows, a fly rod, and a lot of swearing.

The cows kept coming now, coming in waves off the grassy bank. They had no fear of humans, particularly of one who was shouting "Bad cows! Get away! Shooooo, goddammit!"

I even tried yelling "How now, brown cow?" but that didn't work, either.

They just kept mooing.

And coming.

And suddenly, with my arms extended and my hands actually pushing on the head of what appeared to be the Queen of the Cows and my fly rod tucked under my right armpit, I was pushed gently off the gravel bar.

And into the North Platte River.

The pool where the trout were still rising—you have not really seen big trout rising until you've seen them rising at eye level as you float past them—was about eight feet deep, I estimated. I estimated my personal height at, well, less than eight feet. And so I floated. Right up to my chin. The cows drank madly from the very spot where I'd been standing just moments before, seemingly oblivious to the floating, screaming human now headed downstream.

I dragged myself out on another gravel bar on the opposite side of the river about thirty feet downstream, gasping for breath because the cold water had rushed in through the chest region of my waders and had reached all the way to the testicle region. I stripped off the waders and my socks and my long underwear and stood there for a moment, thankful that I had not joined that small list of people who have been killed by brown cows.

I was also thankful that the gravel bar I was now standing on contained several baseball-size rocks which—I wish I was making this up, but I am not—I began launching at the cows while shouting "You sons of bitches!"

Maturity has not always been my strong suit.

The third rock hit a cow squarely on the side of the head and it mooed in what seemed like some pain, and then, standing in my wet boxer shorts alongside a wild river in Wyoming, I felt terribly, terribly sorry.

Specifically, sorry I wasn't able to kick the cow in the ass as she scrambled up the bank and went lurching through the field with her mooing gang of sons-of-bitches friends.

It's been more than twenty years since the cows tried to kill me in Wyoming, and I cannot begin to tell you how much steak I have eaten since then. I'm guessing it's been a ton or two. And wherever I go, I ask for Wyoming beef.

I should probably grow up.

Pontoon Boat Envy

Where Lunkers Lurk

Rich Tosches

Wading in the creeks and streams and rivers and wading into our lakes and ponds and reservoirs, however, apparently is not enough for the avid fly angler. Many years ago, according to fly-fishing historians, a man, probably named Chuck, stood on the shore of a lake, gazed out at the water, and spoke these prophetic words:

"Someday we'll find a way to be out there, away from the shore, our gigantic asses submerged as we float around in some kind of tube."

And the float tube was born.

Today, it is not uncommon on many trout lakes to see dozens of people bobbing around out there, propelling themselves by kicking swim fins that are attached to their feet, their behinds wedged into an inflated truck-tire tube that is marketed as a "belly boat." We gladly pay $200 or $300 for the privilege of climbing into this contraption so we can float around with the fishes. Although in parts of New Jersey you get to do the same thing for free—as long as you're willing to talk to the FBI and rat on Vinny.

And because we are America, we have taken this concept of floating around in a truck tire to astonishing heights. At the top of the line, they are called personal float craft or pontoon craft and can cost $1,000 or more. My personal favorite is the Dave Scadden Pontoon Craft. I am now looking at an advertisement for this fine product that appeared in the September 2001 edition of *Fly Fisherman* magazine. Let's review this ad.

At the top, the ad screams: HOT, NEW! REVOLUTIONARY! NEW!

(Modern marketing, as you know, is 1 percent new idea and 99 percent exclamation points.)

Under this herd of exclamation points in the ad, we find the actual name of the "Hot, New! Revolutionary! New!" device.

It is called: Cardiac Canyon.

This name was chosen by the Dave Scadden Co. marketing department over two other fine suggestions: Massive Stroke Craft and Complete Kidney Failure Boat.

Here now, more of the actual wording in what I stress is a fine, well-made fly-fishing pontoon craft that you and your fly-fishing friends will use and enjoy right up until you drown.

"It's revolutionary, eight-piece frame and 49 lb. weight store easily in our 28x28x12 boat pack!"

I believe the first word of that sentence should have been "its," without the apostrophe.

But frankly, as a fly fisherman, if I have to choose between (a) a company that does not dwell on grammar but chooses instead to concentrate its efforts on making a highly dependable personal pontoon boat; or (b) a company that spends its resources on fancy marketing departments and copy editors who product perfect grammatical advertisements, yet also produces personal pontoon boats that will explode and send me screeching across the lake and over the dam, well, I say you go with that first company.

It's just the way I am.

The ad for the Cardiac Canyon pontoon boat also makes this claim: "Revolutionary 11 ft., 6 in. length."

As you know, for centuries our personal fly-fishing pontoon craft have been either eleven feet long or twelve feet long. The guys with the smaller ones would invariably suffer from what psychiatrists call "pontoon boat envy." The guys with the twelve-footers would walk around with a big arrogant smile on their faces—right up until word got around the bar that they were having trouble "inflating the pontoon," if you know what I mean.

Anyway, we grappled with this monumental problem for a long time before finally someone at the Dave Scadden Co. blurted out this idea: "Hey, I know! Let's make a pontoon boat that's bigger than eleven feet and smaller that twelve feet!"

This caused Dave Scadden himself to jump out of his seat during the board meeting—toppling forward, of course, because he was wearing swim fins—and shout, "Sweet Mary and Joseph! That's revolutionary!"

Another note in the ad proclaims the Cardiac Canyon pontoon boat, which includes a seat that extends a couple of feet above the pontoons, has "zero wind resistance."

Because I was skeptical of this claim, I contacted the chairman of the physics department at esteemed Harvard University. I asked him whether a personal pontoon boat used by a fly fisherman so he could get away from the shore and thus wouldn't keep getting his woolly bugger stuck in the shrubs and have to lurch around on the shore trying to retrieve the $1.99 fly could, possibly, be designed so as to offer "zero wind resistance."

Being an intellectual, the professor responded with a rhetorical question: "How the $%^* did you get my phone number?"

Then he called me an asshole and hung up.

But the point is, if the Dave Scadden Co. has come up with a design so unbelievably thin and streamlined that it offers absolutely *no wind resistance,* I believe what they have created is swimsuit supermodel Elle MacPherson.

Now there's something I'd like to ride across a lake!

Anyway, most of the guys I know have simple float tubes or belly boats that do, indeed, consist of a truck tire tube. This allows us to get out onto the lake where the lunkers lurk. As a bonus, the truck tire tube will eventually burst, which causes us to go skimming across the water at breathtaking speeds in a final act of manly thrill seeking before we drown or, as mentioned previously, go flying over the dam.

The float-tube experience begins near the shoreline. Step number one involves pulling on your waders. If you forget this crucial step, you will find yourself sitting in a lake while wearing pants. After the waders are on, you put swim fins on your feet. If used correctly, these will propel you quickly across the water at speeds reaching one-one-hundredth of a mile per hour. As a bonus, they also put an unbelievable amount of stress on the ligaments and tendons in your knees, eventually crippling you and thus keeping you from skiing, which is a *really* stupid sport.

After you've put on your waders and rubber swim fins, you climb into the tube and begin the graceful walk toward the water. There are two popular methods for doing this. The first is to walk forward. This allows the tips of your gigantic swim fins to catch the ground, toppling you face first into the lake. The more preferred method, of course, is to walk backward. Using this approach, the modern angler is able to stumble over something he cannot see and topple into the lake with the back of his head leading the way.

For the few anglers who ever actually get into the lake without having their lungs fill with water, the next step is to kick the swim fins in a manner that allows you to go around and around in circles until it's time to go home. This, as I understand it, is called "whirling disease" and is a big problem on many trout waters.

My favorite experience in one of these float tubes came in 1997 on an outing with my outdoor writer friend, Karl Licis, who, as I mentioned earlier, apparently doesn't like me. The trip brought us to Spinney Mountain Reservoir some sixty miles west of Colorado Springs, Colorado. On the way up Karl mentioned that the place tends to get a "little breezy."

As I was to find out, this was like saying former President Bill Clinton tends to get a "little horny."

After waddling around the shore for a while with my ass wedged into the float tube, picking myself back up a dozen times after tripping over the swim fins and then taking both the tube and the fins off so I could hike back to Karl's truck, where I had left my fly rod, I somehow found myself drifting away.

I caught a nice rainbow, Karl hooked and landed a huge pike, and then the wind came.

The wind came over the mountains and, to borrow a phrase made popular by Kansas trailer-home owners being interviewed on TV after watching their house take off, "sounded like a freight train."

Suddenly I found myself in a tire tube that was riding up the front of four-foot waves and down the other side, into troughs so deep I expected to find Rush Limbaugh feeding in one of them. The wind was howling at 40 and 50 mph, I would learn from the National Weather Service the next day—after I was done choking Karl.

And it was blowing parallel to the shore. No matter how hard I kicked the swim fins, I could not close the gap between myself and land. I was screaming and flailing my arms and kicking as hard as I could as I went past the spot on the shore where he was standing, having apparently anticipated the "little breeze."

As I went sailing past him frantically waving my hand at him, Karl responded by waving back.

I washed up on a point that extended well out into the lake, some one and a half miles from where I was when the typhoon hit. When I crawled out of the float tube, I tried to stand up and went lurching sideways for about thirty feet, my knees aching and my thigh muscles burning and unable to hold my weight. I lay on my side on the gravel for about fifteen minutes thinking about what a wonderful experience this float-tube thing had been.

And wondering if Karl's proctologist would return my landing net.

Turkey Hunting Unfair?

Lisa Price

I 've had people who don't hunt tell me that they think turkey hunting is unfair. They are against the general theory, that what you're doing is pretending to be a hen, ready to breed.

If a male turkey responds, he is shot, or shot at. People who haven't done it think the whole process is deceitful, or unfair.

But turkey hunters know it isn't really that simple. What we're trying to get a turkey to do is really unnatural. In the turkey world, when the male gobbles the females go to him. We are trying to get the male to come to us, which is not usual turkey behavior.

So I think turkey hunting is perfectly fair. Go against your own instincts? Huge mistake.

And turkey hunting isn't easy. First, there is all the gear you have to lug around and organize in the wee hours of the morning. There is the turkey vest, with its fold out cushion seat, pockets bulging with calls, rangefinder, brush clippers, flashlight, camouflage face mask, hat and gloves. Next the back pack, filled with turkey decoys, and the pop-up blind, slung over your head and one shoulder by its carry strap, and a seat.

You stagger into the woods like some overladen burro with an unbalanced load. In the quest to streamline, I once purchased inflatable decoys, which rate amongst the most stupid things I ever bought.

First, trying to blow them up in a hurry as a turkey gobbled nearby, I nearly hyperventilated and passed out. But, I remember thinking at the cash register, what turkey wouldn't want his very own blowup dolls?

Anyway, one Saturday morning, as the morning sky blazed red at the horizon, I saw a tom turkey strutting silently in the field, just over the crest. I could only see the arc of his tail. I called and he immediately gobbled, coming over the crest enough that I could see his whole body.

Then I caught a flash of movement. A hen turkey was running across the field towards the gobbler, my gobbler, looking for all the world like a Confederate woman holding up her skirts and running pell mell down a dirt road to her man, home after four years in the Civil War. I decided I hated her.

This happens to me all the time in my personal life too, but usually the "hen" is wearing spike heels. The hen and her new friend disappeared into the red dawn in a borderline Hollywood moment. They continued into the woods, no doubt to a secluded clearing where they'd make fun of my blow up decoys.

But for the rest of the morning, I waited there in hopes that the gobbler would return. As I waited I got plenty of exercise, repeatedly chasing down the inflatable decoys as periodic wind gusts slipped them from their stakes and tumbleweeded them through the field.

So much can go wrong when you're turkey hunting. Inflatable decoys can desert you or a real hen can make an interception. You can waste more than an hour stalking what turns out to be a discarded tire.

So people are right. There are many things that are unfair about turkey hunting. But sometimes you get a chance. Or some morning, you see a turkey tail fanned, black and outlined in the rising sun like a scrap of charred paper risen from a campfire, like an artist's rendition of promise and hope.

Those things, chances and visions, are given to you freely, to keep always, and I can't find anything unfair about that.

To Hell with Hunting and other Miscellaneous Items

Ed Zern

Tame swans live in parks, and hiss at people. Wild swans are swans that do not have a park to hiss in.

Positively the Last Chapter About Lions in This Book

The history of lion-hunting abounds in curious and unusual departures from the normal sporting procedure.

During the early days of World War II, two young cadets in training at a Royal Air Force base in Rhodesia fell to boasting of their respective prowess as hunters. Since several lions had been reported in the vicinity, they agreed to a friendly contest, and each put up a pint of Guinness's—the first one to kill a lion to get both bottles.

While one of the cadets armed himself with a borrowed Mannlicher rifle and set out to kill his lion in the conventional way, the other, being somewhat more enterprising by nature, secured permission from the commandant to borrow one of the combat airplanes used in training at the base.

Loading the wing guns with live ammunition he took off hastily, and after reconnoitering for a few minutes, spotted a splendid specimen trotting across the plain. In almost less time than it takes to tell it, he dove at the unfortunate beast, riddled its tawny carcass with machine-gun bullets, and returned to the base, where he quickly polished off both bottles.*

*As far as the writer can discover there is no particular moral to this story, except possibly that a strafed lion is the shortest distance between two pints.

The Case of the Bookish
Fly Fisherman

It was a June day some twenty years ago, on the Brodheads Creek in Pennsylvania, that I met an elderly gentleman fly-fishing the flat water below Charley Rethoret's Hotel Rapids. He was elegantly dressed, with stocking-foot English waders and twenty-dollar muleskin brogues over them, and he was one of the first men I ever saw who used a store-boughten wading staff. I had been sitting on the bank gutting a brace of breakfast-size browns and watching him work his way downstream with a wet fly. He was fishing a short straight line in the precise, almost mechanical way that good wet-fly fishermen often employ, and it wasn't until he was nearly on top of me that I noticed the book under his right arm, held close to his side by the pressure of his elbow. When he saw me, he stepped up on the bank and sat down beside me.

"Not much doing today, is there?" he said, filling his pipe, and I noticed that he still kept the book under his arm.

"Not much," I said, "but it may pick up around four-thirty. Yesterday a nice hatch of Light Cahills came about that time. Do you mind if I ask why you carry that book under your arm, instead of in your jacket or your creel, where it can't fall into the water?"

"Not at all," said the old man. "I carry it under my arm because I've been carrying it under my arm, while fishing, for forty years. Not the same book, of course—they wear out, and I replace them."

"Do you read them when the fishing's slow, or what?" I asked.

"My dear boy," said the man, "I have never read a book in my life—make it a point never to read a word. Strains the eyes, and a true fly fisherman needs to keep his eyesight absolutely keen. A worm fisherman, of course, could be blind as a bat and still catch trout—but I see you're a fly fisherman, and understand these matters. But although I never read books I sometimes look at the pictures, and one time in a book on fly fishing I saw a photograph of a man holding a book under the upper part of his casting arm while he cast. I was just learning to fish with flies, and hadn't had much luck. So the next time I went trout fishing I put a book under my arm, the way the photograph had showed, and, sure enough, on my first cast I hooked a trout. Since then I've always held a book under my arm—guess I always will."

"I've seen those photographs too," I said. "If you had read the text, it would have explained that holding the book under your arm is just an exercise to train you to hold your arm in close to your body, so you'll use your forearm and wrist properly. You're not supposed to hold a book there while you're actually fishing."

"Maybe not," said the man, "but that's the way I do it, and I manage to catch a trout now and then." He went on to say that because the books wore out, or occasionally fell into the water, he bought them by the dozen—when he found one that felt just right, he would order twelve copies. And occasionally on his lunch hour he would visit several bookstores, trying out the new books for feel and fit; it's amazing, he said, how few books are suitable for carrying under one's arm.

When I asked him why he didn't use a piece of wood cut to the shape of a book, which would have been cheaper and wouldn't have worn out or been damaged by water, he said curtly, "A glass rod would be cheap, and wouldn't wear out, but I noticed that you're using a split-bamboo Payne. Good day, sir!"

After he had gone on down the river I walked back to the hotel to get some lunch, and Charley Rethornet came over to the table and sat down for a minute. "Funny thing happened a little while ago," he said. "An elderly gent came in here, in fishing clothes, sat down in a booth and when I went to take his order he asked me to read the menu to him. Said he couldn't afford to risk straining his eyes, or some such nonsense. He had a book under his arm, and kept it there even while he was eating."

"I know," I said. "I met him downstream, book and all."

"Did you notice the title of the book?" Charley asked.

"No," I said, "did you?"

"He left it on the table while he went to wash up," Charley said, "and I saw that the title was something about Alsace-Lorraine. Since that's where I lived as a child, I opened it up and saw it was hollowed out inside, like one of those old books made into a cigarette case. Only there weren't cigarettes in it—just a tin box. So as long as I'd already snooped, I looked in the box, too."

What was in it?" I asked. "Heroin?"

"Worse than that," said Charley. "Angleworms."

The Caribou Went Thataway

Squatting beside the fire that Joshua Ananak had coaxed into life in the lee of a huge boulder, out of the wind that whipped across the empty tundra—using pine sticks he had carried all morning in his knapsack, since there's not enough wood to make a match stick in an acre of this land—I now helped Joshua watch the battered teakettle, and could see there was something on his mind.

John MacDonald had told me Joshua spoke a little English—very little—and would probably be too shy to use it; he was right, and our conversation for the three days of hunting since Slim's party had left had consisted of some eight or ten words. I knew Joshua was twenty-four years old, lived at George River Settlement, wasn't married, and had been one time to the big city (Fort Chimo, pop. 700), but only because John had told me. Otherwise I would occasionally point to an outsize hoofprint and say "Tuktuk!" and Joshua would say "Cah-ree-boo!", and we would thus demonstrate our remarkable fluency in each other's language.

But now, with the natural curiosity of these friendly, extroverted people and perhaps appreciating my effort to communicate and wanting to reciprocate, Joshua looked up and said carefully, *"How... old... you?"* I told him, and he smiled shyly and said *"You... old... man."* (Among Eskimos, whose life expectancy even today is still low, anyone over fifty is venerable and "old man" is a term of respect.) I agreed, and emboldened by his communications breakthrough Joshua said, *"Where... you... live?"* "New York," I said, and Joshua said, *"Noo... Yock."* "That's right," I said. "New York."

Then Joshua asked me a question, and to this day I don't know the answer. He frowned in puzzlement and said, *"Where... that... near?"*

How to Shoot Crows

Over the years a number of readers have written, asking me to provide them with my crow-shooting system as it appeared here a decade or so ago. As both of them are regular subscribers I can hardly afford to ignore their request, and hasten to comply.

The system is based on a study of crow behavior conducted by research biologists at Phelps University which showed that crows have a relatively high level of intelligence and are actually able to count, but only in multiples of three or less, so that the conventional procedure for fooling crows—by sending several men into a blind, then having all but one of them leave—is not likely to work except with very young birds, if at all. Thus, even if six crow hunters go into a cornstalk blind and only five come out, the crows probably won't be fooled, as they will have counted off the hunters in trios and will realize that one of the groups is short a man; as a result they will stay the hell away from there until the frustrated gunner gives up and emerges.

My system for successful crow hunting is childishly simple, and consists of the following steps:

1. Build a blind overlooking a cornfield frequented by crows.

2. Assemble a group of twenty-five hunters, all dressed more or less alike and of nearly equal height, build, and facial characteristics. All the hunters should be clean-shaven, but *twelve of them should be wearing false mustaches.* The group should assemble in a barn or some sort of building not less than 350 yards from the field. (It would be prudent to have a few spare hunters on hand, to substitute in cases of pulled muscles, heart attacks or other contingencies.)

3. All of the hunters should be equipped with 12-gauge shotguns, but it is advisable that these be fairly light in weight, as it is important that *all hunters going to and from the blind must travel at a dead run,* so that the crows will not have sufficient time for their calculations.

4. As soon as a flock of crows comes into the area, eleven of the hunters are dispatched from the old barn to the blind, running at top speed. The instant they arrive, seven of them turn around and rush back to the barn.

5. When the seven hunters get back to the barn, they are joined by six other hunters and the thirteen of them sprint back to the blind as fast as possible; on arrival there, ten of them immediately turn around and dash back to the barn.

6. Before the ten arrive, eight more hunters are sent from the barn to the blind. When they meet the ten returning from the blind all of them switch hats and false mustaches while milling around in a tight huddle, then break it up and resume running to their respective destinations.

7. As soon as the eight hunters arrive at the blind, five of them turn around and rush back toward the barn; on the way they meet nine hunters running from the barn toward the blind, whereupon the hunters divide themselves into two groups of seven, one of which runs back to the barn while the other rushes to the blind, changes hats and mustaches, leaves two of its members there and dashes back to the barn.

8. Of the twelve hunters now in the blind, nine rush across the fields to the barn while twelve of the thirteen hunters in the barn

charge en masse from the barn to the blind; on arrival they immediately turn and sashay back to the barn taking two of the three hunters still in the blind with them, *leaving a single hunter.*

9. It is, of course, essential that all this be done at the highest possible speed, so that the crows will fall hopelessly behind in their arithmetic and in the consequent corvine confusion fail to realize that a hunter is concealed in the blind.

10. Eventually the crows will learn to count faster, so that the system must be modified occasionally to keep ahead of them. In addition to having the hunters run faster, it may be necessary to introduce false beards and quick-change toupees as well as false mustaches, and to build a second blind on another side of the field so that the traffic will be triangular instead of simply linear, requiring the crows to start working on trigonometric permutations and geometric progressions in order to cope. In severe cases the hunters may be equipped with numbered jerseys from 1 to 25 *but with the number 17 omitted and two number 21s.* (This can also be done with roman numerals, when birds are very wary.)

Watch this space next month for an equally simple, foolproof system for outwitting that wily old woodchuck in the back pasture, requiring no special equipment other than a stuffed Guernsey cow and a milkmaid's costume.

A Flagon of Fables

The Ugly Princess

Once there was a princess who was ugly as sin. Her old lady, the queen, used to shake her head and say, "Sure, she's a sweet kid. But boy, she is some ugly!" One day her old man, the king, said, "Kiddo, you ain't never going to make it on sheer pulchritude. What you got to do is take up some sport where guys and gals do something together, preferably where the light isn't too good—that way you'll meet some men, and maybe they won't notice you ain't a raving beauty until it's too late. So get moving."

"Yes, papa," said the princess, and hurried down to the local sporting-goods store. When she told the clerk her problem he looked her over and said, "Princess, you got the build of a natural-born shotgun-shooter. It just happens I got this pigeon-grade Perrazzi with gold inlays and three sets of barrels in stock—let's see how it fits."

After the clerk had sawed a half-inch off the stock it fitted fine, and after buying a shooting vest, a cartridge belt, and a case of trap loads the princess wrote a check for the stuff, drove to the local gun club, and signed up for a course of lessons from the pro. In a week she was busting clay birds like crazy, went 100 straight at skeet her second week, and was smoking the blue rocks from 22 yards.

Sure enough, along came a handsome but somewhat astigmatic duck hunter, who watched the princess powdering clays from all stations, then sidled up to her, and proposed a liaison. "A *what?*" said the princess, partly from starting to go deaf and partly because her vocabulary was not extensive.

"A liaison," said the handsome young duck hunter. "You know, like Shacksville,"

"Oh, that," said the princess. "Okay, but only with, you know, legal documents and a ring and like that."

"Fair enough," said the h.y.d.h., and a few days later they were married and moved into an apartment.

When the duck season opened the h.y.d.h. took the princess to his duck club, set out a rig of decoys and joined her in his blind. When the ducks started to come into the rig and saw the princess, they flared off, and when this happened several times the handsome young duck hunter said, "Sorry, sweety-pie, I got my priorities," and filed suit for divorce.

Moral: Ugliness is only skin deep, but if it flares ducks, that's deep enough.

All About Ice Fishing

I was driving through Pike County, Pennsylvania, one particularly cold and blowy January, and stopped off to visit with Gollup Kuhn, the undisputed champeen free-style liar of Lackawaxen. After he'd plied me with ripe cider Gollup suggested that the big pool in the Delaware, right in front of his house, was frozen good and thick, and that we might do some ice fishing. Sitting in the warm kitchen it seemed like a fine idea, and we went.

That was the first time I'd ever ice-fished, and if I keep my wits about me it will be the last. Three hours later we were back in the kitchen, and pretty soon I had thawed out enough to notice that Gollup was talking.

Some years ago, Gollup said, a local gent had been ice fishing on the same pool and had stepped on a thin spot and gone through. That was the last anybody had heard of him until the following March, when his wife had received a telegram from the Chief of Police of Port Jervis, some twenty miles downriver. The telegram read: YOUR HUSBAND'S BODY FOUND STOP IN VERY BAD CONDITION AND FULL OF EELS STOP WIRE INSTRUCTIONS.

The bereaved lady, according to Gollup, hotfooted it down to the depot and sent off the following directive: SELL EELS SEND PROCEEDS SET HIM AGAIN.

Have a Cigar

This is the end of the book, and I can assure you that it's almost as much a relief to me as it is to you. And in case you bought rather than borrowed this copy, and feel that you didn't get a reasonable return on your investment, I urge you to consider this note which I had from a friend a short time ago, and which I quote in entirety:

> *Dear Ed:*
>
> *I am become a father, although several months prematurely. The baby, a boy, weighed one pound ten ounces, and although he will live in an incubator for quite a while he will be okay, the doctors assure me. Betty is doing fine too, and altogether I am well pleased.*
>
> *However, speaking as one fisherman to another, I feel compelled to remark that in this instance I barely got my bait back.*

Family Interludes

Nick Lyons

He that views the ancient ecclesiastical canons shall find hunting to be forbidden to churchmen, and being a toilsome, perplexing recreation; and shall find angling allowed to clergymen, as being a harmless recreation, a recreation that invites them to contemplation and quietness.
—Izaak Walton

Though the relationship of an avid fisherman to his family may be said to have no season, or to be always "in season," it reaches the peak of its intensity—or aggravation—in the very height of the trouter's year.

There are, I am sure, innumerable arcane and esoteric reasons for this.

But the safe pragmatic reason is simply this: the trout fisher is at his moment of greatest self- and trout-absorption—and least resistance; and his family, flourishing under the beneficence of his year-long support and devotion, and the ideal weather, is at maximum strength.

Days are long; children are indefatigable; wives acquire an alarming propensity for shopping and house-hunting and "just walking together, like a *real* family, in the park." In the early days I did not have an ally among them, and my secret fishing life suffered much at the hands of my family

There were the little things: two missing barred rock necks that turned up under Anthony-the-thief's pillow; a notorious departure from the Schoharie in the midst of a massive Hendrickson hatch, after I had waited three hours for it to appear (my wife called them "Morgans" and pleaded that we leave "this bug-infested place"); innumerable engagements that took precedence; irony; caustic wit to the effect that "grown men" did not act in the ridiculous way I acted about trout. I must be painfully truthful about it, for it all reached a crisis, a momentous crisis, in an incident still painful to recall.

My fishing friends say I am too generous with women and little children. Perhaps. For I suppose Mari, Paul, Charles, Jennifer, and Anthony owe their survival of that Father's Day trip to my extraordinary equanimity. I am not at all sure how I survived.

The spring, troutless and city-bound that year, had been long, but Father's Day weekend was longer.

We left in a flurry, all six of us, on Friday, but despite my best efforts, my speed and my scheming, it was still too late even to make the latest moments of the evening rise on the closest streams. So I settled into a family habit of mind, decided to bide my good time, and set about enjoying a harmless day of visiting friends and swimming on Saturday. After that we could easily fulfill the most prominent of our trip's simple purposes: as I had engineered my wife into saying, "A few solid hours of fly fishing for Dad—poor Dad, who never gets out on the streams anymore because he loves us so much."

Not that I believed her, or had much confidence that at this particular season of my married life I would actually get to drop a few flies—but her gesture seemed sincere and I took it at face value. "A turning point," I thought with quiet satisfaction. Thus, hopefully, I had stashed my little Thomas and my vest carefully in the corner of our rented station wagon. I had heard of such turning points.

The temperature was ninety-eight degrees when we left our friends at three o'clock that Saturday: too hot to fish, no doubt, so I allowed Mari to persuade me that Vermont would be cooler, that we would have time to fish that evening and all day Sunday. "A nice drive will keep us cool," she insisted.

It was little less than one hundred and fifty degrees in the car once we hit the crowded highway: I cannot remember being able to drive faster than thirty-five. But up Routes 5 and then 91 to Brattleboro we went, pausing to examine, while we sped, a half dozen or more promising waterways. It had been part of my plan (cunningly conceived, I must admit) to inject my oldest son, Paul, with the trout fever, and the serum had taken with a vengeance. Before I could see a stream, he'd spot one and call out, "Can we stop here, Dad? It looks like a terrific place for tremendous trout."

He did that several dozen times.

The serum nearly cracked me.

By the time we reached Vermont, all four children were howling wildly, stepping on each other's toes and pride and souls. Dinner took two hours, motel-hunting another hour, and precisely at dusk we were established in cool Vermont, exhausted. Had I been on the Schoharie, at Hendrickson time, I would not have been able to lift my arm to cast.

"Tomorrow we'll get some big ones," I said to Paul as we turned off the lights and settled, all six of us, into the quiet and cool of the air-conditioned room.

"Do you promise, Dad?"

"I promise," I said.

"Can I get some big ones, too" asked Anthony, my four-year-old, in the dark room.

"Maybe."

"Me too?" asked Charles with his foghorn voice. "If Paul does, I want to get some big ones, too."

"Let's sleep now, children."

It was quiet for five full minutes and, motionless, pooped, I was nearly into a pleasant dream about the Green Drake hatch on the Beaverkill when Jennifer whispered loudly, "You'll let me catch some big ones too, won't you, Daddy?"

"Shussssh!" said my wife. And then, sardonically, *"Trout!"*

Well, Sunday it was raining long thick droplets of rain: a day-long pernicious rain if I'd ever seen one.

"Didn't you say fishing was best in the rain, Dad?" asked Paul.

"You *wouldn't* take the boy out in a rain like this, would you, Nick?" asked Mari.

"Not when it's heavy, Paul," I said quietly.

"And you *wouldn't* expect the rest of us to sit in a muggy car while you were out catching pneumonia, would you?"

"We will not fish in this weather," I assured my wife, sullenly.

"You promised, Dad!"

"It will not rain all day," I told Paul. "And maybe it's not raining in New York State."

So we drove and we sang a hundred songs and we munched some of our genuine Vermont maple sugar—which did not quite justify Saturday's trip to cool Vermont, and which made Jennifer dreadfully nauseous—and we made our way slowly through the blinding Father's Day rain that was sure to kill any decent fly fishing for a full three days, along the winding, twisting Molly Stark Trail, and the children stopped singing, and then fought and bellowed, and Mari became irritated and blamed me, and then Paul blamed me for not finding him a "dry trout stream."

We crossed into New York, where it was pouring nails, at about twelve-thirty, had a long lunch, and then started gloomily, for a Father's Day—or any day—down Route 22. The Hoosic River, I noted, was impossibly brown, and the rain still showed no signs of growing less frantic. The Green River, a sprightly spring-fed creek, was clearer, but the rain continued and Mari would have none of sitting in a muggy car while I got pneumonia.

"If you could find us a nice clean beach, where we could get some sun and have something to do for an hour or so. . . But you really can't expect me. . ."

"Scarcely," I said.

"You promised," said Paul.

A disaster either way. Straight home: the only solution.

There is absolutely no question in my mind that I should indeed have gone home. Right then. Tragedy was imminent. Had I simply read the signs of the times, I could have avoided disaster.

Yes, blithely I was heading home, peace in my soul, capitulation painless, when, as we approached Brewster, the sun broke out suddenly—brightly, fetchingly. I could not resist a quick look at the Sodom section of the East Branch of the Croton River.

"We won't do any fishing," I promised. "I just want a fast look at an old friend. I used to fish this stream when I was a kid, every Opening Day. Came up the first time when I was. . ."

"Thirteen. I know. You mention it every time we pass this silly creek."

"Do I really? Do I mention it *every* time we pass?"

"Yes, you do. 'I used to fish the Left Branch of the Croydon every Opening Day when I was a kid.' Every time."

"East Branch. Croton," I muttered. " A short look. Three minutes. Perhaps less."

"I sincerely hope less."

Miraculously, the water below and above the bridge was admirably clear, not crystal but a translucent auburn, perhaps because it traveled to this point over a long cobblestone sluice after shooting down from the top of the reservoir. Interesting, I thought; very interesting.

I scurried back to the car with the happy news.

"Well, if you think you can catch a few trout for supper," Mari said, "you can drop Anthony and me off at a coffee shop for half an hour and take the rest of your children fishing in the Left Branch of the Croydon, or whatever it is."

"*All* of them?"

"I want to go with Daddy," shouted Jennifer.

"If Paul goes, I have to go too, Dad," said Charles petulantly.

"At least make it forty-five minutes," I said.

"With Anthony? In a coffee shop?"

"All right, children: a half hour to catch two fat trout for supper."

"Nick, you haven't brought home a trout in two years. You talk about fishing day and night; read about it constantly; tie those confounded bugs by the evening; go on and on and on—and never bring home any fish."

Since the clock was running, I did not choose to explain that despite the tragedy of being married I still *caught* trout now and then, though I rarely kept them anymore. One such argument, with my mother-in-law, who to this day thinks I keep a mistress on the banks of the "Croydon," led me to stomp out of the room with the profound truism: "Do golfers eat golf balls?"

"Two fat trout for dinner, children—in one half hour."

I dropped my wife off at ten of five, spent seven minutes acquiring some night crawlers, another four setting up Paul's spinning rod, and was on the stream by one minute after five exactly.

"Lovely," I said. "The water's beautiful, Paul. We're going to get four or five."

"Really, Dad?"

"Can't miss. Look: that fellow right under the bridge has one—see him splashing?"

The children crowded together along the bank, watching the brisk battle of a thrashing and leaping eleven-inch brown. I took the time to sneak in six or seven casts, but did not even get a tap.

Then Paul wanted the rod and I gave it to him, telling him how to cast across and slightly upstream, how to hold the rod tip down in anticipation of the strike, how to keep delicate control of the moving bait. He managed his casts well, and I watched eagerly as the night crawler floated downstream and out of sight. Before his fourth cast, Charles wanted his turn too. No, I had promised Paul he'd catch a trout first, I told him gently.

"I want *my* turn, Daddy," said Jennifer.

"We only have one rod."

"No fair. It's not fair, Dad," said Charles gruffly.

"Can't you keep these infants quiet so I can fish?" demanded Paul.

"Don't get nasty," I advised.

"They're bothering me, Dad."

"After Paul gets a fish," I promised Jennifer and Charles wisely, "you two get a turn each."

"Only one," said Jennifer.

"Two trout," said Paul.

But he got no strikes in the next fourteen or fifteen casts, and I noticed that it was now five-eighteen. I was glad I'd left my Thomas in the car. Another ten minutes of this madness—no more.

To get the younger children out of Paul's way, I decided to go up on the bridge itself for the last few minutes, though I noted with alarm how fast the cars sped by. I flattened the children against the edge, warned them sharply not to climb up the low wall, and leaned far over to peer down into the fairly clear auburn water.

A few flies were coming off the water—small darkish flies—but I paid them no heed.

Then I saw it: a long dark shadow, nose upstream, slightly to the left of a large submerged boulder. Now and then it would rise slowly to the right or left and, almost imperceptibly, break the surface of the flat stream. The fish was well over a foot long.

I tried to point it out to Jennifer and Charles, lifting one in each arm so both could see at exactly the same time, but when they scrambled further onto the low wall I spooked and put them back on the pavement, whereupon they raced back and forth across the bridge several times while cars shot by menacingly.

I told Paul about the fish and he promptly climbed up the bank and onto the bridge. He plunked his worm loudly down into the water and it bobbed to the surface and waved there, without the slightest threat of ever being disturbed by a trout.

But the long trout kept rising, once or twice every minute—God, was it really five twenty-three already?—and when I tossed it several bits of a worm, it swirled and snapped at them, though it did not finally take any.

Then a few of the small darkish flies rose to my level and I leaned out incautiously and grabbed several of them.

Dark blue; tiny. Most curious.

What were they? Iron Blue Duns. Not more than three or four a minute, but a steady hatch. *Acentrella*—about No. 18. Weren't they a late-April mayfly, though? No matter. *Acentrella*—nothing else.

Not much of a dinner, but the long trout was unmistakably settling for them. Had I tied a few last winter? Yes, one each, a No. 18 and a No. 16.

The trout rose again—and then again, this time with a definite sucking-down of the water, a turning of its sleek yellow body that showed it to be of considerable size and weight.

Five twenty-eight.

I could stand it no longer. Grabbing Jennifer and Charles by the collars, I rushed back to the car, plucked out my aluminum rod case and vest, and then tugged the children—silent, frightened—down the muddy bank, past a flourishing garden of shiny poison ivy, and toward the downstream section below the bridge.

Swiftly I unhoused and jointed my delicate Thomas, a simple, lovely idea in bamboo. I managed to mount the fly reel and slip the line through the first two guides, but then began to fumble. The line slipped back through to the reel. Then I worked the line through four guides and discovered that it was twisted around the rod after the second. Then it was through all of them, but the spidery 6X tippet would not shake loose and got tangled in itself, and I had to select another. Then I couldn't find my Iron Blue Dun in No. 18. Should I try the No. 16? Or an Adams in No. 18? Or a small Leadwing Coachman?

Finally I found the Blue in with the Adamses, its hackles a bit bent, and I poked the film of head lacquer out after only six or seven tries and then knotted the fly to the leader on my fourth attempt.

Five thirty-five. She would be furious already—even on Father's Day.

"Quiet. You children have got to be absolutely quiet. Not a sound"—they had said nothing—"good children. You're not going to spoil Daddy's sixteen-incher, are you?"

"How big is a sixteen-incher, Daddy?"

"Big, Jennifer, Very big. Quiet. Quiet. Quiet, now."

"PAUL! DADDY'S GOING TO CATCH A SIXTEEN-INCHER!" Jennifer howled in her high-pitched shrilly voice.

"Can I help you, Dad?" asked Charles.

Paul, on the bridge, had leaned far over to see the action. Clouds were forming rapidly in the sky.

"Paul! Get back!" I called, nearly flopping over on the muddy bank. "But WATCH OUT FOR THE CARS! Not too far back!"

Damn, no waders. No matter. The moment was here.

I stepped in boldly—in my Father's Day shoes, in my neatly creased trousers, in my Father's Day sport jacket—tumbled to one arm on a mossy rock, climbed over the riffles slowly, bent my hand to steady myself on another rock (soaking the new sport jacket up to the elbow and along the hemline), and meticulously surveyed the long flat pool.

A few soft small drops of rain began to fall.

"Paul! Paul! Look what Daddy's doing!"

"Dad, can I go wading, too? shouted Charles.

"Can we, Daddy?"

"Will all my very good children kindly be ab-so-lute-ly quiet for ten minutes. I love you all. I really do. But *please, please* be quiet."

"Daddy, Daddy," called Jennifer. "Charles is in the water. Charles is in the water. Charles is..."

"I am not! I am not!"

"Charles! Get out and stay out! Now!"

Another foot. Not too close. Whoops! Almost slipped that time, Don't rain. Don't rain, yet! "Paul! Will you *please* get off that railing?"

"My line's tangled, Dad. And I can't see a thing."

"Then come down. But carefully! Watch out for the cars. And the poison ivy."

"Will you fix my line, Dad?"

"In a minute. In just one minute."

Five *thirty-eight!*

"Charles is in the water. Charles is..."

"I am not!"

"Charles, if you don't stay out of the water I'll break your little arm!"

I could not see the fish beside the boulder, but thought that amid the steady raindrops and bubbles on the surface I detected the characteristic dimple of a trout's rise. "Now," I murmured audibly. I looped out several yards of line, checked behind me for trees or shrubs or sons or daughter.

The old feeling. That glorious old feeling. After twelve full months, it was all still there.

One more false cast.

"Now."

The line sped out, long and straight; the leader unfolded; the fly turned the last fold and dropped, quietly, five inches below the base of the bridge. Perfect.

I retrieved line slowly, watching for drag, squinting into the steadily increasing rain, along the rim of the dark water, to see that tiny dark-blue fly. In another moment it would be over the spot.

There was a heavy splash below me. Then another and another.

"Charles is throwing stones, Daddy. Charles is. . ."

"CHARLES!"

Whammo!

The tiny Iron Blue Dun disappeared in a solid sucking down of the water. I raised the rod swiftly, felt the line tighten along its length and hold. Not too hard. Not too hard, Nick. I did not want to snap the 6X leader.

I had him. A good brown. A really good brown. I felt his weight against the quick arcing of my little Thomas. Sixteen inches for sure. Not an inch less. The trout turned, swirled at the surface, and bolted upstream.

"Daddy caught one!" shouted Jennifer.

There were momentous splashes downstream.

"CHARLES!"

Out of the corner of my wet eye I could see Paul, in his short pants, hopping through the great garden of poison ivy. "Got a fish, Dad?" he called.

"Got a big one, kids," I said proudly, holding the Thomas high, reeling in the line before the first guide to fight him from the reel. "Your ol' Dad's got a good one this time—*whoaaa!*"

Just then Paul slipped on the muddy slope and slid rawly— through more poison ivy—to the brink of the stream.

The rain was steady and thick now, and I felt it trickle down past my jacket collar and along my spine.

The trout had run far up under the bridge and I was playing him safely from the reel. Several times he leaped high into the air, shaking, splattering silver in all directions, twisting like a snake.

"I'll help you, Dad," shouted Charles, splashing vigorously toward me.

"Didn't I tell you—?"

But before I finished, the huge trout began to shoot downstream rapidly, directly toward me. I retrieved line frantically. He was no more than four yards from me and I could see the 6X leader trailing from the corner of his partly opened mouth; the jaw was already beginning to hook.

Charles was quite close to me now, behind me, and I half turned to shoo him back to shore. His hair was plastered flat on his head from the rain, and he had a long thin stick in his hands and was holding it out, in the direction of the trout.

"I'll get him, Dad, I'll get him," he said. His tone was sincere and helpful.

"*No!*" I shouted, and turned to wrest it away from him.

The gesture was too sudden. The leather-soled shoes were no match for the mossy rocks. With gusts of heavy rain pelting my face, I felt my left foot slipping, tried to catch myself and my tangled line, felt my right foot slipping too, and, holding my delicate, my beloved Thomas high overhead, went down, disastrously, flat on my rump, up to my chest, and kept going, the Thomas slamming wildly against a rock...

IF THE WHEEL HAD NEVER BEEN INVENTED

Blowing Away the Media

Steve Chapple

It is a soft spring day in Montana's Hyalite Canyon. The hill is spaced with stumps and Douglas fir. We walk slowly along a path at the 6000-foot level. Below, the rasp of the creek across granite masks the sounds of our breathing. Suddenly, from behind a stand of aspen, there is the glint of a Sony. Strobel levels his .20 gauge and fires but, incredibly, the spray of bird shot only *pings* off the screen. Could the console charge? I drop to one knee and let loose with my .45. There is the satisfying *thunk* of bullet against cathode. Our quarry implodes in a flash of yellow, orange, and blue and spins down the slope, end over end, antenna chasing power cord, until it comes to rest against a lichen-covered boulder at our feet.

"You won't hear any more *Love Boat* reruns in *these* woods," says Strobel.

He's right. It's been a good day's hunting: two Sonys, a Mitsubishi, and a two-point Sylvania. (All TVs tend to be two-pointers, unless rigged for cable, in which case they are considered does and can only be taken in special hunts.) We lay out the gutted televisions in the snow for a trophy shot.

In Montana, you see, we don't watch TVs. We shoot them. We don't have a few beers and catch the game. We have no beers and blow the game away.

Electronic rights activists may squawk, but TV hunting is as American as bait-fishing. Primal recreation.

Typically, a TV hunt such as the one Strobel and I arranged is a stocked, or "New York," hunt, the prey arrayed on separate stumps after being scrounged from rec room and garage or purchased at local pawn and thrift shops. The truly committed pack in generators so that the targets glow blue in the bushes. The element of cultural revenge is stronger in a live TV hunt, since you really get to implode Ted Koppel,

Rush Limbaugh, Barney, or the ever-erroneous weatherperson (take your choice).

Aldous Huxley, the author of *Brave New World,* once wrote: "A society most of whose members spend a great part of their time, not on the spot, not here and now and in the calculable future, but somewhere else, in the irrelevant other worlds of sports and soap opera, of mythology and metaphysical fantasy, will find it hard to resist the encroachment of those who would manipulate and control it."

True. And when Huxley referred to "sports," I don't think he meant TV hunting, since televisions were not widespread in his time, nor, obviously, is the hunting of them a be-fatted spectator sport, which is what he loathed. Though Huxley, as a meek British person, could not come right out and say it, I am sure he would have agreed: TV hunting is the one thing that will save Western civilization from itself.

Undeniably, TV hunting is one of the last freedoms left. There are no government regulations (yet). No bag limits. The hunting of televisions is one of those spontaneous American expressions that surface in the darkest hours, when the *McLaughlin Report* cannot be switched off quickly enough. Something large is afoot here. We need interactive shopping channels about as much as geese need cheeseburgers. There is some brutality connected with TV hunting, admittedly, but there is much violence on television, too.

TV hunting, as a socially redeeming sport, got its start July 4, 1982, on Montana's Sindelar Ranch, when wealthy rancher Brian Sindelar left a cryptic message on his nephew Will McLaughlin's answering machine: "I have a renegade television on my property. I want you boys to come out and help me."

Will, then 15, brought his Winchester 30.06 lever action. Will's high school buddy, Dave Strobel, who years later would be my TV guide for the Hyalite hunt, brought along his grandfather's single-shot 20 gauge. At the ranch they found a trail of cut TV plugs and half-buried bits of copper wire. Sindelar, like most TV hunters, had his rules. If he judged that the set could "see" or "smell" the boys before they saw or smelled it, he rehid the TV. The boys were told to shoot fast, before the channels changed. At the end of the hunt, Sindelar tagged the antennas and Will and Dave hauled the carcasses to the dump. Thus was a sport born.

TV hunting is not for everybody, of course, not even for every decent person with a gun, but if it is for you, there are some things you should know. The white powder that puffs out when bullet bites screen can be quite poisonous, like the powder in fluorescent lights. Let the dust settle before checking your kill. There is also some danger of being hit by shrapnel, especially at close range.

Decoys do not make sense in TV hunting. Practicing, though possible, is not practical, either. You can throw the sets up like skeet, but it's a mess on the ground, like using live pigeons. The ecologically correct—and what hunter these days is not?—spreads canvas or a plastic tarp under the televisions.

Let us beware of image, because television hunting is a sport for our times. Never mind that the media have been careful to ignore the growing phenomenon, so far—and naturally enough. What Santa Monica producer wishes to admit that True Americans live to drill her creations with double O buckshot? The media in this country may be reviled, but they are not stupid.

In fact, TV hunting could easily be co-opted. I can imagine one of those video *verité* shows following hunters into the local Powder Horn, asking which ammo is best for the new flat screens. The tumble of tube down ravine is mighty visual stuff, and it cannot be long before Geraldo films "Men Who Hunt TVs." Others will follow: "2020 with a 30.30." Nintendo will come out with its most popular game: "TV Hunt!"

But if the sport catches on, as I believe it must, Americans will return to their homes purged after a day of stalking the wild Sylvania. A calm will settle into our living rooms. Parents will once again talk with their children, and they will be heard, and the children will smile. Respect will be interactive and mutual. Lovers will make love without video aids, seeing the real person underneath or above them. The musically inclined will pluck acoustic instruments. They will not channel surf. Their weapons will be warm in locked cabinets, and their minds free.

In America, it is tough to beat the media, but, if you're a good shot, it is still possible to cream them.

Exercise your rights.

How to Turn a Perfectly Normal Child into a Fisherman

Paul Quinnett

Several years ago I was consulted by a highly agitated mother who felt something dreadful was happening to her son.

"A fatal disease?" I asked.

"It's worse. At least they're working on cures for fatal diseases."

"What then?"

"He wants to become a fishing guide."

Sometimes in an interview psychologists are required to put in extra effort to keep a straight fa…, uh, maintain our decorum.

I realized that, given my lust for angling and the risk admitting this might have on a potential client, my next question had to be purged of any interviewer bias or excess emotion and delivered in the most impartial, professional voice possible.

"Walleye or salmon?" I queried.

The woman gave me one of those long, penetrating stares clients reserve for the moment when they have confirmed their worst fear, that shrinks need shrinks.

Realizing she'd seen through my professional facade, I acknowledged my prejudice toward fishing and offered to refer her to someone who played golf.

"Oh my God, no!" she cried. "My ex-husband played golf. But since you're a fisherman, maybe you can tell me why they're all so crazy.

I didn't take offense at the question.

In a matter of a few minutes, I had explained that fishermen were no worse than most other sportsmen of passion, and considerably better off than many.

"How?" she queried.

"Well, they tend to be happier, more contented, and less stressed."

"They sound like milk cows," she mused. "But, what about my son? He's obsessed with fishing and thinks of nothing else."

I smiled. "He may have a case of the passions."

"The 'passions?'"

"It's a kind of magnificent obsession with angling," I explained dreamily. "You see, fishing is always rewarding, always satisfying, always challenging, always…"

"Just a minute," interrupted the lady. "You sound as crazy as my son. And he gets that same stupid glint in his eye I see in yours. I tell you I'm worried. He's nineteen and should be in college. What do I do?"

Clients are always asking tough questions like this. For some reason, they want quick solutions to knotty problems. Fortunately, we psychologists are highly trained in dodging obvious queries. If you give advice and it works, you get the credit while the client becomes dependent and doesn't grow. If you give advice and it *doesn't work,* you come off looking stupid beyond belief. If things really go sour, you might get sued. Therefore, the answer to all requests for advice is to ask the same question you were just asked.

"What do you think you should do?" I asked.

"I don't know," said the woman. "Say… what is this? If I could get him to do what I want him to do I wouldn't be in here seeing you."

Another thing they teach in graduate school is how to handle frustrated and angry clients.

Once I explained to the woman I had always wanted to be a fishing guide myself, and that there was no way I could objectively consult her on how she might handle her son's request to spend his college savings on a 20-foot jet boat, she accepted my referral to a non-fishing colleague and we terminated any professional relationship. Of course, I asked if she had one of her son's business cards, and I didn't charge her for the session.

Several years later, I ran into this woman in a department store. She lost the battle with her son and he guided for a couple of years in Alaska before returning to the Lower 48 and starting college. Unless I miss my guess, he did not major in psychology.

Raising Fishermen
Fishermen seem to spring up in non-fishing families with some regularity, as in the case I just described, but more often the child is

aimed at the fishing life by its mother and father. Bulls-eyes are not guaranteed.

Though no one has ever asked me, I have always wanted to tell parents how to raise fishermen. As a father of three and consultant to many, I know about the vulnerabilities of little minds and, therefore, how to implant the sport of angling deep into the psychological core of an otherwise innocent child. As a one-time college instructor in developmental psychology, I am prepared to offer my own formula for rearing anglers. This formula also works to inoculate children against drug abuse and install self-esteem, subjects which will be further explained in the chapter on fishaholism.

Nature vs. Nurture

Are fishermen born to the sport or do they acquire the habit? Down through the centuries, people have pondered this and similar questions regarding great generals, opera singers, world-class athletes and theoretical physicists.

Dr. John B. Watson, the famous behavioral psychologist and learning theorist, once said if given enough time and total control of the environment, he could turn any given baby into a doctor, lawyer or Indian chief.

Can you start with any old baby and turn it into a happy, contented, clear-eyed adult with a love of angling? Sure you can. The research says so. Down through the years Dr. Watson has been proved more right than wrong. Except for some hard-core personality traits and the limitations of genetically determined things like height and eye color, nurture wins.

There is no known anti-fishing gene. If anything, there is probably a pro-fishing gene, so raising fishermen should be no more difficult than raising Democrats. In the bargain, you can end up with an ethical sportsman who loves and respects nature and holds ecologically sound conservation values that last a lifetime.

What more, I ask any parent, could you possibly want?

Start Early

You cannot begin your project too soon. Consider, for example, this fictionalized announcement from the New York Times:

"Born to Mr. and Mrs. Wendell P. Terry, an eight pound, two ounce fisherman. The baby angler was deftly netted by Dr. T.S. Morgan, himself a fly fisherman and long-time member of Trout Unlimited. The baby will be christened Lee Wulff Terry, after the world-famous fisherman of the same name."

There is great power in naming. In ancient times, names were so special they had to be given to you under extraordinary circumstances. Your name could come to you in a dream, or be given you by an elder, but in any event, it was your name and only suited you. It set the course for your life.

Announcing the birth of a fisherman with a strong fishing name, in hopes of casting the die after nine months of pregnancy, though, is probably too late. To get a neonate headed in the right direction, you can actually begin well before the fetus is fully developed.

We know from several research studies that a little one is quite capable of learning while still in the oven. A fetus exposed to pieces by Beethoven while in the womb will, several years later, learn to play those same pieces more quickly than others, providing evidence human learning takes place in the womb. I used to tell my classes this old story about an English woman to drive this pre-birth learning point home.

There was once a recently impregnated woman who very much wanted her child to be both a fisherman and well mannered. To get the desired result, the lady read books on manners and stream etiquette to her swelling abdomen for the entire nine months of her pregnancy.

The nine months passed, but no child came. Then 10 months. Then a year. Then two years and still no child. At the five year mark, the lady was huge and quite uncomfortable, but there were still no signs of labor. A decade passed. Then two decades. After some 35 years, the lady passed away.

When the medical examiner opened her up, he found two, fully-grown English fishermen engaged in the following conversation:

"No, *you* go first."

"No, you. I insist. This is your beat."

"I'm very sorry, sir, but I believe it is your beat and, therefore, you should exit and take the first cast."

"Quite the contrary, my dear man. But thank you, anyway. Now, please, be a good sport, take your leave, and make the first cast."

This absolutely true story suggests several important steps that can be taken by couples hoping to raise an angler.

First, try to conceive the child during a fishing trip. I have no research to document the importance of environmental settings and their influence on matters of conception and eventual outcomes but how could it hurt?

Next, because positive *en utero* influences have salutary effects, I cannot see the harm in the following prescriptions:

Expose the fisherman-in-progress to the sounds of water; babbling brooks, pounding surfs, waves lapping against canoe sides, etc.

Exposures to the sound of a screaming reel, shouts of "One on!" and the general sort of fishing chatter that accrues during a day on the water might give the tyke a leg up on angling jargon later on.

The mother-to-be should probably eat a lot of fish during the pregnancy.

Research has shown that both fetuses and infants are relaxed by the gentle swaying of the mother. What could better ready a child for a fishing future than easy hikes to remote lakes, the rocking motion of a boat, and the rhythmic action of Mom while she whips a fly rod back and forth, back and forth while whispering of rising trout, caddis hatches, and humming those joyful little tunes that sometimes bubble up from the heart during moments of great pleasure.

Both mom and dad might read fishing poems and stories to the swelling belly. As long as twins are not expected and you lay off the etiquette, what possible risks could there be?

Get the Birth Myth Right

All of us have a birth myth. Sometimes the myth is given to us, sometimes we make up our own. For example, if three guys in long beards are guided by a super nova to your mother's delivery room and happen to bring along some incense and myrrh, you're likely to grow up with a lot of people expecting you to do big things.

On the other hand, if you're in a quarrel with your parents about something and think they don't love you anymore, you may create your own birth myth. "There was a mix up at the hospital. I'm someone else's kid." Or, "I must have been adopted."

A fisherman's birth myth might include being born on the opening day of walleye season, or at the height of the green drake hatch, or in the back of a bass boat. Being named "Izaak" after Izaak Walton or "Lee" after Lee Wulff, also fit the bill.

Alexander the Great's birth myth was that he would conquer the world. This expectation was laid on him by his folks, some Macedonian soothsayers, and the fact of his royal birth, and after a little trouble in Asia Minor, he did conquer what he knew of the planet. Whether kings, conquerors, or casting champions, the process works the same. The important thing to remember is that parents have a great deal to do with what sort of myth the kid grows up with, and therefore, his destiny.

The birth myth the fisherman father hands to his offspring will typically include a number of psychological expectations, including the imagined warm companionship that will begin once the child is old enough to become "my little fishin' buddy."

This leads me to an observation about where the trouble begins for half of our population.

How many fathers look at a brand spanking new baby girl and think "fishin' buddy?" Not enough, I can tell you. More parents put a damper on things by seeing fishing as a "boy thing" or referring to angle worms as "icky." If you don't think of girls as fishers from the very start, the odds are heavily stacked against any little girl growing up to love the sport. Almost all the avid fisherwomen I know were brought to the sport by their fathers.

As we expect of children, so shall they grow.

If you want a daughter to grow up to fish with you, give her a fitting birth myth. If it's true, tell her she was born the day the first salmon returned to the river, the day the big pike was caught, or the morning the ice went out of the bay and the lake trout began to hit. Anything. Use visualization to set the goal.

If you're the trouter, close your eyes and "see" her standing side by side with you, knee-deep in your favorite stream. See a rod in her hand. See her dressed in hip boots, a light green vest, and wearing a yellow fishing hat with matching trim. See a smile on her bright little face. Now see that smile widen to a great grin as a nice rainbow rises to take her fly. To get what you want, follow Thoreau's advice, "Print your hopes upon your mind."

Setting Up the Classroom

With a fishing birth myth in place, the next question is "How old should my child be before exposing her to angling?"

Very recent research on newborns indicates that, while we once thought they had poor and blurry vision in the first weeks of life, they actually see perfectly at a distance of nine inches. This is the approximate distance from the mother's breast to her face, and therefore, the recommended distance for early exposure to fish pictures and fishing videos.

I'm speaking here of what psychologists call an "enriched environment." While a lot of research has been done on the possible beneficial effects of enriched stimulation, the results do not strongly support the idea that an especially busy, stimulating, enriched environment actually leads to things like higher IQ. But then again, there are no data to suggest it hurts.

Early exposure certainly won't hurt. Of all the nursery rhymes my mother read me, this excerpt from one by Eugene Field most helped cast the die:

Wynken, Blynken, and Nod one night
Sailed off in a wooden shoe;
Sailed on a river of crystal light
Into a sea of dew.

"Where are you going, and what do you wish?"
the old moon asked of the three.
"We have come to fish for the herring fish
That live in this beautiful sea.
Nets of silver and gold have we."
Said Wynken, Blynken, and Nod.

The old moon laughed and sang a song
As they rocked in the wooden shoe,
And the wind that sped them all night long
Ruffled the waves of dew.

The little stars were the herring fish
That lived in that beautiful sea.
"Now cast your nets wherever you wish;
Never afeard are we!"
So cried the stars to the fishermen three:
Wynken, Blynken, and Nod.

Don't Waste Time Studying Woodcraft: Brush Up On Machiavelli Instead

John Randolph

There has been a great deal of discussion lately in literary haunts and joints about what a sportsman should take along with him to read in hunting or fishing lodges, hotels, and camps.

It is possible to make a fairly exact list. The list is immediately limited by the fact that most of these places already have a great deal of reading material around, most of it concerning hunting and fishing. But there is no advantage for a sportsman in reading what his companions are reading; he has got to have private material for his monologues. Without it, he can hold the floor by persistent roaring, but he cannot astound or impress.

Furthermore, he must be alert to improve his technique as well as increase his material. A man can dominate a conversation by sheer will; with good technique he can overwhelm it. So his reading must all be useful.

Critics and commentators have worked out a reading list that is compact for travel, comprehensive, classical, and guaranteed to enable any hunter or fisherman to talk for hours with authority. It includes no hunting or fishing how-to-do-it stuff, which is dangerous material among strong, hardy outdoorsmen. Here is the list:

Any thick book on economics, old or new. A recent one might be better, since the musical jargon of economics changes from year to year and a word this year might not have the same meaning this year that it didn't have last year. The great advantage of this material is that it cannot be contradicted, any more than a fog can be resisted. Good, strong, technical stuff about the behavior of money and goods can resist any attempt to interrupt and may induce sleep. It is especially effective if bankers or corporation presidents are around.

One chapter of Machiavelli, "On How a Prince Should Keep Faith." This is for instruction in technique. Too many hunters practice lying and dissembling with no other purpose than deception or to hear themselves talk. Nobody can lie or dissemble properly about hunting and fishing without some purpose, such as to prove that he has some quality that he fancies his companions will admire. They never do, but he should have an aim. Machiavelli, in showing him that a smart prince never welshes on a deal just for the fun of it, will lead him gently to sound, effective fishing and hunting lies.

A World War I copy of the *Infantry Drill Regulation,* if he has had no military service. It will help him to talk intelligently to ex-servicemen and even to shout them down. They never read it.

The second volume of *The Decline and Fall of the Roman Empire,* if he has not read the first volume. Gibbon assumed that his readers already knew the facts and chronology of history intimately and could read Latin and Greek. Plunging into the middle of this book will help him to interrupt and take charge of discussions already in progress.

Any heavy catalogue on the gear of hunting or fishing, whichever he may be doing at the time. It will help him to prove that all of his companions are carrying the wrong tackle, guns, and clothing

A cookbook or treatise on gastronomy, or both, the less well known the better. This is important, even vital. Without it, only a true gourmet can criticize the cooking in detail, suggest menus to the hotel or lodge operator, instruct his companions in the preparation and savoring of food, and make himself generally useful in a dietary way. A month or so ago I saw Charles Blake of Braintree, Massachusetts, completely rout a hunter who tried to do these things without first boning up. This man talked loudly and without preparation about food for some time before fixing Blake with a beady eye and demanding:

"Do you know the correct way to cook deer liver?"

`"Yes, I know the correct way to cook deer liver," Charles Blake of Braintree, Massachusetts, snarled. "You throw it in a blasted skillet, fry it, and eat it. That's the correct way to cook deer liver."

He might not have said blasted; might have used some other word. But the ring of authority was there. He had studied the thing.

A sportsman doesn't need any more than that, except a loud voice and a strong will. These books will give him all the material and guidance he needs.

Naturally, he will take along his regular reading. On a rainy day there is nothing like curling up in a window seat with a good comic book.

How to Fish With Your Dad

Jack Ohman

If you're like most Norman Rockwell Americans, your dad probably taught you how to fish. He probably took you to some little pond with sunnies and crappies, and you jerked the poor little fish out of the water into perdition. Then, as you got older, he took you on more sophisticated fishing extravaganzas such as bass fishing or drifting for walleyes, or, if your father was a masochist with a strange sense of humor, fly fishing. But, inevitably, there comes a point in a fisherman's life where he believes that his fishing expertise has outstripped his father's.

"The poor old goat," you may mutter patronizingly, "he's just out of the loop on all the latest developments and technological advances in fishing. I'll take him out and show him how the New Man catches fish."

Your dad realizes that his role as fishing master is about to be

usurped as you uplink with your mainframe on your Personal Depth Finder/Fish Locating System. You're secretly chortling about blanking the old man.

"Gee, Dad, are you really going to use that Lazy Ike? I mean, that's right out of the 1950s. It's embarrassing. Try one of these grape Gummy Bear-flavored Krankbaits with inset neon graphics."

The old man tells you to kiss his ass and ties on the stupid Lazy Ike, embarrassing you, and almost gratuitously adds that "this baby caught a lot of fish before you were the size of pumpkinseed."

Six hours later, you and your depth finder and your neon grape Gummy Bear lure are 0 for 4 and the old man is making the boat list to starboard because his stringer weighs twenty-nine pounds.

The Marshmallow Purists

Jim Dean

Maybe it's the fact that we are away from home and are overcome by the joyous anticipation of adventure. Or maybe it's because we can't resist the urge to redefine our identity in the presence of those who don't know us. Or perhaps it's just that, regardless of age, we are all still kids full of barely contained devilment. Whatever the reason, I have observed that the practical joke is never more tempting than when we gather with new companions to share our common obsession with fishing or hunting in distant places. The most even-tempered among us is very likely to become either predator or prey.

My friend Matt Hodgson, for example, pursues his ruling passion for fly fishing seriously, but like many who have been at it a long time, he sometimes grows weary of the near-religious pedantry and politically correct intolerance that he encounters among some anglers who have been newly baptized in the oft-contrived rituals of this sport. "It gets tedious," he observed as he told me this story.

On a recent trip to fish the Yellowstone River in Montana, he and his companions found themselves one morning in the company of a guide who seemed far too inclined to preach the gospel. "Now, I don't know how you fellows fish back home," he sniffed, "but here we fish only with flies and we release all trout. I would much prefer that you fish with dry flies, but if you have some other notions, we should discuss them."

Matt had hardly anticipated such a sermon. Not only is he unlikely to be taken for a rube, but his experience as a fly fisherman and fly tier far exceeded the guide's.

"Well, to tell the truth," Matt replied, "what I had in mind was a technique we prefer back home in North Carolina. Why don't you fellows go on ahead, and I'll run back into town and get about two hundred yards of stout cord and some 3/0 hooks. This looks like a really good place to set a trotline. You don't right offhand know where I could get a mess of chicken necks for bait do you?"

Sometimes the best way to crush a stereotype is to play to your adversary's worst fears. For a moment, the guide looked as though he had caught a bullet with his teeth, but when the laughter died down and he realized that Matt had no intention of stringing chicken necks across the Yellowstone, he relaxed and joined his peers for an enjoyable day of fly fishing.

Those of us bred and born in the brier patch of southern culture are frequently called upon to diffuse an unfortunate (or fortunate) stereotype when we travel to distant lands where our mother tongue is automatically linked with toothless ignorance and inbreeding. But sometimes it's fun to keep those suspicions alive too.

In the late 1970s, some friends and I journeyed to Pennsylvania to fish the storied limestone streams where Vincent Marinaro, Charley Fox, Ed Koch, and others had spawned a new and highly sophisticated technique for catching wild trout on flies carefully fashioned to imitate terrestrial insects. We had spent the winter tying flies, reading the literature, and preparing ourselves for this crusade to Mecca.

We drove all night and rendezvoused with our Keystone State guides on the stream shortly after dawn. They seemed a bit reserved, but they looked at our tackle and apparently decided that we at least looked like fly fisherpersons. My friends, however, were not about to let such an educational opportunity pass.

As we tromped down to the water, we swapped those precious bits of information that are thinly disguised to reveal our knowledge and establish our credentials. Fly boxes were shared and patterns compared. Just when it looked as though we might be accepted, one of the Pennsylvania anglers asked to see the patterns I'd been tying for this occasion.

Proudly, I produced my fly box and flipped open the lid. Each compartment was filled with tiny marshmallows, sorted by color—white, pink, yellow, green. I was stunned. The Pennsylvanians looked like someone had slapped them with a wet carp.

"But... but," I stammered.

"Yep," said one of my North Carolina companions. "We should have warned you, I suppose. Dean, here, can match any hatch with a marshmallow. Fishes them dry too."

The worst of it was that my Tar Heel buddies had emptied my several hundred flies into a paper sack—it took hours to get them sorted out. But everyone—well, almost everyone—had a good laugh and another stereotype had bitten the dust. We had a grand time fishing together that week.

And one of us had colorful snacks to eat on the stream too.

excerpt from

Crazy Fishing

Almost no one used a fly rod in saltwater thirty years ago when I walked out one summer day on the Fort Macon jetty to try my new nine-foot, ten-weight rod equipped with a three-hundred-grain, high-density shooting head. Friendly fishermen gave me room to cast, curious to see whether I would catch anything, especially since no one seemed to be having much luck soaking bait or casting lures. I doubt they'd ever seen anyone use a fly rod in saltwater. After about a dozen casts, I had a solid strike on a Lefty's Deceiver streamer fly that I had been working slowly along the bottom.

"Got one," I said, in case someone might not have noticed. The fight was strong, though sluggish, but whatever I had hooked ran off to one side a short way, then reversed direction. It did this several times, giving me cause to suspect that it was most likely a flounder or spotted sea trout. You can imagine my surprise when I slid a size ten-and-a-half low-heeled canvas tennis shoe onto the rocks. It was hooked in the tongue, which was not only appropriate but also provided the fulcrum that had caused the shoe to plane first one way and then the other. It had been a convincing performance, and we all looked at the shoe for several stunned moments until finally one of the other fishermen found the right words.

"You oughta cast back out there," he said. "Them kind normally run in pairs."

excerpt from

Where Are You, Ralph?

The one bout of seasickness I remember above all others took place out of Morehead City over thirty years ago on an old converted PT boat named the *Danco*. I had worked that summer to save money for a head boat trip, and sick or not, I was determined to fish. Indeed, I was doing fairly well until I mistook my box lunch for some ripe squid (the sandwiches and bait were passed out in identical paper cartons). I barely made it to the rail, where I managed to throw up right into the gaping maw of a very nice red snapper that another fisherman had just winched to the surface.

The angler was livid and refused to bring the fish aboard. Instead, he cut his line and stalked off to try his luck from another spot along the rail.

I was too sick to enjoy this at the time, but I recall thinking that he could have rinsed off that snapper. Besides, I would have swapped him a brace of untainted black sea bass for it. After all, it isn't often you catch the main course and the stuffing at the same time.

INTERIOR TEMPERATURE OF ALUMINUM BOAT IN SUMMER: °874 KELVIN...

© Jack Ohman

Black Duck Down

Doug Larsen

Although I can accept talking scarecrows, lions, and great wizards
of emerald cities, I find it hard to believe there is no paperwork
involved when your house lands on a witch.
                                                        —*Dave James*

Why aren't there any popular duck hunting movies? If the catalogs
I get are any indication, I can confirm that there are something
like seven or eight thousand duck hunting videos, but you never see a
duck hunting movie. In video, you have titles like *Run and Gun, Whack
and Stack, Stack and Whack, Shellac and Stack, Go Back and Shellac II,
III,* and *IV,* and countless, countless others. Typically, these are low-
budget productions and the plot is predictable. It is always the same,
or so it seems to me. Boy travels to hunting spot. Boy takes boat ride.
Boy meets ducks. Boy shoots ducks. Boy does product endorsement.
Boy shows dead ducks to camera. Then they roll the credits and you
listen for the voice-over that tells you to look for the same boy next
year in another video you cannot miss: *Go Back and Shellac V.*

But I'm not talking about videos, I'm talking about movies—big-
time, big-screen, coming-soon-to-a-theater-near-you, Citizen-Kane-
quality cinema. What could be more compelling or more attractive
than waterfowl hunting? The viewing public was awed by the cine-
matography of *Out of Africa.* Remember the flyovers of the African
plains and the symphonic music? Imagine the same thing in North
Dakota or Alberta or even Louisiana. Big vistas, pink sunrises, waterfowl scattering before the helicopter-mounted cameras. That is what
duck hunting is about, and that is what duck hunting needs. Duck
hunting, grainfields, marshes, and lakes hold the beauty that the
movies need and the moviegoing public feeds on.

Waterfowl hunting also has all the classic stuff they teach in high
school theater and psychology classes about struggle and conflict.
Remember that stuff? I'm going way, way back, but I remember my
bearded psychology teacher, Mr. Dunbar, lecturing a room full of

bored, or at least skeptical, high school seniors on the concepts of man versus man, man versus nature, and man versus himself. It didn't make sense to me then, but throw in duck hunting man versus stubborn outboard motor, and you've probably got a hotter property.

Not that there have not been hunting movies. *The Deer Hunter* was a movie with hunting in the title. But, alas, it was not really a deer hunting movie. It was a war experience movie with deer hunting in it. While it is generally agreed that *The Deer Hunter* was a great movie, anyone who hunts deer, or almost hits them with cars, knows they got the deer all wrong. Theses guys were supposed to be deer hunting in Pennsylvania, but the deer they were hunting looked like little elk or red stag or something. They weren't Pennsylvania whitetails. And, after they shot a deer in this movie, they strapped it to the hood of their car, got all liquored up, and drove through town throwing beer bottles out the window. Just the image of hunting I want my neighbors to see.

Then there was *Deliverance*. Clearly, it started out as a "guys go hunting" movie, until everything went wrong and Burt Reynolds and his pals met the poaching hillbillies who aimed to torture and torment and kill them. Those kinds of encounters generally put a damper on the ol' canoe trip. To this day, if I get really lost in strange country, I start humming the foreboding *Deliverance* banjo music until I get oriented.

As for other hunting films, there was *The Shooting Party* in 1984, and *Gosford Park* more recently. Both were movies about long shooting weekends in England, the pantywaist Brits, and the continued fall of the British aristocracy. These were really more class-struggle movies: those who have, shot the pheasants; the have-nots were beaters, loaders, and the like. Both pictures had to do with shooting, but neither was strictly a shooting movie. *Gosford Park* was more like an Agatha Christie book or a game of Clue, where Colonel Mustard gets clonked on the head with a candlestick in the library. Neither were duck hunting movies. As a rule, any movie where the actual clothes you'd wear hunting would qualify as costumes cannot be a real hunting movie.

As a brief aside, a hunting picture I can recommend to you is *The Ghost and the Darkness*. Not at all a duck hunting movie, but a true lion hunting story, it is well worth the two dollars it will run you to rent it at your local Blockbuster outlet. The film features Michael Douglas as the white professional hunter who is charged with killing two man-eating lions, and Val Kilmer as a family-man hunter who comes of age in a strange country. This is a rare movie for Hollywood, which, starting with *Bambi*, has generally portrayed hunters as callous, uncaring, slothful, trigger-happy, or worse.

The best movie I can think of that has the word duck in the title is *Duck Soup*, a Marx Brothers movie from the 1930s. Like *The Deer Hunter, Duck Soup* wasn't a duck movie; it was an anti-war movie, with Groucho Marx as Rufus T. Firefly, the leader of Freedonia. Not really duck related, but funny if you are a Marx Brothers aficionado. Then, there was *Howard the Duck*, a movie famous—or perhaps infamous— for being about as bad as a movie with duck in the title can be. To save you the trouble of ever having to see it, *Howard the Duck* grew up on a planet where ducks evolved instead of apes. You can either rent *Howard the Duck* or just go out and buy a bottle of Sominex. Either way, you'll get to sleep fast. To be totally inclusive about waterfowling titles, I should mention that Cary Grant starred in an Oscar-winning movie titled *Father Goose* in 1964, which was yet another war movie. Few geese actually appeared in the film.

Contrast these hunting examples with *Grumpy Old Men*. It was an ice fishing movie. For God's sake, if Hollywood moguls can make a movie about ice fishing, which is about as exciting as watching televised chess, surely they can make duck hunting interesting for the silver screen. Then there was *A River Runs Through It*. Now there was a fishing movie that was really about fishing, and people who fished, and how fishing was woven into their lives. People in the fly-fishing business credited the movie for virtually revitalizing the fly-fishing industry and making fly-fishing cool. Plus, while men watched it over and over again to see a great fishing movie, women didn't mind that men watched it over and over again since it had Brad Pitt in it. It was a great movie that did great things for fishing and the outdoors. Movies can do that. Remember *"Crocodile" Dundee*? It was a goofy picture, but it made people realize that Australia wasn't just an island that England still used as a prison. Next thing you know, Sydney is hosting the Olympic Games. The movie *Evita* popularized the notion of a stylish Argentina; tourism boomed, and people took tango lessons. Movies shape people's perceptions.

Duck hunting needs this. We need to be perceived as cool, even though most of us who hunt waterfowl know it is the coolest thing we do already. But I'm afraid that movie studio executive types are not going to take duck hunting at face value. Sure, everyone in Hollywood who doesn't drive a Jaguar drives a Hummer, but they don't drive big trucks for the same reason you and I drive big trucks. The only way they ever take them off road is when they accidentally back over a flowerbed or overshoot the parking lot and drive onto the kids' soccer field. They are going to see duck hunting as plagued by bad weather—muddy, buggy, windy, and cold. At times duck hunting is all of these things. Plus, we'll have to explain all about the guns and shooting, which will take time. But I'm prepared to convince any movie mogul who shows interest.

The African Queen was a huge success, and it was buggy—it even had leeches. *Dances With Wolves* was a great success as an outdoor movie. It showcased the Plains Indians and their great relationship with the land—a really fine example of the genre. It also featured buffalo hunting and cold weather. *Fargo* was sort of a cult success, and Lord knows it was a movie about the cold, given its Fargo, North Dakota, setting. *The Grapes of Wrath* had bugs (locusts) and *The Perfect Storm* showcased big winds and bad weather. While my wife reminds me that the movie also showcased George Clooney, it was a success nonetheless. Even *The Wizard of Oz* featured bad weather. If it weren't for the tornado, well… you know the story.

The problem is, none of these wear-their-sunglasses-indoors-movie-studio slicks is going to want to start from square one, research a great duck hunting story, turn it into a screenplay, and then spend millions of dollars to make a duck movie from scratch. They are out to make money, and if *Ace Ventura: Pet Detective* puts money in the bank… well, there you go. Or if they have to go to New Zealand and spend nine trillion dollars to make *Lord of the Rings,* then that is their prerogative. But for once I'd like to see a movie about a good game warden instead of a bad prison warden, or a good guide or outfitter instead of a bad cop. But maybe if the duck hunting community took some examples of great movies, and then we just worked with the stories or massaged the ideas a little, we'd come up with something they'd buy and produce.

Consider the story of a boastful small-town loner, starring George Wendt (barfly Norm Peterson from *Cheers*) as a guy in his mid-fifties who is a little hard to get along with, so he ends up duck hunting alone all the time. He has a nice boat, decoys, and equipment, but his friends and neighbors are all really hard-core duck hunters and they don't really think he is that much of a hunter. Every time the loner goes out to the big marsh at the edge of town, he returns to his spot at the end of the bar and tells everyone he's brought back a limit. Every day of the season, he gets "the limit." He boasts and brags and claims to be the "king of duck hunting." But nobody ever sees the ducks. He's always "just cleaned them," or just given another stringer of ducks to "some guys down at the plant." Disney would not like it, but we'd call the movie… *The Lyin' King.*

Or consider the touching musical story of an immigrant Austrian family that revels in togetherness—and goose hunting. The entire wholesome family goes on goose hunting road trips each fall when the various family members are not competing in goose calling contests. Like the folks in *The Partridge Family,* they travel in a big school bus, and like the family in *The Brady Bunch,* there are parents, with three or four daughters and several sons. But unlike the Von Trapp family, none of them can sing a lick, so they honk and purr and cluck on Olts, Rich-N-Tones, Haydels, and Big River flutes. All of the children are champion duck and goose callers, but they are a little quirky; they all wear camouflage lederhosen, sewn from old goose camp curtains. In the story, the family roams about the Middle West and up into Canada, goose hunting from their custom school bus, which is filled with camouflage and their possessions. A trailer filled with hundreds of Bigfoot decoys is hitched to the back bumper. The screenplay is titled, *The Sound of Goose Music.*

Another story that will surely be a hit is the suspense-filled tale of several duck-hunting-obsessed Russian navy submariners that band together and secretly crack into U.S. government agencies that are responsible for the atomic clock—and our calendars. Once these diabolical Russians crack into the computer system, they try to lengthen fall waterfowl seasons so they can selfishly shoot more ducks themselves. Meanwhile, U.S. authorities chase them all over the world's oceans as the clock ticks down to opening day. There will be huge, huge drama because, if the Russians succeed and seasons are lengthened, then bag limits will have to be reduced dramatically. Tentatively titled *The Hunt for More October.*

Or how about a story about a little group of guys, maybe three, from a small town in Arkansas—maybe Stuttgart, so we could show the World Championship Duck Calling Contest in the footage at the beginning? We'll make them close friends or brothers or something, and these are guys who just live to go timber hunting. This can be a touching story. We'll make all three of them blond and good looking, and we'll tell all about their relationships (women will like that part), their dogs, and their dead-end jobs, and their mean bosses who get in the way of timber hunting. One will have a health problem or a wooden leg, or he'll be a bad shot, just so the audience will pity him a little more than the others. We'll show beautiful footage of flooded Arkansas timber along with sunrises, boat rides, and the wind whipping through the movie stars' collective blond hair as they race through the flooded woods in the pink sunlight. In the exciting final scene, as we play soulful banjo music, our three stars will be on an afternoon hunt. They'll pick up their decoys and wade from one timber hole to another. And then they'll move again, because the ducks keep landing all around them, but not close enough for good shooting. They'll be frustrated, but they are a tight-knit group, so they'll persevere because they want to get it right. Finally, they'll get limits of mallards… and they'll all smile and slap each other on the back. But then (more banjo music) they'll realize they have become completely disoriented. They have lost their boat and their way home. We'll see a shot of the three stars standing together in a timber hole in their waders. They are looking at each other with the knowledge that they may have to share a common fate. They'll look around anxiously for familiar landmarks. Things will become desperate as darkness begins to fall in the timber. Tentative title: *Waders of the Lost Ark*.

Hollywood, there is some real opportunity here. Are you listening?

Fishing Stories

Charles W. Morton

The time has come to end the senseless competition among writers
of fishing stories: the narrator hooks a fish and (*a*) catches it or
(*b*) loses it. The only items in the story that are at all variable are the
species of fish—and hence its size and habitat—and the kind of tackle
used in his wisdom (or folly) by the narrator. These, along with a few
details, would simply be left blank in the standardized fishing story, to
be filled in as the facts warranted. Thus, whether it all took place at the
headwaters of the Orinoco or the narrows of Spectacle Pond, much
pencil chewing and time-consuming thought will be saved by adher-
ence to the simple rules governing all fishing stories.

The fishing story must begin with a modest statement of the
author's credentials: "I've fished for the mighty —— off Acapulco and
the battling —— along the Florida Keys. I've seen a maddened ——
swamp a dory off Wedgeport, but for sheer power and gameness I've
seen nothing that can equal, pound for pound, a ——."

That's a perfectly workable opening paragraph for any fishing
story. If the reader is foolish enough to doubt its validity when applied
to some notoriously inert species, let him remember that the fill-in of
the battle itself will prove everything that the narrator contends. It's
bound to, for the narrator uses just the same fill-in for a rock cod,
which behaves much like a boot full of water, as he would for a fifty-
pound muskellunge.

After presenting his own credentials, the narrator must introduce
his guide. Guides are always terse, monosyllabic men—which saves
the author from writing much improbable dialogue and dialect. They
grunt or they gesture, but that's about all. The narrator must assume at
this point the disarming role of chump and leave the high strategy to
Joe, the guide. ("We never did learn Joe's last name, but he taught us
all there was to know about ——s.")

Another purpose of the guide is to wake the author up on that
never-to-be-forgotten morning and give him his breakfast: "My head

had hardly touched the pillow, so it seemed, before Joe woke me up. The delicious aroma of ——ing —— greeted my nostrils, and I lost no time in getting out of my blankets."

And so to that mysterious locality, known only to Joe, where the narrator has been assured he will have a chance to pit his cunning against the great-granddaddy of all ——s. It makes no difference whether Joe is a Kanaka or a Canadian, or whether they travel by express cruiser, mule, or pirogue—their destination always disappoints the narrator when he gets there: "It looked like the last place in the world to try for ——s, but Joe merely grunted and gestured vaguely at the water. '—— here,' he said. 'Big one.' "

Joe of course was right, the author ruefully confesses. His first lure, a —— (spinner, fly, minnow, or grapnel baited with a small shoat—it's all the same) had hardly touched the water when down went the rod, out screamed the line! It was all the author could do to keep his footing against that first wild rush of the ——.

The next two hours are crammed with action, while the author brings in one gigantic —— after another, certainly the biggest he has ever seen and one of them looking as if it would go for at least —— pounds on the club scales. But hold on. What's wrong with Joe? He seems disgusted. He grunts contemptuously. Bored stiff. The author, still the chump and slow to catch on, presses Joe for comment. Joe grunts. "Big —— still here," Joe replies, gesturing at the water, and the author begins to realize that Joe is talking about a —— of a size never reported in all the annals of —— fishing.

Comes the final cast. Nothing happens. No —— of any size seems to be interested. The length of this interval of writing depends on how much space the author is trying to fill. If need be, he can reminisce of bygone feats against giant clams, electric eels, or things that have nothing to do with ——s.

Suddenly, a few yards beyond the lure, the waters swirl: "Some vast, invisible force was causing a submarine upheaval. Spellbound, I watched a great tail appear for an instant as the monster lazily rolled over and submerged again. I turned to Joe. "Don't tell me that was a ——! I whispered. '——s don't get *that* big.' But Joe only grunted. 'Big ——,' he replied."

The author realizes that his tackle is far too light for a —— of this size. Joe had really known what he was talking, or grunting, about. But it's too late now. So: DOWN goes that rod again. OUT screams the line.

Even with a —— pound drag, the ——'s rush carries all before it. Crash! The leviathan hurls himself far out of the water and comes down with an echoing splash. The author vainly tries to reel in precious line.

"My rod bent almost double. Pandemonium reigned." Sooner or later, as the line races from the screeching reel, the author does a very foolish thing: "I tried to brake it with my thumb." Naturally enough, he gets a bad burn on his thumb. More leaps, lunges—a page or so of them.

"Suddenly, my line went ominously slack. I began frantically reeling in. '—— gone,' Joe grunted."

True enough. The tale is almost told. Remains only the unbelievable circumstances of the leader when the narrator finally winds it to the surface. Gut, wire, or ⅜-inch log chain, its condition never varies: "*Bitten clean through!* Mute evidence that the —— had met man's challenge—and won!"

They prepare to leave. "But suddenly the waters were convulsed again as the mighty —— broke the surface in all his majesty and, with a final derisive smack of his great tail, disappeared—still the Monarch of ——" (Spectacle Pond, the Upper Orinoco, Hillsboro Inlet, etc., etc.).

158

Guiding Guys

Ian Frazier

The beautiful McIllhenny River rises timelessly from the foot of the Rocky Mountains in the anglers' paradise that we at Pools and Riffles Guiding Service and Angling Supplies call home. Tumbling from a cleft in a fawn-colored cliff, it runs clear and cold as chilled gin across lovely rocks in headlong flight, only to spread in easy, wadable flats harboring monster brown trout if you know where to look; then it doubles back on itself the opposite way for seven miles in a blue-ribbon section where overhanging ponderosa pines dapple its surface and the play of rose-pink on the sunset ripples of the feeding pods of fish can make you wonder why you ever…

May I put you on hold for a second?

Hi, I'm back. Anyway, it's a river to dream of, and at Pools and Riffles, we do. I'm Steve, the owner, chief guide, and chairman of the board. Some years ago I gave up helping folks with their 401(k)'s at Crane White down in the big city. Moved here with my wife, Larissa, and never looked back once, except for the alimony thing. Been here almost two and a half years, every day kicking myself that I didn't do this sooner. The river is in my blood now, it *is* my blood itself, and I dream of it—waking and sleeping I dream of the river. (And also of hitting a small bearded man in a fedora about the head with a carrot.)

Take a look at our brochure: Pools and Riffles is just off the interstate and a short drive from Camas International Airport, with daily service to all major hubs. We'll pick you up in our special van and take you to your accommodations; or, if you choose, you can reserve our streamside lodge with all the amenities, including fax and secretarial. Whether you're an experienced fly fisherman or have a Visa card that was issued just last week, we can provide a consummate angling adventure for everyone. If you don't have your own gear, we'll be happy to rent it to you while explaining that if you're really serious you're going to wind up buying all this stuff eventually anyway so in the long run it'd be cheaper just to go ahead and buy it now. But in this, as in everything, the ultimate decision rests with you.

Maybe you live in a crowded, built-up, urban area filled with urban-type people and their hairdos and CD players. That's your business. Personally, I can take it or let it alone. Up here you'll find that the urban-type environment seems awfully far away. At Pools and Riffles our goal is to make you forget that world and immerse yourself in ours—in our pristine, crime-free streams and rivers, our clear blue skies (we get over three hundred days of sunshine a year!), and our many acres of motels where you usually never have to lock your doors.

To guarantee you the finest fly-fishing experience available, Pools and Riffles has assembled the most outstanding staff of licensed angling guides in the Rocky Mountain region. Whether you're looking for an afternoon float trip, an overnight, or even a week's excursion into the backcountry, we know we've got the perfect trout-hound for you, whatever your personal preference or style. Allow me to introduce you.

First, there's *Craig,* our resident mountain man. Craig is big—need I say more? Craig'll run about six foot seven and about 260, 275 pounds. We're talking big, and that's not even counting the beard. Craig doesn't say much. He doesn't have to—just "Yep," "Nope," and "Like some freshly ground black pepper on yer salad, hoss?" On a trout stream he can do whatever's needed, from tying a size 24 midge fly out of pocket lint to patching through a call to your broker in Tokyo on your cell phone. He practically grew up on these waters since he moved here from Seattle in '96. Wild and free as the mountains themselves, he's always happy to run back to the car and get you any little item you desire. He'll put you onto some trophy fish and himself onto a much-deserved tip, you can be sure.

Potter is from one of the oldest families on Philadelphia's Main Line, but he'd never tell you that himself. Back in the days of silk fly lines, Pot's great-granddad was the fellow who taught J. P. Morgan the double-haul. But ol' Pot's just guiding for the sport of it, and he's every bit as regular as you or me. If you've got a problem with your casting mechanics, Pot will see it right away and take care to point it out each time you cast. He's famous for encouraging his clients with old angling sayings like "I *beg* you to cast that fly to four o'clock!" and "I *can't* believe you missed that strike!" Shiny, high forehead, old-fashioned shades with side panels, big grin, bottle of Pouilly-Fumé in the cooler, Hasty Pudding anecdotes—that's Pot. Your angling education isn't complete until you've spent long hours on the water with him. Did I mention he's a gourmet cook?

Stan is by far the most dedicated trout angler you will ever meet. He lived in a sleeping bag in a cave above Twelve-Mile Reservoir for eight years, fishing with mouse patterns all night long, if that gives you any idea. His wife's the one that ran off with Claus von Bulow. Stan is in a program now and has begun to take responsibility for some of the problems from his past. Stan has learned to redirect hurtful emotions the way any sensible guy should—straight into fishing, and more fishing after that. There's not a dime's worth of "quit" in Stan.

Unlike the rest of us, *Bethany-Anne* is not a man. As the result of an amicable sex-discrimination lawsuit, we are happy to add her to the team. Despite lacking the upper-body strength required for high-wind casting and pulling the boat out of the water, Bethany-Anne can do some things. Beyond that I'm not at liberty to say. If you happen to arrive with a spouse or girlfriend or other non-fishing guest, a trip with Bethany-Anne might work out just fine.

President Jimmy Carter joined our staff last fall, and we're honored that he did. Everybody knows what an avid fly fisherman Jimmy is. Historians add that Jimmy is the first President or former President to guide. It costs a little more to fish with Jimmy, and it's worth it, too. (When you're sitting around the campfire, get him to tell you about how he shaved that Secret Service agent's head that time.) He's as personable and friendly and laid-back as they come, just so long as you don't lose any of his tackle or get cigarette ashes in the boat or anything. Jimmy may be the only recent President never to have been indicted, but don't let the record fool you: He can outsmart anything that swims. As you shake his hand goodbye at the end of a once-in-a-lifetime angling epic, remember that the customary gratuity for former heads of state is 33 percent. Gentlemen, we give you the President!

A word of advice, just between us: During the months of June through October, our bookings are usually very heavy, so it's a good idea to schedule far in advance. To help with your plans, Pools and Riffles has set up its own toll-free number predicting stream flows and fishing conditions for the next five years. A taped announcement of upcoming conditions indicates what you can expect on the dates you have in mind: Condition 1 (Best Fishing I've Ever Seen), Condition 2 (Best Fishing in Twenty Years), Condition 3 (Excellent,

Excellent Fishing), Condition 4 (Great Fishing, for This Time of Year), Condition 5 (The Guys Have Been Catching Some Great Fish), and Condition 6 (Great Fishing, Far as I Know, So C'mon Up!).

Occasionally we get questions from potential clients about the incidence of whirling disease in local waters and its possible consequences in a sharp decline in trout populations. However, according to a study we have read, the latest data indicate that there is no such thing as whirling disease.

Out West, the federal government puts out a lot of this misinformation in order to collect its confiscatory taxes and keep down the number of fishing guides. (We offer discounts for payments in cash!) As far as we're concerned, the best people to manage a resource are working anglers who see the river year in and year out, not some bureaucrats somewhere. In our effort to promote wise use, we practice a strict but voluntary policy of catch-and-release. This means that every fish caught will be measured, weighed, photographed, recorded with a tracing of its outline on butcher paper, and returned to the river so that it can have the same experience another day. If this offends the meat fisherman, so be it; no angler we'd care to fish with would do otherwise.

Many of our clients keep coming back to us year after year, we find. All kinds of folks head our way—they're middle-aged, approaching middle age, or in their forties or fifties or mid-fifties; gray-haired, balding, or having not very much gray hair; they might be doctors, lawyers, entertainment attorneys, physicians, bankers, stockbrokers, accountants with law degrees, or surgeons. What they share, and what we at Pools and Riffles prize, is an infectious enthusiasm for being out on the river with a fly rod and fishing and laughing in a particular way just all the time.

At Pools and Riffles we understand that the quality of the angling experience doesn't depend on how many fish you catch, so long as you catch a lot, but rather on their size and on nobody else's being bigger. Such incidentals are the trophies we truly treasure. The light sparkling on the wet clothes of a friend who fell in, the disappointed expression on the face of your partner when you land one, or the complimentary beer in the late afternoon by the boat launch with the car radio playing as you sign the receipt—these are the intangibles. This is what we offer at Pools and Riffles, where the finest in fly-fishing is as near as a few phone calls, cab ride, an airport, another airport, a third airport, and a courtesy van ride away.

Bad Advice

Ian Frazier

Some years ago, on a camping trip in the pine woods of northern Michigan, my friend Don brought along a copy of an outdoor cookbook that appeared on the best-seller lists at the time. This book contained many ingenious and easy-sounding recipes; one that Don especially wanted to try was called Breakfast in a Paper Bag. According to this recipe, you could take a small paper lunch sack, put strips of bacon in the bottom, break an egg into the sack on top of the bacon, fold down the top of the sack, push a stick through the fold, hold the sack over hot coals, and cook the bacon and egg in the sack in about ten minutes.

I watched as Don followed the directions exactly. Both he and I remarked that we would naturally have thought the sack would burn; the recipe, however, declared, "Grease will coat the bottom of the bag as it cooks." Somehow we both took this to mean that the grease, counterintuitively, actually made the bag less likely to burn. Marveling at the "who would have guessed" magic of it, we picked a good spot in the hot coals of our campfire, and Don held the sack above them. We watched. In a second and a half, the bag burst into leaping flames. Don was yelling for help, waving the bag around trying to extinguish it, scattering egg yolk and smoldering strips of bacon and flaming paper into the combustible pines while people at adjoining campfires stared in horror and wondered what they should do.

The wild figures that the burning breakfast described in midair as Don waved the stick, the look of outraged, imbecile shock reflected on our faces—those are images that stay with me. I replay the incident often in my mind. It is like a parable. Because a book told us to, we attempted to use greased paper as a frying pan on an open fire. For all I know, the trick is possible if you do it just so; we never repeated the experiment. But to me the incident illustrates a larger truth about our species when it ventures out-of-doors. We go forth in abundant ignorance, near-blind with fantasy, witlessly trusting words on a page or a tip a guy we'd never met before gave us at a sporting-goods counter in a giant discount store. About half the time, the faith that leads us into the outdoors is based on advice that is half-baked, made up, hypothetical, uninformed, spurious, or deliberately, heedlessly bad.

Greenland, for example, did not turn out to be very green, Viking hype to the contrary. Despite what a Pawnee or Wichita Indian told the Spanish explorer Francisco Vásquez de Coronado, there were no cities of gold in western Kansas, no canoes with oarlocks made of gold, no tree branches hung with little gold bells that soothed the king (also nonexistent) during his afternoon nap; a summer's march on the Great Plains in piping-hot armor presumably bore these truths upon the would-be conquistador in an unforgettable way. Lewis and Clark found no elephants on their journey, though President Jefferson, believing reports from the frontier, had said they should be on the lookout for them. And then there was Lansford W. Hastings, the adventurer and promoter of Sacramento, purveyor of some of the worst advice of all time. He told the prospective wagon-train emigrants to California that he had discovered a shortcut (modestly named the Hastings Cutoff) that reduced travel time by many days. Yes, it did cross a few extra deserts and some unusually high mountain ranges; the unfortunate Donner Party read Hasting's book, followed his route, and famously came to its grisly end below the narrow Sierra pass that now bears its name. According to local legend, the air in the Utah foothills is still blue from the curses that emigrants heaped on Lansford W. Hastings along the way.

People will tell you just any damn thing. I have found this to be especially so in establishments called Pappy's, Cappy's, Pop's, or Dad's. The wizened, senior quality of the names seems to give the people who work in such places a license to browbeat customers and pass on whatever opinionated misinformation they please. When I go through the door of a Pappy's or Cappy's—usually it's a fishing-tackle shop, a general store, or a bar—usually there's a fat older guy sitting behind the counter with his T-shirt up over his stomach and his navel peeking out. That will be Pappy, or Cappy. Sometimes it's both. Pappy looks at me without looking at me and remarks to Cappy that the gear I've got on is too light for the country at this time of year, and Cappy agrees, crustily; then I ask a touristy, greenhorn question, and we're off.

Cappy, backed by Pappy, says the rig I'm driving won't make it up that Forest Service road, and I'm headed in the wrong direction anyhow, and the best place to camp isn't where I'm going but far in the other direction, up top of Corkscrew Butte, which is closed now, as is well known.

What's worse is that I crumble in this situation, every time. I have taken more wrong advice, have bought more unnecessary maps, trout flies, water filtration devices, and assorted paraphernalia from Pappys and Cappys with their navels showing than I like to think about. Some essential element left out of my psychic immune system causes me always to defer to these guys and believe what they say. And while the Lansford W. Hastings type of bad advice tells people they can do things they really can't, the Cappy-Pappy type of advice is generally the opposite. Cappy and Pappy have been sitting around their failing store for so long that they are now convinced you're a fool for trying to do anything at all.

Complicating matters still further is Happy. She used to be married to Cappy but is now married to Pappy, or vice versa. Happy has missing teeth and a freestyle hairdo, and she hangs out in the back of the store listening in and irritatedly yelling statements that contradict most of what Pappy and Cappy say. The effect is to send you out the door as confused as it is possible to be. What's different about Happy, however, is that eventually she will tell you the truth. When you return your rented bicycle or rowboat in the evening, Pappy and Cappy are packed away in glycolene somewhere and Happy is waiting for you in the twilight, swatting mosquitoes and snapping the elastic band of her trousers against her side. You have found no berries, seen no birds, caught no fish; and Happy will tell you that the birds were right in front of the house all afternoon, the best berry bushes are behind the snow-machine shed, and she herself just caught fifty fish right off the dock. She will even show you her full stringer, cackling, "You gotta know the right place to go!"

Of course, people usually keep their best advice to themselves. They'd be crazy not to, what with all the crowds tramping around outdoors nowadays. I can understand such caution, in principle; but I consider it stingy and mean when it is applied to me. There's a certain facial expression people often have when they are withholding the one key piece of information I really need. They smile broadly with lips shut tight as a Mason jar, and a cheery blankness fills their eyes. This expression irks me to no end. Misleading blather I can put up with, and even enjoy if it's preposterous enough; but smug, determined silence is a posted sign, a locked gate, an unlisted phone. Also, I think it's the real message behind today's deluge of information-age outdoor advice, most of which seems to be about crampons, rebreathers, and synthetic sleeping bag fill. What you wanted to know does not appear. Especially in the more desirable destinations outdoors, withheld advice is the most common kind.

I craved good advice one summer when I fished a little-known Midwestern river full of brown trout. Every few days I went to the local fly-fishing store and asked the guys who worked there where in the river the really big fish I had heard about might be. The guys were friendly, and more than willing to sell me stuff, but when I asked that question I met the Mason-jar expression I've described. I tried being winsome; I portrayed myself as fishless and pitiable, told jokes, drank coffee, hung around. On the subject of vital interest, nobody offered word one.

I halfway gave up and began driving the back roads aimlessly. Then, just at sunset one evening, I suddenly came upon a dozen or more cars and pickups parked in the high grass along a road I'd never been on before. I pulled over, got out, and crashed through the brush to investigate. There, in a marshy lowland, was a section of river I had never tried, with insects popping on its surface and monster brown trout slurping them down and fly rods swishing like scythes in the summer air. Among the intent anglers along the bank I recognized the fishing-store owner's son, one of the Mason-jar-smiling regulars. The experience taught me an important outdoor fact: Regardless of what the people who know tell you or don't tell you, an off-road gathering of parked cars doesn't lie.

In case you're wondering, this particular good fishing spot was on the Pigeon River near the town of Vanderbilt, Michigan, upstream from the dam. It's been years since I fished there, so I can't vouch for the up-to-dateness of my information. But unlike smarter outdoorsmen, I am happy to pass along whatever I can, because I myself am now gabby and free with advice to an embarrassing degree. I noticed the change as I got older; I hit my mid-forties, and from nowhere endless, windy sentences of questionable advice began coming out of me. An old-guy voice takes on its own momentum, and I seem unable to stop it even when I have no idea what I'm talking about. Sometimes when strangers ask me for directions on a hiking trail or just around town, I give detailed wrong answers off the top of my head rather than admit I don't know. When my hearers are out of sight, my reason returns and I realize what I've done. Then I make myself scarce, for fear that they will discover my ridiculousness and come back in a rage looking for me.

Outdoor magazines I read as a child featured authoritative fellows in plaid shirts and broad-brimmed hats who offered sensible tips about how to find water in the desert by cutting open cacti, how to make bread from cattail roots, or how to predict the weather by the thickness of the walls of muskrat dens. I wish I had down-to-earth wisdom like that to impart, but when I search my knowledge, all that comes to mind is advice that would cause me to run and hide after I gave it. The one piece of real advice that I do have is not outdoor advice, strictly speaking; I think, however, that its soundness makes up for that drawback. It is true virtually every time, in all lands and cultures. I offer it as the one completely trustworthy piece of advice I know, and it is this: Never marry a man whose nickname is "The Killer."

Other than that, you're on your own.

The Book of John

Bill Heavey

Around this time each year a loud thump outside the house announces to millions of American sportsmen that the new Cabela's catalog has just hit the front porch, flattening any flowerpot, bicycle, or dog on which it lands. After burying Duke in the vegetable patch, the breathless recipients attach a heavy chain from their ATV to the document and drag it into the bathroom for a first look. This lasts, on average, half an hour. Then, a simultaneous flushing of toilets causes reservoirs nationwide to fall 6 inches, injuring thousands of jet skiers and proving once again the existence of a just and loving God.

The word *catalog* comes from the Greek *katalogos*, literally "words causing income to vanish." But *catalog* hardly begins to describe this magical work. A quick perusal yields information to live by. For instance, raise your hand if you knew any of the following three facts:

- A box of Weatherby Magnum Ultra-Velocity ammo in .30/378 Weatherby Mag., 200-grain Nosler Partition, will run you $90, or about $4.50 per shell. At that price, you might want to let that Cape buffalo get really close before wasting a shot.

- For about 50 bucks more you can get a pair of Cabela's Kangaroo Upland Bird Boots, which weigh almost nothing, are a whopping 62 percent stronger than cowhide, and will still be going strong when you are pushing up chokecherry. Of course, state law prohibits their shipment to California for fear of offending celebrity animal rights activists.

- Nothing screams "good taste" to your houseguests like a $60 clear-acrylic toilet seat in which fishing lures, bullets, or hooks are embedded.

The most recent catalog runs to 711 pages and weighs more than some Korean automobiles. The day is coming when a *cabela* will refer to a unit of weight. You will buy crushed stone and pig iron by the cabela. Diet pills will promise to help you shed those unwanted cabelas. Olympic lifters will bow their heads in silent tribute to the brave Ukrainian champion who was crushed when he attempted to clean and jerk what would have been a new world record of 100 cabelas.

Dick Cabela's empire started out small. Back in 1961, he placed a three-line ad in a magazine offering five hand-tied flies to any customer who would cover the 25-cent postage. Orders were processed at the company headquarters, Dick's kitchen table in Chapell, Nebraska. The flies were sent back with a mimeographed sheet listing other sporting items for purchase. The operation has been so successful that nearly 6,000 employees now work in that kitchen. Mary, Dick's wife, is said to be tired of having to make them sandwiches every day and thinks it's about time to build a cafeteria.

The Cabela's catalog has long exercised a strange power over otherwise rational men. As you consider it in the privacy of the best seat in the house, it starts to seem like a good idea—no, a responsibility—to buy not only what you need immediately but also gear that you *might need some day*. Thus, guys who live on fishing boats in Alaska suddenly crave 17-inch camo snake boots. Others who have difficulty opening the hood of their truck covet the titanium-handled Leatherman Charge XTi with nine double-end bits should they ever run out of gas in the wilderness and have to drill for oil. Guys who've never bushwhacked through cover worse than the azaleas in their front yard must have the Filson Double Tin Cloth Chaps that stop the smaller shotgun loads at close range.

I recently ordered the handheld Thor 10-million-candlepower spotlight. Why? Because let me ask you something: How stupid are you going to feel when hordes of eye-sucking aliens invade Earth and your entire family dies just because you lacked the wattage to signal other planets for help?

My personal weakness is footwear. I'm the kind of guy who can't be happy if my feet aren't. That's why I need the Trans-Alaska III pacs endorsed by the winner of the Iditarod and rated to minus 135 degrees. Overkill? We'll see who's laughing when the next ice age hits. And I know the chances that the editors of this magazine will call to say "Heavey! Next plane to Alaska. Bighorn sheep" are slim. But slim is not none. That's why I need the $270 boots handcrafted by Austrian elves and featuring the Vibram multigrip outsole and removable Air-Active footbeds designed for precisely that kind of hunting.

I could go on. I'd like to. But my daughter is banging on the bathroom door and calling me a doo-doo head. Don't forget the camo bedding on page 327. The Mossy Oak Shadow Grass window treatments are particularly spiffy. And now, jet skiers of America, say your prayers

Scents and Sensibility

Michael A. Halleran

Two eyes like burning coals stared out from the dark interior of the dog box. Inside a nervous shuffle, and an impatient paw at the grated door, digging and scratching. The longer we waited for the guys to get their gear together, the more insistent the digging became.

"Which dog is that?" someone asked from two trucks away.

"Oh, that's mine," said a quiet fellow in a Filson vest, "his name is Benzedrine."

I first met Benzedrine the Brittany about two years ago while hunting quail in Northeast Kansas. His master was pretty laid back, about 50 or so, and vice president of the local credit union. A brother-in-law to one of the regulars, he drove a nice Chevy, swung a nice Beretta double, and was an amiable fellow, a nice addition to any hunting party. His dog was not nice, though—he was insane.

The guys picked through their gear and the dogs assembled. When Master finally opened Benzedrine's dog box, a huge iron casemate with two locks on it, he had to brace it with his forearm, the way you'd keep a Grizzly inside a refrigerator. Then, with a check cord in the other hand, he quickly snapped fast the cord on the steel reinforced battle-ship cable that he used for a collar.

"That's a pretty stout collar," I said.

"Yeah," Master said ruefully, "I had to get one with metal on it—he's chewed through three nylon collars and two leather ones."

"How the heck does he do that?"

"I haven't the slightest idea," Master said with a pensive look.

With the tailgate up and with the check cord lashed to a cargo hook, Benzedrine surveyed his domain, exerting enough pull on the rope that it was practically smoking. He was mostly white, two broad orange patches along his back and a half orange face which gave him a cock-eyed look like a Barbary pirate. His head was broad and his nostrils flexed open and closed ceaselessly, sniffing, taking it all in. Every now and again, apropos to nothing, he curled his lip, baring just his front incisors and let out a little snort.

There were five hunters and two shorthairs, a Brittany and a big-running pointer milling about the vehicles and Benzedrine tied fast to the Chevy, scowling. He gave a quick glance over the party from his elevated perch and you could see him sizing everyone up.

Snort. Master. Some guy. Another guy. Two shorthairs (idiots). Snort. A pointer (slow). A couple guys. A Brittany (another idiot). Not much competition today… Snort.

Everything ready, Master's hand went to the tailgate latch slightly easing the tension on the check cord; that was all it took. Trailing the cord, Benzedrine went airborne over the endgate like a busted bottle rocket. Five hundred yards out he bumped a good sized covey, snapping shark-like at the slower singles. He chased them for a good fifteen hundred yards due north along the fence row at slightly under the speed of sound, checked only by a rabbit. Radar locked, he tore back south after it in a crazy jig-saw pattern. Just as suddenly, he abandoned the cottontail and veered back towards the hunters for about 200 yards. Then he locked up solid under a big hedge tree. The pointer backed and the other dogs followed suit, the hunters sprinting forward, guns ready.

His point was awfully ugly—more like a nose guard than a bird dog—both feet out, ready to spring, head down, hind end up high. When we got within twenty five yards of him, he moved.

The skunk moved too, but not before hitting Benzedrine with a green double espresso straight to the snoot. In a microsecond, several things happened at once. Everyone ran for cover, the skunk backed up and Benzedrine charged.

The old timers say that a skunk can spray seven times before its tanks are empty. Although it's difficult to count such things while running backwards as fast as you can, not to mention being partially blinded with the animal equivalent of Dioxin, the skunk got in three more shots before Benzedrine pounced and dispatched it with a smart shake. Reeking but triumphant, with the skunk held aloft in his jaws, Benzedrine made straight for the hunters, and discipline collapsed. In a grotesque game of tag with the pointer and shorthairs in hot pursuit, he headed for each hunter in turn, undeterred by their avoidance. It might have looked like he was seeking praise for his derring-do, but he just wanted to watch us run like hell.

Suddenly at my elbow, Master appeared.

"Did you get much on you?" he asked.

I nodded, keeping my gag reflex in check with a firm jaw.

"Well," he said thoughtfully, "I guess I better go get that skunk away from him—he'll carry that thing around all day if I let him."

"Has he done this sort of thing before?" I asked as he walked off to find his dog.

"Hydrogen peroxide and baking soda," he said blandly over his shoulder, "really cuts the smell—don't bother with tomato juice—doesn't do a thing."

He's right, you know. If you're hunting with Ole' Benz, stock up on the peroxide, a crate ought to do, and save the tomato juice for a double Bloody Mary. Or two.

Stalking the Red-Nosed Captain

Max Shulman

Until a year ago I knew absolutely nothing about salt-water game fishing. Today I am an expert, loaded with lore. I have learned how to tempt a tuna, master a marlin, seduce a sailfish, beguile a barracuda, and tell big lies.

I've been attracted by deep-sea fishing for many years, but somehow I never got around to it. It seems like every time I planned to go, something annoying would come up to prevent it, like root canal or a job. But early in November of 1968—it was shortly before Election Day—I looked over the list of presidential candidates and it was clear to me that if ever there was a time for a man to go fishing, this was it.

Asking advice from knowledgeable friends, I was directed to a recently opened resort in the Bahamas—Great Harbour Cay, a sun-blessed, breeze-kissed isle which has been turned into a paradise for fisherman, yachtsmen, golfers, and other unemployables. I arrived at Great Harbour Cay late one afternoon, unpacked my deep-sea gear (a kapok T-shirt, inflatable drawers, and six bottles of Dramamine) and turned in early for a good night's sleep.

The next morning I boarded my chartered fishing boat, the *Uninsurable,* a trim craft with merrily gurgling bilges and a captain named Rummy Rafferty, an attractive red-nosed man with palsy. The mate, a lovable native named Black Power, cast off the lines, the Captain threw the throttles open, and we leaped away from the dock with a roar.

Some hours later, after a passing dory pulled us off the sandbar, we reached open water. What excitement flooded my breast as I gazed for the first time at the incredible blues and greens of the Bahamian sea! How my pulses pounded and my eyeballs shone as the mate baited the hooks with mullet and balao and dropped them over the stern!

"Captain," I said eagerly to the Captain, "what kind of fish will we catch?"

"Bless you, sir," said the Captain, "what kind would you like?"

"Are there any marlin around?" I said.

"Lordy, yes!" said the Captain. "Why, I declare we must have raised thirty or forty yesterday."

"Where?" I said.

"Bless you, sir," said the Captain. "Right here where we are."

Marlin! I fairly trembled with anticipation. Could it be that I—a tyro, a novice—would catch the mightiest fish in the sea on my very first trip? No, it was too much to hope for.

But suddenly my reel was whirling and shrieking and my line was running out at blinding speed!

"Oh, joy!" I cried. "A strike! A strike! Oh, joy!"

"Shut up and reel," said the Captain.

Now began the titanic struggle: man, the wily hunter (me) against raw, savage, and elemental nature (the fish). Back and forth the battle seesawed, the outcome always in doubt. I reeled in; he ran out. I reeled in again; he ran out again. Sometimes I thought my strength would give out, but somehow, I know not whence, at the last second I summoned up just a little more. And under the waves my adversary too was finding hidden reserves. A hundred times it seemed he could fight no more, but a hundred times he turned and plunged and fought again. How long the battle lasted I truthfully cannot say, for I was unaware of time or space. In all the world there were only two things—I at one end of the line, he at the other.

At last it was over. One final plunge and then—his noble heart broken—he came to the side of the boat and the mate's sharp gaff slashed downward.

My every sinew aching, my voice a dry croak, I said to the mate, "What is it?"

"Kelp," said the mate.

"However, sir," said the Captain, "that's no reason not to have a drink."

We drank. We trolled. We waited. Then we drank and trolled and waited some more.

"Can't understand it," said the Captain. "They were sure here yesterday."

"Where do you think they've gone?" said I.

"Aha!" said the Captain. "I know exactly where they've gone, the foxy devils." He pointed off to his left. "See that rip?"

"Yes," said I.

"That's where they are," said the Captain and whipped the wheel hard aport.

Some hours later, after the mate had replaced the broken rudder with a toilet seat, we reached the rip. And—you're not going to believe this—no sooner did we get there when—wham! zap! zowie!—I had another strike!

I will not attempt to recount the landing of this one; even Herman Melville's powers would be strained to describe the action and passion, the drama and strife, the cosmic contest of atavistic guile against brute protein. Suffice it to say that when it was over, the monster lay gaffed in the boat.

"Marlin?" I said to the mate.

"Barracuda," said the mate to me.

"Oh, " I said, crestfallen. But my spirits quickly rallied. "Well," I said, "it must be the biggest barracuda ever taken in these parts."

"I doubt it," said the Captain. "Looks to be about 4 pounds."

"But a fighting fool!" said I.

"Officially, the record for barracuda is 103 pounds," said the Captain. "*Officially,* that is. Actually I got one last year that went well over 120."

"Do tell," said I.

"Happened on my way back to port one evening," said the Captain. "Getting around sundown when she hit. Lordy, how she hit! Three and a half hours I fought that 'cuda. Pitch dark it was when I finally pulled her in. Got back to the dock and the weighing shed was closed for the night. Had to leave her on the dock till morning—which is how come I don't have the record."

"Goodness," I said. "What happened?"

"Tinker Bell," said the Captain. "That's my cat, Tinker Bell. She came out during the night and must have ate 50 pounds off that fish."

"Heavens to Betsy," I said.

"If you think *you're* surprised, imagine how I felt when I saw Tinker Bell next morning," said the Captain. "Bigger than a St. Bernard, she was."

"Where is she?" I said. "I'd certainly like a look at her."

"Dead," said the Captain. "Choked to death on her flea collar, poor thing."

"Have a drink," said I, "and see if you can remember some other world records you got tragically diddled out of."

"Much obliged," said the Captain. "Well, sir, I guess the most tragic happened back on April 17, 1961, when I caught the record blue marlin."

"How big?" said I.

"Can't say for sure," said the Captain. "All I can say is I've seen the *official* record marlin—814 pounds—and mine went anyhow twice as big, maybe three times."

I wiped away a tear.

"Hooked her off the Isle of Pines about eight in the morning," said the Captain. "Fought her all that day and half the night. Dragged me all over the sea, she did, but I hung tough. Finally I brought her in and lashed her to the boat and headed for the nearest land. If only it hadn't been that particular night!"

"What particular night!" said I.

"April 17, 1961," said the Captain. "Bay of Pigs."

Later that day I learned some more of the Captain's heart-rending history. Not only had this gallant, luckless man been bilked out of the records for marlin and barracuda, but also for dolphin, sailfish, and tuna. His dolphin, at least 180 pounds, was hijacked by a Japanese trawler. His sailfish, 200 pounds by the most conservative estimate, was carried away by Hurricane Esther. His tuna, 1,200 pounds if it was an ounce, was lost when the Apollo 7 spacecraft landed on his leader.

I could well sympathize with the Captain's misfortune, for I had a little of my own that day. Three times I got tremendous strikes, and three times the fish got off.

"What a crying shame!" said the Captain after each loss. "You had a marlin."

"Did you see him?" I asked each time.

"Plain as day," said the Captain.

"Oh, mice and rats!" I cried, stamping my foot testily, but the Captain passed the bottle till I was calm again.

And so with good talk and good fishing the day raced by. Before we knew it, the setting sun was turning the sea to gold, and the

Captain set his course for home. (Actually, as it turned out, we landed in Haiti because he neglected to compensate for drift in the toilet seat. How we chuckled over that in the days ahead, the Captain and Papa Doc and I!)

But I digress. I was speaking of the end of my first day's deep-sea fishing. Tired but content, I sat and looked out at the burnished sea and reviewed what I had learned. Even to one as new at the game as I was, certain profound truths were already clear. To wit:

1. Fishing boats leak.
2. Fishing boat captains drink.
3. Any fish you lose is a marlin.
4. Fishing was always better the day before you got there.
5. Though deep-sea fishing is a very difficult sport, it can be mastered by any man or woman with average strength and inherited money.

Cartoonists

There are as few cartoonists specializing in hunting and fishing subjects as there are magazines buying cartoons about field sports. Many of the best "outdoor" cartoons are found in book collections by the prolific John Troy, Bruce Cochran, and Jack Ohman. This wasn't always the case. In the 1950-60s, the "laddie" magazines, *True, Argosy* and *Playboy,* carried many smart cartoons, often in two and four colors, and cartoons in the adventure magazines were commonly used to sell all sorts of men's products such as Barbasol shaving cream, Kaywoodie pipes and Kools cigarette (Willie the Penguin). Virgil F. Partch, a *Collier's* cartoonist stands out with his take on hunting and fishing.

The single and glaring exception to this current scenario is the active sponsorship of cartoonists by the New Yorker magazine. The very best cartoonists, or rather the very best humorists with pen and ink wash, found in that magazine set a very high standard in both art and content. Peter Arno, George Price, Charles Addams, George Booth, Bill Woodman, and many others have covered and continue "outdoor" traditions with great wit and style. And the New Yorker cartoonists started early. For example, from 1925 to 1965, there were over 170 cartoons with a fishing theme, over 230 with a hunting theme. Of course, some of the earlier subjects, such as foxhunting and whaling, are now dated but the themes of man against nature with nature the winner, in the field and at home, are nicely sketched. And the early cartoons seemed drawn by individuals who really knew what they were talking about. From 1965 to 2004, there were over 100 "fishing" cartoons and over 150 hunting cartoons and, along the way, a perspective from the "harvested" grew—first, from netted commercial fish (a thought nicely updated in the movie, Finding Nemo) and then on with game fish, ducks, deer and other "managed" game animals. A sampling of the New Yorker's very best are on the following pages.

"And that's how ya clean a deer!"

"Any nibbles yet, hon?"

"And another thing. Keep your flaps down."

The Watch Dog

Henry Morgan and George Booth

This is a distant cousin to the pointer. As a matter of fact, he *is* a pointer but he's no danger to partridges or pheasants.

This animal is especially bred for his work and needs no training. What he does is in his blood… and the finer the blood lines, the more accurate the dog.

Your typical hunter has only one watch and it's a pretty good one, so he doesn't like to wear it when he's out in the fields. Also, it's much harder to tell time by the sun than you think. Besides, there's not always a sun out to tell time *by*. This is where your watch dog comes in handy.

What you do is set twelve sticks upright in the ground in a large circle. Make one stick about six inches higher than the others. It stands for "twelve."

Now you place your dog in the exact center so that he faces the tallest stick. Let's say, for purposes of illustration, that the dog's name is "Gentlemen."

What you do now is get outside of the circle. Then you turn around and face the dog. Then you give the command: "Time, Gentlemen, time, please!"

The dog will then stick out his tail and turn, pointing to the current time. A really fine watch dog can point within one or two seconds of the exact time.

When summer comes, you merely set your dog one hour ahead, reversing the process in the fall.

Mr. G. Morfit of Baltimore, this country's leading authority, has a dog named, "Split." He works in tenths of a second.

Mr. Morfit oils his dog once a month.

The Way it Really Was(n't) When it all Began

Andy Duffy

In the beginning God created the heavens and the earth. He created Eve with a brain and Adam with a desire to hunt and fish. After placing the two of them in a garden he evaluated the situation, and the woman he called good.

Then came the fall.

Since football hadn't been invented yet, Adam tied a string to a stick and went hunting. He called the string and stick a bow. Making the bow was almost a sin. But since the wheel hadn't been invented yet and he couldn't compound the thing, Adam got a pass. Sin didn't come until later.

Adam got frustrated because he couldn't get close enough to the deer for a shot. He invented a naughty word. That was Adam's curse.

He took apples from the tree and made a bait pile. That was the original sin. To make matters worse, he took a bite from one of the apples.

Adam still couldn't get a deer. Nothing was hanging around his bait pile except that old serpent. That was when Adam started feeling a little exposed. Because he hadn't managed to get a deer yet, Adam put on a fig leaf and urged Eve to do the same. That was the first camouflage.

Adam never did become a good archer. It took God to harvest the first game. He fashioned clothes for Adam and Eve to wear from the skins of the game He took and then banished them from the garden. Men have been looking ever since to try to find the happy hunting ground again.

Eve, remember, had a brain. She realized at once that they would have to work to make a living. Seeing some sweet-smelling grass nearby, she said, "Adam, why don't we raise some cane?"

Adam, of course, being a guy, couldn't spell. He thought she said to raise Cain. So they had a baby; that's what they did. Guys have been raising a little Cain whenever they're able ever since.

A time of real hardship came as fall turned into winter. Adam tried doing some ice fishing, but as Peter wasn't around to show him how to walk on water, Adam kept falling through the ice.

Back then, of course, since the earth was young, seasons passed quickly. Spring came and Eve, being wise, wanted to plant a garden. While Adam was off trying to call in a turkey, Eve worked up a little plot of ground. Adam was so busy trying to invent the box call that he'd forgotten his bow when he left. Eve took some worms she unearthed while working up the plot of ground, unstrung Adam's bow to use for a fishing rod, and caught some fish.

When Adam got home and saw what Eve had done, he was very angry. He was angry because he had never caught a fish, but he thought he was angry because Eve had gotten his bowstring wet. He began waving the string around to dry it out. That was the beginning of fly-fishing. Because Adam couldn't catch a fish with a dry fly, he invented baseball. He got all the animals together and arranged a game. Naturally, the Tigers lost. That is pretty much where we are today. Women do all the work, men are still trying to talk with turkeys, and no one can catch a fish with a dry fly. Oh, and the Tigers are still always losing. But men still think they have all the answers.

Bare Bones Fly

Andy Duffy

A few years ago I encountered what I think is the hottest new fly to come along in years. It is now being fished around the world by a tiny group of very elite and tight-lipped fishermen. But don't look for it at your local fly shop.

Until just recently kept a close secret by its inventor, who lives a highly reclusive life, and by a small group of trout fishermen fanatical about keeping the fly secret, word of the fly has now leaked out to a few local trout bums. Knowing that the fly can be kept secret no longer I've decided to go ahead and publish information on it for the first time so the fly's originator, who still wishes to remain anonymous, can receive due credit as its inventor.

The fly is called the Bare Bones fly. It was originally tied for those times when the fishing was so good that the fish would take a bare hook. Since then, a small number of dry-fly purists have begun using it to match the hatch when nothing is hatching.

I think the fly will become the next Adams. Just as the Adams has evolved into an entire family of flies, I think the Bare Bones will come to be tied in many styles with equally good results. It makes an attractive fly tied as small as a size #28, and I've seen it used by a tiny handful of progressive saltwater fishermen tied on size 1/0 streamer hooks. The fly's versatility is one of its real strengths.

The fly can be adapted to any style of fishing. It can be tied as a dry-fly, wet-fly, or a streamer pattern. Technically, only the dry-fly is a Bare Bones. Used as a tandem tie and fished over huge gulpers, it is called a Wish Bone. Tied streamer style and used for Bonefish, it is called the Bone Bone. Tied on a midge hook and dressed with plenty of dry-fly floatant, it is called a Dry Bone. A doctor friend of mine tied an abbreviated version which he calls a Sawbones. One can tie a loop of scarlet floss on a Bare Bones to create a Royal Bones. (If you do this, it is considered proper etiquette to store the fly in a sarcophagus rather than in a fly box.) If you hook yourself with one that hasn't been debarbed, the fly is called a Royal Pain in the Butt Bone.

The fly is used to satisfy demands in a number of situations. As previously mentioned, it was originally tied to be used when fishing was so good that the fish would take a bare hook. It is also appropriate for other circumstances.

I was once fishing on Michigan's Clam River with Jim Procter of Gulliver, Michigan, who had on a nice little brookie, when he noticed another angler approaching his hole. Jim is a secretive guy and didn't want the approaching angler to become aware of the hot spot, so he simply gave the brookie lots of slack line. With the brookie sulking on the bottom, Jim exchanged some pleasantries with the intruder, exchanged some fishing advice, discussed Goethe, Kant, and Quantum physics, and the man went on his way. After he was out of sight around the bend, Jim played in his trout and creeled it. The river could have been entirely fishless for all that stranger knew.

We've probably all been faced with similar situations. My solution now when someone is approaching territory that I've staked out for myself is to simply tie on a Bare Bones. I can beat the water to a froth and never catch a thing. Any onlooker would swear that hole was the coldest spot on the river.

When your mother-in-law arrives for the week and announces that she would like you to catch her a nice mess of trout for a fish fry is another good time to use the Bare Bones. I once fished for a solid week using nothing but a Bare Bones in exactly that situation. It was great! I never caught a thing.

The Bare Bones is tied from remnants of the Emperor's Clothing. Tied from such remnants, the fly has a wonderful translucency, almost bordering on transparency, which exactly imitates the outstretched wings of a tiny spinner in the surface film. The problem with using remnants of the Emperor's Clothes is that they are so hard to find. Many fly shops no longer stock the material since it is getting rather rare and is in short supply. It is getting rather expensive, too. If you encounter a situation where you cannot find the material, if the afternoon is cold and snowy, simply keep looking at all the fly shops you know of until you find some. It's an exceptionally pleasant way to spend an afternoon. I once was able to visit 15 fly shops in a single weekend by looking for the Emperor's clothes.

But be forewarned. Employees of some fly shops say they have it in stock when I really don't think they do. I have difficulty finding it on their shelves. I still don't know how to deal with this situation. I get tired of saying, "Where was that stuff again? I can't see a stinking thing."

If you absolutely, positively cannot find any of the Emperor's clothes, try using Poppycock feathers instead. If you find that you have to resort to this tactic, though, be sure you use only the finest, least webby of the hackles. But they work.

True, it is difficult to find the Emperor's clothes. Poppycock, on the other hand, is easily obtained at any fly shop or along the banks of any decent trout stream. Although Poppycock is considered by most to be an acceptable substitution, real traditionalists insist that the resultant fly should be called a Poppycock instead of a Dry Bones.

Bare Bones are *the* fly to try when the fishing is the toughest. I remember a frustrating situation that occurred a few years ago while I was fishing the Ranch section of the Henry's Fork. A hatch of some little bit of nothing began that caused the big browns to stare scornfully at all of my offerings. Finally, in desperation, I tied on the smallest little Bare Bones I could find in my fly box. Now equipped with 8x tippet and a little Bare Bones, I made a downstream, slack-line presentation to the biggest snottiest trout rising in the area. I continued fishing through the area catching as many trout with the Bare Bones as I had before I tied it on.

I also like to use the Bare Bones where fishermen are the most sophisticated. On North Carolina's Davidson River, I once saw a fisherman catching one trout after another with an itty-bitty bit of fluff. Following my inquiry, he told me he was using a #28 Adams. "You must be really good," he told me. "I can't even *see* what you're using!"

Be careful when using the Bare Bones. It can sometimes lead to an argument. I remember one time I was using a fly that I thought was a Bare Bones. An angler wandering down the stream wondered what I was using, so I showed it to him. He asked what it was, so I told him and explained a little about the fly

"That's poppycock," he snorted, and walked away.

"It is not! It's a Bare Bones," I retorted angrily. But I looked at my fly again and discovered it was pure Poppycock.

I've successfully used Bare Bones flies when I didn't want to catch fish as large as 22 inches. Of course, because of the fly's success, I was able only to estimate the fish's length. It might have been 24 inches. Only rarely will a little brookie you don't want to catch take the fly. On those occasions. I suspect the fly was a poorly tied one.

I like my Bare Bones flies tied very sparse. Use a little bit of nothing to dub the body. The wings and tails come from the tiniest threads of the Emperor's clothes. The flies actually are not difficult to tie. I honestly believe anyone who is capable of inserting a hook into a vise is capable of tying one. Give this fly a try on your next fishing trip. It's the ultimate in a sparsely tied fly.

"Geez Lady... I'm trying to fish here!"

The Wood Duck

James Thurber

Mr. Krepp, our vegetable man, had told us we might find some cider out the New Milford road a way—we would come to a sign saying "Morris Plains Farm" and that would be the place. So we got into the car and drove down the concrete New Milford road, which is black in the center with the dropped oil of a million cars. It's a main-trunk highway; you can go fifty miles an hour on it except where warning signs limit you to forty or, near towns, thirty-five, but nobody ever pays any attention to these signs. Even then, in November, dozens of cars flashed past us with a high, ominous whine, their tires roaring rubberly on the concrete. We found Morris Plains Farm without any trouble. There was a big white house to the left of the highway; only a few yards off the road a small barn had been made into a roadside stand, with a dirt driveway curving up to the front of it. A spare, red-cheeked man stood in the midst of baskets and barrels of red apples and glass jugs of red cider. He was waiting on a man and a woman. I turned into the driveway—and put the brakes on hard. I had seen, just in time, a duck.

It was a small, trim duck, and even I, who know nothing about wild fowl, knew that this was no barnyard duck, this was a wild duck. He was all alone. There was no other bird of any kind around, not even a chicken. He was immensely solitary. With none of the awkward waddling of a domestic duck, he kept walking busily around in the driveway, now and then billing up water from a dirty puddle in the middle of the drive. His obvious contentment, his apparently perfect adjustment to his surroundings, struck me as something of a marvel. I got out of the car and spoke about it to a man who had driven up behind me in a rattly sedan. He wore a leather jacket and high, hard boots, and I figured he would know what kind of duck this was. He did. "That's a wood duck," he said. "It dropped in here about two weeks ago, Len says, and's been here ever since."

The proprietor of the stand, in whose direction my informant had nodded as he spoke, helped his customers load a basket of apples into their car and walked over to us. The duck stepped, with a little flutter of its wings, into the dirty puddle, took a small, unconcerned swim, and got out again, ruffling it feathers. "It's rather an odd place for a wood duck, isn't it?" asked my wife. Len grinned and nodded; we all watched the duck. "He's a banded duck," said Len. "There's a band on his leg. The state game commission sends out a lot of 'em. This'n lighted here two weeks ago—it was on a Saturday—and he's been around ever since." "It's funny he wouldn't be frightened away, with all the cars going by and all the people driving in," I said. Len chuckled. "He seems to like it here," he said. The duck wandered over to some sparse grass at the ege of the road, aimlessly, but with an air of settled satisfaction. "He's tame as anything," said Len. "I guess they get tame when them fellows band 'em." The man in the leather jacket said, "'Course they haven't let you shoot wood duck for a long while and that might make 'em tame, too." "Still," said my wife (we forgot about the cider for the moment), "it's strange he would stay here, right on the road almost." "Sometimes," said Len, reflectively, "he goes round back o' the barn. But mostly he's here in the drive," "But don't they," she asked, "let them loose in the woods after they're banded? I mean, aren't they supposed to stock up the forests?" "I guess they're suppose to," said Len, chuckling again, "but 'pears this'n didn't want to."

An old Ford truck lurched into the driveway and two men in the seat hailed the proprietor. They were hunters, big, warmly dressed, heavily shod men. In the back of the truck was a large bird dog. He was an old pointer and he wore an expression of remote disdain for the world of roadside commerce. He took no notice of the duck. The two hunters said something to Len about cider, and I was just about to chime in with my order when the accident happened. A car went by the stand at fifty miles an hour, leaving something scurrying in its wake. It was the duck, turning over and over on the concrete. He turned over and over swiftly, but lifelessly, like a thrown feather duster, and then he lay still. "My God," I cried, "they've killed your duck, Len!" The accident gave me a quick feeling of anguished intimacy with the bereaved man. "Oh, now," he wailed. "Now, that's awful!" None of us for a moment moved. Then the two hunters walked toward the road, slowly, self-consciously, a little embarrassed in the face of this quick incongruous ending of a wild fowl's life in the middle of a concrete highway. The pointer stood up, looked after the hunters, raised his ears briefly, and then lay down again.

It was the man in the leather jacket finally who walked out to the duck and tried to pick it up. As he did so, the duck stood up. He looked about him like a person who has been abruptly wakened and doesn't know where he is. He didn't ruffle his feathers. "Oh, he isn't quite *dead!*" said my wife. I knew how she felt. We were going to have to see the duck die; somebody would have to kill him, finish him off. Len stood beside us. My wife took hold of his arm. The man in the leather jacket knelt down, stretched out his hand, and the duck moved slightly away. Just then, out from behind the barn, limped a setter dog, a lean white setter dog with black spots. His right back leg was useless and he kept it off the ground. He stopped when he saw the duck in the road and gave it a point, putting his head out, lifting his front leg, maintaining a wavering, marvelous balance on two legs. He was like a drunken man drawing a bead with a gun. This new menace, this anticlimax, was too much. I think I yelled.

What happened next happened as fast as the automobile accident. The setter made his run, a limping, wobbly run, and he was in between the men and the bird before they saw him. The duck flew, got somehow off the ground a foot or two, and tumbled into the grass of the field across the road, the dog after him. It seemed crazy, but the duck could fly—a little, anyway. "Here, here," said Len, weakly. The hunters shouted, I shouted, my wife screamed. "He'll kill him! He'll *kill* him!" The duck flew a few yards again, the dog at his tail. The dog's third plunge brought his nose almost to the duck's tail, and then one of the hunters tackled the animal and pulled him down and knelt in the grass, holding him. We all breathed easier. My wife let go of Len's arm.

Len started across the road after the duck, who was fluttering slowly, waveringly, but with a definite purpose, toward a wood that fringed the far side of the field. The bird was dazed, but a sure, atavistic urge was guiding him; he was going home. One of the hunters joined Len in his pursuit. The other came back across the road, dragging the indignant setter; the man in the leather jacket walked beside them. We all watched Len and his companion reach the edge of the wood and stand there, looking; they had followed the duck through the grass slowly, so as not to alarm him; he had been alarmed enough. "He'll never come back," said my wife. Len and the hunter finally turned and came back through the grass. The duck had got away from them. We walked out to meet them at the edge of the concrete. Cars began to whiz by in both directions. I realized, with wonder, that all the time the duck, and the hunters, and the setter were milling around in the road, not one had passed. It was as if traffic had been held up so that our little drama could go on. "He couldn't o' been much hurt," said Len. "Likely just grazed and pulled along in the wind of the car. Them fellows don't look out for anything. It's a sin." My wife had a question for him. "Does your dog always chase the duck?" she asked. "Oh, that ain't my dog," said Len. "He just comes around." The hunter who had been holding the setter now let him go, and he slunk away. The pointer, I noticed, lay with his eyes closed. "But doesn't the duck mind the dog?" persisted my wife. "Oh, he minds him," said Len. "But the dog's never really hurt him none yet. There's always somebody around."

We drove away with a great deal to talk about (I almost forgot the cider). I explained the irony, I think I explained the profound symbolism, of a wild duck's becoming attached to a roadside stand. My wife strove simply to understand the duck's viewpoint. She didn't get anywhere. I knew even then, in the back of my mind, what would happen. We decided, after a cocktail, to drive back to the place and find out if the duck had returned. My wife hoped it wouldn't be there, on account of the life it led in the driveway; I hoped it wouldn't because I felt that would be, somehow, too pat an ending. Night was falling when we started off again for Morris Plains Farm. It was a five-mile drive and I had to put my bright lights on before we got there. The barn door was closed for the night. We didn't see the duck anywhere. The only thing to do was to go up to the house and inquire. I knocked on the door and a young man opened it. "Is—is the proprietor here?" I asked. He said no, he had gone to Waterbury. "We wanted to know," my wife said, "whether the duck came back." "What?" he asked, a little startled, I thought. Then, "Oh, the duck. I saw him around the driveway when my father drove off." He stared at us, waiting. I thanked him and started back to the car. My wife lingered, explaining, for a moment. "He thinks we're crazy," she said, when she got into the car. We drove on a little distance. "Well," I said, "he's back." "I'm glad he is, in a way," said my wife. "I hated to think of him all alone out there in the woods."

Excerpts from

A Good Life Wasted

Dave Ames

I was guiding the First Baseman and the Shortstop. The Shortstop was legally blind, and the First Baseman had lost most of the feeling in the left side of his body after a stroke. The Shortstop couldn't see the strike, and the First Baseman couldn't react to it. Helping people help themselves; it's the essence of guiding. I found that if I yelled "FISH-FISH-FISH!" in the Shortstop's ear when a trout ate his fly, and spun the boat to tighten the line to help the First Baseman set the hook, then all those missed strikes started turning into jumping fish.

Both rods were doubled over with tugging fish when a peal of thunder rumbled across the hills. I beached the raft on a gravel bar alongside the other boats. There's no good place to wait out a thunderstorm on a river but we did our best, as far as possible from the nearest trees, huddled in the lee of a shallow hole in a limestone cliff while the full fury of twenty-five-thousand-foot-high cumulonimbus cloud broke around us.

We were so close to the center of the storm that sound and light arrived simultaneously in jagged bolts of electric blue thunder. There aren't many jobs where you get to be a hero, and I was replete with vicarious fish-catching pleasure. Those old guys in my boat had appreciated the day so much. Then, without any warning at all, Cappy darted out into the pelting rain.

He left like a sprinter from the blocks, if the sprinter is wearing waders over a Humpty-Dumpty costume. Cappy had always been stout, the team catcher, with a center of gravity so low he must've been an immovable object when defending home plate. A lifetime of good food and drink had extended that center of gravity considerably. Cappy gave it everything he had, but you can only do so much when you're eighty-one and round as a grapefruit.

Cappy said later he had to run. He said it was like a command coming from everywhere at once, he could do nothing else buy obey, and it probably saved his life. Cappy thanked his Guardian Angel but I think he ran for secular causes. He was compelled to enter his first race in fifty years because he was the geriatric version of the bionic man, his premonition simply a positive charge building up on all the metal he packed around inside him.

Cappy was held together with pins and plates, a legacy of his hard-fought athletic career. He had steel knees, steel hips, two hearing aids, a pacemaker, an oxygen tank for emergencies, and a battery pack in a shoulder harness that delivered electrical pulses to stimulate the muscles in his back. With all that to go wrong, you wouldn't think it would be the back that would finally catch up to him.

Cappy ran downstream directly away from the upstream trees as if he really had been warned, so fast he kicked up squirts of gravel with every step. A dozen strides later he was still accelerating when the top of the tallest cottonwood tree vaporized in a resounding crack of lightning that wasn't nearly as loud as Cappy's high-pitched scream. The backpack spit a stream of yellow sparks and blew soft puffs of white smoke; Cappy pitched forward facefirst into the gray, sticky river mud.

We all leapt out into the rain. The air stunk of sweet ozone, and the backpack sizzled in as the Kingfish sliced Cappy free of the harness with a bone-handled sheath knife. I helped roll him over on his back. The Kingfish leaned forward to check Cappy's vital signs.

"Does he have a pulse?" I asked. "Is he breathing?"

"Not only that," said the Kingfish, "he's smiling."

Cappy was, too, a beatific smile, like he knew something that nobody else did.

"Quick!" he said "Call my wife."

I was thinking *Last Will and Testament,* but the Shortstop knew better.

"A stiffy," he said, and there was wonder in his voice, "Cappy has a stiffy."

And there it was, the telltale bulge in Cappy's waders.

"Geez," said the third baseman—and there was wonder in his voice, too—"anymore just going to the bathroom is about as much fun as I can handle."

"Oops," said Cappy. "Never mind."

The team at this point was of a single emotion. Their long, sad faces and slack jaws all told the same story: Some things are worth dying for. Cappy's friends weren't concerned, they were jealous. Cappy had come within a whisker of frying like a grub on a griddle but every man there would gladly have traded places with him.

And these were wise, learned men.

It's a lesson I've never forgotten.

Hunched over the camera on her tripod, Heidi could hear an engine coming half a mile away. The motor knocked as it died fifty yards of thorny rose thicket away. Doors creaked open, then slammed shut; a tall brown Indian with long black braids and four white men in baseball caps sauntered into Heidi's view along the edge of Beaver Head Rock. The five men gazed down on the river where four fishermen were already fanned out on the gravel bar, two with fish bending their rods.

"Shit," said a man in a Mets cap, "they're in our spot."

"I told you we needed to leave earlier," said a guant man in a green parka.

"I told you we needed to leave earlier," mimicked a man who held his head like it hurt.

Long Black Braids rubbed his hands together as if he were making fire. "I think it's time the Indians staged an uprising," he said.

Green Parka wrung his hands. "What are you going to do?" he asked.

Mets Cap smiled. "You sure are a sneaky bastard," he said appreciatively.

"Remember that," said Long Black Braids, "when you're writing a check for the tip. Now you guys go get ready to move fast. Put on all your fishing stuff."

The men disappeared. Car doors creaked; then it was quiet. Heidi was zeroed in on a lark as it shredded a piece of orange baling twine to use as lining for its nest. The motor drive on her camera whirred as Green Parka's reed-thin voice said: "What are you looking for?"

Long Black Braids replied in his radio announcer's baritone. "Someday," he said, "I gotta clean out under this seat. I know that tape from the last powwow is here somewhere."

A car stereo suddenly boomed, ceremonial drums and guttural chants storming like avenging ghost riders over Beaver Head Rock. The echo of three quick high-powered rifle shots startled Heidi enough that she bumped her head on the bent sticks at the top of the blind. The fishermen on the gravel bar looked nervously over their shoulders as they fished. Moments later Long Black Braids danced into sight at the edge of the bluff.

He brandished a half-gallon bottle of whiskey with one hand, a lever-action deer rifle with the other, all the while stomping up a miniature cyclone of dust as he skipped a tight circle to the beat of the pounding drums.

The music got faster and faster, building to a feverish crescendo. Long Black Braids stopped as suddenly as the drums. He now stood facing the lake with his legs spread and arms up, the whiskey and rifle silhouetted against the blue morning sky. Just to be certain he had the undivided attention of the four cowering fishermen below, he squeezed off another round.

"Hey," he called, "you white guys won't mind if me and about twenty of my buddies come down and do a little shoot-and-release fishing, will you?"

The drums started up again. Long Black Braids danced slowly back out of sight.

"Get ready," he said. "They'll come up that path there. We'll go down over here."

As if it were choreographed, the four fishermen on the river hurriedly gathered their gear and left by the quickest trail out, their heads popping up and down at the edge of the bluff like worried gophers. Meanwhile Long Black Braids and his crew ran a back-door play through a narrow cut between the granite outcrops that formed the head and shoulders of Beaver Head Rock. The displaced fishermen wandered around scratching their heads for a while, wondering where all the Indians went. After much discussion they finally decided that since the coast appeared to be clear they should go fishing again, but when they walked back to the bluff they found that someone had taken over their sweet spot on the gravel bar.

"Hey," said a man in rose-colored glasses, "isn't that the guy with the rifle down there?"

He pointed to the lake where Long Black Braids was walking between fishermen. Every time he stood beside one of them he'd say something, and the guy would catch a fish.

"He looks like a guide," added Rose-Colored Glasses.

They stood there quietly. They still hadn't quite figured it out yet.

"He is a guide!" said Rose-Colored Glasses.

They talked big for a while about going back down to the lake, but they weren't fooling Heidi. Those four were in way over their heads. In a boardroom they might have had a chance with Long Black Braids, but maybe not even then.

Dancin' With Shirley

Alan Liere

The pheasant opener would have been better. Had they really known anything at all about hunting and hunters, they would have waited until then to stage their protest. In just two more weeks they might have enlightened mankind and saved all birddom by assembling in the friendly rolling wheat land just south of Spokane. But here? At the bottom of one of the steepest canyons in the Snake River Gorge? They had ventured much too close to the essence of it all.

Like others before them who had joined similar causes, this tiny group of anti-hunters would allow, even encourage, their own exploitation. In the big picture, their protests served only to pad the pockets of the fat cats who headed their organization—the fat cats whose goal was job security rather than victory or even some noble enlightenment. Take on a winless, unpopular cause, gather lonesome, lost, misinformed fanatics as your disciples, fill your coffers with pledges for the "fight," and enjoy the good life. Perpetual employment. Not a bad scheme.

So here they were in Wawawai Canyon with instructions to disrupt the early chukar opener in eastern Washington. Other than that, there were no definitive objectives. Good enough that there was something to stand for. Good enough that they did not have to spend the week-end alone.

Encouraged and directed by a scowling, blustery man in his mid-60s, a middle-aged fellow wearing a dark beret, a navy-blue tie, and leather street shoes confronted me as I swung from the cab of my pickup. "Do you intend to hunt partridge?" he inquired stiffly.

"Partridge?" I questioned. "You must mean chukars. No one I know calls them 'partridge', though." I pulled my shotgun from behind the seat. "That's what I'm going to do, all right." I glanced critically at his outfit. "How about you?"

The man looked back at the fat cat who was ignoring him and toward others in his group who were approaching a second hunter on the pull-out beside the road. "Sir," he said, "I intend to make sure you have a miserable day."

"Well, that's very thoughtful of you," I said, "but I probably won't need your help. This is chukar country, partner. Look at those hills. In two hours I'll be standing up there on that highest ledge and my tongue will be draggin' the ground right about where you're standing."

"You'll not dissuade me," the man said. "I am sworn to disrupt your hunt. Today, sir, you will not upset the balance of nature. Today, not a feather will fall."

"You must have seen me shoot before," I said. As if to emphasize my deficiency, I stuffed another box of shells in my vest. Then, seeing no need for further conversation, I hefted my 20-gauge and started up the hill. The man scrambled to get ahead of me. "By the way," I called as he stumbled over a field of basalt, "my name is Alan. What's yours?"

"Surely," he said, "you don't expect me to reveal..."

"Then Shirley it is," I said as he huffed and clawed, trying to maintain his balance. "I understand how that goes; had a male cousin once named Karen." I stopped to tighten a boot lace. "But I tell you, Shirley, I wouldn't go scrambling along like that on all fours unless you're immune to snake venom."

The man slammed to a stop, poised like a dog on point. His head jerked around and I could see nothing but white in his eyes. "Snake venom?"

"Western rattlesnakes," I said. "They're pretty pathetic compared to a copperhead or a cottonmouth, but for their size, they pack a real wallop." I picked my way through the talus toward his frozen form. "You might be better off to take it a little slower, Shirley. Maybe you'd be even happier walking along beside me for a spell."

The man pondered my offer briefly. "I know what you're trying to do," he said, "but it won't work. To disrupt your hunt I must stay ahead of you and encourage the partridge to fly. It says so in the manual."

"They don't take much encouraging," I said, "but go ahead if that's what the manual says. Watch out where you put your feet, though, and try to keep your hands off the ground. This is a wonderful dance if the snakes don't get ya. And don't step on your tongue," I added.

Tentatively leaving his frozen crouch, the man made a slow but admirable effort to get above me again, sucking in the sweet morning air and exhaling it noisily as he climbed. When he had gone a hundred yards, I turned to the east and began cutting across the face of the hill to where a patch of wild onions grew. Chukars often went there to feed at first light and I hoped to intercept the first flock before they moved to their rugged loafing areas on the rock faces.

"Hey!" The thin voice echoed down the canyon. "Where… are…you…going?" The words had long pauses between them as if he was having difficulty getting his breath.

"I'm chukar hunting, Shirley," I hollered back. "Remember? I'm out here upsetting the balance of nature!"

"Yeah," he shouted, "but…I'm…way…up…here…and…"

"…and I'm not going that way anymore," I finished.

The man didn't say anything for a long time. Then, he got up from where he had sprawled and began slipping across the hillside—on all fours once again. "Wait up," he called hoarsely. It was louder, but the way his words seemed to stick between his lips, I could tell he had cotton mouth.

The sun, which had been only a promise a half hour before, now clawed impatiently at the rim of the canyon. In just a tee-shirt and jeans, I was slightly chilly, but in an hour it would be hot. Broiling hot. And though I hated the extra weight of the two-quart canteen, I would be thankful for every drop before the day was over. I looked down at the speck that had been my truck. I loved seeing where I'd been, smug with the knowledge that the man who can hunt chukars still has some good years ahead.

"Misss-terrr!" A sorrowful call interrupted my reflections. "Could you give me a hand?"

Shirley had taken a shortcut and gotten himself hung up on a rock face. He now hung precariously by his fingertips from a lava outcropping with at least eight feet of air between his soles and the next ledge. Climbing slowly, I edged up beneath him. "Those shoes must be uncomfortable," I said.

"Miss-terrr!" It was pathetic.

"Okay, okay," I said. "I'll have to catch you. Just let go."

"No way!" he whined. "You'll drop me."

"Well, that's a possibility," I said, "but Superman is busy. His sister is getting married this weekend, see, and…"

I caught Shirley around the waist, staggered back a few feet, and recovered without falling. When I put him down, however, he just kept going, melting into an amorphous mass with a silly little beret on top. "So what do you think of chukar hunting so far?" I asked.

The blob moved slightly and a head emerged. It studied my boots several moments, then sat up. He tried to lick his lips, but the tongue was dry and stuck in the corner on the outside of this mouth, and he couldn't speak.

"Sometimes," I continued, "it's even better than this. Sometimes I see huge herds of mule deer. Usually there's a coyote or two, and once I even saw a bobcat."

"Wha 'bout paridge?" Shirley asked, fighting to return his tongue to his mouth. "Dis a paridge hun, iddint it?"

"Chukars," I corrected. "Chukars. I see those, too, but you've got to put in a lot of miles. Shoot, Shirley, we haven't gone more than a few hundred yards." I reached for my canteen and took a sip. Already, the water had lost its icy edge. I offered him a drink which he accepted and which seemed to help him with the tongue problem.

"I think I'll just walk behind you for a time," he said meekly. "I guess I don't need to disrupt your hunt all at once."

"Suits me," I said. "I'll be on my way, then."

Two hours later, I flushed my first birds, and as is my custom, missed badly. A hundred yards behind me, Shirley hollered something quite unintelligible. "What's that?" I hollered back at him. "I couldn't hear you."

Closing the distance between us like a drunk trying to run in a room full of marbles, Shirley threw his arms in the air and shouted incredulously, "You missed?"

"Yes," I affirmed, "I do that quite regularly."

"But I wanted to see a partridge!" he gasped when he finally stopped just a few yards below me.

"Help yourself," I said, pointing down the hill. "They went that-away."

Shaking his head, Shirley plopped down on a flat rock. "Never make it," he panted. "Blisters everywhere."

"That's a shame," I sympathized, "'cause the trip down is worse."

"I was afraid you'd tell me that," he groaned, quietly looking out over the ribbon of water far below. "Kind of like falling down stairs, huh?"

"Not really," I replied. "More like tumbling out of an accelerating truck. How's your forward roll, Shirley? Gymnastic experience is very helpful up here."

Shirley said nothing after that, and we sat silently admiring the view. Several times he shifted uncomfortably and cleared his throat like he was about to start a conversation, but not until I stood up to leave did he speak.

"I don't get it," he said. "You climb mountains, you slide, you fall down. Your water gets warm, your lungs begin to burn, and it feels like there's a bonfire in your boots. You walk five miles then miss the only birds you see. How am I suppose to disrupt a hunt like that? It's already disrupted! You don't even care if you shoot a par... a... a chukar!"

"Oh, I wouldn't go *that* far," I said, "but I've got to admit chukar hunting—any hunting—is a lot like a Thanksgiving turkey; it's the stuff that goes with it that makes it good. I guess you don't really need a gun to chase chukars, but I'd feel awfully silly stumbling around up here without one."

"I know the feeling," Shirley said.

"You might try the want-ads," I suggested. "You could probably get a good used 20-gauge for three-fifty."

"I don't feel *that* silly," Shirley said, gingerly removing a shoe and sock. "This country is magnificent, but I don't think I'll be shooting any chukars." He rubbed his big toe and grinned up at me. "I guess it's not so bad if you do, though."

"That's kind of the way I see it," I said. "You go to your church and I'll go to mine."

Shirley stood up and looked far down the canyon to where an explosion of red-tinted sumac caught the sun. "But maybe we could meet in the middle sometime. Maybe I could follow you around again when my feet are in better shape. Maybe you'd let me shoot your gun once or twice—just to see."

"That's a possibility," I said, smiling. "This is a great dance, Shirley, and anything, don'tcha know, can happen at a dance."

To Hell with Scurrilous Discourse!
(1974)

Don Zahner

"**O**ur Father Walton would not have expressed it in such a course manner."

I turned on my stool at the long mahogany bar of the Antrim Lodge to identify the source of the thin but cultivated little voice that had suddenly sliced through the soaring decibles of anglers reporting the triumphs and frustrations of their day on the Beaverkill and the Willowemoc.

I had found solace in the words of a nearby angler as he told his companions of a particularly uncouth spincaster who had violated the waters of Junction Pool with a Lazy Ike obviously designed for pike or tarpon, putting down a finer fish the angler had been working for over an hour. His friends chortled appreciatively as he recounted the rather bizarre and anatomically challenging instructions he had called out to the interloper as he finally surrendered the water to him.

The owner of the voice was himself equally thin and little, with a pink, wizened face sharpened by a full head of white hair and a pair of steely gray eyes slightly misted from drink. He did not appear to be real.

"Pity," he muttered as I acknowledged his presence to his satisfaction. "Our brothers of the angle today have lost the grace of language and thought that our great mentor both cherished and bequeathed us."

"That's true," I allowed, with the wisdom of many years spent on bar stools next to blithering idiots. If you're too agreeable, however, they eventually pull out pictures of their first wife or their last salmon, and this requires equally balanced measures. "But you heard what he said about the big Lazy Ike. The bast–"

He waved a tiny finger at me. "Ah-ah-ah! Walton hears you. I commiserate with the poor fellow, but not with his language. Father

Walton spoke to us all when he laid down his thoughts upon sacrilegious and lascivious language and jests. 'A Brother of the Angle,' he had Piscator tell Corydon, 'that is cheerful and free from swearing and scurrilous discourse is worth gold.'"

He paused to make communion with Father Walton by taking a rather large gulp from his slowly withering martini, and I also reflected on Izaak's warning about not trusting "men warmed by drink." But he quickly resumed with his Waltonian vesper service.

"'Give me,' Father Walton said, 'a companion who feasts the company with wit and mirth and leaves out the sin which is usually mixed with them.'" He paused for a quick communion, then continued.

"A sylvan trout stream is, of course, a cathedral of the spirit. I too have encountered frustration and hooliganism upon the stream, but I have also managed to chastise the offender without profaning the sacred air about me."

I had begun to shape my lips to ask "How?" when I realized that he was going to tell me anyway, so I used the convenient aperture to pour down a slug of medicinal scotch and listened.

"I recall the time that I took a week's fishing on the Miramichi. It was greased-line casting with a dry fly over a productive yet shallow hold. A most boorish type whom I cannot dignify by the word 'gentleman' had the affrontery to cross the run no more than twenty feet above me. When I glared at him, he cursed me roundly, but I did not lower myself to his level. I became excessively worked up over this, I admit, and climbed from the water, but not before I looked back over my shoulder angrily and cried out, 'Spawn of an empty redd!' I believe even he understood my reference, and I was able to sublimate my anger in a most satisfactory and Christian manner."

I was suddenly impressed. There was a certain fire in his pale eyes as he repeated his mild curse. Father Walton would have approved.

His eyes took on a sparkle. "And I was not found wanting that day on the West Branch of the Ausable when I found a young man perched precariously on a large boulder in midstream. He remained there for two hours, dominating the pool and flailing the water in all directions. I finally left, but not before I was able to deliver a parting shot."

I leaned forward eagerly. "Which was?"

"May your next cast, sir, be plaster!"

I rested my hand on his shoulder, which served to steady us both. "Sir, you have opened up a new world of invective for me and for that angling fraternity of which we are all members." I had already moved into his tranquil world, and besides, I thought Walton might really be listening.

Then I told him of the shocking encounter with an inebriated worm fisherman on the Pere Marquette who had challenged me to a fishing contest for money. We had quite a confrontation, exchanged many coarse words, and almost came to blows—the only thing that kept me from thrashing him was the fact that he was at least six-and-a-half feet tall.

How much more satisfying it would have been had I merely said, quietly and calmly, "May your fate be that of the Tups Indispensable!"

I spoke of this with my new mentor and he chuckled roundly. "Splendid, splendid," he cried. "You will find many more now that you have found the true Waltonian spirit." Then he further confided in me. "I have always found this one to be most satisfactory in reprimanding wayward fishermen." He leaned over confidentially and whispered, "Your grandmother fishes riffles!"

The high frivolity that this recollection engendered caused a mild seizure, during which he teetered drunkenly on the edge of the stool and fell into a paroxysm of coughing and laughter. He found the fresh martini placed in front of him an effective antidote, giving me time to think this all out.

Unseen vistas suddenly lay exposed before me. That time on the Upper Peninsula while fishing the Black River, when I found another fisherman chumming a particularly attractive pool with the innards of a recently cleaned fish. How appropriate it would have been in Hemmingway country to have drawn upon the words of the master by sneering at him, "I spit on the silk of your Muddler!"

Oh, the countless times I could have dignified the occasion with the appropriate invective, satisfying both to self and to the memory of dear Izaak.

"Your father was a worm rancher!"

Or… "May you go penniless to a Catskill fee pond!"

One could even direct one's ire toward a fish that had thrown the hook; more than one poor salmonid had been the target of my profane curses. Instead, why not "You son of a grilse!" or, "May you develop gout in your adipose fin." At once creative, yet recreative, a catharsis to flush the soul and the mind of sinful thoughts and gutter jargon.

The possibilities are infinite. "May your next hatch be in your fly box!" I was just relishing "May Ed Zern defame you in his next book!" when I glanced back at my friend to see him slowly and majestically sliding from his perch like a small piece of silly putty.

I reached out to steady him, but in so doing I knocked his drink over, olive and all, drenching his shirt front and waking him suddenly from his shaky reverie. He cried out in alarm, bringing the bartender over to ask what had happened.

He pointed his trembling little finger at me, his face maroon with anger, and screamed unbelievably—"This sonofabitch spilled my god-dam martini all over me!"

I rose from my stool, shocked and disappointed. Then reflexively, I countered him with a terrible oath, gleaned possibly from an earlier encounter with an icthyological glossary.

"Male catostomidae!"

He turned to me with a stunned look,—hoist, so to speak, by his own petard—then marched unsteadily out of the bar and upstairs to his room.

I smiled and hoped he looked it up.

"We haven't seen a duck in two hours. Think I'll get out and stretch my legs."

Lewis Grizzard, the Georgian humorist who passed away much too young in 1994 wrote widely on a number of subjects with great humor and strong, informed opinion. He was always railing, on our behalf, against what he called the Thought Police yet rarely turned his attention towards field sports. I think he and his dog, Catfish, would have appreciated the traditions and trappings of chasing upland game birds. A city kid who preferred birdies on the golf course, Grizzard claimed he wasn't really against hunting. In his book, It Wasn't Always Easy, But I Sure Had Fun, *he offered his Revised Rules of Hunting Down Deer and Blowing Them Away. His rules were simple: if you shot a deer; you had to eat it. All of it. (He allows a pass on the pancreas and large intestine.) You can't shoot another deer until you have eaten all of the first deer, which a game warden will confirm by inspection of your freezer. If you've gotten ahead of yourself, you have to eat the pancreas of the second deer but you can fix it any way you want.*

Grizzards love for his dogs shows up in a great story about a man buying a bird-dog. It's best listened to on his recording, Addicted to Love, *yet easily stands alone in good humor.*

Addicted to Love

Lewis Grizzard

A black Lab, I think, is the finest dog a man can have. I mean black Labs are loyal and they're great, you know, and I come from a long line of black Lab trainers. My Uncle Grover was a black Lab trainer and he's a big duck hunter and everything, and he also ran a fruit stand down in Moreland and one day a Yankee tourist came by and got talking about duck hunting.

He said: "You know, I'd like to go duck hunting. I've never been duck hunting before." (Highly inflected Yankee accent—Editor)

Uncle Grover said: "You keep talking like that and you ain't going with me neither! Tell you what, I'm going take you out here on my farm, they got some ducks and I'm going to let you see how this all clicks in."

So they came to the store, got him a jacket with leather pouches, little holes for shotgun shells and whiskey and all that, L.L. Bean shoes and all that kind of stuff. Got this little black Lab puppy sitting right next to him, this fellow from Massachusetts. Duck flies over, *Boom*, he knocks him down. The black Lab jumps in the water, swims over, gets the duck, brings it back, puts it right down next to the Yankee. He's impressed. He's never seen nothing like this. Another duck, *Boom*. Got him. Dog jumps in the water, swims over, gets the duck. They do this all one morning. He is very impressed. He had a little cocktail over there with Uncle Grover after all this was over and said: "You know, I have some friends in Massachusetts who'd really enjoy this. I know where I can get a pond. But now, can I get one of these dogs in Massachusetts?"

Uncle Grover says, "Fool, of course, you can. I'm going to tell you something cause you're my friend. You're from up north, don't know nothing about dogs. You can lose your money real fast on a black Lab if you ain't smart. There's one thing you've got to check on a black Lab. You've got to make sure the black Lab's little ol hinny ain't too wide."

He said, "Why is that?"

He said, "Well any fool knows. If a black Lab's little hinny is too wide, when he jumps in the water to go get the duck, he'll fill up with water and will float to the bottom and you'll be out a dog. Now just make sure you check any black Lab, make sure you check it."

He goes back up to Massachusetts, gets him a pond. Gets his friend. Comes time to buy the dog. He looks up the phone book and finds a dog breeder. Calls him up and says, "Yes, I'm going to do some duck hunting. And I need a dog. Do you have such a dog known such as the black Lab?"

"Oh, yes, I got a new one. Just out of a champion. Love this dog. $1500. It's a steal."

He said, "Well, that sounds good but I, of course, know something about the black Lab and I must come over and examine him first."

He says, "Well fine, come on over." Gets over, trots out the little puppy. Gorgeous little baby saint in that dog. Just happy, running around, just great.

"Oh, but it's a beautiful dog but I got to examine him first."

"Go right ahead, do what you want to do."

So the fellow from Massachusetts took his finger and inserted it into the dog's little hinny and he pulled it and said, "Can't buy this dog, uh-uh, don't want this dog."

He said, "Well, why not?"

"Well fool, his lil' hinny's too wide, everyone knows if you get a black Lab, why when he jumps in the water, he'll take on water and sink and I'll be out a dog."

Dog breeder says, "OK, well, just a minute, I understand it."

And reached up under the little black Lab puppy, grabbed him in his most private, tender parts, squeezed 'em as hard as he could and gave him one turn like that. Little ol black lab's hinny got about *thiiii-iiiis* big.

And the intelligent fellow said, "I'm sorry, I had him set for quail."

"I told you that goose was too big for the pup!"

Excerpts from

Red Smith on Fishing

Red Smith

Anglers' Club

I t was in the Anglers' Club of New York a few years ago that a pet-
rifying potion called martini-on-the-rocks ("O true apothecary!
Thy drugs are quick") was encountered for the first time. It was an
experience never to be buried deep in memory, and recently there were
stories in the papers which brought it back to the surface.

The stories told how scholars at Princeton had discovered "startling
similarities" between Izaak Walton's *The Compleat Angler* and a work
called *The Art of Angling* published seventy-six years earlier than Izaak's
master opus. The boys at Princeton didn't like to say so bluntly, but the
facts seemed to be that the revered Mr. Walton was a skulking plagiarist.

Inevitably a question presented itself: What manner of depth
charge were they consuming in the Anglers' Club, now that the truth
was out?

"Just the usual thing," a member reported in a tone that was like a
shrug. "Did I say the usual?" he asked "That may be stretching it a bit.
Back in prohibition days we not only mixed our own recipes but made
up our own ingredients. Once somebody making up the gin forgot to
add the distilled water. There was a dinner featuring straight grain
alcohol flavored with essence of juniper."

"The speeches," the member recalled happily, "never were so witty
before, and haven't been since."

But how about those horrifying revelations regarding The Master,
whose "delightful innocence" charmed Charles Lamb, whose "fascinating veins of honest simplicity" bewitched Washington Irving? To
discover now that Father Izaak was a contemptible literary thief—

"Pooh," the member said. "You're talking about that book of
Kienbusch's. We knew it all the time."

Recently Carl Otto v. Kienbusch, of New York, came upon the only copy of *The Art of Angling* which is known to exist.

"Kienbusch," said the Brother of the Angle, "is a member of the club. He showed the book around to all of us. It may be big news at Princeton, but we've known for a good while that Walton swiped from everybody whose stuff he read, same as all those writing johnnies do. How did Kipling put it—

> " 'When 'Omer smote 'is bloomin' lyre,
> He'd 'eard men sing by land an' sea;
> An' what 'e thought 'e might require,
> 'E went an' took—the same as me!' "

All the same, it comes hard to think of the gentle old ironmonger as a calculating hack lifting paragraphs and passages from authors who had gone before him, and never giving credit to his sources. It wasn't as though he were a young guy struggling to get into some slick-paper paradise like *Sports Illustrated.*

Izaak was a churchly man and no rookie in the writing dodge when he produced the first edition of *The Compleat Angler, or The Contemplative Man's Recreation* in the sixtieth year of his life. He had already done two biographies—of the poet John Donne, and his old fishing companion, Sir Henry Wotton—and if there wasn't an aura of sanctity about his graying skull he managed to create one.

"Anglers," he wrote, meaning himself, "they be such honest, civil, quiet men." Honest? Why, the old rummy! A fellow pictures him now in that little stone hut of his which had three sides facing the River Dove so he might see if a trout were dimpling the water. He's dipping into barley wine, "the good liquor that our honest forefathers did use to drink—the drink which preserved their health and made them live so long and to do so many good deeds," and poring through the works of his betters for passages that he could steal.

It is not easy to believe this of Walton. A guy would as lief believe that Dame Juliana, who wrote the very first treatise on fly-fishing—

"Dame Juliana!" said the member of the Anglers' Club. "Good heavens, don't you know about her? Fact is, she probably wasn't a her. The language used in her *Treatyse of Fysshinge wyth an Angle* went out of style seventy years before the time she is supposed to have been born, and the chances are that whoever faked her stuff was a man, not a woman."

From beginning to end, these had been shaking discoveries. One would have thought that the mere unmasking of Walton as a plagiarist would have shaken the Anglers' Club until the stuffed trout fell from its walls.

"You mean those big fish hanging over the doors?" the member said. "Don't worry about them. One was caught on a worm, one was netted and the other was killed with a pitchfork."

Nothing is scared.

The Beamoc is a Trout With Two Heads

At 6 AM the climate of the Catskills was dropping as the gentle rain from heaven upon the place beneath. In this instance the place beneath was a swatch of muddy turf outside a window of the Reed Cottage in Roscoe, New York.

As anybody knows, if he can read either English or the rod and gun columns, the stroke of 6 AM is to the angler as the clang of a bell to an old fire horse. In this case it was like the clang of a bell to an English heavyweight. There were snuffling sounds, such as a man makes breathing resin, and the creak of bedsprings as a body rolled over and snuggled deeper.

Two hours later the voice of Sparse Grey Hackle, angler, filled the house. The rain had abated, but this was a trick. It was lying in wait. It lay in wait through the hurried two-hour breakfast and the drive to the "Big River." Then it pounced, in hissing, gleeful torrents, mixed with one pounding rush of hail.

Harry Darbee, angler and flytier, had joined the party and suggested starting on the "Big River"—the Beaverkill below the Junction Pool, which is formed by the confluence of the Willowemoc and the upper Beaverkill, or "Little River." The theory was that with the water high and roily the "Big River" would be less crowded than the smaller streams.

It wasn't exactly deserted, except by trout, but there was less congestion downstream than, for example, at the Junction Pool, where worm fishermen lined the banks. The Junction Pool is always patronized enthusiastically in the hope of landing a beamoc. The beamoc is a brown trout with two heads, one of which gazes longingly down the Beaverkill, while the other hankers for the Willowemoc. Unable to make up its minds, the beamoc lives its life out in the Junction Pool. Harry Darbee wears a portrait of one on the shoulder patch of his fishing jacket.

Mr. Darbee lives in Roscoe and these waters speak to him with a thousand tongues. On opening day he listened to all the tongues and what they said brought him no joy. Neither did Mr. Hackle's thermometer, which said the water temperature was forty-two degrees. Harry said this meant the trout, if any, would be logy and disinclined to battle the savage current in midstream.

He advised working the slack water along the shore, where the malingerers would be loafing. The advice proved sound. In less than two hours, during which a tempting variety of bucktails, wet flies and nymphs was offered on four rods, there came a strike. Meade Schaeffer, angler and artist, got the strike but not the fish.

Now and then a pale, domestic brand of sunshine was produced. If a guy happened to be out of the water detaching his fly from a willow branch, a semblance of circulation was restored at these moments. During one such interval it was decided to try the "Little River."

There the traffic was heavier and the fishing better, loosely speaking. That is, Meade Schaeffer caught a number of small trout on a spruce fly, and Harry Darbee had one strike which felt good, he said. Mr. Schaeffer said his were all gray trout, hatchery fish, and he released them. The other members of the party said nothing of interest.

Later in the afternoon a worm fisherman walked up and splotched his rig in where a fly fisherman was working a streamer. The fly fisherman reeled up, backed off, and asked: "Any action?"

"I got eight," the worm fisherman said bitterly. "No size. I'm fishing a pool, feller comes along, throws his bait right where I got my line. So I got to leave. So he catches a twenty-inch brown and an eighteen-inch brookie. Right in my pool!"

"Some people," the fly fisherman said, "have no manners."

"You said it," the worm fisherman said.

He splotched his bait in again and caught a large sucker.

"Do you want it?" he asked politely.

`"No, thank you." It was time to quit, anyhow, and go see what the boys were having in the Antrim Lodge. They were having plenty. This may account for the fact that traffic was lighter on the "Litter River" the next day.

That second day was raw and splattery with a yammering wind

which snatched flies out of the air and flung them into treetops. If there were trout in the treetops, they didn't seem to be feeding. The day's bag totaled one fish, caught, naturally, by Meade Schaeffer.

It was suggested that May would tell a different story after the water warmed and the hatches began.

"Yes," Harry Darbee said, "sometimes you can hook into a nice one. I tied into a pretty fair one last summer. He straightened out a bend in the river and took out two covered bridges before I landed him. And then I had to turn him loose."

"Why?"

"The water level," Mr. Darbee said, "dropped when I took him out. Would've ruined the fishing."

Swinging Door County

A pair of Baltimore orioles—the lowercase kind that can't hit, either, but can fly—swung their woven hammock from one apple tree, and in another nearby lived a family of kingbirds on a bough directly over the badminton net. When guests at Bay Shore Inn tried to use the court, the kingbirds dived at their heads in silent, persistent fury. The kingbird is a flashy dresser and will fight anything; if he could swear at umpires, you couldn't tell him from Durocher.

In the waters which cool the Door County peninsula, the black bass waited to be fed, queued up like tourists in front of a Miami cafeteria. The bass are always there and always ready to fight at the drop of a worm.

There are not, to be sure, so many now. There were a month ago. July was given over to their slaughter, and the fingers now pecking at the typewriter are delicately tinted with bass blood.

Door County is a limestone spur on the northeastern shoulder of Wisconsin, a buffer created by nature to keep the bass of Lake Michigan from quarreling with those of Green Bay. All along both wooded shores are rocky coves and craggy points where the fish congregate and wait for handouts from vacationists.

In the early morning and at evening, they can be taken close to the shore with fly rod and bugs or streamers or poppers or feather minnows. When the sun is high they loaf near the bottom on rock ledges or shoals offshore. Then they are attracted only by delicatessen served in the depths—night crawlers or minnows or soft-shell crabs or hell-grammites or Green Bay flies.

Some of these tidbits are local products unfamiliar to eastern eyes. The crabs, for example, aren't the round things you get deviled or au gratin in Baltimore. They are immature crawfish, shaped like tiny lobsters and served both on fishhooks and in saloons, where they are boiled with dill and salt and washed down with beer.

Green Bay flies are soft-bodied mayflies maybe an inch long, with transparent wings. They hatch by the million on these waters and fly ashore at night to die in huge drifts around streetlamps and lighted shop windows. Their carcasses give off an evil bouquet which bass prefer to Chanel No. 5.

An occasion is recalled when a monstrous hatch swept into Cleveland while the Indians were playing a night game, and the contest was almost flied out. Clouds of bugs settled on the players, fluttered into batters' eyes, flew into fielders' mouths, got squashed in typewriters in the press box. Students of international relations might make something out of the fact that in Cleveland and Detroit these smelly pests are called Canadian soldiers and in Windsor, Ontario, they are known as American soldiers.

Several years ago the hellgrammite was described here as a green and ugly little monster collected in swamps by Wisconsin fish-bait tycoons. This brought a letter of furious protest from the eastern angler, Mr. Sparse Grey Hackle, who wrote that hellgrammites were black and found in creekbeds. Nobody ever saw a green hellgrammite, he insisted, except people who also saw pink elephants habitually, and he suggested that the proper name of this peninsula must be Swinging Door County.

Be that as it may. If true hellgrammites are the black larvae of dobsonflies, then these aren't true hellgrammites because they're the pupae of dragonflies, but they're still green, and bass here call them hellgrammites and dote on 'em.

Among freshwater game fish, the bass is the neighborhood tough who wears a derby hat, smokes big, black cigars and never shaves. He swaggers through these waters pawing over the free lunch counter and offering to lick any —— in the house. He doesn't always win but he's always ready to try.

A few hundred yards from Bay Shore Inn is a reef where a lumber schooner went down long ago. On a calm day the bones of the old vessel can be seen easily through the clear water. This summer a huge population of bass kept house among the ribs and spars.

On most days it was no problem at all for a fisherman to take his limit off the wreck. These fish seldom ran longer than ten, eleven or twelve inches and came to be known contemptuously as "wreck-size," though on a fly rod a smallmouth of these dimensions can make more trouble than two blondes.

The wreck had another attraction not possessed by the reefs farther from shore. It is within easy earshot of a cottage occupied by baseball fans. Every little while, an angler dreaming in his boat could hear a little girl call to a neighbor, "They're still five to five in the eleventh." Thus he kept abreast of current events.

No need to ask who "they" were. In this country there is only one baseball team, the Milwaukee Braves. All others are beneath mention.

If you are hunting a safe distance from home for at least a couple days, there will be a night that you and your hunting party will want to go to town. All types of appetites encourage this outing. If you plan to eat indoors at the Pickled Boar's Snout Saloon, no need to shave or anything equally foolish, just clean up like you were going to the Elks for the smelt fry. And gulp a handful of breath mints.

Such a visit to these most foreign parts was greatly described by a comedy writer and non-hunter out of the 1950s and '60s who moved his Japanese wife Reiko, number one son, Bobby, and menagerie to the wilds of Canada to run a fishing lodge. A sample of their "night out" from Jack Douglas' book Shut Up and Eat Your Snowshoes *will have a familiar ring—to hunters on the road.*

Excerpt from
Shut Up and Eat Your Snowshoes

Jack Douglas

"Then it's all set," I said. "We'll all meet at the Empire Room of the Chinookville-Hilton next Saturday night. Okay?"

Next Saturday night turned out to be the rainiest Saturday night in the history of mankind. The trip across the lake to our soggy Land Rover was one long bailing operation, which never removed more than one-quarter of the water sloshing over our shiny-new going-to-town shoes.

In connecting up the battery in the Rover, everything was so wet I almost electrocuted myself, and later, sliding and skidding down the hairy timber road, I wish I had. And the Rover's headlights were helpless against the downpour. A Greek marathon runner with a damp torch would have given more light and also something to guide us, because the road was just a rumor so far as visibility was concerned.

Route 365 was not much better and the two one-way bridges which traversed the now-wild, raging Chinookville River undulated ominously. Bear droppings mixed with rain gave the tire tread nothing to grab, and driving through this superslippery mess bestowed on us the overall feeling of confidence one gets while iceboating with a drunk. On a lake not quite frozen over.

When we reached the Trans-Canada Highway, with its thundering multi-ton tractor-trailers, driving faster than the speed of sound, plus the usual Saturday night daredevils, playing chicken and dying, we breathed a sigh of gratitude and relief. We were safe at last.

Reiko and Bobby and I were the first to arrive at the Empire Room and were shown an easily arranged ringside table. The room was small and the decor consisted mainly of dusty balloons badly in need of air and long streamers of lifeless twisted paper streamers, strung across the black, greasy-looking ceiling. Apparently the Empire Room had once been used, back in Chinookville's frontier days, to smoke hams and bacon, because the air still had a slightly porcine flavor. Not unpleasant, but hardly a Mardi Gras aroma.

Four aboriginals were chained to the bandstand, where they twanged, banged, pounded and plucked a guitar, drums, piano-organ, and bass violin. These apes were not long from the mother tree, and with the proximity of our ringside table, which I was beginning to regret, they gave off a strong indication that Alpo played a major role in their dietary laws. Alpo laced with hot buttered gin.

Two go-go girls, who had seen better days—but God knows when or where—were caged on each side of the bandstand. Looking at them—even casually, which was all they deserved—I was surprised to see a pan of water and a half-eaten can of salmon in one of the cages. At least, I thought, *someone* cares.

The go-go girls were much too arthritic to keep up with the rock group, and their scanty costumes revealed a rainbow of varicose veins in their pipe-stem legs. Until they started to do, what *they* thought was an exciting shimmy, I had no idea they were topless. Their breasts were like dusty wind socks at an abandoned Arizona airport. And the wind wasn't blowing east or west or north or south. No matter how hard these Medicare houris tried to shimmy up a breeze, their wind sock bosoms remained listless at half-mast. Still in mourning for McKinley. Or maybe Lincoln.

Sandra Trilby was the first to arrive. She warped up to our ringside table like she was docking a full-rigged schooner. I was so astonished at her array of finery I didn't recognize her. I just sat in my chair and gaped. She was wearing her ancient wedding gown, which had been drastically shortened to a mini-skirt, revealing her knees, which had been left there by the glacier. Her legs were difficult to describe. She was neither bowlegged nor knock-kneed. Sandra Trilby had one of each. And apparently she was wearing a mammoth-skin body stocking—hair side out. Her mackinaw was thrown carelessly over her shoulders like a stole, and she was using a lorgnette with one lens missing to size up the room and the rest of Chinookville's jet set. In the dim light, I thought she was wearing a human bone through her nose in the style of a New Guinea headhunter, but it turned out to be her wet cigar, which had been smashed in the revolving door as she entered this charming Chinookville *bolte*. I was disappointed.

"Where's Lambert?" I said.

"Oh, he's parking the sled," Sandra said. "And tying up the dogs."

"*Sled!*" I said. "Whaddya mean?"

"Sorry," she said, her reptilian eyes darting around the room to see who was there. "It's been so *long* since we've been to the city. Not since our wedding day."

"You're kidding," I said.

"No, I'm not," she said. "Lambert and I are really married."

"I didn't mean *that*," I said. "I meant—"

"Lambert and I lived together for eight years before we decided to make it legal," Sandra said, charmed by her own daring admission. "We got married right after the monkey came."

"What?" Reiko said.

"Yes," Sandra said, "my brother sent us a little pet monkey from South America and we decided it wouldn't be fair to him for us to be living in sin."

"What's 'living in sin'?" Bobby wanted to know.

"It's a town near here," I said.

"It's not there anymore," Sandra said.

Before things got really puzzling to all of us, Lambert Trilby suddenly was sitting with us, wearing a tuxedo which was badly in need of mowing.

Excerpts from

Out of My Head

Henry Miller

Angler Survives in a Vegetative State...

"**A**nybody home?" I asked, rapping on the door.

I was visiting my good friend and a former fishing fanatic, Milt Axelroot.

His wife, Sunflower Moonglow Kowalski-Axelroot, after an epic battle that lasted years, had converted Milt to vegetarianism a couple of months before. I thought I'd stop by and see how it was going.

Coming from the back yard was a swishing sound followed by the rending and tearing of plant life, much like the noises you hear on a National Geographic special when a herd of stampeding elephants flattens a banana plantation.

Peering around the corner of the house, I saw Milt, clad in waders and fishing vest, standing in his daughter's wading pool and making false casts over the garden with his favorite 9-foot, light-action graphite fly rod.

"Hi, Milt, how's it going?" I asked cheerily.

"Shhhhh," he said angrily. "You'll spook the cukes."

He launched a greenish fly into a tangle of vines, mended the slack, then reared back on the rod.

An 11-inch cucumber, impaled on the No. 6 hook, tore loose from a vine and wobbled and rolled across the lawn as Milt reeled in.

He scooped it up in a small trout landing net, detached the hook, admired it for a moment, then placed it gently into a wicker creel at his waist.

"A couple more like that and we'll have a dandy salad," Milt said with a grin.

"I took a 4-pound casaba from the same spot a couple of weeks ago," he said, gesturing toward a dirt mound of melon vines. "It was tricky getting it in, though. It wrapped the line around a sprinkler head while I was fighting it."

"I see you've made the adjustment to being a nature nutloaf," I observed as Milt began false-casting again, shifting his position in the wading pool.

"Yea. It was tough. When Sunflower told me I'd have to give up fishing and hunting, the marriage almost went into the dumper.

"But with little Lotus Ankh just turning 4, and the community-property laws being what they are, this seemed like a more acceptable compromise."

It wasn't easy at first, Milt said, allowing the line to shoot out into the garden.

He said he had to set up his fly bench to tie tomato horn worm and apple maggot imitations.

And it was during one outing to test the apple flies that the police arrested him casting over an abandoned Grannie Smith orchard near Corvallis, Milt said.

His explanation to the officers led to a 72-hour hold for psychiatric observation at the Oregon Home for the Bewildered, he continued. But once Sunflower showed up and explained what was going on, the justice system relented.

Since then, things have been going along pretty smoothly, Milt said.

"I caught a mess of tomatoes with a couple of cabbage butterfly imitations this morning," he said. "A couple of them were pretty small, but I had to keep them because they were pulp-hooked."

Milt said he was pretty busy most nights tying up this assortment of agricultural pest imitations for his upcoming vacation.

The family was planning a tour of U-pick farms in northeastern Oregon and southern Washington, he explained.

"Missing real fishing isn't so bad," Milt said, a shade of wistfulness in his voice. "Hell, next week I'm going out on a charter boat out of Depoe Bay to go kelp fishing.

"And a healthy-sized kohlrabi or carrot will give you a good fight trying to get it out of the ground, especially on light tackle."

Milt began false-casting again over a likely looking stand of pole beans, which he referred to as the panfish of the vegetable kingdom,

"It takes a mess of them to make a meal," he said, detaching a wax bean from the hook and adding it to the creel.

I decided to leave him to his fun, but I couldn't resist asking just one more question.

"Milt, I can see you've adjusted pretty well to being a compost head when it comes to fishing," I said. "But you were such a hunting fanatic. How did you learn to live without that?"

A grin spread on his face from ear-to-ear.

"Come on inside the house," he said, reeling up the line and tucking the fly rod under his arm. "I'll show you my 14-pound watermelon. I had the rind mounted.

"I got it right through the stem at 150 yards. Didn't ruin any of the meat."

One word of caution, though: Always remember the furnace analogy.

Combinations such as smoked oysters, canned chili and camp margueritas have a tendency to start the human equivalent of a flue fire.

My name is Henry, and I'm a carnivore...

It must be Indian summer. There's lots of hot air, but very little light.

A column about the feverish anticipation of hunting season brought a chorus of responses from anti-hunting readers.

In deference to their arguments, I've seen the error of my ways. I've decided to forgo eating anything that didn't die of natural causes.

If that attitude is adopted by all of us, it would mean requiring to see a death certificate for any animal consumed by those weak-kneed slackers such as myself who can't live without eating critters higher on the food chain than a stalk of wheat.

Which could lead to news items such as:

"The steer died after a lengthy illness brought on by eating a load of green hay laced with tansy ragwort," it will say in the meat-for-sale section of the obituaries. "Viewing will be in the freezer case from 11 a.m. until 1 p.m., following which there will be a barbecue cremation at Wallace Marine Park."

If the trend catches on, people will be forced to compete for the slim supply of meat.

"We have a 2-year-old white-faced Hereford on a respirator at Our Lady of the Packing Plant animal hospital in East Waterford," the auctioneer at Sothebys will say.

"The cow suffered a massive coronary from an excess of butterfat. What am I bid for the hindquarters?"

Or...

"Slightly damaged rump roast, $217.89 a pound.

"The victim jumped a fence and was hit by a semi while trying to make it over both lanes of Interstate 317 just east of Dead Man's Corner near Weem's Junction."

Or...

"Winter kill. $157.22 a pound.

"Extra lean venison from a herd trapped on the high Cascade summer range by an unexpected blizzard. Some freezer burns."

Or...

"For sale: Tornado-plucked chickens, turkeys and some ducks. $58.95 a pound.

"Sale is forced by a twister hitting several coops and pens in Woebetide, Kan. Storm-damaged pullets at reduced prices. Ask about our monsoon special.

"Also available, some slightly cyclone-fence-strained turkey parts suitable for soup stock or gravy. $56.22 a pound. Ask about our bulk specials. There's a 27 cents-a-pound discount if you bring your own plastic bags and shovel."

Out-In-Left-Field Guide

Gary Cox and Mike Beno

Sometime around September, certain wild species begin to change plumage—shedding their colorful feathers for drabber attire, fashioned to blend in with the damp environment these birds will migrate to for the season. At first, the molt seems to make the varied species look alike, but on closer inspection, and with the expert advice provided on these pages, you may be able to identify some of the more common birds.

Take a moment during a break in the action this season to look *inside* the blinds and hunt clubs for a sampling of the characters who turn out for this sport called duck hunting. You may find comfort in the fact that the health of a habitat is judged by the *variety* of species it supports.

Gluttonum immensus

Common Names: Tiny, Bubba, Earthquake.
Range: Commercial sized.
Call: "Errrp."
Behavior: A large, lumbering species, Ol' Lunch-in-the-Blind cannot hunt in any blind, for any length of time, without doing something involving food. Will feed on anything that cannot bite back or at least get away. Uses more grease than Jiffy Lube. Fries everything, including coffee, and should be voted arteriosclerosis poster child. Wears clothing with more pockets than a pool hall, all the better to stash and carry vast stores of provender, bits of which will be found in those pockets with balled-up Kleenex for seasons to come. Graduate of the Fatback School of Nutrition. Can belch in seven different languages.

Trendii catalogus

Common Names: Dirk, Chad, Huntington.
Range: $100,000 to $500,000 (with perks).
Calls: "On the Gold Card, please."
Behavior: Owns the latest in outdoor gear from his hand-ground shooting glass lenses right down to his polar-expedition boots, yet has never been sighted in a marsh. Goes "gunning," never hunting. Most of that is done over chablis and brie at parties long on French phrases and short on straight English. Wishes Volvo or BMW would come out with a pickup truck. Will be the first at the athletic club to own one when they do. Is under psychiatric care because of nightmares about actually cleaning a bird. It's murder on the manicure. But he actually has very little to worry about in this regard. The closest he'll ever come to a duck is at the end of a fork at Chez Paul. Mouton Rothschild '54, please. Daddy went on a safari in 1954.

Nostalgic aristocratus

Common Names: The Colonel, The Old Man, Retired.
Range: Where the Good Old Days are still good.
Calls: "I remember when…" "Years ago we didn't…"
Behavior: Characterized by rheumy eyes and fetid pipe smoke, this species brings new meaning to the term "antique." Has an endless arsenal of stories designed to elicit sleep, or, more mercifully, deep coma. Stridently claims to have known Mr. Nash and Fred Kimble personally, even though he spent his entire life thousands of miles from either. Nothing invented or thought of since 1936 is worth knowing about. Disrelishes the plastic in decoys and shell casings. Finds automatic shotguns an abomination. Fiberglass boats and Gore-Tex have desecrated his sport. Sits in the Library with snifter and ascot, carving, pining and staring at dusty books. Is never seen outdoors.

Nimrod obsessus

Common Names: Donald, Drake, Blue Bill (when not hunting).
Range: Gun shops, sport shops, sportsmen's clubs, conservation hearings. (This information deemed reliable during off-season only. During hunting season you'll never find him.)
Call: Make that "calls." He owns 17 of them.
Behavior: Stockpiles enough guns to fight a war and has more boats than the Iranian Navy. Owns sufficient insulated underwear and boots to clothe the boat people. Had over 400 ducks and geese on display in his home at last count (his wife's, not his). Can recite federal hunting regulations, as well as those for 20 states, by heart. Is working diligently on the other 30. This multifaceted species displays many interests including dog training, shell loading, boat building, equipment purchase and repair, hunting magazines, gun cleaning, game cleaning, game cooking, trap and skeet, hunting videos, blind building, home taxidermy… Is commonly divorced.

Pestum afield

Common Names: Black Plague, Get Lost! @#$!**!
Range: Any place you are hunting.
Calls: "Mind if I hunt here?" "Duh."
Behavior: Enthusiastic but somewhat unwary, this species has even been known to hunt itself on occasion. One can only speculate on its mating habits, but judging from sheer numbers, it must be doing something right. Known to assemble peculiar heaps of hunting gear by begging and borrowing. If an individual of this species lives in your neighborhood, it will slowly acquire most of your hunting equipment. If one is not nearby, it will find you sooner or later. Easily identified in the field—look for overturned boats, mud-plugged guns, filled waders, pink flamingoes in the spread. Listen for discordant yelling, equipment fumbled into the bottom of a boat and calling that sounds like breeding time at a jackass ranch. For identification in the hand… well, you don't want to get that close.

Excerpts from

Gun Dogs & Bird Guns

Charles J. Waterman

Roller Derby

Dogs are in the smell business. For example, an odor that can immobilize an over-sensitive human can be exhilarating to a dog.

A dog has what I shall call a broad odor-appreciation range. For example, let's take a silky-eared English setter who can smell a woodcock on the other side of a bush which contains a family of field mice, two old bird nests, and a dead weasel. Here we have a sensitive creature with true odor appreciation.

Now while seeking a woodcock or quail smell this setter comes upon a raccoon which has been dead for eleven warm autumn days. Reluctant to leave this treasure trove of olfactory delight, the setter hurriedly rolls on it before going on with his hunting. Then, by accident, he finds an irritable skunk and investigates it. After rubbing some of the results of this encounter from his eyes he continues seeking the scent of woodcock or quail. At this point his master questions the old bird hunter's rule of always working a dog upwind but the day is still young.

While happily loping along with his aura of deceased raccoon and living skunk the setter winds a covey of quail and comes to what we shall call a "classic point" from a distance of thirty feet, scenting the quail through heavy wiregrass and a little broom sedge which contains a gopher tortoise. The gunner comes up and, holding his breath briefly because he approaches downwind from the setter, he walks into the covey of quail and shoots one of them with an expert swing of his 12-gauge improved-cylinder and modified Holland & Holland, using a one-ounce load of Number 8 shot. (Even in these hypothetical situations I like to maintain accuracy as to detail.)

The bird falls some distance from and out of sight of the setter, who begins hunting dead and finds it where it has fallen beside a rotting log with the discarded skin of a corn snake draped over it. On the way back to his owner the setter scents a sleeper that did not flush with the other quail, and after blowing a wing feather of the dead quail from his nostrils he makes another classic point. The hunter shoots this bird and the setter tries to retrieve both of them but drops one. By now I believe you follow me in the matter of selective scenting and odor appreciation. Of course the setter is offended that he is put in the kennel that night and not allowed to sleep by the fireplace, despite the insistence of my old hunting friend that setters should be kept by fireplaces, even in warm weather, for aesthetic purposes.

Dogs and people approach things a little differently. For example, I am very fond of pizza but have never had a desire to roll in it. Rolling in more or less odorous things may be somewhat mysterious but I assume the idea is to collect a choice odor and take it along. Still, there is something else about it I can't put my finger on. For example, a dog that has smelled as nearly like a rose as a dog can smell for most of his life is likely to go on a roll when accompanied by another dog he wishes to impress.

Like the time we took Tex on the trout fishing trip with our friends who had the new car. We even debated taking the gleaming car but decided we'd be nowhere that it could get scratched, even though we were going into a Western pasture—with Tex the Brittany and our friends' dog of impeccable poodle ancestry. The pasture was well occupied by Angus cattle and as soon as we opened the door Tex climbed out and showed that coiffed poodle how a real he-dog handles a cow pasture. I got him fairly clean but I had to do it in a pretty cold trout stream and without soap.

But up to now this has been just so much padding to get to a report on the rolling aptitudes of the Duchess of Doonesbury, my sixty-two-pound English pointer. Until I met the Duchess I had paid little attention to the techniques of rolling, considering it a routine move, like sitting down or scratching. The Duchess changed all that.

I trust you have observed rolling. A dog making a serious roll on or in something that smells puts his nose to the ground just a little before he gets to the object. He then sort of slides his nose and the side of the head up alongside it and slowly rolls so that his shoulders strike that optimum spot, whereupon he flops over, momentarily out of control, and then wriggles carefully with his feet in the air. Since he soon acquires the aroma of the rolled-on object I have always wondered why it is that after he stands up concluding the process and shakes himself he then turns to the target and takes another long sniff.

Anyway, that is the pattern of the routine roll for something that smells a little or a great deal. It had never occurred to me that it required any special technique and the matter of accuracy had not come up in my experience until we acquired Dutch. I soon learned that she took rolling seriously but that she was remarkably inaccurate. This came up for the first time when I kicked off my hunting boots and socks and was preparing to head for the shower and heard a scraping sound. It was Dutch endeavoring to roll on my socks but missing them by a good eighteen inches. As time went on I realized she had a serious problem with her rolling, having a misunderstanding of rolling trajectory and failing to lead her target properly, thus ending up rolling some distance away. A few days later she tried to roll on my shoes (evidently for practice) when I was wearing them and sitting in a lounge chair. She ended up partly under the chair with her tail caught in a complex mechanism that allows a chair passenger to lie back with his feet up.

Our dogs are generally barred from the bathroom but in a little shack we live in while hunting we cannot conveniently make the bathroom off limits. One evening I heard strange sounds from there and Debie told me it was Dutch with the bath towels. I jumped to my feet and started that way but Debie said not to worry.

"She's been doing this pretty regularly," Debie said. "She pulls the towels off the racks and tries to roll on them but doesn't seem to hit them. No hurry about going in there as they're already on the floor and she won't roll on them."

Shortly afterward, Dutch appeared in the bathroom door and glared at me but I did not laugh.

In approaching a rolling target, Dutch's eyes take on a calculating stare and she gathers herself for the effort, measuring distances and seeking the proper foot placement. She lowers her head with clocklike precision and becomes tense in anticipation. I watched this many times and, assured that persistent practice would succeed, I guess I lost interest. But rolling is important.

It was early season in grouse country, warm sun and a long day. Dutch had done her best but there weren't many birds and I was mentally measuring my way to the truck as I stumbled out of a dense patch of aspen and listened for Dutch's bell. I hadn't heard it for a couple of minutes. As I broke from the aspen into open pastureland, I froze in despair.

Two hundred yards away, its presence heralded by a breeze-borne whiff, even from that distance, was a dead cow. And visible too were Dutch's legs, pointed skyward and waving in the snappy, jerky pattern of a dog's luxurious roll in super smell.

I screamed before I had sense enough to blast on my whistle and before me flashed the long ride home in a Ford Bronco with Dutch and her treasured carrion. Finally, Dutch heard me, the waving legs stopped and at last she stood up and ran toward me. Did you call, boss?

Averting my face, I waited until she was at my feet, and holding my breath I gradually turned to eye her. But I needn't have worried. Dutch missed the cow.

I had two friends named Jack and Jerry (real names) who got a highly touted and expensive German shorthair by mail-order from a southern kennel. They had him on two weeks' trial, and they lived way up north where seasons open early. After the dog ate all of Jack's and Jerry's birds, the seller had to take it back. Jack commented, however, that such a dog was a very easy keeper, requiring hardly any dog food.

Even with careful planning there are awkward moments. A friend of mine walked up to a ranch house door to inquire about Hungarian partridge hunting. He'd left his Brittanies in the car, but one squeezed unseen through a partly opened window.

The rancher at the door seemed preoccupied and stared over Ben's shoulder.

"Oh, I guess it's all right for you to hunt," he said. "But I think you should tell your dog to put down my duck."

Fish Naked

Jerry Dennis

Naked we come into the world and naked we leave it, but deciding what to wear in the meantime can be a pain in the duff. I consider shopping for clothes about as much fun as shingling condominiums, so I like to wear the same blue jeans and corduroy shirt most days, and would probably wear them *every* day if my wife and kids didn't complain. I'm not lazy or undisciplined or unclean, just uninterested.

But when I was in my early twenties, my fishing friends and I were fashion paragons, on the cutting edge of what would eventually become known as the grunge look. We grew our hair long (and yes, Dad, you were right: Someday we *did* look back at the photos and cringe) and dressed only in jeans, tees, and flannel shirts. Because we were too obsessed with fishing and hunting to land good jobs, money was scarce. It condemned us to sleeping in our cars when we traveled and fishing with cheap waders, mid-range fiberglass rods, and decent but not great Hardy reels. We filled mismatched plastic boxes with flies we tied ourselves and stuffed them inside vests so stained with sweat and blood and spilled dry-fly floatant they looked as if they'd been kicked around on the floor of an automobile repair shop that doubled as a slaughterhouse.

For a few years in the mid-seventies, Mike McCumby and I drove west every September to fish the waters in and around Yellowstone Park, a region that even then was a center of outdoor fashion. Mike and I stood out from the rest of the crowd. When we entered fly shops the proprietors looked at us the way a famously conservative congressman from northern Michigan looked at hippies—as road dreck that arrived in town with one pair of underwear and one five-dollar bill and no intention of changing either of them. Mike and I weren't hippies, but neither were we in the market for Wheatley fly boxes or a hundred-dollars' worth of Japanese-tied Humpies and Bitch-Creek Nymphs. To get useful information we had to spring for a couple spools of tippet material and endure the head-to-foot glances of customers who wore more money on their backs than Mike and I earned in two weeks of pounding nails. Screw 'em, we said. Our outfits sucked, but man, we *fished*.

One year we spent every day for a week on the Firehole. We concentrated on the meadow sections of the river, in the midst of geyser fields, mud pots, and boiling streams. It's hard to imagine water more unlike the stained, cedar-shrouded rivers we had grown up fishing back home in Michigan. We became a bit delirious with the novelty of casting where there were few trees to snag our backcasts and where large fish fed recklessly on the surface in midstream, at midday.

The Firehole's trout see a lot of skillfully presented artificial flies and can be fussy about which ones they eat. Mike and I did okay, fooling a few good fish every afternoon during mayfly hatches and taking rainbows and browns to eighteen inches on weighted nymphs deaddrifted through some of the deeper riffles. That was during working hours, when we had much of the river to ourselves. On the weekend we had to share.

We knew the Firehole was popular, but we were not prepared for the crowds that gathered at every bend and riffle that bright September Saturday. Much of the competition was composed of deeply intent young men and women who dressed as if they had been assisted by personal fashion consultants and cast as if they had been tutored from the crib by tournament champs. Mike and I were a little intimidated. On previous trips to less fashionable places in Wyoming and Montana, we had shared the water with locals wading wet in dusty blue jeans and cowboy hats, carrying Band-Aid boxes of flies in their shirt pockets, and casting heavy glass rods with most of the paint chipped off. They were after-work anglers, good at muscling Woolly Worms into the wind and keeping their freezers stocked. Although Mike and I considered them kindred spirits, they dismissed us as effete fancy-pants purists because we wore chestwaders with only a few patches on them and preferred long leaders and smallish dry flies over the giant, gaudy, subaquatic patterns that were standard in most Western fly boxes in those days. One afternoon on the Madison an elderly cowboy casting large nineteenth-century-style wet flies on snelled hooks laughed out loud when we told him we were using #20 Blue-Winged Olives and 6X tippets. Later, surrendering to the when-in-Rome principle, we ambushed the Madison with Spruce Flies the size of neotropical songbirds and caught just as many fish as we were accustomed to catching, but they averaged half a foot longer.

On the Firehole we kept running into expert midgers casting thousand-dollar rods and wearing outfits like the folks in the Orvis catalog. They looked us up and down in frank appraisal, bent over to read the logos on our rods and reels, and more often than not began furiously dropping names. "I fished this stretch once with Ernest," one yawning dude said, sliding up to Mike and me on the bank of a drop-dead pool where a few minutes earlier we had watched a brown trout big enough to eat a muskrat rise, just once, during a brief hatch of minuscule gray somethings. The dude didn't specify which Ernest he meant, and we were too polite to ask. Then, later, while Mike worked a gravel run downstream and I stood on a rock casting dry flies and watching a streamside geyser erupt, a meticulously dressed gentleman with a cosmetic suntan walked to within twenty feet of me and began casting into the same pool. As I reeled in he leaned my way and said "I helped Jack Hemingway land and release a twenty-eight-inch brown trout from that exact spot a month ago."

Well, I was glad to hear it. I've always wanted to catch a twenty-eight-inch brown trout, and any rumor of one's existence is encouraging. But I had seen enough superbly dressed, superbly equipped, and superbly connected fishermen for one day, so I excused myself and rounded up Mike and we hiked through a stand of lodgepole pines to intercept the river in an area the map showed was as far from roads and boardwalks as any stretch of the Firehole gets. It was a hot day, grasshopper weather, and we walked a fair distance. We were sweating like wrestlers when we finally spotted sunlight flashing on water through the trees.

But then we saw the glint of a rod and stopped. Pilgrims were everywhere on this holy water. We were pilgrims too, of course, but after fishing an uncrowded river all week it was hard to be charitable. We walked to the edge of the woods to see what we were up against.

Facing us from the shallows on the opposite bank was a powerfully built man wearing skin-tight, skin-toned waders, with a landing net hanging below his waist and a fly rod waving around his head. Two heartbeats later, in a kind of cognitive double-take, I realized that the man was wearing neither waders nor clothes. He was stitchless, buck-naked, bare-assed as a baby. And there is no delicate way to say this: That thing hanging to his knees was no landing net. The guy was a freak of nature. P.T. Barnum could have made a fortune off him.

Mike and I drew back into the woods and hunkered down to

think. We stayed quiet, not wanting to alert the guy to our presence. It sounds strange now, but we were spooked. Seeing a naked man fishing is odd enough, but this naked man brought to mind the biological concept of dominance hierarchy. We were six-point bucks intruding on a twelve-pointer's territory, and we sure as hell didn't want him to think we were challenging him for it.

"Did you see that?" Mike whispered.

"I'm not sure," I said. "You're talking about the nude guy in the river?"

"Yea. But did you see *that?*"

We stepped to the edge of the trees. The man was gone. In his place was a woman, knee deep in the river, placing short, splashy casts to midstream. She too was starkers. And her physique was just as extraordinary as the man's. She had the kind of body that is considered out of fashion nowadays but can be seen on glorious display in Greek statuary, saucy Renaissance paintings, and turn-of-the-century French postcards. Venus with a fly rod.

Now we were really spooked. Where was the man? And what would he do if he caught us spying on his girlfriend? We cut through the woods, taking frequent glances behind us, and came out on the river a long bend downstream, in open terrain, where we could keep an eye on the woman above us and see anyone approaching when they were still a hundred yards away. But now the naked woman and the naked man were together, standing side by side and casting in synchronized rhythm, like the original innocent anglers of Eden. If Mike and I had been first-time visitors to the planet, we might have assumed we were witnessing some form of ritual courtship display.

We had a stretch of river to ourselves, at least, so we took our time and fished carefully. A middle-aged man wearing tight waders and a slouch hat furred with dozens of flies passed us on the bank and gave a jolly hello. We returned his greeting and watched him walk upstream to the bend where Adam and Eve fished. He stopped beside them and exchanged words as if there were nothing unusual about encountering naked people on the Firehole. It was disorienting. Mike and I wondered if we were terribly misinformed. Maybe nude angling was a local tradition, promoted by the West Yellowstone Chamber of Commerce and celebrated with effusive prose in travel magazines. Maybe it was a *tactic*.

We cast nymphs for an hour or so, but the trout seemed to have hightailed it to the headwaters. No insects were hatching, and the river was shallow and empty of life. All the time we fished we watched the man and woman. They never raised a trout. If nudity was a tactic, it didn't work.

It occurred to us that we might be witnessing a fashion statement. Maybe the nudists were protesting designer labels and de rigueur fishing duds, casting off all superfluities and announcing bravely to the world that only the river and the fishing mattered. The idea was nice, but it probably didn't apply. My guess is it just felt good to take your clothes off and stand in the water and show off a little. Mike and I laughed about it as we made our way downstream. For the first time all week we were the best-dressed guys on the river.

"Those guys behind us are the lousiest callers I've ever heard."

How to Perpetuate your Myth

Nelson Bryant

If, plagued by the various ills that aging flesh is heir to, you wonder how to sustain your reputation as a rock-hard, immensely clever hunter or fisherman, do not despair, for there are some only slightly dishonest ways of perpetuating the myth.

Let us consider the deer camp. The deer camp is not a place where the animals gather, but some log cabin, shack or lodge in the woods that serves as a base of operations for a group of hunters.

If you are the oldest fellow in the camp and have been there several times before, you know more about where the deer are than do your companions, and you also often have a chance to suggest what territory each man should hunt.

It's usually a relatively simple matter to assign yourself the best hunting area and the younger men the worst. You can get around the mild moral discomfort you may feel by telling yourself that deer often change their habits, that a ten-year pattern may be broken this time around.

If it is a well-run camp, the breakfast dishes will be cleaned up just as the tops of the spruces become visible against the eastern sky, and if the thought of lurching up the mountain before your joints have become properly loosened appalls you, there is a way out.

Inform the others that you have a special stew or casserole you wish to delight them with when they return from the hills that evening. Use a little arrogance. Tell them that—just because no women are about—there is no reason to live on canned swill.

With a little foot-dragging, much of the morning can be consumed in that project, and by that time you probably will have reached the stage where you can walk without stumbling. If you happen to be a writer, you needn't bother with cooking—simply make a show of getting out your notebooks, remarking that some people have to work for a living, even when hunting.

Eventually, of course, you'll have to go into the hills. If all has gone well, you'll set for about 10:30 A.M. Perhaps the hot spot you have set aside for yourself will produce a deer immediately; in which case you will drag it triumphantly back, ahead of everyone else, remarking when they arrive empty-handed that you can't understand their problem, that the woods are full of deer.

In youth, taking a deer early in the game is a disappointment, because your hunt is over. Later, you'll welcome this event. It not only relieves you of any more hiking, but frees you to read the book of poems you tucked away in your duffle bag, to toss scraps of food to the camp's Canada jays and chipmunks and to take long naps.

If you fail to get your deer on opening day, there is still an almost effortless way to enhance your reputation. Plan your hunt so that you are, by early afternoon, propped against a sun-warmed boulder on the southwestern slope of the mountain. Settle yourself comfortably, and before long, sleep will come. Remain there the rest of the day, perhaps kindling a tiny fire to heat a cup of tea and to ward off late afternoon's chill.

Near sunset, move slowly downhill toward the camp, but stop a quarter of a mile short of it. Tarry there as darkness fills the woods.

Wait until you hear the others return, until lamplight gleams from the cabin windows, until you know that your friends are becoming concerned about you. This is particularly effective if it has begun to snow, conjuring thoughts of the old-timer being lost in a blizzard.

You may if you wish remain there until someone goes outside and fires a signal shot into the night sky, but that is carrying it a bit too far.

Arise, tousle your hair, slap your face to make it red, as with exertion, sprinkle pine needles on your garments—or snow if it's possible—and stride to the cabin, kicking the door open and demanding a tot of bourbon.

Stomp your feet on the cabin floor and hang your rifle on the wall, and, glass in hand, immediately launch into a saga that might go something like this:

"I walked clear to hell and gone over Terrible Mountain. On the backside of it I picked up the trail of a big animal that led me down into Black's Swamp. Damndest mess of blowdowns you ever saw. I poked around in there all afternoon. Twice I saw a deer ahead of me, but I couldn't be sure it was the big one. I hung around until near sundown, hoping he'd show. That's a good buck. I'm going back in there tomorrow."

Then, lest you be queried too closely, advance to your stew, give it a stir and say: "Probably shouldn't have wasted my time with this after breakfast, but it sure smells first-rate."

The waterfowl hunter is more restricted in his image-creating maneuvers, particularly if he shares a blind with someone. About all you can do when you have a duck-hunting companion is to avoid all distant shots. Hold off until you can see the bird's eyes—30 yards or less away—and if you still manage to miss, rub the shoulder where you took a bullet in the Normandy invasion and softly curse the sniper who spoiled the uncanny coordination of eye and hand you once possessed.

If you are angling, trout fishing offers the best chance for self-inflation. You can't, for example, fool someone who is standing beside you in the pounding surf, flinging lures at the same school of fish. Fly-fishing a trout stream, however, you and your companion will separate, and as soon as you are screened from each other there need be no limit to your imagination. It is a good idea to enjoy several pipes on the bank of the stream, while you fashion the tale you will tell at the day's end.

If you wish to remove all doubt—or most of it—from your friend's mind, insist on fishing waters in which all trout must be released. Catch-and-release trout fishing has helped spawn a new breed of anglers who have found total contentment in equipage and approach, in mastering the entomology of stream insects, in tieing the flies designed to represent those insects and in creating new fly pattern and angling techniques about which a seemingly unending spate of books have been written. Some of these titles that come to mind are *Nymphs I Have Known, Caddis Madness and Fly Dry,* not forgetting of course, the privately published—1,000 signed copies—*Reeling About,* a singular probing of the inconsistencies of trout, women and wine.

But even if you are flogging a stream where the fish may legally be kept, there is no reason you have to trouble yourself catching them.

Steal along the stream, making sure you don't cast your shadow on the water, thereby startling the fish. Indeed, the best approach is to cast nothing on the water for if you do you may hook an overhanging branch and lose one of the flies—the only ones you ever carry—given you by Lord Purslane when you angled his stretch of the Itchen as war clouds were gathering over Europe.

And when the cattle are lowing and winding slowly over the lea and the setting sun flames in the west, seek out your companion, who, insensitive to the new tradition, has a lovely brace of 16-inch rainbows in his creel, and tell of how, for the third time in as many years, you managed to fool Old Cannibal, the monster seven-pound brown trout that has spent more than a decade in Dairymaid Pool.

Tell how the big fellow's deep, bronze sides gleamed in the last light from the dying sun as you slipped him back into the water, slide your silver flask from your hip and propose a toast to old trout and old friends, and, disarmed by good brandy, your companion will soon cease to doubt your tale.

Given time, so will you.

All I Really Need To Know I Learned By Having My Arms Ripped Off By a Polar Bear

Andrew Barlow

For me, wisdom came not at the top of the graduate-school mountain nor buried in the Sunday-school sandpile. For me, wisdom arrived during a visit to the home of our trusted friend the polar bear. Actually, I suppose "trusted friend" is something of a misnomer, because last year I had my arms brutally ripped from my torso by a fifteen-hundred-pound Norwegian polar bear. How and why this happened is an interesting story. For now, though, let's take a look at some fun lessons about our good friend *Ursus maritimus*, the polar bear. Here's what I learned:

—Share everything. You might be thinking, Really? Even with polar bears? Yes, share especially with polar bears. Actually, the word "share" does not exist in a polar bear's vocabulary, which consists of only about three hundred words. Give everything you have to a polar bear and do not expect him to share it. It did not occur to the polar bear who took my arms from me to share them in any way afterward.

—Polar bears are meticulous about personal cleanliness. A typical polar bear will feast for about twenty to thirty minutes, then leave to wash off in the ocean or an available pool of water. The polar bear who feasted on my arms did exactly this, leaving to scrub up in a nearby lake. Good hygiene is fundamental.

—In nearly all instances where a human has been attacked by a polar bear, the animal has been undernourished or was provoked. In my case, the bear was plump but deranged. Consequently, my attacker bear was spared the execution that typically follows an assault. My proposal—that my polar bear have his arms ripped off by a larger polar bear—was rejected by the authorities. No lesson here, I guess.

—The town of Churchill, Manitoba, is known as the "Polar Bear Capital of the World." According to legend, when a bear ambled into the Royal Canadian Legion hall in Churchill, in 1894, the club steward shouted, "You're not a member! Get out!," and the bear did. This story is almost certainly fictitious. During the first ten minutes that a polar bear was removing my arms from my body, I repeatedly shouted, "Stop!," "Get away from me!," and "Please—oh my God, this polar bear is going to rip my arms off!," but the animal was unfazed. The lesson in this is that you can't believe everything you hear.

—Beware of blame-shifting. The authorities speculated that the nasty scene may have begun when I grabbed onto the polar bear's fur. At first, I thought, Gee, maybe that's right—I must have done something to get him sore. But now I reject this suggestion. Why would I grab his fur?

—Things change. As a child, I used to delight in early-morning "polar-bear swims" at my summer camp. Now I don't even feel like swimming anymore, because I have no arms.

—Summing up: 1. Do not run from a polar bear. 2. Do not fight back. 3. Don't just stand there. Whatever you do, it will teach you a lesson.

—Never judge a book by its cover. Polar bears hate this.

—When a male polar bear and a human are face to face, there occurs a brief kind of magic: an intense, visceral connection between man and beast whose poignancy and import cannot be expressed in mere words. Then he rips your arms off.

My First Deer, and Welcome to It

Patrick F. McManus

For a first deer, there is no habitat so lush and fine as a hunter's memory. Three decades and more of observation have convinced me that a first deer not only lives on in the memory of a hunter but thrives there, increasing in points and pounds with each passing year until at last it reaches full maturity, which is to say, big enough to shade a team of Belgian draft horses in its shadow at high noon. It is a remarkable phenomenon and worthy of study.

Consider the case of my friend Retch Sweeney and his first deer. I was with him when he shot the deer, and though my first impression was that Retch had killed a large jackrabbit, closer examination revealed it to be a little spike buck. We were both only fourteen at the time and quivering with excitement over Retch's good fortune in getting his first deer. Still, there was no question in either of our minds that what he had bagged was a spike buck, one slightly larger than a bread box.

You can imagine my surprise when, scarcely a month later, I overheard Retch telling some friends that his first deer was a nice four-point buck. I mentioned to Retch afterwards that I was amazed at how fast his deer was growing. He said he was a little surprised himself but was pleased it was doing so well. He admitted that he had known all along that the deer was going to get bigger eventually although he hadn't expected it to happen so quickly. Staring off into the middle distance, a dreamy expression on his face, he told me, "You know, I wouldn't be surprised if someday my first deer becomes a world's-record trophy."

"I wouldn't either," I said. "In fact, I'd be willing to bet on it."

Not long ago, Retch and I were chatting with some of the boys down at Kelly's Bar & Grill and the talk turned to first deer. It was disgusting. I can stand maudlin sentimentality as well as the next fellow, but I have my limits. Some of those first deer had a mastery of escape routines that would have put Houdini to shame. Most of them were so smart there was some question in my mind as to whether the hunter had bagged a deer or a Rhodes Scholar. I wanted to ask them if they had tagged their buck or awarded it a Phi Beta Kappa key. And big! There wasn't a deer there who couldn't have cradled a baby grand piano in its rack. Finally it was Retch's turn, and between waves of nausea I wondered whether that little spike buck had developed enough over the years to meet this kind of competition. I needn't have wondered.

Retch's deer no longer walked in typical deer fashion; it "ghosted" about through the trees like an apparition. When it galloped, though, the sound was "like thunder rolling through the hills." And so help me, "fire flickered in its eyes." Its tracks "looked like they'd been excavated with a backhoe, they were that big." Smart? That deer could have taught field tactics at West Point. Retch's little spike buck had come a long way, baby.

At last Retch reached the climax of his story. "I don't expect you boys to believe this," he said, his voice hushed with reverence, "but when I dropped that deer, the mountain *trembled!"*

The boys all nodded, believing. Why, hadn't the mountain trembled for them too when they shot their first deer? Of course it had. All first deer are like that.

Except mine.

I banged the table for attention. "Now," I said, "I'm going to tell you about a *real* first deer, not a figment of my senility, not some fossilized hope of my gangling adolescence, but a *real* first deer."

Now I could tell from looking at their stunned faces that the boys were upset. There is nothing that angers the participants of a bull session more than someone who refuses to engage in the mutual exchange of illusions, someone who tells the simple truth, unstretched, unvarnished, unembellished, and whole.

"Even though it violates the code of the true sportsperson," I began, "I must confess that I still harbor unkind thoughts for my first deer. True to his form and unlike almost all other first deer, he has steadfastly refused to grow in either my memory or imagination; he simply stands there in original size and puny rack, peering over the lip of my consciousness, an insolent smirk decorating his pointy face. Here I offered that thankless creature escape from the anonymity of becoming someone else's second or seventh or seventeenth deer or, at the very least, from an old age presided over by coyotes. And how did he repay me? With humiliation!"

The boys at Kelly's shrank back in horror at this heresy. Retch Sweeney tried to slip away, but I riveted him to his chair with a maniacal laugh. His eyes pleaded with me. *"No, don't tell us!"* they said. *"Don't destroy the myth of the first deer!"* (which is a pretty long speech for a couple of beady, bloodshot eyes).

Unrelenting and with only an occasional pause for a bitter, sardonic cackle to escape my foam-flecked lips, I plunged on with the tale, stripping away layer after layer of myth until at last the truth about one man's first deer had been disrobed and lay before them in all its grim and naked majesty, shivering and covered with goose bumps.

I began by pointing out what I considered to be one of the great bureaucratic absurdities of all time: that a boy at age fourteen was allowed to purchase his first hunting license and deer tag but was prevented from obtaining a driver's license until he was sixteen. This was like telling a kid he could go swimming but to stay away from the water. Did the bureaucrats think that trophy mule deer came down from the hills in the evening to drink out of your garden hose? The predicament left you no recourse but to beg the adult hunters you knew to take you hunting with them on weekends. My problem was that all the adult hunters I knew bagged their deer in the first couple of weeks of the season, and from then on I had to furnish my own transportation. This meant that in order to get up to the top of the mountain where the trophy mule deer hung out, I had to start out at four in the morning if I wanted to be there by noon. I remember one time when I was steering around some big boulders in the road about three-quarters of the way up the Dawson Grade and a Jeep with two hunters in it came plowing up behind me. I pulled over so they could pass. The hunters grinned at me as they went by. You'd think they'd never before seen anyone pedaling a bike twenty miles up the side of a mountain to go deer hunting.

I had rigged up my bike especially for deer hunting. There were straps to hold my rifle snugly across the handlebars, and saddlebags draped over the back fender to carry my gear. The back fender had been reinforced to support a sturdy platform, my reason for this being that I didn't believe the original fender was stout enough to support a buck when I got one. My one oversight was failing to put a guard over the top of the bike chain, in which I had to worry constantly about getting my tongue caught. Deer hunting on a bike was no picnic.

A mile farther on and a couple of hours later I came to where the fellows in the Jeep were busy setting up camp with some other hunters. Apparently, someone told a fantastic joke just as I went pumping by because they all collapsed in a fit of laughter and were doubled over and rolling on the ground and pounding trees with their fists. They seemed like a bunch of lunatics to me, and I hoped they didn't plan on hunting in the same area I was headed for. I couldn't wait to see their faces when I came coasting easily back down the mountain with a trophy buck draped over the back of my bike.

One of the main problems with biking your way out to hunt deer was that, if you left at four in the morning, by the time you got to the hunting place there were only a couple of hours of daylight left in which to do your hunting. Then you had to spend some time resting, at least until the pounding of your heart eased up enough not to frighten the deer.

As luck would have it, just as I was unstrapping my rifle from the handlebars, a buck mule deer came dancing out of the brush not twenty yards away from me. Now right then I should have known he was up to no good. He had doubtless been lying on a ledge and watching me for hours as I pumped my way up the mountain. He had probably even snickered to himself as he plotted ways to embarrass me.

All the time I was easing the rifle loose from the handlebars, digging a shell out of my pocket, and thumbing it into the rifle, the deer danced and clowned and cut up all around me, smirking the whole while. The instant I jacked the shell into the chamber, however, he stepped behind a tree. I darted to one side, rifle at the ready. He moved to the other side of the tree and stuck his head out just enough so I could see him feigning a yawn. As I moved up close to the tree, he did a rapid tiptoe to another tree. I heard him snort with laughter. For a whole hour he toyed with me in this manner, enjoying himself immensely. Then I fooled him, or at least so I thought at the time. I turned and started walking in a dejected manner back toward my bike, still watching his hiding place out of the corner of my eye. He stuck his head out to see what I was up to. I stepped behind a small bush and knelt as if to tie my shoe. Then, swiftly I turned, drew a bead on his head, and fired. Down he went.

I was still congratulating myself on a fine shot when I rushed up to his crumpled form. Strangely, I could not detect a bullet hole in his head, but one of his antlers was chipped and I figured the slug had struck there with sufficient force to do him in. "No matter," I said to myself, "I have at last got my first deer," and I pictured in my mind the joyous welcome I would receive when I came home hauling in a hundred or so pounds of venison. Then I discovered my knife had fallen out of its sheath during my frantic pursuit of the deer. Instant anguish! The question that nagged my waking moments for years afterwards was: Did the deer know that I had dropped my knife? Had I only interpreted it correctly, the answer to that question was written all over the buck's face—he was still wearing that stupid smirk.

"Well," I told myself, "what I'll do is just load him on my bike, haul him down to the lunatic hunters' camp, and borrow a knife from them to dress him out with." I thought this plan particularly good in that it would offer me the opportunity to give those smart alecks a few tips on deer hunting.

Loading the buck on the bike was much more of a problem than I had expected. When I draped him crosswise over the platform on the rear fender, his head and front quarters dragged on one side and his rear quarters on the other. Several times as I lifted and pulled and hauled, I thought I heard a giggle, but when I looked around nobody was there. It was during one of these pauses that a brilliant idea occurred to me. With herculean effort, I managed to arrange the deer so that he was sitting astraddle of the platform, his four legs splayed out forward and his head drooping down. I lashed his front feet to the handlebars, one on each side. Then I slid up onto the seat ahead of him, draped his head over my right shoulder, and pushed off.

I must admit that riding a bike with a deer on behind was a good deal more difficult than I had anticipated. Even though I pressed down on the brake for all I was worth, our wobbling descent was much faster than I would have liked. The road was narrow, twisting, and filled with ruts and large rocks, with breathtaking drop-offs on the outer edge. When we came hurtling around a sharp, high bend above the hunters' camp, I glanced down. Even from that distance I could see their eyes pop and their jaws sag as they caught sight of us.

What worried me most was the hill that led down to the camp. As we arrived at the crest of it, my heart, liver, and kidneys all jumped in unison. The hill was much steeper than I had remembered. It was at that point that the buck gave a loud, startled snort.

My first deer had either just regained consciousness or been shocked out of his pretense of death at the sight of the plummeting grade before us. We both tried to leap free of the bike, but he was tied on and I was locked in the embrace of his front legs.

When we shot past the hunters' camp, I was too occupied at the moment to get a good look at their faces. I heard afterwards that a game warden found them several hours later, frozen in various postures and still staring at the road in front of their camp. The report was probably exaggerated, however, game wardens being little better than hunters at sticking to the simple truth.

I probably would have been able to get the bike stopped sooner and with fewer injuries to myself if I had had enough sense to tie down the deer's hind legs. As it was, he started flailing wildly about with them and somehow managed to get his hooves on the pedals. By the time we reached the bottom of the mountain he not only had the hang of pedaling but was showing considerable talent for it. He also seemed to be enjoying himself immensely. We zoomed up and down over the rolling foothills and into the bottomlands, with the deer pedaling wildly and me shouting and cursing and trying to wrest control of the bike from him. At last he piled us up in the middle of a farmer's pumpkin patch. He tore himself loose from the bike and bounded into the woods, all the while making obscene gestures at me with his tail. I threw the rifle to my shoulder and got off one quick shot. It might have hit him too, if the bike hadn't been still strapped to the rifle.

"Now that," I said to the boys at Kelly's, "is how to tell about a first deer—a straightforward factual report unadorned by a lot of lies and sentimentality."

Unrepentant, they muttered angrily. To soothe their injured feelings, I told them about my second deer. It was so big it could cradle a baby grand piano in its rack and shade a team of Belgian draft horses in its shadow at high noon. Honest! I wouldn't lie about a thing like that.

If seasoned swabbies can be called "old salts," there should be special words for well-seasoned big game guides like Fred Webb. Others have said if you are in a jam in a remote Canadian setting, a Fred Webb is the type of person you want to see on the horizon. If you are jammed up, however, in a less remote reading room, a Fred Webb is the type of person you want to enjoy on the page, and his editors let his unique voice roar through.

The Whiskey Expert

Fred Webb

We meet a lot of interesting people in the hunting business. One of them we remember as the "Whiskey Expert from California."

Most hunters that I know appreciate the occasional toddy. Certainly, a drink around the campfire at the end of a pleasant day afield adds to the enjoyment and camaraderie, for which many of us journey to the far places. However, in hunting camps, where safety is a prime consideration, the use of spirits must of necessity be governed by some rules. When one is a couple of hundred miles out in the Barren Lands, in case of an accident dialing 911 is definitely *not* an option. Perhaps in this regard I have a reputation for being a bit "hard assed," but will live with that image, rather than go down in history as the Genial Drunk who let the idiots kill themselves.

Having been a student of human nature as it applies to hunting camps, for a good many years, I have also noticed that the guest who plies the guides with booze, so as to be entertained by the antics of the simple rustics or the colorful natives, is usually the first to complain when things go amok. They are quite outraged when some fun-loving soul fires a couple of shots through the tent, or fails to show up at the crack of dawn, bright-eyed and bushy-tailed. We therefore have a few simple rules regarding social intercourse between guests and staff when booze is involved.

As with all rules, of course, there are bound to be some people who insist on stretching them. Such was the gentleman from California, who professed to be the world's foremost authority on whiskey, bourbon whiskey in particular. A guest at one of our Arctic caribou camps, he arrived with a very pleasant group of people, and along with everyone else had received a copy of the camp information, including our policy on giving liquor to the staff.

In this particular camp, all of the guides are Inuit from the Central Arctic. They are excellent guides, combining the skills of a people who live on the land, with years of experience in our employ guiding southern guests on trophy-hunting expeditions. Like guides everywhere, myself included, they do enjoy a drink, and indeed a beer ration is supplied when space on the aircraft allows. Beyond that, all understand that the "hard stuff" is off limits until we are clear of the camps. Like people of any culture, however, they are susceptible to persuasion.

We were only into the hunt a couple of days when it became apparent to myself and Dan, the camp taxidermist, that the Whiskey Expert not only left his booze lying around prominently, but didn't appear to believe in our camp policy of not treating the help. Dan had already quietly advised him that we would be happier if he didn't insist upon taking his guide into the tent before supper every evening to "treat" him.

Evidently being a Whiskey Expert, to the point that he said he could identify fifty brands, by taste alone, blindfolded, he assumed that everyone else had his practice in handling it. He was also, I suspected, one of the type who would work the guide to death, bribe him with booze, and leave him with no gratuities beyond the empty bottle and a hangover.

Needless to say, I was not too happy with the situation, but thinking that perhaps a friendly chat would remedy the matter, I attempted to keep a happy face on things. One should, I suppose, give the guest the benefit of the doubt, before calling in an airplane to get rid of him. I tried to convince him that the guides were all family men, they needed the job and their end of the season bonus, and thus if any rewards were in order, a cash tip at the end of the trip would do them more good than a smash of bourbon before supper. All to no avail.

One must realize here that the guide involved was one of my best employees, a good friend, one who ordinarily was no problem whatever. Now he was sort of stuck in the middle. To the best of his ability, he was trying to please the guest, while at the same time not letting me down. Though technically stretching the camp rules, he was responsible enough to have just one, say, "Thanks, I'll see you in the morning" and let it go at that. He certainly didn't want to get himself in a mess, let us down and lose his season's bonus.

Dan the Taxidermist was probably even more upset about the situation than I was. As a special friend of the guide, he felt that the Whiskey Expert was taking advantage of him, attempting to bribe him with booze to increase an already outstanding effort.

Finally came the last day of the hunt. Everyone had been successful in taking great caribou trophies, and were now out fishing and taking photographs. After the boat crews are all away from the beach, one of the duties of the taxidermist is to shut off the oil stoves in the guest cabins and sweep them out. In the middle of cleaning, Dan came up to the cook shack and when he left took a water glass with him, a fact which puzzled the cook enough to ask me what he was up to. I promptly forgot all about it, with plenty on my mind getting the next day's airplane charters organized by radio.

By late in the afternoon all the parties were back in, everyone happy as clams at high tide. It had been an extremely successful week; many of the trophies taken would make the record books. Up at the taxidermist shack, as they all gathered around taking pictures of the caribou racks and comparing scores, I noticed the Whiskey Expert, with his usual glass of amber liquid in hand. I also noticed that Dan and the guides were throwing glances his way as they worked at padding the racks for shipping out the next day. One of the guests remarked, "Boys, it has been a wonderful trip, but I am glad we are heading out of here. It was really chilly out there today. Winter is on the way."

"Yup," says the Whiskey Expert, "I came in chilled right to the bone, but after a couple of damn good belts of this bourbon, I'm starting to thaw out pretty good."

For some reason, the guides drop what they are doing and sneak around behind the shack, where I find them doubled up with laughter. "Come on down to the cook shack," Dan blurts out, "I've got to tell you something, and I want the cook to hear. She will appreciate it."

Mystified, we gather in the kitchen. "OK Dan," I demanded, "what in hell is going on?"

"Well," he said, "you know how many times I told that old bastard to keep the booze to himself?"

"Yes, and so did I."

"Well, last night I asked him once again very politely if he would just simply take that jug of whiskey off the table and put it under his sleeping bag, where it wouldn't be tempting any of us."

"Yes," I said, "and I asked him to do the same thing, but I guess he isn't the kind who will listen."

"Well, sir, this morning," says Dan, "I took that water glass down to his cabin."

"Jesus, Dan, drinking the guests' booze is something I have never known you to do."

"No, no," says Dan, "I didn't drink a drop of it. I simply poured out a whole water glass, took it outside and poured it down that squirrel hole behind the tent."

"Weren't you afraid he would miss it was gone from the bottle?"

"Hell no," he says, "I just pissed the glass clear full and poured it back into the bottle, so it was right back up at the same level."

The cook and I can't believe what we are hearing.

"Yep," he goes on, "when the guide came in I told him about it, so he turned down the supper drink this time. Now I guess we've got a couple of things settled. The guides will be damn leery about accepting drinks from now on, and we know that that old son of a bitch isn't such a great Whiskey Expert after all."

"The Whiskey Expert," from *Home From the Hill* by Fred Webb, copyright © 1997 by Fred Webb. Used by permission of Safari Press. www.safaripress.com

Native Queen, "a celebration of the hunting and fishing life" is an unexpected self-published pleasure from a newspaperman in Tennessee. Buy his book and slowly savor stories that have resonance in all areas of a life spent outdoors. You will read "Bill" and "First Pinch" to your best friends.

The Fish Dog

Mike Sawyers

My fish dog is a combination of springer spaniel and Hungarian sheepdog, as hairy a canine conglomeration as has ever gone afield.

Being one-half bird dog and one-half work dog, he is neither good at hunting nor tending the flocks. Discovering this, I was content to let him remain curled up in a corner of the room where I couldn't tell his head from his tail.

During that period, his only contributions to my fishing trips were a few locks from his long coat, which had a beautiful breathing action when tied into a streamer fly.

His name, Wolf, is derived from the fact that his face resembles a werewolf straight out of the Saturday night horror show, and not because he shares the characteristics of his canine cousins.

Occasionally, I would take Wolf along on a rabbit hunt. His uncontrollable enthusiasm actually worked to my advantage. If I could guess which was his next burst of speed would take him, I could position myself properly and let him drive the cottontails my way. It was a sort of rabbit-dog-hunter checker game.

I'll admit that I had wondered if his sheepdog ancestry might give him the desirable ability to herd brown trout. But remembering that trout have heels at which he could nip, I gave up on the idea.

Sheer accident was the way I discovered Wolf's affinity for trout. One warm spring morning I had arisen early and sipped a cup of coffee in the yard as I watched the sun perch on the horizon. "An ideal morning for a little fishing," I happened to think aloud.

Wolf broke into a howl, the likes of which were usually reserved for the Irish setter bitch across the street. He obviously wanted to go along. But for what? His involvement in my fishing trips so far, not counting his hair for flies, had been in licking the tails of the trout I'd bring home.

I relented. "Sure, Wolfer. You can go," I said, whereupon he sprung onto the hood of the car.

Creature of fishing habit that I am, I drove to a nearby stream that is my bent to flail. The river is a jungle of overgrowth and steep-sided banks. Occasional stretches of water are unencumbered with the thick overstory and allow room for a short backcast. It is in these areas that the brown trout will feed in the mornings and evenings. During the day they remain incarcerated in their jails of roots, branches and undercuts.

I had turned Wolf loose in the nearby fields to chase butterflies and otherwise stay out of my way. I was sitting on the bank looking for rises or other indications of trout activity. Should I encounter such omens, I fully intended to beguile the offending fish with a beautiful size 16 blue dun which I would drop a foot or two above the trout's nose.

At last. As I watched a yellow warbler flit among the branches of a willow, it came. Slurp!

I swung my head in time to see the rings of disturbance riding the surface rapidly downstream.

Slurp!

This time on the other side of the hole.

Slurp! Slurp!

Instantaneously, I recalled the hundreds of facts that a fly fisherman must in his piscatorial computer when he moves into an ideal situation such as this. Fish the tail of the pool first. Wade softly. Cast smoothly. Don't spook the fish with the leader. Make sure the fly will float high.

The browns would be mine.

Directly behind me was an opening in the brush, obviously placed there by fate to allow my backcast. I stripped enough line from my reel so that my 10-foot leader would turn over properly. Everything was in tune, functioning perfectly. Measure the distance. The first cast counts. Now... this time.

I followed through with precision, and the fly dropped just short of a willow leaf and rode the water as would a natural insect which had fallen from the streamside vegetation.

I could see the brown trout on the river bottom. As the fly alighted, I thought I detected a nervous twitch in the fish's left pectoral fin. The fly floated on.

There. I was sure of it now. The brown flipped its tail and moved back a little to the left so as to be in better line of attack when the fly reached its position.

Slowly, the fish began to ascend, a look in its eye that I've seen in the orbs of truck drivers as they peruse the menu on the wall of the diner.

Cheeseburger—$1.95. Large French fries—90 cents. "Here it comes, brown trout," I thought. "Cheeseburger, fries and a big malt. Put a rush on that order, Henry."

As the fish reached mid-depth, the speed of its ascent increased. Then, silhouetted against the azure May sky, an unidentified flying object appeared. True to a man intent on the matter at hand, I paid little attention. The depth perception out of the corner of my eye is not great and the vision could have been a mosquito hovering near my hat brim or a Boeing 747 soaring at 30,000 feet.

Actually, it was a flying rag mop. It was Wolf.

His momentum must have been significant because he sailed off the five-foot high bank with the greatest of ease. His appearance coincided directly with the submergence of the trout. The brown was so close to taking the fly that, as it arched its back to descend, it scraped the point of the hook and left a small cycloid scale impaled there.

Sploosh!

Wolf has landed.

The temperature outside is 61 degrees and the time is 8:37 a.m. We hope you had a pleasant trip. Thank you for flying Wolf Air.

Wolf surfaced a few feet downstream from where he had entered. Helped by the current, the dog paddled my way. I remember thinking that if he were a spitz he should probably have been named Mark.

"Why are you just standing there?" every splash of his paws seemed to ask. "I flushed this big trout and I thought you would be catching it."

Using his floating ears as outriggers, he maneuvered onto shore. After mutual greetings, I noticed a bad sign.

The first symptom is a little twitch of the tip of Wolf's tail. By the time you see that, however, it is too late to take shelter. The quivers become convulsions as they travel toward his head.

The cold spray from Wolf's shower of river water sobered me that morning. And, although I didn't remonstrate with Wolf, I didn't have the craving to sneak up on any more fishing holes either.

I've taken Wolf on other fishing trips since then. But we have an understanding now. When he doesn't go, he knows that he'll have a fish tail or two to lick at day's end.

When he does go, I know that I'm fishing just for the fun of it.

Jackrabbit Fishing

Mike Sawyers

My big break in the field of outdoor writing came when I got the chance to interview Jim Dowden, the famed—nay, infamous—jackrabbit fisherman of Bozeman, Montana.

Anybody who has tried to break into the big three of the outdoor writing industry (in outdoor writers' jargon that refers to *Outdoor Life, Sports Afield* and *Field & Stream*) can tell you that they are tough nuts to crack. Even the editors of those magazines will tell you the same thing by way of a form-letter rejection slip. It is really simple arithmetic.

There are three magazines that buy, say, for the sake of discussion, 1,000 articles each year. There are, say, for the sake of discussion, 4,186,745 outdoor writers. When you divide 1,000 by 4,186,745 you get… well, it is a very small number.

Editors tell new writers that if they will come up with unusual stories, the kind that will make the busy reader pause long enough to buy the magazine, they may eventually see their words and their names in print.

That was my chance. My wife always told me I was unusual. First, I tried a manuscript about using pasta balls to catch carp imported from Italy. That went over like a can full of worms at a fly fishermen's dinner.

Next, I sent a manuscript that dealt with the effect of the solunar tables on fishermen's wives. Apparently, based upon the number of rejection slips I acquired, that item was as popular as sand in a spinning reel.

I was as disillusioned as a guy who finds a misspelling in the dictionary.

Finally, I met Jim Dowden. I had been running article ideas through my brain long enough to recognize a winner when I stumbled on it. Dowden's career as a jackrabbit fisherman had not garnered a lot of press when I met him in a dimly-lit roadhouse in Montana's Bitterroot Valley in the winter of '69. He was shooting nine-ball and quaffing a mixture of distilled liquids that would probably have burned in a camp lantern.

After beating me five straight games he looked up, just before he was ready to break, and said, "You ever fish for jackrabbits, Bud?"

Well, of course, the answer was "no." I was given and accepted a libated invitation to meet Dowden the next morning at a sagebrush flat crossroads where he would take me fishing for the huge bush bunnies.

When morning arrived, Dowden opened the trunk of his battered '55 Chevy and pulled out sections of a fly rod that, when put together, made up one of the longest and strongest whoosh-sticks I have ever seen. To the butt of the rod he attached what could be described more accurately as a winch than as a fly reel. On the reel was a length of reinforced fly line that ended in a wire leader.

Just one look at the assembled monstrosity and the viewer could easily see how Dowden had developed his massive upper body. A day of jackrabbit fishing with such a contraption was easily more of a workout than a day in the weight room at Fatoff, Inc.

I followed Dowden through the sagebrush. I was more intent upon watching and learning than in doing any actual jackrabbit fishing myself. I was content to put all my efforts into taking notes and snapping photographs of the encounter than in making the catch.

We hadn't been out for five minutes when Dowden stopped and cocked his left ear upwind. Something unheard by me had come to the attention of the crafty wielder of the desert fly rod.

"Listen," he said. "There's one feeding off to the left."

I listened but only to the silence of the desert; a silence that is sometimes so complete that it is deafening.

But Dowden was insistent. "Naw, he's up there," he remarked at my inability to hear the critter. "Sounds like he's working on some spring grass."

Dowden pulled a box from his jacket and began groping through the contents. I was certain, from his actions, that he knew what he sought but it took him some time to find it.

"There it is," he shouted in a whisper, pulling a long, green, yarn-like whisp of a thing from what was obviously a fly box. "I haven't used this since I took a 12-pounder down in the sage flats near Vernal."

Dowden reached for his tippet and deftly removed the orange carrot fly he had planned to use. On went the fake grass fly and he began to false cast.

There was a slight breeze blowing toward him and it took the larruper of lagomorphs quite an effort to finally get enough line out. But then it was done and with a final thrust he used a double-haul and banged 35 yards of fly line through the Montana morning.

The green grass fly paused in the air and dropped to the sagebrush as softly as the closing of a baby's eyelids. There the fly hung. No action. Then Dowden pointed the rod tip directly at the fly and with smooth wrist action imparted a little side-to-side action to the grass fly. "Simulates the wind," he whispered from the side of his mouth, never taking his stare from the area of the fly.

Then, without so much as a "getting a bite," Dowden pulled back on the rod. The reel began to sing as a fully-grown white-tailed jackrabbit streaked through the sagebrush. Occasionally the rabbit's rear quarters would show as the critter bounded into momentary view. My motor driven camera was clicking profusely.

To shorten what is becoming a long story, let me tell you that Dowden landed that rabbit as he had countless others, letting the bunny play itself out to the point of exhaustion.

It was a simple maneuver to remove the barbless hook from the jack's lip and shake the bunny a little until it revived and bounded on its merry way. Of course, Dowden occasionally keeps a rabbit for the pan but in the last few years has leaned more and more to the catch and release theory.

"There's just not enough jacks in some areas to go around anymore," he said.

The day afield had been one of my most memorable. Although I wasn't able to score with the big three of outdoor magazines, the trip allowed me to be published in a new market, Jackrabbit Fisherman's Annual, a publication that has since gone out of business and put all of its back issues through the shredder.

Rainbow Trout Obituary

Mike Sawyers

3-Pound Rainbow

SMOKE HOLE, W. VA – 3-pound rainbow trout, age 3, of Low-Water Bridge Hole, succumbed Saturday after mistaking a metal spinner for real food.

Born in January of 1994 at the Reed Creek Hatchery in Pendleton County, Mrs. Rainbow was the daughter of the late Mr. and Mrs. Brood Trout.

Surviving are thousands of siblings in such waters as Lost River, Thorn Creek, Seneca Creek and the North Fork of the South Branch of the Potomac.

Mrs. Rainbow was best known for her ability to capture and ingest sculpin from between rocks at the bottom of the river.

A memorial photograph of Mrs. Rainbow will be placed on the wall of the angler who caught her.

The State of West Virginia will honor Mrs. Rainbow with a Trophy Fish Citation including art work by Duane Raver.

There are few outdoorsmen of good humor that can tickle a sportsman's funny bone from the stage and on the page but twin brothers, Gene and Barry Wensel, are double trouble on all fronts. Their humor is infectious, relaxed and wide-ranging. Of course, they are master whitetail bow hunters and their how-to books and tapes are best sellers. But let these "Rambling Rednecks" start telling you what happened on the way to the deer stand on their tape Camp Fire Memories, *for safety sake, you'll have to pull over to the side of the road*

Excerpts from

"...And the Horse You Rode in On!!!"

Gene and Barry Wensel

I went to school in Indiana, where fox squirrels are pretty common. During my freshman year, a fox squirrel I eventually named Harvey discovered that by climbing a certain tree, he could jump to the window sill of the dormitory where I lived. Whenever he found the window open with no one home, he'd come on in and scrounge around my junk food supply. Not only did Harvey eat some good stuff, but he made a real mess in doing so. The last stone was cast when he got into a big box of cookies Mom sent from home. I made plans to teach him a lesson he'd never forget.

Laying a trail of peanuts from the window shelf up to my desk, I set up a box trap held up by a pencil with a string on it. I got in my closet and waited. A half hour or so passed, when here came Harvey, the fattest squirrel in Indiana. When he worked his way under the box, I jerked the string and nailed him. Harvey got pretty irate over the whole thing. But if he thought he was upset then, all he needed to do was wait a few minutes. I borrowed a pair of electric hair clippers from a guy down the hall. Using a leather glove, I pinned down ol' Harvey and went to work with the shearers. I shaved the whole rear half of his body, including his tail. We're talking stark naked. Ol' Harvey looked like a rat with his pants off when I finally let him go. I left the front half of his body unshaven. I'd see him around campus on occasion, but he usually kept his distance and for sure stayed clear of my room.

All this happened in early September. Along about November I was sitting in class one day when I happened to look out the window to see good ol' Harvey sitting on a limb close by. Right away I noticed something went wrong. Mother Nature must have compensated wrong or something. The front half of his body was really bushy, with the longest hair I've ever seen on a squirrel, while the back half had not much more than a five o'clock shadow. Lucky for Harvey, we had an easy winter. I made a pair of pants for the old boy, but he never stopped by to pick them up.

Riding trail, or at least getting several horses in single file, makes for some interesting observations. All horses love to pass gas at their colleague following right behind. They've also mastered the sport of dumping a load WHILE they're walking. I mean they don't even miss a step most of the time. Some horses stop, but most experienced mountain horses don't even get out of step. Try it sometime and you'll see for yourself that it's no easy trick. Very impressive.

I have to admit that Wile E. Coyote and the Roadrunner has always been one of my favorite cartoons. I question my faithfulness because I want to someday see that coyote catch and eat that little commie. Then again, last year I shot a chicken stealing coyote and when I walked up to his carcass, I couldn't help but mutter a low "meep-meep" under my breath.

Dinner With Pete

Jim Enger

When I first got to know the Boardman River I had another, secret, name for it. My private name for it was the "Compromise River."

I called it that because the Boardman ultimately empties into Grand Traverse Bay, an arm of Lake Michigan, right in downtown Traverse City, a sophisticated northern Michigan resort town known for—among other things—its shopping. Once upon a time, when I had to be concerned about such things, I could drop the lady in my life in town with the cash and scoot a few miles out of town for some fishing. So everybody was happy, more or less. Though sometimes I would get, "But I thought we were going to spend our vacation *together!*" Never mind that there are 168 hours in a week and I was going to hog a mere 6 of them for myself. Besides, I would tell her, when you're having lunch on the terrace at the Bean Pot, look down at the river and remember that the water you're seeing flowed right around my waders a little earlier. It's sort of like being together.

That's how I came to secretly call the Boardman the "Compromise River." You can bet that I had dozens of no-compromise rivers all over the state, but trout streams being what they are, you don't usually find them flowing through the basements of designer-label boutiques. The Boardman is a real Christian river in that regard and I was thrilled to discover its benefits. I even thought about presenting a marketing proposal to the Chamber of Commerce—"SHE SHOPS/YOU FISH!"—but had second thoughts when I realized the idea was self-defeating in the long term. True, the local merchants might have been grateful. But I couldn't imagine a trout fisherman on every bend of the river for one thing. For another, I'd know that they were stooping to my level of sickness—paying (literally) for a few stolen moments. It wasn't a club I wanted to start.

The Boardman really does flow right through downtown Traverse City and actually gets a limited salmon and steelhead run. The salmon are captured at a permanent harvesting station and stripped of their eggs, practically in the shadow of Milliken's Department Store. At certain times of the year you'll see mom and dad and the kids with their noses pressed against the viewing windows of the egg-stripping station, Gucci shopping bags overflowing. I swear I once saw a guy cooling his credit cards in one of the raceways.

The steelhead are passed by the weir, and one of the hot spots is the park behind the main post office, although there's not much cover there and the fish are real spooky. (If you're fly fishing on the boardwalk on the post office side, you must roll cast. Otherwise your backcast will hit the building.) But I once saw a kid not more than seven or eight years old hook what appeared to be about an eight-pounder on a Snoopy rod. His buddies dropped their rods, with their lines still in the river, and ran shrieking up and down the bank following the action. The kid's line was soon tangled in the others and a rod shot off the bank as the startled fish made a lengthy run. After two or three minutes the fish threw the hook and the kid retrieved a tangled mess of monofilament and the other Snoopy rod. His buddies offered high-fives while shouting "awesome, awesome!" And to think, some of us started out on sunfish.

I've caught steelhead off the sandbar at the mouth of the river right behind the Holiday Inn, once in a suit and tie. In an earlier life I used to get to Grand Traverse City on business and once—having been through a serious nonfishing spell—I pulled into the parking lot of the Holiday Inn, popped the trunk, pulled on my waders, and grabbed my rod. Two minutes later I was waist-deep in Traverse Bay, and about five lucky minutes after that I was fast to a small steelhead that had mistaken my Mepps spinner for a cocktail-hour hors d'oeuvre. I presented the trout to the chef at the Holiday Inn, who promised me his best effort. (Yes, there were guests who seemed skittish at the appearance of a man in waders walking through the lobby and dining room with a largish, still-wet fish.) I checked in at the front desk, and not long after that I was at the bar in the cocktail lounge, contemplating a wonderful dinner and thinking kind thoughts about a firm that would send one of its employees to Traverse City, Michigan. The bartender said—as he set my martini down—"I just heard that some jerk walked through the restaurant in waders."

South of Traverse City the river flows through the lovely Boardman valley, finding its way through mixed pine and hardwoods, and then through meadow land. Here it's a trout stream and a pretty good one if you know its secrets. Over the years it had become a favorite, and my buddy Pete and I fished it often. We liked it as an occasional alternative to the Au Sable and other rivers that could get crazy with canoes on holiday weekends. We stayed at a strange place called Ranch Rudolph—in the summer a combination mid-western dude ranch, campground, sometimes fishing camp, and in the winter a roaring snowmobile enclave. The river runs through the grounds and I especially like the isolated, narrow meadow stretch just below the ranch. Now there is a privately owned horse operation on one side of the river where over-grazing has turned that once-pretty little meadow into a hellish mess.

But there are miles of good water. From above the ranch to Brown Bridge Pond it's mostly woodsy. Just upstream from where the river enters Brown Bridge Pond (really a small lake) Pete once caught an enormous brown trout during the Hex hatch. But the river has deep holes there and you have to know what you're doing. Especially at night. Below Brown Bridge Pond and downstream from Garfield Road, there's a lot of meadow water where grasshopper patterns can be deadly during the late summer months. Bob Summers, the famous bamboo rod maker, lives and works on this stretch.

Early one Saturday, just before first light, Pete parked the car on a turnoff in the woods above the ranch. We had pulled an all-nighter, leaving Detroit at the bewitching hour. Pete drove; I kept the coffee coming.

For those of you who have done this, you'll know that there are intermittent lapses throughout the night that are potentially fatal when the driver and the navigator have them simultaneously. For those of you who haven't, you might remember all-nighters for high school or college exams. You'll recall drifting off, and then waking with a start. But safely at your desk. It's another thing to wake up on the wrong side of the road in the deadly glare of oncoming highbeams and the desperate roar of an eighteen-wheeler's horn. This in the cause of the supposedly gentle sport. (The adrenaline rush is about the same as your first Atlantic salmon on a dry fly.)

We rigged up in the dim pale of the trunklight. I was uncertain what to start with and finally settled on a slender streamer, a Black-Nosed Dace. I couldn't see what Pete was tying on, but I knew it would be something wet. We spoke in whispers, as though not wanting to wake the red squirrels, or the tiny chickadees, or the big black bear surely sleeping just behind yonder bush.

The plan was to fish downstream, leapfrogging each other, and end up at the ranch precisely at cocktail hour late that afternoon. There we would corral someone from the ranch to drive us back to the car, something they were always glad to do.

We got in near a giant old white pine that leaned precariously across the river. Many of its branches were rusty brown, a sure sign that the tree was nearing the end of its long life. These old warrior white pines still exist here and there, memorials left over from Michigan's incredible post-Civil War logging boom. There has been a lot written about the early logging industry in Michigan, but in his wonderful little book *Waiting for the Morning Train*, Bruce Catton, the noted Civil War historian, wrote about growing up in Michigan and visiting some of the camps as a young man. Catton puts the Michigan logging industry in perspective, writing that enough pine boards were produced in Michigan by 1897 to build ten million six-room houses. That's one hundred and sixty billion feet of lumber, according to Catton. Michigan was literally awash in big timber. The preferred tree was the white pine. There were millions of them, they grew tall and straight, and they floated high in the shallow rivers of Michigan, making them the easiest to drive to the mills. By the early 1900s what had been one of the densest stands of pine east of the Mississippi River had been mostly leveled. Michigan had been transformed from a land of deep forest to a land of scrub.

The root mass of this big pine was pulling away from the bank and its tentacles were alive with ants, spiders, and other small critters. But it was very shallow there and no trout would hold under that potential smorgasbord, at least not with daylight coming on. So I stuck with my Dace and waded downstream, working out line and getting my arm loosened up. Minnows scattered and I felt pretty good about the fly. There was a nice little morning breeze and the sun was just beginning to break through the forest. Shafts of light did pirouettes on the river's surface. I watched Pete slide quietly into a pool of diamonds just downstream.

My first trout came to the Dace from a small pool below a snarl of tag alder. It was a brown, not large—as none of the fish in this stretch would be. It was a beautifully colored trout and I held it up and whistled. Downstream Pete smiled and gave me a thumbs-up.

I was very pleased, as I always am, with my first trout of the day. Sure, there is the satisfaction of knowing that—at least momentarily—you've got the right fly. Moreover, it's also knowing that things are right with the world, at least in my little corner of it. After that first trout, especially if it has any size to it, my anxiety level drops tremendously. Suddenly I'm hearing birds, aware of water noises, smelling the smells of the forest, and actually realizing that I have a cigar in my mouth and am tasting it.

I released the fish and watched it scoot back into the pool. I climbed out and walked the bank down to Pete. I had the thermos in the back of my vest,

"That was the icebreaker," Pete said. "What was it?"

I told him. "You want some coffee?"

Pete was warming to his task. He was working a small logjam. Cast, strip, strip, strip, cast, strip, strip, strip—and so on—until something or nothing happens. We have fished together for years and he is an intense fisherman for the first couple of hours. But not competitive. (He once caught three, twenty-five-pound steelhead on the same day on a visit to a British Columbia river, which I learned about practically by accident months later.) We glory in each other's successes, large and small.

"What I'd really like is a beer," he said. "I feel like I've been up all night."

"Well, we have been except for one little indiscretion."

"That could have been a serious whoops," he said. And then, a little pointedly, "Why don't you sit the hell down or move back. You're casting a shadow on my pool here." Subtlety is another of his attributes.

I did, in fact, find a very comfortable spot on the bank where, after unslinging my vest, I poured some coffee, relit the cigar, and enjoyed the beginnings of a beautiful day. I watched Pete work the little jam. His fly landed next to a log and there was a wonderful boil and he was fast to a fish. The trout zipped out into the current, changed its mind, and charged back toward the jam. Pete led it carefully away from the logs and minutes later had it in hand, a twin of the brown I had caught earlier.

He admired it for a moment or two and slipped it back in the water. It darted back under the logjam.

I asked Pete what he was using. He held it up as he waded to the bank. He was smiling. A Royal Coachman streamer.

"Now I'll have some coffee. But I'd rather have a beer. You got any more of those cigars?"

"This is the last one."

"Right."

He reached toward my mouth and I swatted his hand away. Then he was going through my vest.

"That's what I thought!" he said, unwrapping the dark A.C. Grenadier. "Two packs! And here's the lighter."

It was warming rapidly and I took off my jacket and stuffed it in the cargo pocket in my vest, noting that a package of cigars had disappeared.

"You're welcome," I said.

"Thank you," he replied, grinning like a lotto winner.

"Need anything else while I'm at it?"

"I think I'm fine for now," he said, blowing a puff of smoke. "Unless there's a beer in there." I shook my head.

"Then maybe you'd walk back to the car for the cooler?"

I flicked my still-lit cigar butt at his waders. He was laughing as he jumped out of the way. So was I. It was going to be a great day.

We fished downstream, doing exactly what we had planned, with a lot of jazz going back and forth about who was getting the better water. There were intermittent requests for cold beer. We each picked up a couple more trout nearly identical to the others, one a little larger, pushing thirteen inches. As the day wore on we began to see some bugs and finally some rising fish. Just above the ranch I saw what appeared to be a decent fish working below a riffle, but tight against the bank. So I camped on the spot and added some tippet material to my leader. The bugs were sparse and I couldn't tell what they were, so—what else when on the Boardman?—I tied on a small Adams, a fly that generations of anglers have used with success almost everywhere trout are found. The Adams was born on this very river in the 1920s, developed by local angler/tyer Len Halladay, who named it after an angling friend from Ohio. Little did he suspect back then that it would one day be famous on trout waters the world over.

I wasn't sure it would actually match what was hatching, but that of course is the beauty of the Adams. Besides, I wanted to fish with the fly on its home water.

At that moment Pete came by on the bank. "I see you have the juicier water again," he said.

"This little nothing of a riffle? I stopped here just so you could have that good pool right around the corner."

"I'm touched. But I don't suppose that fish over there that's sucking down flies every ten seconds had anything to do with it?"

"Is there something rising over there?" I said, shading my eyes. Like a machine, the fish rose again.

"If that's a five-inch brook trout *I'll* go get the beer," he said. "By the way, these cigars are very good."

"I'm glad you're enjoying them," I said. "I suppose you're going to stand there and watch?"

"Of course. I want to see you blow this one."

But it was too easy. A freshman at the Orvis school could have caught this trout. The fly landed a couple of feet upstream from the fish, rode a line of slick water, tumbled onto the eddy at the bottom, and was neatly snatched.

The trout bolted downstream and it was clear that this was a better fish. The river was shallow and the fish scampered everywhere, the light tippet slicing the water.

"There's still time to screw it up." This came from up on the bank.

Gradually the fish tired and I heard Pete slip into the river behind me. He was at my shoulder as I worked it in. It was another brown, a nice one, a couple of inches past the twelve-inch marker when laid against my rod. The small Adams was snug in the corner of its mouth. I faced the trout upstream, letting the oxygen-rich riffle water pour through its gills. A minute later it shot away, leaving a long wake.

Pete stuck out his hand, a big smile on his face. "Nice fish, pal."

I was appropriately modest.

I then went way down, leaving Pete a series of good pools, all on tight bends with deeply undercut banks. I was ready to call it a day, particularly after that trout. But I continued to fish as I moved along and took a mixed bag of browns and brookies, mostly in the ten-inch class, all of them on the now scruffy-looking Adams. Finally, I came to the ranch, its long, broad lawn running down to the river's edge. I climbed out, propped my rod against a handy birch, slipped out of my vest and stretched. It had been a long but satisfying day.

I walked up to the lobby of the main building and inquired about a room. The kid behind the desk grinned when he saw me standing there in still-wet waders. I got the room key and went into the rustic bar, where I felt a lot less sillier, and bought a few cans of cold beer. "How'd you do?" the bartender asked.

Back down by the river, I sat on the bank, popped a beer open, and relaxed. It felt good to get the wader suspenders off the shoulders.

Presently Pete came around the bend upstream, reeled in, and lit the afterburner when he saw what I had. I never saw a guy in waders go that fast in the water. I handed him a cold one and he drained it. "That was the best beer I've ever tasted," he said with a belch.

We freshened up in the room, retrieved the car, and headed for the bar. Over cocktails, we discussed the day. Pete had also taken several more fish on dry flies, and a nice one to boot. He'd seduced them with Bivisibles, or so he said, a fly I've never fished and probably never will. But he likes the damned thing. ("It has class. Class and it works," he claims. Class? It's a brown and white fuzz ball.) At any rate, we both agreed that the Boardman had given us a good day, good at least for that stretch of it. Streamers in the morning, some satisfying dry-fly fishing in the afternoon. No outsized fish, but we didn't expect any. Just some classic fly fishing.

We were pooped and hungry and left the bar and found a table. The restaurant was nearly full. Most were out-of-state-tourist types—"fudgies," as they're called. They had that look. (There are nearly as many fudge shops in northern Michigan as there are pine trees.) There was a group on the patio clustered around a big, half-barrel barbecue. Whatever was getting scorched smelled pretty damned good.

A chipper little waitress came over and handed us menus. I drained what remained of the martini I had carried over from the bar and ordered another one.

I didn't have to look at the menu. I knew that a dude ranch—even a Midwestern version—would have a stockpile of steak in the kitchen. A couple of different kinds, as it turned out, and I ordered the biggest cut. So did Pete. Our waitress leveled with us and said the kitchen was a little backed up so it might be awhile, but she could bring our salads. I said fine and she looked at Pete. His eyes were closed.

"Sir?" she said.

Pete jerked awake.

"She wants to know if you want your salad now?" I said.

"Yeah, sure." His eyes fluttered. I said I was going to go out on the patio for a few minutes—I'd watch for the salad delivery. The waitress said fine; Pete mumbled something.

The group around the grill turned out to be a congress of adult Boy Scout leaders. There was much talk of merit badge training and so forth. My martini was the focus of so much lip-smacking attention I thought the glass was going to melt. I stood near a corner of the patio and watched a guy fish one of the ranch ponds stocked with rainbow trout that you can see but not catch. I have fished for them with grasshopper patterns (the grounds are alive with them at times) all the way down to Tricos on 7X. If the ranch ever becomes famous, it will be for a strain of rainbow trout that do not eat.

Turning, and peering through the window, I could see Pete, chin on his chest, eyes closed.

A guy sidled up to me and said quietly, "If I slip you ten bucks would you get me a double one of those—pointing at my drink—and take it around to the front of the building?"

I said sure, but there was the bar just ten feet away through the open door. I was curious—why didn't he just hop in there and get his own?

"Because some of the organizers of this little shindig are from Baptist churches, and they have a real thing about certain types of refreshment. I've got a flask stashed in my tent for a quiet little nightcap later. These guys are okay, but a Saturday night cookout without a see-through is un-American."

I was glad to do my good deed for the day, and as I maneuvered through the dining room I discovered that salads had been delivered to our table. Pete was sleeping, sitting up with his arms crossed on his chest.

I carried that big wet silver bullet through the lobby, thrilled to be part of a clandestine operation. It added a little extra excitement to an already outstanding day. Out front I found my panting scoutmaster.

"You get the Citizenship merit badge!" he exclaimed as we introduced ourselves.

"I already got it thirty years ago."

"Good for you. Then I'll put you in for an Oak Leaf Cluster or something," he said between sips. "And here, take these." He handed me a film canister. Inside were half a dozen of the prettiest Hendricksons I had ever seen. "I saw you get out of the river. I've been staring at these all day. I was hoping to get in some fishing myself. I tied 'em," he said modestly.

I thanked him, wished him luck, and back in the dining room gave Pete a shake. There was barely a response and I could tell that the lad was about done for. But I thought he wanted to eat, so I gave him another shake. This time his head came up and he looked at me through half-closed eyes. "Pete, there's your salad," I said.

"Rest my eyes for a minute," he mumbled. In an instant he was breathing deeply, his chin in his chest once again. I went to work on my salad, while I examined in more detail the fortuitously acquired Hendricksons, which now sat perkily on the tabletop. Our thirsty scoutmaster was, indeed, a lovely tyer.

The waitress came by with a basket of bread and gave Pete the eye. She looked at me with raised eyebrows. I smiled, my mouth full of salad. "Your steaks will be out in a minute," she said. "Should I bring his?" I nodded affirmatively.

Minutes later she was back. The entrées were truly beautiful, big and sizzling and just what the doctor ordered. I gave Pete a couple of good shakes—"Pete! Pete!"—and got no response except for a gentle snore.

I assaulted my steak, eating too fast, but luxuriating in every mouthful. I eyed Pete's, wondering.

And then suddenly, with a big sigh, Pete leaned forward, crossed his arms on the table around his plate, and rested the side of his face directly on that big, perfectly grilled porterhouse. A sixteen-ounce, medium-rare pillow. I kept eating, but with less enthusiasm because I could see that my chances for a double portion had diminished.

The waitress rushed over, horrified, "It's okay," I said. "He likes to sleep with his head on meat."

"Is he okay!?"

He was fine, I assured her. He was snoring steadily and attracting the attention of other diners, who were smiling and pointing, doubtless having never seen a man sleeping on his supper.

I helped myself to his side order of onion rings.

The snoring got a little louder and his exhalations were having an eroding effect on his vegetable selection. At regular intervals peas skipped off his plate and across the table. I thought about him possibly inhaling a couple and wondered if *that* would wake him. A little girl came by and stood and stared. People in the farther corners would stand and stretch for a look, smile or laugh, and sit back down.

I finished eating and thought about various ways of raising Pete's head to get at that steak—I'd slip the bread under there—but thought better as I recalled watching him smear himself with bug repellent a couple of times during the day. I couldn't imagine that Deep Woods Off would improve a steak. The mother came and collected the little girl, but not before giving my fishing partner a good looking-over.

I ordered cognac, two of them, in case Pete came around. But he didn't, so I was forced to drink his.

Finally, I started to get a little tuckered. I signed the check, left a tip, and after many minutes of prodding was able to partially rouse the sleeping beauty. In a daze he put an arm over my shoulder and I guided him out of the dining room—to a smattering of applause—and ultimately to our room, where he collapsed onto his bed. I removed his shoes, and that's all I remembered until the next morning.

I wakened to hear water running in the bathroom. Pete came out, pointed to his face, and asked, "How did I get these crosshatch marks on my cheek?"

Sex and the Single Retriever

Some Labs Have a One-Track Mind

Bruce Cochran

My first Lab was 95 pounds of hard-charging, ill-tempered retriever madness. His favorite pastime was retrieving everything that fell within his field of vision. His second favorite pastime was having sex with anything smaller than a Volkswagen. Throw in eating, sleeping, peeing on everything, and growling at anyone who approached me and you have a good idea of Splash's personality.

Splash took his job as a meat dog seriously. His freshman year began when he was only eight months and by mid-season he was everything I wanted in a working retriever.

I often hunted alone in those days, if you are ever truly alone when you're with a Lab. Toward the end of the season Splash and I had a memorable hunt at a nearby reservoir. In early morning darkness I rowed across a small cove, put out a couple dozen mallard decoys and snuggled down in my boat on a weedy point to await legal shooting time. It was one of those rare mornings when things went right and I bagged a limit of ducks within an hour.

As I was preparing to leave a lone white front cruised over the decoys. I scrambled for my shotgun, dropped the big bird and Splash bounced out of the boat and flawlessly completed his first goose retrieve. Soon we were on our way back across the cove.

I had a lot to carry when we reached shore: blind bag, thermos, a limit of ducks, shotgun, parka, boat cushion. So I gave the goose to Splash to carry in his mouth and started walking up the muddy road to my truck.

As I neared the halfway point I realized Splash was not beside me. Had he dropped the goose and wandered off to inspect something more interesting? Or worse, had he started eating it? The mental image of a hundred pound dog holding my delicious specklebelly down with his paws and ripping chunks of feathers and flesh from my dinner flashed through my mind. I turned to look and quickly breathed a sigh of relief. Then I began to laugh. Splash had dropped the goose but he definitely wasn't eating it. My poor, abused specklebelly lay in the mud with Splash hunched over it, that dreamy look in his eyes, pursuing his second most favorite pastime.

Babe, my second Lab, was the most faithful of all. She went everywhere I went, which eventually led to a problem.

My wife and I and our kids were camping on our farm one evening. We had spent the afternoon fishing and swimming in the creek, throwing sticks in the water for a wet and happy Labrador. As the evening cooled I built a fire and grilled hamburgers, then we sat around the fire telling stories. After putting the kids to bed I poured my wife and I a drink and we relaxed as the last of the embers died away. Babe curled up under one end of the camper trailer near my feet and began to snore softly.

We talked a while and as the conversation progressed each of us revealed an interesting fact about ourselves—neither of us had ever made love in a car.

A big romantic moon was shining down through the trees, the kids were asleep and the huge back seat of our four-door station wagon beckoned seductively. My wife and I tippy-toed to the station wagon and proceeded to rectify this terrible omission in our personal histories.

At the exact moment when one *never* wants to be interrupted I felt the cold, wet nose of a Labrador in a place where one *never* wants to feel it. You guessed it, faithful old Babe, waking up and realizing I wasn't beside her, had tracked me down.

I let out a surprised whoop. Reflex action took over and I jerked upward, smashing the rear dome light with my balding head. Blood streamed down my forehead. The station wagon lurched and groaned on its springs. Babe barked, and of course the kids woke up and started asking all sorts of embarrassing questions. My wife started giggling hysterically as I wiped the blood from my face with a T-shirt.

They say there is no such thing as bad sex—only good sex and better sex. They're wrong.

My next Lab, Maxine, was every bit as serious about retrieving as Splash. And even though she'd been spayed she was evidently still pretty sexy. At least Jake, my partner Bob's yellow male Lab thought so.

Jake was a blond version of Splash, without the mean streak. Everything in Jake's world fell into one of four categories: something to eat, to retrieve, to pee on or to have sex with. Occasionally some unfortunate object fell into all four categories.

One morning, Bob and I were hunting in separate blinds several hundred yards apart. A small group of mallards appeared, gave each of us a few out-of-range circles, and then pitched into my decoys. I dropped a big greenhead just outside the blocks but he landed head-up and I couldn't get off a killing shot before he disappeared into the smartweed. I released Maxine and she rocketed out of the blind. As she swam toward the area where the bird had fallen, I jumped in and waded through the shallow water hoping to spot the duck and finish him off. But Maxine disappeared ahead of me into the woods and before I had cleared the decoy spread she reappeared with the live drake in her jaws, prancing proudly through the shallow water with that look-what-I-can-do swagger that a good dog gets when she's doing what she was born to do.

Then Bob's booming voice shattered the morning stillness: "Darn it, Jake! No!"

I turned and saw a blond blur splashing across the flooded field, bouncing over muskrat houses and hummocks of smartweed. Jake had reached the breaking point while watching the action from afar. His hormones had kicked in, and he had decided to join the fun. Bob's whistle blasted continuously with no effect.

I wanted Maxine to bring me the duck so I could dispatch it, but she was no amateur and she knew where ducks belong. She charged straight for the blind, the greenhead looking around nervously from her jaws. Bob's whistling, bellowing and swearing grew louder, but Jake continued to close the gap. He caught Maxine 10 yards from the blind and mounted her in one gigantic, splashing leap.

The next few minutes would have made wonderful footage for *America's Funniest Hunting Videos*. Maxine, undaunted by a hundred pounds of sex-crazed blond bomber on her back, plodded resolutely toward the blind with the drake still clamped in her jaws. She reached the ramp leading up to the dog hole and entered the blind, scraping Jake off in the process. Jake, always the master of rapid recovery regained his composure and entered the blind behind her, intent on completing the job at hand. The old blind shook violently. Loose nails popped out and fell into the water. Aging boards creaked and split.

The situation deteriorated as rapidly as the blind. The mallard seized this opportunity to escape and wriggled free, squirting out the dog hole into the water and disappearing beneath the blind. I had long ago placed a concrete block outside the blind door as a step for getting in and out. In my hurry to wade around the blind and chase the drake that was swimming away, I tripped over the block and fell face-first into the water. I came up spitting mud and smartweed, but I finished off the greenhead with a desperation shot before he disappeared behind a muskrat house.

At the sound of the shot, Maxine, who had never been known for steadiness, leapt from the blind looking for something—anything—to retrieve. Jake was right behind her, intent on continuing his unwanted advance. By this time Bob had showed up, out of breath from wading several hundred yards while yelling and blowing his whistle. He clamped a lead on the big blond Romeo and we both stood in the water, panting and laughing.

"You read about this stuff all the time in the newspaper," I said, taking the drake from Maxine. "But I never thought my dog would experience it firsthand."

Bob looked confused. "Experience what first hand?" he asked.

"You know," I said. "Sexual harassment in the work place."

"If we get close enough to the water before we get stuck, we can hunt out of the jeep!"

The Old Man and the Boy Revisited

With apologies to Robert Ruark

Bruce Cochran

It was one of those days when the bobolinks balanced on the bending grasses in the breeze and the Baltimore Orioles scattered notes
around like millionaires throwing coins. I was sitting on Miss Lottie's
big front porch listening to rap music and reading a software manual
when I saw the Old Man come driving down the white oyster shell
street and I knew I was in for one of his famous lectures. He had
cashed in some of his mutual fund shares several months ago and
traded The Liz for a $46,000 SUV. It had a CD player, a thermometer,
a sun roof, four wheel drive, and a built in global positioning system
to keep him from getting lost (and to allow Miss Lottie to keep track
of him). Your ob't sv't had hoped he'd be reluctant to take this chariot
into his more back woodsy haunts for fear of scratching the clear coat
paint job and he'd quit bugging me about hunting and fishing, but so
far that hadn't come to pass.

His big ears stuck out from under his old wool cap and his tobacco
stained mustache drooped over the stem of his pipe. He had just gotten off work from his job as a greeter at Wal-Mart and his little blue
vest with the name tag peeked out from under his old mackinaw. He
ambled up onto the porch and sat down beside me, then he stabbed me
with his pipe stem and his eyes and said, "If you can take that
dodlimbed radio out of your ear without snagging you ear ring and dis-
figuring yourself I've got a suggestion for you."

I ignored him. If I could study a software manual and listen to
Korn at the same time I could add the Old Man's voice into the mix
with no ill effects.

"Not your cup of tea, huh?," he said, sucking on the stem of his pipe. "Okay. How about if I whistle up Frank and Sandy and we see if we can find that covey of quail down by the pea field?" Frank was a blue-ticked Llewellyn and Sandy was a big lemon and white English setter.

I rolled my eyes back in my head like the condescending little smartass I had become. "You must've forgot," I said. "When the big German-owned pig operation moved in they turned the pea field into a series of plastic-lined lagoons full of pig poop. Can't you smell it?"

"Danged if I can't," said Himself, sniffing the air. "How could I dis-remember something as rank as that?"

I turned back to my reading and tried to find where I'd left off. I had just installed a new program that would allow me to do all my homework in thirty seconds, which would mean I could spend more time hanging out at Big Woods Mall. The courts had decreed that, by way of mitigation, the corporation that built the mall had to name it after all the trees they destroyed when they built it. What could be fairer than that? In my opinion it was the best thing that had ever happened to Wrightsville Sound. It had several totally bitchin' computer stores where you could buy all sorts of games. Some of them only cost thirty or forty dollars. It had four video arcades that were way cool, an eighty-five screen movie complex, five nail salons where lots of hot babes hung out, ten movie rental stores, eleven restaurants, and six micro-breweries. It was a most fascinating spot to be young in.

The Old Man wouldn't let me off the hook. "Well," he said, "we could always get Jackie and go see if we can shoot twenty or thirty squirrels." Jackie was a little dirty-yellow fice dog who fairly lived to hunt squirrels.

"You must be off your medication again, Old Timer," I said. "They cut down all the trees when they built the mall. Besides, I don't want to get too attached to Jackie or Frank or Sandy or any of the other dogs till we're sure which ones you're going to have to get rid of. You know the city has an ordinance against owning more than two dogs, and counting the hounds, Belle and Blue, I think you've got about fifteen or twenty."

The Old Man took a lot of time lighting a big red-headed match and shielding it from the breeze as he cupped his hand around his pipe and relit it. I stood up, opened the door and went inside. The Old Man started to follow but I closed the door real quick-like.

"Oh no you don't," I said. "I may have to listen to your homespun philosophy but I don't have to breathe your second hand smoke. What're you trying to do? Give me lung cancer? Stay outside with that foul smelling thing."

"Oh, all right, dagnabbit!" he said. "I'll just scrape it out and stick it in my pocket. Hand me that Barlow knife I gave you for Christmas."

"Can't," I said. "It kept setting off the metal detector at school so I had to get rid of it."

The old man followed me into the parlor. A big fire was going in the stove. It was one of those big old square wood burners that lit up rosy when she really got to jumping. He liked to enjoy the stove as much as possible because he said the EPA would probably pass a law any day now that would make him a criminal just for burning fossil fuels. He sprawled in a rocker in front of the fire, his feet spread whopper-jawed out toward the flames, and took a little drink of his nerve tonic in deference to his years.

"You know how Grandma feels about you drinking in the house," I said.

"It's a sad day when a man can't have a dodlimbed drink in his own home," said the Old Man. "Thank the Good Lord we ain't sunk *that* low yet!" He took another pull on the jar of clear liquid. "And besides," he said, "Miss Lottie won't be home from her NOW meeting for another couple of hours. Then she'll just barely have time to nuke our TV dinners before she takes off for the big PETA shindig over at the Senior Citizen's Center."

As autumn turned to winter, week after week went by with skies the color of putty and a North wind that bored holes in you. Christmas came and went, with plastic trees and electric lights and thousands of shoppers. Big Woods Mall became so crowded I could hardly walk from the computer store to the video arcade without getting trampled.

As spring came on I began to notice some changes in the Old Man. He didn't get on my case about playing computer games or watching TV or chatting with my cybergeek buds on the internet all the time. I could hang out at the mall all day on Saturdays if I wanted without him trying to drag me off to help build a duck blind of fix up the old boat. I had earned some money programming VCRs for old people and he didn't even dis me when I spent it all on a new joy stick instead of a shotgun or a fishing rod. You might think this would be a welcome relief to me, and it was. But in a way it worried me, too. The Old Man seemed happy, but he seemed tired all the time. He still spent some time on the cedar bench with his friends, or hung out in the pilot office or the pool room, but mostly he seemed to spend more time with Grandma. Of course he couldn't sit around the big stove in Jimmy's store like he used to because a huge new supermarket now stood in its place.

I bitched about him rambling on and on about the outdoors all the time but I did love the old dude and I knew that, what with him being so much older than me and all, the day would come when the Old Man would no longer be around. I don't mind telling you I dreaded that day more than I like to admit, even to myself.

I began to notice something different about Grandma, too. For years she had been so cranky that I guess I had gotten used to it. But lately she had begun to hum softly to herself as she popped dinner into the microwave. She even quit bugging me about my tattoos and my shaved head. Now she usually had a big smile on her face. I began to put two and two together and figured she was just trying to put on a cheerful show because something bad was wrong with the Old Man for sure.

Then one Saturday morning it all came together for me. I was just heading out the door for a day at the mall. The Old Man was sitting in the porch swing whittling a duck decoy out of a block of cork that had washed up on shore at Wrightsville Beach. A fruit jar of his nerve medicine sat on the floor beside him. Frank, Sandy, Jackie, Blue and several newcomers I didn't recognize were asleep on the plank floor around the swing.

"You, Boy!" he hollered. "Come here. I got a favor to ask if it ain't too much trouble." I picked my way through the dogs, trying not to step on any or kick over his fruit jar, and stood before him on the porch. I could hear a mocking bird singing in the big magnolia tree.

Like most old people the Old Man took a lot of prescription medication. He was never one to worry about his health and he wasn't as careful as he should have been about following the doc's orders. He would sometimes let a prescription lapse, but lately he had been more careful about one in particular, which worried me even more.

"I called in a prescription to the drug store for a refill," he said. "Long as you're going that way how about picking it up for me on your way home?"

He sucked on the stem of his pipe and took a sip from the fruit jar.

"You *are* coming back before evening, aren't you? I'm plumb out of this stuff and I don't like to go too long without it."

I spent a normal Saturday at Big Woods Mall, hanging with my friends, playing video games and watching the babes come and go at the nail salon. We went to two movies and ate a lot of junk food, but mostly we just hung out and annoyed people.

Toward late afternoon I decided I'd better get home and see what Miss Lottie had planned for supper. If she was feeling real frisky she would nuke us each one of those frozen meals in a little plastic tray. When I was younger I used to like to take the trays out of their cardboard boxes and cut a slit in the plastic covering. It was about the only legal way a boy could use a knife. Or, if she was worn out from watching people argue on TV all afternoon, she would just order us a pizza.

Luckily I remembered to stop by the drug store and pick up the Old Man's medicine. I say "luckily" because that's how I figured out what was going on with him. And let me tell you, I was relieved. I took one look at the label on that pill bottle and knew I didn't have to worry about the Old Man anymore. Funny how one little word can wipe away all your fears. Especially if that word is on a medicine label and it's spelled V-I-A-G-R-A.

Pheasant Dogs I Have Known and, uh, Tolerated

Bruce Cochran

Pointers, setters, Labs, Brittanies, German shorthairs, Shepnell Crosses (that's what you get when you cross Old Shep with Old Nell), you name them, and I've hunted over them. Or tried to when I could find them and see them.

A friend's big German shorthair stands out in my mind to this day, even though I hunted over him only a few times and that was years ago. I don't even remember his name because I never heard his owner call him by it. He was always just "You blankety blank blank-a." You get the picture.

So I'll just call him "Rambo." He was the undisputed leader of the pack, the Alpha dog. This was always the first topic of discussion among the dogs when they hit the ground and began their sniffing and strutting ritual. Any disagreements were settled quickly, often right on the tailgate of Rambo's owner's pickup.

Rambo was a good pheasant dog… if you didn't plan on eating your pheasants or having them mounted. He thought of pheasants as a feathered doggy treat complete with a few mouthfuls of meat; his reward for pointing and retrieving the birds.

And then there was "Rocket." You've heard that dogs often look like their owners? Not this dog. Rocket was a big, lanky, liver-and-white female pointer. Her owner was a short, fat guy (with no liver spots that I could see). According to her owner, Rocket was a great pheasant dog. I had to take his word for it. I never saw Rocket after he released her from her crate. At least I never saw her up close. We did occasionally catch a glimpse of her bounding across a stubble field a half-mile away; putting clouds of pheasants in the air while her owner swore and blew his whistle.

I often wondered why he didn't lose weight chasing her through CRP fields, leaping creeks and climbing over deadfalls in pursuit of his aptly named track star.

Three labs ago I owned a black female named "Babe." Her bloodlines were suspect from the start, and her conformation wasn't exactly what you'd want. She was, well, funny looking. But she had a nose that would put the wariest whitetail buck to shame. She put this God-given trait to good use, too. After the hunt was over. She always knew when we were headed back to the truck, and no matter how tired she was, she would break into a full gallop ahead of us, reaching the truck long before we did.

You wouldn't think a 70-pound dog could eat 120-pounds of donuts, cinnamon rolls, cookies and sandwiches in the few minutes it took us to catch up with her, but I've seen it done. We would usually arrive at the truck to find her sitting on the tailgate, burping and trying to look innocent, Ding Dong wrappers strewn about and white icing stuck to her whiskers.

I once hunted on a game preserve with the most ancient German shorthair I've ever seen. His name was Old Bob. Not just Bob. Old Bob. I don't know how old he was, but I wouldn't be surprised if he was a pup when our grandfathers were shooting paper shells in Damascus barreled side-by-sides. The pheasants were pen-raised, and the cover in the small fields was light, so Old Bob's job was easy. He would roam casually a few yards ahead of us, swinging his old, gray muzzle from side to side sniffing the shifting air currents. When he located a bird, there was no fancy point and no energetic flushing. He would simply lie down beside the bird. I know this isn't considered good form, but it got the job done and conserved Old Bob's energy so he could live to hunt again.

Of course, these dogs are no longer with us, having departed to wherever dogs go when their time on Earth has ended. But I like to think that Rambo has completed some sort of celestial conflict resolution course and is chomping on an endless supply of poultry instead of other dogs. Rocket is happily bounding around in that Big Corn Field in the Sky. Babe is, of course, fat and lazy, lounging in the back of a heavenly pick-up surrounded by an endless supply of Ding-Dongs, Ho Hos and donuts. And Old Bob? Well, Old Bob probably outlived them all. And somewhere he's lying in a soft grass field talking to his buddies, saying, "Hey, how many times did I tell you guys? You gotta take it easy!"

The Fishing Hall of Shame

Bruce Nash and Allan Zullo

Jorge Martínez
Sea of Cortez, Mexico, 1978

Given a choice between catching a fish and tossing his son overboard, Captain Jorge Martínez didn't hesitate for a second—he threw his boy into the drink!

During a 1978 trip to Mexico, Al McClane, fishing editor for *Field and Stream,* wanted to go after Pacific sailfish. So he hired Captain Martínez to take him out into the Sea of Cortez. Martínez's charter boat, *El Diablo,* was the archetypal single-engine wooden boat, which the captain steered from a forward station. The boat was so rickety, McClane accidentally stuck his thumb through the transom.

Nevertheless, it was a beautiful day and McClane enjoyed the company of Martínez and the captain's nine-year old son, Juan, who acted as the first mate. An industrious, obedient boy, Juan helped out by rigging the baits and serving lunch.

Unfortunately, by late in the afternoon there was not so much as a little tug on any of the lines. McClane was ready to give up when, to his joy, he finally got a strike. It was a feisty sailfish. Amazingly, while McClane was playing the fish, a second sailfish came up and took the bait from another line.

Captain Martínez tried to maneuver his boat without losing the two battling fish. But it was an impossible task. He had to do something—fast. After all, McClane was a world-renowned fisherman. Not wanting to lose the second sailfish, the captain grabbed his son, stuffed him into a canvas-covered cork vest, gave him one of the rods, and threw him overboard to keep the fish on the line.

"Your son! Your son!" cried a shocked McClane. "What about the sharks?"

"Oh, don't worry, señor," replied Captain Martínez. "These are the only fish we've had today, and I have more sons."

McClane, fearing for the safety of little Juan, clamped down on the drag and played the fish as fast as he could. Once McClane landed the first sailfish, the boat chugged toward the boy, who was found two and a half miles away bobbing along with the second sailfish. McClane then finished catching that fish—after first hauling in the waterlogged boy.

Excerpts from

Uncle Homer's Outdoor Chuckle Book

Homer Circle

A fisherman had been chunking big plugs for muskies all morning without so much as a follow. Disgusted, he decided to halt for lunch and pulled over under the shade of a mammoth sycamore tree.

As he munched a sandwich, he happened to glance at the root of the big tree, and was puzzled to see a hickory nut right at the water's edge. As he pondered what was a hickory nut doing beneath a sycamore tree, he saw a squirrel scramble down the tree and crawl up to the nut. At that moment a huge muskie shot from the water, seized the squirrel in its toothy jaws, and disappeared from sight. He hardly believed what he had just seen and wished he could have filmed it. Again, he wondered how that nut got there. At that moment he saw a big swirl close by the same root. Out of the swirl emerged the big, toothy head of the muskie and it gently put the hickory nut back on the root.

On one of our fishing trips Zern shared this keeper memory with me. He was fishing in the far north, his only companion an Athabaska Indian guide. They had been together for a week and although the Indian spoke very little English, by now they were fishing buddies, getting by on spare words, nods, smiles, and hand signals.

Suddenly, here it was, their last evening together, tomorrow was departure day. Now Zern knew, as all there must learn, you never give an Indian alcohol in any form. They appear to believe an opened bottle is meant to be emptied. But on this special occasion, Zern had poured two small paper cups with wine he had brought along for the occasion. Handing one to his new buddy, Zern smiled over his extended cup and said: "Salute!" The Indian smiled across his extended cup and said: "Sal-loot!"

Then, Zern noticed the Indian frowning and thinking, as if some words were struggling to get out. Zern kept smiling to encourage him, then, tilting his head, he hesitantly asked: "Where…you…from?" Zern grinned, extended his cup, took a sip, and replied in the same meter: "New…York…City." The Indian shook his head, blinking his eyes in thought as he observed Zern across the campfire's flickering illuminance…some words obviously forming in his mind. Zern smiled, and nodded his head in encouragement.

Raising his eyebrows in question, the Indian said slowly: "New…York…City? …hmnnn. What… big… town… that… near?"

The veteran duck hunter was in his blind before daybreak, everything in its place, waiting for daybreak to bring mallards to his neatly "J-hook" decoy arrangement.

At first light he could barely hear the hunter in the next blind humming…as he looked he could see light glint from an upended bottle. He couldn't believe anyone would violate the fundamental rule of no booze while hunting. Next he heard the man singing in falsetto, then came some loud snoring.

The sun rose very bright and he knew ducks would be scarce. After a couple blank hours, he saw one duck winging his way at least 60 yards high. He took a desperation shot but missed. As the lofty duck passed over the drinking hunter's blind, he saw him jump up, heard him snort, fire one shot, and down the duck came, stone dead. He couldn't help applaud the marksmanship, so he hollered: "Great shot, I've never seen a better one!" "Oh, I dunno" (hiccup) replied the other hunter, "I us-us-burp-usually get two 'er three outuva flo-flo-flock like that!"

News item in a small town newspaper: Lottie Primrose was granted a divorce from her husband, Zekie, champion tournament fisherman. She sued on grounds that he had spoken to her only three times in the past three years. She was granted custody of their three children.

New Ted Nugent Cologne Tested On 'Every Goddamn Animal We Could Find'

The Onion

ALPENA, MI—Ted Nugent held a press conference Monday to unveil his new signature fragrance "Heartland," which the veteran rocker touted as the most extensively tested cologne in history. "We tested that sumbitch on ferrets, weasels, deer, elk, squirrels, bison, trout, crickets, gibbons, iguanas, donkeys, capybaras, koalas, hyenas, penguins, woodpeckers—every goddamn animal we could find," Nugent said. "And, just to be extra-certain it was safe for consumer use, we injected it into a kitten's bloodstream, sprayed it on otters with open wounds that we inflicted, and forced cows to drink it through their nose. We also squirted it in a duck's eyes. Then we ran out of cologne and just started punching the duck." The cologne, now available in stores, features an ivory bottle stopper and comes in a genuine tiger-skin pouch.

—*February 12, 1998*

Milton Berle's Private Joke File

Milton Berle

Two men were out on the lake. Tucker wasn't getting bite one. Wilson was pulling them in every minute. Exasperated, Tucker said, "I can't understand it. My equipment is better than yours. I have better bait. I even spray mine with stuff guaranteed to get them to bite. Damn, I haven't had a bite yet."

Wilson said, "Tuck, it's playing hunches that does it."

"What kind of hunches?"

"It's like this—when I get up in the morning, if my wife is lying on her right side, I fish the right side of the boat. If she's on her left side, I fish the left side of the boat."

"What if she's on her back?"

"I don't go fishing!"

A group of duck hunters were trying to smoke out some mallards. They had no luck until one fat duck popped down out of the sky and started to hover three feet from the head of one of the hunters. Excited, the hunter shot away at the mallard and missed. Not a feather was ruffled. As if in disdain, the bird flew off. Afraid that the other hunters would make fun of the bad shooting, the hunter who'd missed called after the mallard, "And don't you ever come back again!"

"**A**ny luck shooting?"

"I shot fifteen ducks."

"Were they wild?"

"No, but the farmer who owned them was!"

Bubba Talks:
Of Life, Love, Sex, Whiskey, Politics, Foreigners, Teenagers, Movies, Food, Football and Other Matters That Occasionally Concern Human Beings

Dan Jenkins

Deer Hunting

Bubba enjoys going deer hunting once a year, but it's usually for the camaraderie because you hardly ever see a deer on Sidewall Thornton's lease.

Bubba knows one thing about it, though. Deer hunting is a little like the first time you sleep with a woman.

You've got your stalk, your chase, your excitement, you fire your shot—and then realize you've got a hell of a mess on your hands.

Dove Hunting

It is essential, Bubba says, that you and your friends go out and kill several hundred doves every year. This helps prevent the evil doves from taking over the entire western half of the United States.

But there is a right way and a wrong way to go dove hunting. The right way involves the following steps:

1. Store up enough whiskey and food for the weekend.
2. Make sure the bimbos can find the cabin.
3. When the bimbos find the cabin, tell the Mexicans to go kill the doves.

Treasury of Wit and Humor

Jacob M. Braude

Two ardent fishermen met on their vacation and began swapping stories about the different places they had fished, the kind of tackle used, the best bait, and finally about some of the fish they had caught.

One of them told of a vicious battle he once had with a 300-pound salmon. The other man listened attentively. He frankly admitted he had never caught anything quite that big. However, he told about the time his hook snagged a lantern from the depths of a lake. The lantern carried a tag proving it was lost back in 1912. But the strangest thing of all was the fact that it was a waterproof lantern and the light was still lit.

For a long time the first man said nothing. Then he took one long last draw on his cigarette before rubbing it out in the ash tray.

"I'll tell you what I'll do," he said slowly. "I'll take 200 pounds off my fish, if you'll put out the light in your lantern."

An Angler's Dictionary

Henry Beard and Roy McKie

Billfish   An informal term for any of the large salt-water game fishes, such as the sailfish and swordfish, whose upper jaws extend into sharp spears. They are called billfish because, following a day's outing in search of one of these magnificent creatures, the captain of a sport-fishing boat traditionally presents the angler who chartered her with an enormous bill in a short, but emotional dockside ceremony.

Flying Fish   *1.* Remarkable tropical fish capable of skimming over the waves for 100 feet or more on tiny winglike fins. *2.* Any undesirable fresh-water or salt-water fish, such as carp or scup, which, after being caught by an angler seeking more valuable fish, is propelled violently through the air with a brisk arm movement.

Grayling   Beautiful and very shy game fish, once quite common in the U.S. but now only found in Canada and Alaska. It's hard to generalize about this fish, but very broadly speaking, the best time to fish for grayling is an hour or two before you arrive at a stream or shortly after you leave. As far as lures go, almost any fly not in your fly book or vest is a pretty good bet, though you might have had some luck with the one that got hooked in your pocket. There's a good deal of debate about casting methods, but whether you let the fly drift by the fish so gently that it doesn't notice it or tweak it so it spooks it, the results are about equal. As for the likeliest places to find grayling, the best spot to be is on the other side of the river, 10 miles upstream, or back at that pool you passed 3 hours ago.

Kapok   *1.* Silky fibers used as stuffing in boat cushions. *2.* Promising backfiring sound made by outboard motor after 30 pulls of the starting cord. *See* MUMMICHOG.

Tuna   There are a number of varieties of this tasty game fish, but from the sport fisherman's viewpoint, the most important is the giant bluefin, examples of which have been known to exceed 1,000 pounds. It's hard to imagine a fish of that size, but perhaps a few comparisons will help: a half-ton bluefin would be equal to 2,345 sandwiches, 880 gallons of tuna-noodle casserole (standard recipe), or a bowl of tuna fish dip 28 feet in diameter and 7 feet deep!

1936. Ernest Hemingway catches a carp while trout fishing and decides not to write about it.

What it Takes To Be a Good Hunter

Lawrence Lariar

D r. Livingston started it all by saying: *"A man must have a stout heart to hunt. He should also have a good trigger finger, a good trigger, a gun, bullets, and at least one eye."*

(The italics are mine. So is the quotation. Dr. Livingston rarely spoke to anybody but gibbons and most of his gibbon talk is unprintable.)

Alexander the Great said: "ΠΓΔΦ ΣθΨΨ."

(This ancient quotation can best be appreciated by Greeks. A Greek friend of mine named George Popopuloropupopupuopulis claims the translation to be: *"One cup of coffee and apple pie."* George should know. He owns the Popopuloropupopupuopulis Coffee Pot down on Main Street.")

Youth

Ken Jacobsen

While deer hunting in Georgia, I came upon a young boy hiding behind a tree, looking up into the air. I must have startled him because he jumped straight up when I spoke to him. On the other side of the tree was a pile of squirrels. There must have been fifteen or twenty, maybe more.

I explained I wasn't the game warden and he didn't have anything to worry about. And it would be OK for his friend to come out. He said he was alone, but I figured that one boy couldn't have shot that many squirrels.

"Where's your gun?" I inquired.

"Got none," replied the boy.

Now, I knew for some reason the boy was lying.

"How did you kill them squirrels then, huh?"

"This here smooth rock," answered the boy.

Then all of a sudden we heard a rustle high up in the tree and the boy instinctively whipped off the rock, which struck the squirrel in the head. We walked over to pick up his stone dead squirrel.

"Well, I'll be. I never saw such a feat," I said. "You just must be the best left-hander I ever saw."

"Ain't left-handed," said the boy, a little indignant.

"Now son, you don't have to lie to me." (I thought he might be one of those habitual liars.) "I saw you throw that stone left-handed."

"Ain't left-handed!" the boy snapped back. "I'm right-handed."

It didn't make sense to me. I used to pitch when I was younger and knew a good thrower when I saw one.

"Well, if you're right-handed, how come you throw left-handed?"

"Papa made me throw left-handed," he said. "Throwing right-handed, I tore 'em up too bad."

Excerpts from

Wildlife of the New Millennium

Buck Peterson

GOOSE (giant)

ALIASES: Canadian honker, sky carp, tundra maggot (lesser)

SCIENTIFIC NAMES: *Branta Canadensis maxima*

PERSONAL STATISTICS: An average adult stuffed with a serious amount of goose doo will weigh up to thirteen pounds average (this same adult can drop up to one pound of doo a day). Stretched out, the goose will measure twenty-two to forty inches long.

WHERE TO VIEW: General distribution is over and on any golf course. The best place is in the movie *Fly Away Home* (1996), or in Canada, where their citizenship papers are valid. The worst place is in the above movie, or on your private membership golf course.

WHEN TO VIEW: At tee-off time.

WHAT TO LOOK FOR: Scat, everywhere. Like high-priced athletes, they just DOO it! Also on the sixth day of Christmas, when any self-respecting true love hands out six geese a-laying.

TIPS TO INCREASE LIKELIHOOD OF SEEING: Play golf.

TIPS TO DECREASE LIKELIOOD OF SEEING: Double up on the use of the pesticide diazinon.

OLD DIET: Plants high in protein, assorted grains, grasses, and aquatic vegetation.

NEW DIET: Any properly mowed and fertilized grass, especially Kentucky blue grass and other succulents found on the fairways and aprons of golf course greens.

OLD BEHAVIOR: Like cranes and ducks, geese don't have homing instincts and must be learned from adults. Imprinting, a technique developed by the Austrian ethnologist Konrad Lorenz in the 1930s, taught greylag geese to bond, sometimes with Konrad, a lot of times with the carpet in his study.

NEW BEHAVIOR: Canada geese used to mate for life in their second or third year. Urban geese will find another mate should their first lovebird fall out of the sky, and in the new century, may imitate the infidelities of the other bird brains in the park. They will also become active in petitioning golf course managers to initiate predator control programs for egg-sucking raccoons.

LIKELIHOOD OF SIGHTING IN NEW MELLENNIUM: Excellent.

LIKELIHOOD OF GOING ON A WILD GOOSE CHASE IN THE NEW MILLENNIUM: One hundred percent.

FUTURE: A giant subspecies, once thought to be extinct, was discovered near Rochester, Minnesota, and have so successfully recovered on a diet of golf-course grasses that they want to join the PGA as non-dues paying members. The "new" goose waddles on plastic cleated webbed feet; with its bad memory, it will put a great amount of effort into hatching range balls in the rough,

Attention Golfers! If your golf ball accidentally "lodges" in a Canadian Goose, you can, without penalty, place another ball near the place where the big dumb bird was when the "lodging" occurred.

CATCH-AND-RELEASE FISH

ALIAS: Rainbow trout.

SCIENTIFIC NAME: *Salmo giardneri*

PERSONAL STATISTICS: Will weigh up to forty pounds and be up to three feet long.

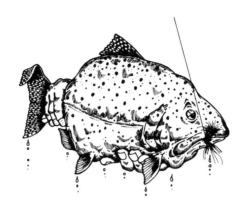

WHERE TO VIEW: General distribution is within a false cast of any Orvis shop or approved lodge, and urban males flyfishing through a midlife crisis. The best place is the Madison River, the South Platte River, the Yellowstone River and in Norman Maclean's *A River Runs Through It*. The worst place is Robert Redford's *A River Runs Through It* (1993), or anywhere else flyfishermen have their fly down.

WHEN TO VIEW: During the false hatch.

WHAT TO LOOK FOR: On shore, look for Land Rovers, barn jackets, wicker picnic baskets, Cabernet-Merlot wine blends, and warmed Brie and walnuts. On the fish, look for net burns.

TIPS TO INCREASE LIKELIHOOD OF SEEING: Fuss with your flies until it's dark.

OLD DIET: Insects, in all their forms.

NEW DIET: Artificial nymphs, dry and wet flies.

OLD BEHAVIOR: Native rainbows fight, look, and taste better than other trout. A wild rainbow outside the hallowed honey holes of the flyfishing elite is a marine marvel.

NEW BEHAVIOR: Codependent on the survival and growth of flyfishing. A plump cutthroat or brook trout in a Montana spring creek has been caught, kissed, and released so many times that fly fishermen should be sued for alienation of affection during off-season. Even trout fry tire of this seasonal exercise and at some point yearn only for a swim in garlic butter.

LIKELIHOOD OF SIGHTING IN THE NEW MILLENNIUM: Ninety-nine percent or less.

FUTURE: The catch-and-release rainbow trout in slow western waters are in trouble with a parasitic disease that causes young fish to spin in circles until they die. Early research indicates a link to the worms in waders priced over $100. Flyfishing elders spinning through assorted mid-life crises are befuddled on how to match this whirling hatch; a manager of a hatchery contaminated with the infection said, "Hey, at least they're more fun to catch!"

TOURNAMENT FISH

ALIASES: Lunker, hawg

SCIENTIFIC NAME: *Mictropterus salmoides*

PERSONAL STATISTICS: Adults without lead weights average two pounds. With lead weights, they tip the scales at five pounds. Both are around a minimum twelve inches in length.

WHERE TO VIEW: General distribution is wherever bass competitors lie in waiting. Or just lie. The best place is near any gear-banging group activity. The worst place is at the fish fry celebrating the winners at the end of the tournament.

WHEN TO VIEW: At the weigh-in, before the biggest are rolled in beer batter inside the judge's tent.

WHAT TO LOOK FOR: Beer in cans, beer in bottles, beer in barrels.

TIPS TO INCREASE LIKELIHOOD OF SEEING: Follow the beer trucks.

OLD DIET: Worms, insects, frogs.

NEW DIET: Plastic worms, insects, and frogs, crankbaits, spinnerbaits.

OLD BEHAVIOR: Getting everything bass-ackwards.

NEW BEHAVIOR: Getting everything back-asswards.

LIKELIHOOD OF SIGHTING IN THE NEW MILLENIUM: One hundred percent. The business of tournament fishing is booming.

FUTURE: Bass and the other tournament fish are subject to intense fishing pressure once a year, then the big money players move on to yet another fishery. During their brief life in the spotlight, tournament fish live quite well. Once a "keeper" is brought to the boat, it is gently unhooked and placed in an aerated water well which has been treated with a chemical formula that replaces lost slime, treats any kind of bacterial infections, and calms the fighting fish. The tranquilizer reduces the weigh-in jitters of the competitors, finned or otherwise. If a fish dies in transport, competitors place the deceased in their opponent's not-so-live well. Once the fish have been weighed and the snot squeezed out of them, state officials take the smaller ones (ones the judges don't want) for their annual department fish fry, because they know best how to fix them.

HATCHERY FISH

ALIASES: Chump salmon, fish-like fish, farm animals, swimming hot dogs, salt water guppies

SCIENTIFIC NAME: *Oncorhynchus doltus*

PERSONAL STATISTICS: The adults always weigh the same and are about the same length.

WHERE TO VIEW: General distribution is wherever the will to ignore the needs of wild fish is alive and well. The best place is in the Pacific Northwest. The worst place is in the Pacific Northwest.

WHEN TO VIEW: When they surface on a wild stream looking for their hatchery pellets, or when they are being trucked on their migration to the sea.

WHAT TO LOOK FOR: A puzzled look when they see natural foods on the bottom of a wild stream. A good sign of the presence of

hatchery fish is the cormorant. These scavengers prefer the easy pickings of concentrated fisheries.

TIPS TO INCREASE LIKELIHOOD OF SEEING: Move to the Pacific Northwest.

OLD DIET: Guppy Chow

NEW DIET: Second helpings of Guppy Chow.

OLD BEHAVIOR: Bred to be caught by sport and commercial fishermen so they do as they have been programmed. Either that or spawn too early.

NEW BEHAVIOR: Want to return to the hatchery where the fast food is to die for. Instead they bump into the fish ladders that are supposed to lift them past the damn turbines to bathe in the warm backwaters.

LIKELIHOOD OF SIGHTING IN THE NEW MILLENIUM: One hundred percent. The outrageous lack of cooperation and political will between the interested parties assure a continual supply.

FUTURE: Hatchery biologists continue to experiment with hybrids to meet recreation expectations, while trying to accommodate deterioration in habitat. Hatchery salmon are pre-programmed by hatchery habitat to live in the long concrete aqueducts that drain the Los Angeles basin.

BEAR (black)

ALIASES: Smokey, Teddy, Winnie, Yogi (Jellystone)

SCIENTIFIC NAME: *Ursus americanus*

PERSONAL STATISTICS: Adults weigh two hundred to seven hundred pounds and are 4½ to 6½ feet in length. Bears seem longer when the length stands up and woofs.

WHERE TO VIEW: General distribution is Alaska, south through the Rockies, east to northern tier states, small populations throughout south, and a very "smokey" subspecies in Yellowstone National Park. The best place is in a box of animal crackers. The bear is the only species with two postures in the Barnum collection—one standing and one sitting—but the way the crackers dump load the boxes, you may only get one. The worst place is inside their den, where a sow with cubs would put a good scout spin on the term den mother.

WHEN TO VIEW: At their convenience. A black bear's view is limited by poor eyesight. Can you imagine the frustration of being the big dummy that "went over the mountain, to see what he could see"

and the "other side of the mountain was all that he could see"? This frustration leads to inappropriate behavior best controlled by a fifty-five gallon tank of red pepper spray.

WHAT TO LOOK FOR: A U.S. Forest Service parade float.

TIPS TO INCREASE LIKELIOOD OF SEEING: Rub peanut butter on window sill; fry a pan full of bacon with the window open and exhaust fan turned on high up at the lake cabin; wear bells on clothing as park bears respond to dinner bells that, as your life flashes before you, toll for thee.

TIPS TO DECREASE LIKELIHOOD OF SEEING: Run a pack of Karelian bear dogs outside your cabin. Stay home, locked up in your room.

OLD DIET: The original three preferred porridge. Yogi, a cartoon mutant, preferred picnic basket food. Visiting bears from darkest Peru enjoy marmalade. Black bears from the land of sky-blue waters enjoy a tall cold Hamm's.

NEW DIET: Corn, melons, berries, *Ulee's Gold* (1998), prickly pear cactus fruit, feed pellets for horses or horses full of pellets. Hal Jam, the literary bear in *The Bear Went Over the Mountain* ordered pies, ice cream, pitchers of honey and maple syrup, cakes, and Cheesy Things on the cuff of a New York publishing house. Less literary bears like oats for breakfast.

OLD BEHAVIOR: Endlessly answering the question about its call of nature in the woods. In the fall, bears eat large quantities of food, then plummet into an extended state of inactivity. This coincides with the football season in which the oxygen intake of other sloth-like creatures is halved and heartbeats slow until touchdowns.

NEW BEHAVIOR: Smokey is over fifty years old and like other boomers, suffers from typical aging problems: memory loss, and inappropriate behavior in impromptu social settings. Stand your ground should you take an informal meeting. The black bear likes to bluff and old Smokey may forget why he's charging you. If you draw a young boar, you won't forget his charging you. If you draw Sonny "the Bear" Liston, you lose.

To decrease your likelihood of being eaten, let your spouse stand his or her ground, or let your "cubs" go play with theirs. If a black bear decides you are the plate du jour, one bite of your nasty hide will return the carnivore to a diet of moth larvae and pine tree nuts.

To increase your likelihood of eating black bear, go to Taiwan and put your mitts on some bear paw soup. The brew is alleged to create sexual vigor. The market for other spare parts in Asian folk medicine is equally strong. Wildlife enforcement agents estimate that for each bear killed legally in the United States, another is poached. However, for many palates poached bear is much too tough. A cut is preferred.

LIKELIHOOD OF SIGHTING IN THE NEW MILLENNIUM: One hundred percent. For the price of a Twinkie, it's easy to find a big park bear hug.

The likelihood of sighting a humanized brown-phase black bear in the new millennium depends on if the Ewoks return in any of the *Star Wars* prequels.

The likelihood of being bitten by a black bear in the new millennium is less than being bitten by a wild horse, yet pound for pound, horse meat is much too tasty to waste as bear bait.

FUTURE: The teddy bear, a black bear named after the first President Roosevelt (and not a popular feminine undergarment), can and will be found wherever stuffed animals are held in captivity. Teddy Ruxpin is a lost voice in that retail wilderness. Black bears living in Yellowstone during the big fire of 1988 are still really black.

COYOTE

ALIASES: Trickster, prairie or brush wolf, barking dog, Wile E.

SCIENTIFIC NAME: *Canis latrans*

PERSONAL STATISTICS: Adults weigh twenty to fifty pounds, slightly more in the East where they mate with wolves and other immigrants. They measure thirty-two to fifty inches in length with a ten- to fifteen-inch tail.

WHERE TO VIEW: General distribution is in all lower forty-eight states, particularly in South Dakota, the Coyote State, and in almost every habitat, but not in Hawaii, except when various subspecies from the species PAC, C.O.Y.O.T.E. are cited in the lobbies of big convention hotels. The best place is in any suburban shadow around any Western city. The worst place is at your picnic table, in your dog kennel.

WHEN TO VIEW: In the dawn's early light, some enchanted evening, near any spring pasture full of livestock.

WHAT TO LOOK FOR: Tracks around your Weber grill.

TIPS TO INCREASE LIKELIHOOD OF SEEING: Don't clean the grill, leave old charcoal hardened by drippings in bowl, let your pets out at night, leave your trash out on the curb the night before pick-up, use wide mesh on the bottom of your rabbit hutches, stake lambs at night in an open field.

OLD DIET: Juniper berries, acorns, apples, peaches, corn, and all melons, rabbits, watermelons, beetles, grubs, snakes, lizards, rodents above and below ground, insects, ducks, domestic turkeys, Bambis, more Bambis, and especially newborn antelope.

NEW DIET: Any lamb that looks like a newborn antelope, any cat or dog that looks like a newborn antelope, any pet in Westchester County that looks like a newborn antelope.

OLD BEHAVIOR: Foiled by roadrunners and fooled by other hapless animals on Saturday morning cartoon hell. Coyotes like to steal other predator foodstuffs, but as the backwoods bruin in William Kotzwinkle's *The Bear Went Over the Mountain* claims, "you have to bang them against a tree real hard, which knocks the wind out of them. Then they behave."

NEW BEHAVIOR: Chasing hapless suburban animals all the live-long day, doo-dah, doo-dah. Interested in reclaiming small rural towns caught in the agribusiness pincher. No longer fooled or foiled. Will not deign mating with lesser suburban canines. Prefers to mate

with wolves but the latest Canadian arrivals in Yellowstone are unfamiliar with American dating behavior. The new coyotes are applying for associate membership in the National Sheep Herders Association, posing as cattle herd dogs. The bravest urban coyotes are the healthiest, and their progeny are urban renaissance dogs that love to harmonize with fire and ambulance sirens.

LIKELIHOOD OF SIGHTING IN THE NEW MILLENNIUM: In a western suburb, 99 percent in the first month; other locations, 99 percent in the first year. (In either location, add 1 percent for presence of a Weber grill.)

FUTURE: City departments of animal regulation take thousands of complaint calls a year about "inappropriate" coyote behavior. Expect the hours of the Coyote Café to expand. Their adaptable behavior, panache, chutzpah, and social system guarantee survival. Population control only stimulates increased reproduction and immigration. Everything the federal government threw at the coyote couldn't eradicate the high plains drifter. This urban guerrilla and equal opportunity eater had evolved into a super-sly dog with a cultivated taste for flame-broiled steaks—fearless and capable of great patience, one coyote will decoy the rube in the barbeque apron while another turns the steak on the grill—hard to trap, and harder to poison, even with a large overdose of Worcestershire Sauce.

Excerpts from

Endangered Species Cookbook

Buck Peterson

Whooping Crane
Grus Americana
North America, Mexico

In the 1800s and early 1900s, these large, tall birds with wingspans that can stretch over seven feet, lost important nesting and winter habitat, lots of feathers to the military trade, and an occasional tail-feather to a hapless goose hunter. By the early 1940s, there were fewer than twenty birds left. Subsequent protection was so successful that a major childhood cough was named after the crane by the U.S. pharmaceutical industry, the sound of the cough resembling the cry the whooping crane made when being plucked for hat feathers. Cranes now nest in protected Canadian refuges and winter in similar refuges in Texas. During the mid-1970s, scientists at the protected breeding centers shipped eggs to Idaho to put in surrogate nests of sandhill cranes. Successfully raised by the non-endangered sandhill cranes, these confused young whooping cranes now winter with the sandhills in New Mexico.

Whooping cranes mate for life and are well-known for their courtship dance. To make whoopee (and little whoopies), cranes first whoop it up with dances full of flapping, head-bowing, leaps, and loud noises, making the whooping crane an obvious candidate as a symbol for any adult service club.

Since the average whooping crane weighs at least three times as much as a wild goose, plan on spending three times as much energy plucking the bird. Prepare three times as much wild rice stuffing. Cook it three times as long as an Aleutian Canada goose.

The Aleutian Canada goose is another natural kidder who has filed for and been granted federal protection in both its breeding and nesting grounds. A small subspecies of the common Canada goose, the *branta canadensis leucopareia* are typically marked with a white ring at the base of the neck. Their major decline came from the introduction of Arctic fox into the Alaskan breeding areas by the Russians and Americans in the early 1800s and the main breeding area, Buldir Island in the western Aleutians, is one of the few island without furry egg-eaters and home of one of the three remaining nesting populations.

It's difficult to distinguish the Aleutian Canada goose from another subspecies, the non-threatened cackling Canada goose. When flying over confused goose hunters wary of game wardens, these natural kidders have been suspected of cackling until out of range of the long guns.

Excerpts from

Buck Peterson's Complete Guide to Deer Hunting

Buck Peterson

NATURAL SIGNS

Tracks: Deer have hoofprints that are easy to follow and look like this:

You can also easily tell the difference between does and bucks. Buck tracks are heel-heavy, more authoritative. Doe tracks are light and flighty.

Does typically have a wider rear due to a pelvis for birthing, or this could be a bow-legged young buck from Texas.

A small buck

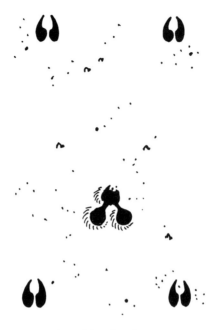

A real big buck!

Tracks are indications of the activity of the moment. Buck has tracked deer through California cannabis, easily catching up with doped deer giggling through the brush. Young deer will drag their feet on the way to a deer event with their folks. Standing deer may have one extra-deep track if they are counting hunters entering the woods.

More unusual tracks include:

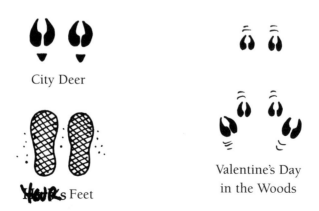

City Deer

Hunter's Feet

Valentine's Day
in the Woods

The White Lies of Deer Hunting

We always see deer here!

I've never seen a game warden in this area.

You start dragging—I'll take over when you get tired!

I'll settle up with you when we get back home!

I'll be back with help!

That looks like a legal buck to me!

Try this—it's really good!

Naw, you don't need a license this far back!

I wouldn't take that kind of crap from him!

Loan me your knife for a while!

No, Honey, this is not a new gun.

Yes, Boss, I'll be back bright and early on Monday.

They'll never find it here!

I'm doing this because you're my best friend.

That's where I hit it!

It's in my other billfold.

Sunrise and Sunset Time Schedule

Except in Wisconsin, where resident hunters shoot both day and night, state laws consider a full day of hunting to start about a 1/2 hour before sunrise until 1/2 hour after sunset. Several states are considering 1/2 day licenses for those who can't stay put in their stand but until these exceptions are made, you're expected to put in a full day.

To determine the start of your hunting day, measure from the time guideline that goes through Buck's stand in northern Minnesota the distance to your stand and add five seconds for each mile west or subtract five seconds for each mile east or vice versa depending on which direction you're facing. In Canada, add one minute either way for each kiloliter of Molsons you drink on the way to the stand. If you are driving deer east of Buck's stand, drivers must shoot first in the early morning but not required in the west. Legal sunrise and sunsets are listed below. Sunrise can often be misjudged with car headlights on high or full moon and sunsets are real tricky sometimes. On a long distance

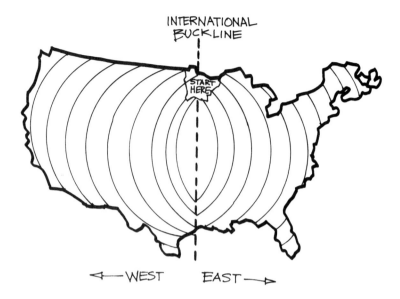

INTERNATIONAL BUCKLINE

START HERE

←—WEST   EAST—→

shot, your deer might be still legal while your shot is questionable! In these borderline cases, stay legal by shooting only in the direction the sun is moving.

International Buckline

Sunrise: October 01 to December 31, any year.
Starts at 7:11 A.M. ends at 7:56 A.M.

Except for late October/early November when the clock is set back an hour for breakfast, add a minute a day or so to determine the legal sunrise.

Sunset: October 01 to December 31, any year.
Starts at 6:54 P.M. ends at 4:34 P.M.

Allowing for a dinner break mid-season, subtract a minute or so each day.

Odds and Ends

As you review these end-pieces, remember this sage, healthy advice: "You're only young once but you can be immature forever."

Limey Lunkers Best Left Behind

The Brits have a distinguished history of eccentric humor yet there is little on hunting and fishing other than a few early fox hunting pieces, cartoons in *Punch* magazine, and gun-room prints by Jaques. One significant exception is the collection of odd stuff called *Oh Cod, the Funny Side of Fishing*, a comedy television special starring Jim Bowen and other comedians. The show is stuffed with quips like: "The only reason he married his wife is because she had worms."

P.S. A decent early take on the fishing guidebook is Cliff Parker's *The Fishing Handbook to End All Fishing Handbooks*. His guide, "Gilhooley," short for "Seamus Nigel McGregor Taliesen Hussein Francois Adolf Guiseppe Abraham Homey Gilhooley," ("I wanted him to feel at home wherever he went, the darlin' boy," said his mother) casts far and wide in his description of the sport on British waters.

R.I.P. National Fishhead Radio

Once broadcast live from the same dusty desert shared by Art Bell outside Parumph, Nevada, Stray Horn Spadewater, the "Voice of the Rainbow" purveyed "barbless wit and tacklebabble" on all fishy subjects. Strayhorn was a Rush Limbaugh with his exaggerated sense of humor sans the hard political spin and as tight an observer of daily routines as Paul Harvey. If you like silly, salty outdoor radio and never heard of National Fishhead radio, you missed a good one, and unlikely to return in this new age of clear channel easy listening mush.

Better Baits Done Dirt Cheap

Novelty fishing lures have hooked anglers for years. The more popular ones are beer bottles and cans (marketing gurus have identified a link between fishing and drinking), AC® spark plugs (a link between fishing and old outboard motors), cigars (a link to a more innocent, non-PC past) and DeKalb® corn cobs (a missing link outside Iowa) with hooks. There are collectibles from political campaigns, from plastic peanuts with an overbite for Billy Carter to Bill Clinton "crank baits" that don't hang up in the bush. Each part of the country has its homegrown varieties. In the Seattle suburb of Ballard, a popular item is a snoose can with hook taken from the history of Norwegian fishermen on the shore spitting into the salmon runs, triggering a homey olfactory high.

Fishing Twenty-Four Frames Per Second

Humorous fishing movies are rarely found on the big screen. There is the mild *Gone Fishing* with Joe Pesci and Danny Glover, and the less recent but very funny ice-house antics of Walter Matheau, Jack Lemmon and Burgess Meredith in *Grumpy Old Men*. In more innocent times, Tim Conway, "America's favorite comedian reels in laughs tackling a new sport," played the lead character in *Dorf® Goes Fishing*. Conway rolled his words like the Swedish chef on the Muppets, and acted out the history of fishing with bait, bow and arrow, and net. He also did an early take on the shopping channels with D.I.P. (Discount in Price) Shopping Network, and an overlong skit with his wife outfishing him. No matter how dated the material seems, the tape is saved by a hilarious take by Conway as Julia Child in her kitchen. For a Goofy take on fishing, check out Walt Disney's 1942 mini-classic *How To Fish*.

Ice fishing is perhaps the most under-served areas of outdoor madness, which is amazing given the conditions ice fishermen must put up with. It's rare to find a wordsmith superstar on thick or thin ice (like Tim Cahill in his *A Wolverine is Eating My Leg*), but in the crazed nonsense category, do not overlook jazz genius John Lurie's pseudo-fishing show *Fishing with John*. As described in the liner notes, "John Lurie knows absolutely nothing about fishing, but that doesn't stop him from undertaking the adventure of a lifetime on *Fishing with John*." Traveling with his special guests to the most exotic and dangerous places on earth, John Lurie battles sharks with Jim Jarmusch off the tip of Long Island, goes ice fishing with Willem Dafoe at Maine's northernmost point, braves the Costa Rican jungle with Matt Dillon, takes Tom Waits to Jamacia, and searches for the elusive giant squid with Dennis Hopper in Thailand. The ice fishing segment alone is well worth the price of this DVD from the famed Criterion Collection.

Catch and Release Tunes

There is no shortage of fishing songs. Light humor continues to be sung for and about fishermen. Today's songs are mostly targeted at gear guys, especially Southern bass fishermen with lots of foot-tapping, knee-slapping, guitar-picking tunes, served country-fried. One of the best collections is an old one, available only on cassette, titled *Gone Fishing, The Greatest Collection of Country and Blues Fishing Songs Ever Recorded.* Sam Chatmon's "Fishing Blues" and Little Milton's "Fishing in the Right Stream" (fishing as a metaphor for "amour") are keepers, and equal to Taj Mahal's take on Henry Thomas' "Fishing Blues."

Songs about Dad, fishing holes, ol' Blue, worms and whoppers are heavy on nostalgia but occasionally a collection includes real suprises. Fishhead Productions' assembly titled *Goin' Fishing* not only includes Taj Mahal's 1974 live performance of "Fishing Blues," but also "Catfish Boogie" by Tennessee Ernie Ford, "The Fishing Hole" by Andy Griffith, and an absolutely delightful "Gone Fishing" duet by Bing Crosby and Louis Armstrong.

It's hard to imagine how a fly-fisherman's song would sound, probably silence, punctuated by more silence, with an occasional voiceover of a cricket rubbing its legs together. Or an orchestral imitation of brook a-babbling, pipe a-smoking, merlot a-breathing, brie a-melting, dainty #20 hook in the ear a-removing.

One of the most recent top-selling songs on the subject is, "The Fishing Song—I'm Going To Miss Her." Written by Brad Paisley and Frank Rogers and sung by Brad, the song is a fresh take on the common theme of "I'm fishing darling so don't let the door slam on your butt on the way out."

One the funniest songs about fish and fishing, however, is in an eclectic collection simply titled *Fishing Songs* from www.laughinghyena.com. The delightful "What Have You Got Against Fish," was written by the late, great Shel Silverstein, popular children's book writer (*A Light in the Attic, Where the Sidewalk Ends, The Giving Tree*), poet, and raconteur. The lyrics of this number are snot-blowing when sung.

Novel Approaches to Fishing

Crazies populate the outdoor world in fiction, and there are few you'd want as next door neighbors. On rare occasions, a true eccentric with access to a printing press will appear on the scene, with a worldview deserving of their own cul-de-sac. One such man is Milford "Stanley"

Poltroon, a former ad guy that took exile in west Yellowstone a number of years back and whose body of work comes as close to Edward Lear's nonsense as anyone. His books, *How to Fish Good, The Happy Fish Hooker,* and others, are pastiches of antique artwork, whacked phrases, upside down copy, and rants and whistles in the dark, all seemingly to encourage even more nonsense. As editor and publisher of his "piscatorial periodical," *The Wretched Mess News,* Poltroon has earned his own cabin at Camp Nonsense.

Carl Hiassen's book, *Double Whammy* doesn't need much updating (first published in 1989) but his caricature of the big mouths of large-mouth fishing tournaments with corrupt big-mouth evangelistic hooligans is a lunker.

A small category of outdoor humor that outdoor writers most appreciate is the subject of being an outdoors expert. One good take is John Gierach's chapter on "Expertizing" in his book *Sex, Death, and Flyfishing.* Of course, Red Smith could fillet a self-styled expert with a casual aside. A very clever piece on word-smithing, particularly manuscript submissions, is Don Zahner's "A Treatise on Writing with an Angle" from his very funny book, *Anglish Spoken Here.*

Another good riff on the world of an outdoor fishing guide was an occasional piece in *Forbes FYI* magazine titled "Coyote Jack, Outdoors Guide." This whacked guide and his dissolute friend Reback disappeared over a decade ago but the column was a perfect send-up on the lore and lives of fly-fishing poseurs. The author, Peter Bowen, now pens the successful Gabriel Du Pre mysteries.

Most fly-fishing books are illustrated as dryly as their flies. A notable exception is the classic *Curtis Creek Manifesto.* Softcover, staple-bound and in large format, Sheridan Anderson's illustrated guide to "the art of fly-fishing on moving water" is a terrific introduction to an often-difficult sport. Anderson explains all aspects of beginning flyfishing through both words and cartoons with great humor. For many, Anderson, a self-described "foe of the work ethic," could be a novice's best (and certainly least expensive) professional fishing guide.

Calendar Guys and Doll

Very few major outdoor magazine covers have featured humor. That is not quite the case with posters and calendars. A very early (1908) poster titled "Shoot Them and Avoid Trouble" by "Winchester Loaded Shotgun Shells" had a kid on each end of a hollowed out log, one with a long stick, the other in the foreground jumping from a just-poked skunk in hot exit. Western Ammunition was a regular supplier of wall humor. A 1924 calendar had a dog pulling the quilt from a hunter in the sack whose alarm didn't ring titled, "Saving the Day." A 1928 Western poster had hunting buddies by the side of the house trying to capture a pal sawing wood, obviously moving through a "honey-do" list, and under the watchful eye of his wife seen through the kitchen window. In the racy calendar category, "Girls in Waders" are common, but one pinup to remember is *Field & Stream*'s "centerfold" of Phyllis Diller, "Miss Fun Fishing 1973," all decked out in chest waders, cowboy boots, a massive rhinestone choker, white gloves, and a cigarette holder. Fang must have been very proud.

On and In the Air

Prairie Home Companion® has a small but good collection of contributor outdoor humor on their web site. But, for the most part, NPR is so urban you can hear rush-hour traffic jams if you cup your ear toward a blue state. The station is such an addiction for some that during a recent fundraiser, one subscriber said she took the radio with her on canoe trips into northern Minnesota. With headset on her head and paddle in her hand, she would not be the only loon on the lake. NPR used to include more varied humor selections. One of the better features was *I Gotta Go* by Ian Shoales, a Duck's Breath Mystery Theater regular. Shoales ranted with humorous authority long before Dennis Miller bought his first beard trimmer.

Picking on the White Folks

"Ole and Lena" and "Sven and Ole" jokes are the HDL in the humor veins of transplanted northern Europeans. This safe humor is jocular, and different ethnic names are substituted to fit the audience. Here are two examples of Scandinavian outdoor humor.

It's opening day of deer season and, you betcha, Sven and Ole go up north together. Sure as shooting, as you'd expect, both in the same swamp, Ole accidentally plugs Sven. Ole jumps into the truck, drives to the nearest tavern and calls the ambulance and soon, the paramedics, cops, and game warden all show up at the scene of the hunting accident.

The paramedics work frantically on Sven while a nervous Ole waits nearby. Finally an exhausted medic comes over to Ole and says: "I'm sorry, Ole. We did everything we could to save him."

"Oh, no," cries Ole. "My only brudder. Vat could I have done to save him?"

"Well," says the paramedic, "it would have helped a lot if you hadn't gutted him before dragging him out of the woods."

Ole was carrying a large fish in a bucket of water away from the lake when a game warden stopped him. The warden asked, "Do you have a fishing license?"

"Don't need one," Ole replied. "This is my pet fish."

"Pet fish?"

"You betcha. Every day I take my pet fish down to the lake for a good swim, and when he's done, he jumps back in the bucket and I take him home."

"That's impossible," said the warden.

Ole looked at the warden. "Want me to show you?"

"Yes, this I gotta see."

Ole puts the fish in the lake and stands on the shore waiting. After a few minutes, the warden gets impatient and says "Well?"

"Well, what?" says Ole.

"Well, when is your fish swimming back?"

"What fish?

Park Plus

Animals in the wild stimulate adventure and sport. Wild animals in a zoo seldom stimulate any humor, unless you view Nick Park's short film, *Creature Comforts*. The comic genius behind Wallace and Gromit®, Park's collection of brief interviews with zoo animals about their daily lives is wildly funny, especially when you learn that many of the voices are nursing home residents. Rent it once and you'll buy it.

Rusty Iron John

An outdoor activity took root in Minnesota during the eighties in which an all men's group movement, started by poet Robert Bly, drummed their way to a higher consciousness. Known as the father of "the expressive men's movement," Bly's followers have been easily caricatured. The absolutely best view on middle-age white men, beating drums, and chanting in the piney woods belongs to Sherman Alexie, the Spokane Indian who writes with great grace, honesty, and humor. In an essay titled, "White Men Can't Drum," he seeks out the local chapter of Confused White Men, and tries to set the record straight. For suburban "warriors" screaming to release the inner animal, Alexie reminds the drumming, barking at the moon white guys that great warriors often don't have an animal inside them. In fact, "If there happens to be an animal, it can be a parakeet or a mouse just as easy as it can be a bear or wolf."

One of the softest and shortest pieces of light outdoor humor is A.A. Milne's *Pooh and Piglet Go Hunting*. Pooh and Piglet's tracking of woozles in the snow is as nice a tale as any about following "pawprints."

Graphic Outdoors

New Yorker cartoonists are fearless on all subjects including endangered species. Very few writers make funny with the subject of endangered species; a notable exception is Catherine Schine's *Save Our Bus Herds* (1982), reprinted in the *New Yorker's* humor collection titled *Fierce Pajamas*. An exceptional book that many took exception to is Buck Peterson's *The Endangered Species Cookbook*, found only in logger bars right next to the jar of pickled eggs.

Postcards of hunters tied to fenders/hoods of old cars are pale imitations of the cartoons in *The New Yorker* at mid-twentieth century. Charles Addams' cartoon of a moose driving a car with a hunter strapped to a fender appeared in 1941. A small, out-of-print art book called *Dennis Adler's High Country Prints* is a decent reversal of roles, moose and bear chasing humans in the woods. His artwork reminds a reader of R. Crumb and his illustration of a naked human on high howling at a full moon and frightening the little moose and bears in camp is worth the Internet search.

Of Zebra Fat and Herter's

If you were lucky enough to grow up in the midwest in the 1960s, Herter's was the sportsman's catalog of choice. The history of the company is well documented elsewhere but for sheer outrageous delight, read George Leonard Herter's books, especially *George the Housewife*. Nowhere else can you find good solid information like: "The fat of zebra is highly prized in Africa for rubbing on women's breasts, supposedly keeping them well filled out and from sagging. ... I know a lot of American women that could stand a treatment or two of zebra fat. Continual dieting and over bathing is reducing American women to a race with pendulous poorly filled breasts." And to think, this book was co-written with his wife, Berthe.

Black Outdoor Humor

There has been little Black or African American outdoor humor unless the black-faced humor of early minstrel shows tickles your fancy. Langston Hughes put it nicely when he wrote, "humor is laughing at what you haven't got when you ought to have it." This helps explain why Black in-jokes are hardly complimentary to the teller or listener and, unless you've walked in their shoes, an outsider feels uncomfortable with older Black humor material.

Funny Black guys are all city kids, but we know Bernie Mac could play a great character in any outdoor setpiece. Danny Glover played a comic character with Joe Peschi in a fishing movie, yet there are few other contemporary examples of Blacks in hunting and fishing predicaments.

That's not to say there wasn't the potential for great fun. Imagine if we had: Pigmeat Markham presiding over Fish & Game violations with *"Hear ye, hear ye! Courts in session. All rise 'cause here come de judge!"* Or George Kirby mc'ing a Bass Pro® tournament; or Slappy White debating the politics of gun control; or better yet, Redd Foxx, Slappy White, and Moms Mabley running an Orvis® Lodge.

Redd Foxx falls into the category of Humorists We Would Have Wanted More Of. His long career is distinguished not only because he lasted so long in a grinder industry, but that he was exceptionally helpful to other Black comics. His best (of few) outdoor jokes is found on his *Restricted* or *The Very Best of Redd Foxx: Fugg It!* albums, describing alligator hunting as "two white guys in a Chris Craft, pulling two Negroes through the Okefanokee Swamp on water skis."

Urban Legends

The Internet is largely responsible for far-fetched tales about sportsmen that have little basis in fact. Older readers may recall an occasional skit on the Jack Parr show when he would have a number of multilingual guests and by the time a phrase from the opposite end of the couch reached Parr, the message was so mangled you couldn't even guess the original piece.

A recent example of an urban/rural legend involves a couple of hunters in a northern state who want to duck hunt on a frozen lake. In the story, the driver had just purchased an expensive SUV and once on the lake, decided to open some water for ducks with dynamite rather than an ice auger. They threw a stick of dynamite with a short fuse and their champion Lab raced to retrieve the "bird." They shot at the returning dog with buckshot, which made him hide under the new SUV. Once the smoke cleared, no dog, no new SUV, just six years of big payments.

These legends supposedly come out of game/fish courtrooms and hospitality suites where law enforcement officers share their favorite tales but are notoriously closed lipped to the general public. The best place to find these stories is in *Field & Stream* magazine where Bill Heavey has announced the Elmer Awards to commemorate hapless Elmer J. Fudds afield that are/were accidents ready to happen.

Beverly Hills .30-.30

The Hollywood movie industry is anti-gun and anti-hunting. In *Doc Hollywood,* when the doctor and his vegetarian girlfriend pee around a deer stand, we stand hunters know it is a good joke to play on a brother-in-law, but the movie intentions were not as pure. Independent movies are no better. In *Winged Migrations,* waterfowlers are portrayed as another health hazard for birds (one serious waterfowler noted the filmmakers used the wrong "voice" for the drake mallard). An extreme example of this take on hunters is in the fairy tale *Fly Away Home.* Imprinted geese follow an ultra-light airplane south to stop a major commercial development, and on the way have to avoid crudely drawn waterfowlers in a blind. Jeff Daniels, best known for his role in *Dumb and Dumber,* wrote and directed a movie titled *Escanaba in Da Moonlight,* an unfortunately confusing tale of a buckless Da Yooper in a deer camp where game meat farts rule. Even *Crocodile Dundee* takes a potshot at outlaw 'roo hunters.

The Golden Age of Hollywood hunting movies was Looney Tunes. The most memorable are the Bugs Bunny and Daffy Duck pairings about duck and rabbit seasons in *Rabbit Fire* (1951), *Rabbit Seasoning* (1952), and *Duck! Rabbit! Duck!* (1953), all directed by the amazing

Chuck Jones. Other early favorites include *Porky's Duck Hunt* (1937), *Daffy Duck with Egghead* (1938), and *To Duck or Not to Duck* (1943). In *Daffy's Southern Exposure* (1942), Daffy stopped migrating altogether. Elmer Fudd (first appearing as Egghead), the bulbous-headed, chipmunk-cheeked hunter chasing the wascally wabbit was America's first cinematic hunting hero. It wasn't too long ago that Elmer still stood proudly with flap hat in front of Warner Brother stores.

Outdoor humor is even rarer on the small screen. Early *Hee Haw* had quips like, "Hey Ezra, is it raining outside? I don't know. Call the dog in and see if it's wet." *The Red Green Show* is another long shot even though he deals with "men-craft," but fishing and hunting are rarely if ever a theme.

Internet Interbreeding

The Internet has replaced the fax machine for ethnic, cultural, and racial jokes. Speeding down the information superhighway are mock game licenses and diagrams of the "Smithinski & Wessonovich target pistol" (barrel pointed backwards). A U.S. Fish & Game "official" notice tells of breeding coho salmon with the walleye, producing the "cowal." The fish was not improved through secondary breeding with the muskie, as it produced the "cowalskie," a hybrid that doesn't even know how to swim.

Politically Correct Dullards

Really good humor produced by urban herbivores is rare. Even those who want to take a potshot at those of us who stand high in the foxhole like the NRA aren't clever and certainly aren't very funny; to wit:

Mad Magazine was once home for many of the best American comic artists and writers. Their January, 1999, take on the NRA is witless: a "Seasons Greeting from the NRA" Christmas card with Charlton Heston sitting in a big chair, holding what appears to be an AR-15, next to a roaring fireplace with a suspicious looking Rudolph mounted over the mantle. An earlier (January, 1992) spoof on NRA membership recruitment is a full page ad with a deer dressed and armed, titled "I'm the NRA" (Nature's Revenge Association).

Flash forward to *Deer Avenger*, a parody of the phenomenally successful interactive PC game called *Deer Hunter*. Loaded with such clever hunter calls such as "Free beer here!" and "Help, I'm naked and have a pizza," Rambo Buck armed with M-16s, bazookas, and slingshots pursues "big-belly trophies" in Minnesota, Connecticut, and West Virginia. (It's obvious dummies wrote this material. Minnesotans know there are bigger beer bellies in Wisconsin). *Deer Avenger 2, 3D,* and 4 followed in quick succession, feeding juvenile anti-hunter sentiments in a gaming world dominated by irresponsible violence. As could be expected, even less witty games continue on.

Stand-up Guys

Redneck humor deserves its own category. The broad brush used by anti-hunters to paint sportsmen and women as rubes and rednecks has caused some to celebrate and market. Jeff Foxworthy and his blue-collar touring pals are an established comedy troupe and occasionally these professional rednecks wander into the woods. Ron White is the kind of guy you'd like to hunt and fish with. He drinks, smokes, and sees humor in everything. In his DVD *Tater Salad,* he says he doesn't hunt because "it's early in the morning, it's really cold outside, and I don't want to go" and then moves into a family deer hunting story that's worth the price of admission.

Foxworthy talks a little deer hunting and fishing in his autobiographical *No Shirt, No Shoes—No Problem.* His three tapes sponsored by Bill Jordan's Realtree® (*Incomplete Deer Hunter, The Return of the Incomplete Deer Hunter,* and *Incomplete Deer Hunter 3*) are the best example of his redneck deer hunting humor.

Larry the Cable Guy dresses like he just left the deer shack in his trademark grungy old plaid flannel shirt with the sleeves torn or bit off. In his *Git-R-Done* DVD, he talks about hunting only once, starting with "I got a deer at 300 yards with my Ruger. It was at the zoo, don't count."

Parody, Satire, and Things That Go Bump in the Forest

The funniest parody of the Sergeant Preston legend was done by B.K. Taylor, a contributing artist to *National Lampoon* from 1975-1987. "Timberland Tales" was populated by Dr. Rogers, a Mark Trail-type character, his wife Kathleen, Maurice the Indian Boy "an unbelievable naïve and bulbous teenager," and Constable Tom "a dimwitted, muscle-bound Canadian Mountie." The characters were in full-time high tension, aided and abetted by the over-sexed Foamy the Dog.

The second best take on Preston is a television series that ran its course much too quickly. *Due South* teamed a Canadian Mountie with a Chicago street cop and the clash of cultures, with an occasional appearance of Leslie Neilson, is worth the on-line purchase of the pilot program. Very funny stuff, indeed. Light years beyond was the strange brew of Bob and Doug McKenzie's *Great White North*.

Big Game Routines

To some, the golden years of big game hunting in Africa were in the 1950s and 1960s. Interest in safaris was such that cartoons on the subject even appeared in *Playboy* magazine. One of the wildest stand-up routines ever on an African hunt was on Broadway where Paul Lynde started a career of kinky, misogynistic comedy with a bit in a review titled "New Faces of 1952." A splendid take on a "Trip of the Month" as reported to a women's garden club, Lynde's travelogue with slide show was a wild, free-associating ride to very foreign parts.

Chrome-plated Wit

If Dorothy Parker was correct that wit has truth in it and wisecracking is simply calisthenics with words, the sporting world will never be short of bumper-sticker humor. Here are a few examples:

Give a man a fish and he will eat for a day. Teach a man how to fish, and he will sit in a bar and drink beer all day.

Give a man a fish and he will eat for a day. Teach a man how to fish and you will get rid of him for the whole weekend.

Give a man a fish and he will eat for a day. Teach a man how to fly-fish and he will become a woman.

The following should be bumper stickers:

Ever consider what pets must think of us? I mean, here we come back from the grocery store with the most amazing haul—chicken, pork, half a cow. They must think we're the greatest hunters on earth!
—Anne Taylor

It's a good thing we have gravity or else when birds died, they'd just stay right up there. Hunters would be all confused.
—Steven Wright

If an infinite number of redneck hunters riding in an infinite number of pickup trucks fire an infinite number of bullets at an infinite number of highway signs, they will eventually produce all the world's great literary works in Braille.
—Author unknown

Cooking with PETA

A restaurant in Saskatoon, Canada, uses the slogan: "There's Plenty of Room for All God's Creatures—Right Next to the Mashed Potatoes." The quip is a perfect call for the group People Eating Tasty Animals, a thorn in the side of the humorless at the other PETA. Camp food humor revolves around well-seasoned "meals" in duck shacks, and deer and fishing camps. A common tale is a long involved recipe where a merganser is carefully prepared on a board and once baked, thrown away and the board eaten.

The potential for humor must surely start in a sportsman's grocery cart. What hunter hasn't packed the cart with food you wouldn't dare bring home: beef bologna, white bread, Velvetta, SPAM®, Twinkies, Hostess Cupcakes, Little Debbie Snackcakes, bags of remaindered Halloween candy, and chips and dips of many flavors?

In his more serious guidebook *Bobs, Brush, and Brittanies*, Joel Vance repeats a joke about who gets to be the camp cook (the first one who complains about the food):

While the rest are out hunting, the hunter stuck with the cooking walks out and spots a big, fresh cow-pie (stack of moose turds) thinking he'll fix his buddies by baking a pie with these fresh ingredients and the first guy who complains gets the apron. He makes the pie in a nice store-bought crust and serves it at dinner. The first hunter at the table ready for dessert takes a big bite out of the cow-pie and howls, "Hey, this tastes like cowpie (moose turds)." Then quickly adds, "It's good though!"

Readers looking for good humor and strong opinions in food writing need go no further that Jim Harrison (game), especially his *The Raw and the Cooked* and Calvin Trillin (non-game).

Postcards from the Edge

The greeting card business occasionally produces a good laugh: a Santa sitting next to a surprised diner at a lunch counter saying "What the hell, I'll have the venison." Postcards are quite often more explicit. A good source of fishing humor postcards is Derek Mills' *The Fishing Here Is Great.* You'll find photos of monster fish leaping over canoes, trying to swallow bank fishermen, strapped to horses and railroad flatbeds and ridden by bait-casters. It is much harder to find good hunting cards unless you run across one with a cowboy bent on a Leanin' Tree® card display or enter the world of Duckboy Cards, a Montana image company.

Outdoor Books Best Left Outdoors

The following are press releases from the files of the under-funded, currently helm-less Literary Coalition to Save the Great Pulpwood Forests.

Worst Outdoor Book of 1999 Finally Announced. The Literary Coalition to Save the Great Pulpwood Forests has selected *Bambi* by Jane Schulman as the worst outdoor book published in 1999 and a serious contender for the worst outdoor book of all time. The citation from Executive Director, Salvatore Palatino, reads: "The gratuitous violence reprinted in this adaptation of an already ridiculous forest fable leads the reader to think dying in a forest fire started by an unattended campfire is just desserts for someone who poked a hole in Bambi's mom. What did you expect? The "new" Boy Scouts don't teach campfire skills anymore! What's worse is the dead man's jacket on page 46 looks like a L.L. Bean wool cruiser. No decent author would waste such a good jacket, not when it could have gone to a needy, alive person in another book."

A cottonwood sapling will be planted on the north edge of Big Babe Lake to mark this announcement.

Worst Outdoor Book of 2000 Finally Announced. The Literary Coalition to Save the Great Pulpwood Forests has selected the worst outdoor book published in 2000. In the citation, Executive Director, Salvatore Palatino notes: "Nevada Barr, a summer park ranger for the National Park System, sets her mysteries in exotic yet publicly funded national recreational areas. Her current book, *Deep South,* is no exception. The female protagonist, Anna Pigeon, solves the author's mysteries, but not the biggest national park system mystery, "Why can't they fix the roads in Yellowstone?" If they would only divert a few dollars from the fund to put more wolves at Little Red Riding Hood's door, taxpayers could enjoy a leisurely drive through what was once our premier national park. We encourage Barr to set her next mystery in Yellowstone but assume the book would be too long due to the characters delayed at roadblocks during high season."

A cottonwood sapling will be planted on the north edge of Big Babe Lake to mark this announcement.

Worst Outdoor Book of 2001 Finally Announced. The Literary Coalition to Save the Great Pulpwood Forests has selected *Fish!* by

Stephen C. Lundin, Harry Paul, and John Christensen as the worst out-door book of 2001. The citation by Salvatore Palatino, Executive Director, reads; "An unsuspecting reader would think this book is a helpful guide to one of America's favorite outdoor pastimes. Wrong. This is another slimy, fishy self-help book for small businesses. No advice on favorite lures or flies, water conditions or which bass boat to buy. No cautions on fishing with high explosives. No discussion on which caliber to use when gunning spawning beds. The thrust of this book is throwing overpriced Copper River salmon fish, not catching fish in Seattle's Public Marketplace where fishmongers pitch fish 15 feet to wrappers with as much interest to a real sportsman as frozen turkey bowling."

A cottonwood sapling will be planted on the north edge of Big Babe Lake to mark this announcement.

Worst Outdoor Book of 2002 Finally Announced. The Literary Coalition to Save the Great Pulpwood Forests has singled out 2002 as being the worst year for publishing outdoor books. Despite excuses of post 9/11 distress from the largest publishing windbags, absolutely wretched books were shoved on shelves this year. Executive Director Salvatore Palatino laments that, "The award categories have to be expanded to accommodate such deserving titles as Bo Derek's neigh-sayings, *Riding Lessons: Everything That Matters in Life I've Learned from Horses,* and someone else needs to do the stupid business of read-ing them. I'm out of here." Director Palatino is currently being treated for clinical depression with a variety of medications, none of which are working at press time. He was last seen communing with a cottonwood sapling on the north edge of Big Babe Lake.

Liars Clubbed

Tall tales or tall "talk" occupies a small niche of published outdoor humor, the size deserved as the tall tales integral to everyone's hunting and fishing camps are best spoken. The tradition of tall story grandil-oquence and boasting have frontier roots, when Colonel Davy Crockett grinned down tree-rats (raccoons) and, in Salvanus Cobb, Jr.'s world, impossibly long-shot bullets were salted so the meat would-n't spoil before recovery. Brevity is an unusual virtue in tall tales. The legendary newscaster, Lowell Thomas collected some of the very best in his book titled *Tall Stories: The Rise and Triumph of the Great*

American Whopper (1945). Liar's contests are now the contemporary stage for tall-tale tellers and Bill Lepp, five-time winner of the West Virginia State Liars Contest, is an acknowledged champion of the form.

In the Key of Buckshot

Funny hunting songs are among the rarest of beasts. There are a few current practitioners of note from the Midwest, where good-natured humor is a brain food group. Da Yoopers come from da UP (Upper Peninsula) of Michigan and on the comedy album *Culture Shock* you'll meet among others, "Da Couch That Burps" and wear out "Second Week of Deer Camp." Good, solid beer and brat humor!

Duck and goose hunting music includes cursing, splashing sounds as decoys are set in the dark, oars a-banging, and labs a-moving. For a good lick of hardcore duck country tunes, Louisiana's Duck Commander "Duckaholic's Anonymous" on *There's No Cure* CD will seriously stir your waters.

Gas in the Great Outdoors

One of the joys of the field is the opportunity to belch and fart with little fore- or after-thought. At least out in the open air. Farting in a small deer shack can, however, disrupt the balance of nature. Musical fruit is a comic stand-by, a popular character in movies with no artistic pretensions. In print, farting doesn't stink so badly and one of the most helpful short pieces is tucked inside Roger Welsch's fine cookbook, *Diggin' in and Piggin' out*. His formula for taking the anger out of beans is as good as remembering Buddy Hackett's observation that women don't fart, but often stand near dogs that do.

Credits

Every effort has been made to contact the copyright holders of each of the selections. Rights holders of any selections not credited should contact Willow Creek Press, P.O. Box 147, Minocqua, WI 54548 in order for a correction to be made in the next reprinting of this book.

Excerpts from *A Good Life Wasted* by Dave Ames. Copyright © 2003 by the author and reprinted with the permission of The Globe Pequot Press.

"Comatose - God of Fishing" from *Scandinavian Humor & Other Myths* by John Louis Anderson. Reprinted with the permission of the author. "The New Scandinavian Gods" first appeared in *MPLS/ST. PAUL* magazine.

"#6" by Nancy Anisfield. All rights reserved. Reprinted by permission of the author.

"All I Really Need To know I Learned By Having My Arms Ripped Off By A Polar Bear," copyright © 2002 by Andrew Barlow. Originally appeared in the *New Yorker* and reprinted by permission of the author.

Fishing definitions excerpted from *Fishing: An Anglers Dictionary*, copyright © 1983 by Henry Beard and Roy McKie. Used by permission of Workman Publishing Co., Inc., New York. All rights reserved.

From *Milton Berles's Private Joke File* by Milton Berle, copyright © 1989 by Milton Berle. Used by permission of Crown Publisher, a division of Random House, Inc.

"Out-In-Left Field Guide" by Mike Beno and Gary Cox. Originally appeared in *Ducks Unlimited Magazine* and reprinted with the permission of the publisher.

"Hunting Camp Cook" from *Horseshoes, Cowsocks & Duckfeet* by Baxter Black, copyright © 2002 by Baxter Black. Used by permission of Crown Publisher, a division of Random House, Inc.

"The Watch Dog" from *Dogs* by Henry Morgan and George Booth. Illustration reprinted by permission of the artist.

Braude's Treasury of Wit and Humor, (Englewood Cliffs, NJ: Prentice-Hall, 1964), copyright © 1991 by Jacob M. Braude.

"Prairie Dog Hunting" from *The Cosmic Wisdom of Joe Bob Briggs*. Copyright © Joe Bob Briggs. Reprinted by permission of Sawdust Joint Productions.

"Big Game Taxidermy" and "Tall Fish" by Reynold Brown. Originally published in *Outdoor Life* (1952, 1954). Reprinted by permission of Mary Louise Tejeda Brown.

Contributors

Nancy Anisfield is currently the senior editor of the *Upland Almanac* magazine and creative energy behind the Ugly Dog Hunting Company. She lives in northern Vermont where she also serves as an upland hunting instructor and occasional guide.

John Louis Anderson is a good Norwegian/Swedish/American boy, who grew up in New Ulm, Minnesota, attended a good Lutheran college in Augustana, Sioux Falls, and got his M.A. from the University of Minnesota in Theater Photography. He has worked as a photographer for the Guthrie Theater, Chanhassen Theater, and a number of national magazines in both the United States and Scandinavia. He has written about Scandinavia and other topics (some op-ed) for *MPLS/St Paul* magazine, *Minnesota Monthly*, the travel section of the *Minneapolis Star & Tribune* and WCCO Radio.

Dave Ames spends much of his time in pursuit of trout and grayling. He has written for the *Chicago Tribune, Cleveland Plain Dealer, Sports Afield, Fin and Feather*, and *Montana Magazine*. Ames' books are *True Love and the Wooly Bugger* and *A Good Life Wasted: or Twenty Years as a Fishing Guide*. He lives in Montana.

Andrew Barlow is the co-author of the humor book *A Portrait of Yo Mama as a Young Man*. His pieces have appeared in the *New Yorker*, among other publications. He lives in New York City.

Henry Beard founded the *National Lampoon* along with Doug Kenney and Rob Hoffman. Prior to *National Lampoon*, Beard collaborated with Kenney at the *Harvard Lampoon* during the late 1960s, producing nationally distributed parodies of *Life* and *Time* magazines and a book length parody of *The Lord of the Rings* called *Bored of the Rings*. Since leaving *National Lampoon*, Beard has authored and co-authored over 30 humor books.

Mike Beno's feature articles have appeared in *Audubon, Sports Afield*, and *National Wildlife*. Recently retired as editorial director for Reiman Publications, Milwaukee, Wisconsin, he's been officially deputized as a Loon Ranger for the Sigurd Olson Environmental Institute.

Milton Berle is remembered by some for his vaudeville years but his major debut was as the star of NBC's Texaco Star Theater in 1948. This comedy variety show was the most popular series in the early years of TV and where Berle earned one of his first Emmy Awards. NBC valued Berle so much that he was signed to a "lifetime" contract in 1951, which paid him $100,000 whether or not he performed. Berle was a popular emcee, TV guest star, character actor, and nightclub comedian—in character for over 60 years until his death in 2002, at the ripe age of 93.

Baxter Black, cowboy, poet, and humorist has been described by *The New York Times* as "probably the nation's most successful living poet." This former large animal veterinarian is a popular figure through his public appearances, his column, and on National Public Radio. Baxter lives in Benson, Arizona, and on www.baxterblack.com.

Harry Bliss, **Michael Crawford**, **Matthew Diffee**, and **Frank Modell** are *New Yorker* cartoonists. Their work and that of others can be discovered at www.cartoonbank.com

George Booth is a quintessential *New Yorker* cartoonist. Born in Cainsville, Missouri, Booth grew up on a vegetable farm. He attended the Corcoran College of Art and Design, the Chicago Academy of Fine Arts, the School of Visual Arts, and Adelphi College. Drafted into the U.S. Marine Corps in 1944, he was invited to reenlist and join the Corps' *Leatherneck* magazine as a staff cartoonist. Drafted for the Korean War, he was ordered back to the *Leatherneck*. As a civilian, he moved to New York where he worked as an art director in the magazine world. Fed up, he quit and pursued cartooning full time, beginning a successful career phase in 1969 with his first *New Yorker* cartoon sale. Over time, his cartoons have become an iconic feature of the magazine. In a doodler's style, they feature everyman beset by modern complexity, goofballs perplexing their spouses, cats, and very often a fat dog. One signature element is a ceiling light bulb on a cord pulled out of vertical by another cord attached to an electrical appliance such as a toaster.

Jacob Morton Braude was a prolific collector of stories, quotations, anecdotes, and toasts. His books are classics in the field of public speaking.

Joe Bob Briggs is a multi-media shock force. Infamous for Joe Bob's Drive-in Theater, his long running and top-rated network show on the Movie Channel, Briggs has enthusiasm for, and the last word on, the cinematic fringes. Briggs was also a commentator on Comedy Central's *The Daily Show* during its first two years. The Joe Bob Report on www.joebobbriggs.com is an informed rant on movies and other popular culture and a high traffic e-shopping mall. His latest book is *Profoundly Disturbing Shocking Movies That Changed History*. Buy it!

Reynold Brown was one of the premier illustrators of movie posters before embarking on a career of fine art in the early 1970s. Brown produced over 250 movie poster campaigns for Universal, Disney, MGM, and AIP for such movie classics as *Ben Hur, Spartacus, The Alamo, The Time Machine, Son of Cochise,* and the *Creature from the Black Lagoon.* His campaigns included stars like Elizabeth Taylor (*Cat on a Hot Tin Roof*), James Stewart (*Shenandoah*), and James Cagney (*Man of a Thousand Faces*). Brown died in 1991. His wife, Mary Louise, continues a fine art career in pastels.

Nelson Bryant "at onetime or another, has been employed as a farm hand, cook, deck hand, logger, gravedigger, carpenter, oyster fisherman, and for 13 years—managing editor of a small daily newspaper in New Hampshire." Now he devotes himself to writing his columns for *The New York Times* and doing whatever he can to "assist man in establishing a decent and functional relationship to the natural world."

Steve Chapple is the author of eight books and two screenplays. *Kayaking the Full Moon: A Journey Down the Yellowstone River to the Soul of Montana* was chosen as a Notable Book of the Year in the Travel and Science category by *The New York Times*. It also won a Lowell Thomas Award for the best travel book of the year. He co-wrote David Brower's *Let the Mountains Talk, Let The Rivers Run.* A former staff columnist for the *San Francisco Chronicle*, he writes on politics and the environment, adventure and travel for *The New York Times, Los Angeles Times, Christian Science Monitor, National Geographic, Travel & Leisure, Outside, Rolling Stone, Premiere, Audubon, Men's Journal*, and many other magazines. He is a contributing editor of the *San Francisco Examiner Sunday Magazine* and the 1997 winner of the Polar-Tek challenge.

Russell Chatham is a world renowned landscape artist "whose unique style permeates all of his interests." Visit his fine art gallery, his Livingston Bar and Grill, and the latest publications from his distinguished Clark City Press at www.russellchatham.com. Chatham's books *The Angler's Coast* and *Striped Bass on the Fly: A Guide to California Waters* are collectibles and he has illustrated books by Jim Harrison and Guy De La Valdene. From 1988, for five years, Russell Chatham, founder, publisher, and editor released nearly 30 books of superior quality and Clark City Press now continues its literary tradition.

Homer Circle, or rather "Uncle" Homer has been the angling editor for *Sports Afield* for twenty-four years, retiring in 2001. He's been president of the Outdoor Writers Association of American and has received the Lifetime Achievement Award from the American Sportfishing Association. Circle lives in Ocala, Florida.

Bruce Cochran is a humor powerhouse. Writer-illustrator for Hallmark Cards from 1960–1962, freelance cartoonist, illustrator/writer since then. Creator of *Fun 'N' Games with Cochran!*, the daily sports cartoon in *USA Today* from 1983–1991. Frequent cartoon contributor to *Sports Afield, Field & Stream, Playboy, Penthouse, National Lampoon, Kansas Wildlife & Parks, Pheasants Forever Journal, Wall St. Journal*, and many other national publications from 1960 to present. Regular cartoon features: "Marsh Madness" in *Wildfowl* magazine, "Way Outside" in Kansas Wildlife & Parks magazine, "Humor Corner" in *North American Hunter*. Writer and illustrator of over 10 books on outdoor subjects, recently *Antlers Away*, a heavily-illustrated humor book about deer and deer hunting, published by Willow Creek Press.

Raymond Coppinger, Ph.D. majored in literature and philosophy as an undergraduate at Boston University. His Ph.D. thesis in biology at the University of Massachusetts is on the effect of experience and novelty on avian feeding behavior. He joined the founding faculty at Hampshire College in 1969, where he is professor of biology. He teaches and does research on animal behavior, especially the behavior of canines. Ray and his colleagues and students have published over 50 papers on his dog research. His favorite publication, however, is the book *Fishing Dogs*, a humorous and iconoclastic look at dogs, fishermen, and professors.

Gary Cox is a freelance illustrator/designer living in rural Black Earth, Wisconsin. He produces *Puddler* magazine—a children's natural history publication for *Ducks Unlimited*, and contributes illustrations to *Ducks Unlimited* magazine. Other clients include Fish and Wildlife Service, Wright Group/McGraw-Hill, various regional magazines, and local environmental organizations. When not working, he can be found standing in a spring creek untying knots in flyline.

James W. (Jim) Dean began writing for publication in 1964 while he was a lieutenant in the U.S. Army, and after his discharge, he worked as outdoor editor for the Burlington, N.C. *Times-News* for four and a half years. In 1969, he was employed by the N.C. Wildlife Resources Commission as a staff writer and assistant writer for *Wildlife in North Carolina*, and in 1979, was named editor, a position from which he just retired. With Lawrence S. Earley, he co-edited the book *Wildlife in North Carolina*, published in 1987 by the University of North Carolina Press. In his spare time, he is a freelance editor and photographer for outdoor magazines, including *Outdoor Life, Field & Stream, Sports Afield, Fly Fisherman, Gray's Sporting Journal, Sporting Classics*, and others.

Jerry Dennis has earned his living since 1986 writing about nature and the environment for such publications as *The New York Times, Smithsonian, Audubon, Orion, Field & Stream, Wildlife Conservation*, and *National Geographic Traveler*. His books, *A Place on the Water, The River Home, From a Wooden Canoe*, and most recently, *The Living Great*

Lakes: Searching for the Heart of the Inland Seas, have won numerous awards and have been translated into five languages. He lives on Old Mission Peninsula, near Traverse City, Michigan

Jack Douglas shared a 1954 Emmy Award for comedy writing and wrote material for such performers as Bob Hope, Bing Crosby, Woody Allen, and "Laugh-In" hosts Dan Rowan and Dick Martin. During the 1950s and 1960s, Douglas was also a frequent guest on the Jack Paar Tonight Show. His funny books include *My Brother Was An Only Child, The Adventures of Huckleberry Hashimoto, Never Trust a Naked Bus Driver*, and *The Jewish-Japanese Sex, and Cookbook and How to Raise Wolves*. Douglas died in 1989.

Andy Duffy resides in Evart, Michigan, and writes freelance outdoor copy for the *Cadillac News* and other publications. Some of the publications actually use the material he writes for them.

Dick Ellis is the syndicated columnist behind *Dick Ellis' Wisconsin Outdoors*, a popular program carried in over 50 Wisconsin newspapers. He is a six-time recipient of national awards presented in 2004 and 2005 including first place in Humor/Excellence in Crafts Contest at the Outdoor Writers Association of America annual convention. Ellis is married to Lori and they have a daughter named Taylor Rae. He can be reached at (262) 549-5550 and write@execpc.com

Jim Enger's book, *Incompleat Angler: A Fly-Fishing Odyssey* is so fine, even the forward by Ted Williams is worth clipping and sending to your friends. As one reviewer nicely put it, "At heart, this book is a quest for the innocence of near and far away places, for paradise lost, the company of good friends."

Ian Frazier is a writer and humorist, born in Cleveland in 1951. Frazier attended Harvard University where he was on the staff of the *Harvard Lampoon*. After graduating in 1973, he worked briefly as a magazine writer in Chicago and then moved on to New York City; he joined the staff of the *New Yorker* where he wrote feature articles, humorous sketches and pieces for "The Talk of the Town" section. In 1982, Frazier moved to Montana. His books: *Dating Your Mom, Nobody Better, Better than Nobody, Great Plains, Family, Coyote v Acme, It Happened Like This, On The Rez*, and *The Fish's Eye*.

Charles Gaines is the author of 23 books, among them *Stay Hungry*, a final nominee for a National Book Award in fiction and the international bestseller, *Pumping Iron*. He is an award-winning writer for film and television and has published over 200 magazine articles in *Esquire, Playboy, Men's Journal, Town and Country, Sports Afield, Field & Stream, Audubon, Outside, Architectural Digest, Sports Illustrated, Forbes FYI,* and many other periodicals. A collection of some of his angling articles from all over the world, *The Next Valley Over*, was published by Crown in 2000.

Lewis Grizzard was described by *The New York Times*, as "a Mark Twain for our times." From 1979 to 1994, his column from the *Atlanta Journal & Constitution* was syndicated by 450 newspapers. His concerts and his best-selling books led to appearances on *The Tonight Show, Today, Larry King Live*, and *Designing Women*. The titles of many of his books are first indication of the good humor within, such as: *Does a Wild Bear Chip in the Woods* and *Don't Bend Over in the Garden, Grammy, You Know Those Taters Got Eyes*. Grizzard died much too early at age 47 in 1994 from a congenital heart defect. Grizzard lives on in a show created by his widow, Dedra, and his best friend, Bill Orbst. Visit www.lewisgrizzard.com for an introduction or remembrance of this fine Southern humorist.

Richard Guindon's first cartoons, dealing with a character called Hugger Mugger, were published in the *Minnesota Daily*. Hugger Mugger eventually was syndicated and appeared in 100 college newspapers. Guindon then went to New York where, as a freelance cartoonist, he sold his work to *Downbeat, Playboy, Esquire*, and *New Yorker* magazine. The *Realist* sent him abroad for a year as a kind of cartoonist-correspondent in Greece, Turkey, Egypt, Jordan, and Israel. Guindon was born December 2, 1935, in St. Paul. He began cartooning after he finished three years in the army, joined the *Minneapolis Tribune* in 1968, and completed his fine career at the *Detroit Free Press*. A quote: "Always remember to keep your sense of humor. It's the one thing that separates us from the scum."

Mike Halleran was born in Boston but grew up in Kansas. A freelance writer and practicing attorney in the Flint Hills of Northeast Kansas, his articles have appeared in *Shooting Sportsman, Upland Almanac, Midwest Outdoors*, and *Fur Fish Game*. A devoted husband and father, he enjoys hunting pheasant, quail, prairie chicken, and defense counsel.

Bill Heavey is a freelance writer in Arlington, Virginia. He was an obsessed fisherman as a child, got over it, then re-discovered angling when some friends gave him a spinning rod for his 21st birthday. This led him into a downward spiral and he soon found himself both fishing and hunting. He is especially fond of bow hunting and has never believed that a lack of skill should dissuade anybody from doing anything, with the possible exception of certain kinds of surgery. He writes regularly for *Field & Stream*. (Editor's note: Heavey not only writes for *Field & Stream*, he has deservedly stepped into Ed Zern's waders.)

Ken Jacobsen is a hunter activist with a long history of outdoor and wildlife related advocacy: five years President of the Seattle Chapter of Ducks Unlimited, First Vice President of the American Brittany Club, Founder of the Hemingway Chapter of Trout Unlimited, and a lifetime member of NRA. He also actively supports Safari Club International, FNAWS, REMF, and the TRCP. Jacobsen is an artist, sculptor, nationally recognized field trail judge, camp cook, inventor, and marketing consultant.

Dan Jenkins is the author of *Semi-Tough, Dead Solid Perfect, Baja Oklahoma, Life Its Ownself, Fast Copy,* and *The Dogged Victims of Inexorable Fate.* He was a senior editor for *Sports Illustrated* for better than two decades and has written a monthly sports column for *Playboy,* essays for *Golf Digest,* and a general interest syndicated newspaper column.

Doug Larsen is the author of two best-selling waterfowling books, *Don't Shoot the Decoys* and *The Duck Gods Must Be Crazy,* both products of hunting for waterfowl and funny stories for over three decades. His work has appeared in *Ducks Unlimited, Shooting Sportsman, Sporting Classics,* and a number of other popular magazines. He currently lives in western Pennsylvania with his wife, Katie, three children, and a young Labrador.

Lawrence Lariar, a prolific writer, was perhaps best known for his novels but was a student of cartooning, with collections: *Best Cartoons of the Year 1943, Cartooning for Everybody,* and *You've Got Me In Stitches: A New Collection of the Funniest Cartoons of All Time about Doctors, Patients, and Hospitals.*

Tom Lehrer staked out his position as one of the best musical satirists in the 1960s with his infamous "The Vatican Rag," "Smut," and his ode to spring pursuits, "Poisoning Pigeons in the Park." His nuclear holocaust anthem "We Will All Go Down Together When We Go" and "Pollution" set a high standard for political satire. After his big hit, the 1965 album *That Was the Year That Was,* Lehrer returned to a quiet academic life—a rare performer who didn't have the need for a fawning audience to shore up self-esteem. A three-CD box set of his collected works, *The Remains of Tom Lehrer,* is now available from Rhino Records.

Franz Lidz is a *Sports Illustrated* senior writer (who doesn't particularly like sports), a *Golf Connoisseur* contributing editor (who doesn't play golf), a *The New York Times* TV essayist (who lacks a TV), and author of *Ghostly Men: The Strange but True Story of the Collyer Brothers* and *Unstrung Heroes: My Improbable Life with Four Impossible Uncles,* which was made into a 1995 Disney feature film. Lidz has been a commentator for Morning Edition on National Public Radio and a reporter for *ABC Wild World of Sports*. His humorous writings have appeared in more than two dozen anthologies. He once appeared on David Letterman's show with his pet parrots Peter Rabbit and Mrs. Falbo, unsettling the host with the observation: "Peter speaks 16 bird dialects, including loon. He's learning Waring Blender, but I can't let him get too close to ours. He thinks it's a Jacuzzi."

Alan Liere is an award-winning humorist and columnist for *Wildfowl, Upland Almanac*, and three (northwest, southwest, and eastern) flyfishing magazines; he also writes a weekly newspaper column for the *Deer Park Tribune* and *Spokane Review*. He has a BA in Education and a MFA in non-fiction writing. Between voluntary skirmishes with his word processor and hostile engagements with assorted other hateful mechanical devices, he hunts, fishes, and attempts to find a bird dog that will treat him with respect. Liere has retired from academia after 30 years of flirting with early senility and bladder failure as an English teacher in the Mead School District near Spokane, Washington. His collections of wit include *Bear Heads and Fish Tales* (1988) *...and pandemonium rained* (1996), and *Dancing' With Shirley* (1998), which can be ordered via alanliere@yahoo.com

Nick Lyons is the author of more than four hundred essays and twenty books. For twenty-five years he wrote the famous and beloved "Seasonable Angler" column for *Fly Fisherman* magazine. Born in 1932, Lyons was a faculty member at Hunter College of the City University of New York from 1961–1968, where he became a professor of English. From 1964-1974, Lyons was executive editor at Crown Publishers in New York and was founder and president of Nick Lyons Books (now Lyons Press, a Globe Pequot Press imprint) from 1978 to 1999. Nick not only was and is of good humor, more importantly, he took risks in publishing a wide variety of outdoor humor.

J. Angus McLean is a wildlife illustrator living on a hilltop outside Vernonia, Oregon, expanding and refreshing the traditions of sporting art. His silk screen clients include Fred Meyer, Wal-Mart, GI Joe's, Made in Oregon, PAC 10 colleges, Olympia Beer, Jansport, and others. Leanin' Tree, the greeting card company, acquired his comic oil "Splashdown" for greeting cards and McLean's fishing bears, bugling elk, and mallard ducks are marketed on apparel internationally. "Sourdough" McLean has illustrated all of Buck Peterson's books and the logger bar they call "the office" is under surveillance. Contrary to the view of junior art directors, McLean maintains there are no stinking puffins on the Oregon Coast.

Wayne McLoughlin was born in Wales in 1944. His interest in nature began as a young explorer of Hampstead Heath, London, and later, of the swamps of Northern Florida where he collected water moccasins, turtles, and lizards for local schools. His interest in art began simultaneously, and he often recorded his hunting and fishing experiences in sketches and paintings. His career creating illustrated humor parodies for national magazines, including *Esquire, Omni, Next, Yankee,* and *National Lampoon* was in addition to creating commissioned award-winning project and campaign pieces for major corporations like Citibank, Ford Motor Company, IBM, Motorola, and Master Card. An experienced outdoorsman, McLoughlin served as a regular contributor to outdoor magazines like *Sports Afield* for over 20 years, and more recently, to *Sporting Tales.* He has been a contributing editor to *Field & Stream* for over a decade, where he explores the humorous side of the sportsman's life in prose and pictures. He continues to produce fine paintings; visit www.blueloonfinearts.com.

Roy McKie teamed as illustrator with Henry Beard on a number of very successful books including *Sailing: A Sailor's Dictionary* and *Computers: A Hacker's Dictionary.*

Patrick F. McManus was born in northwest Idaho in 1933. At Washington State University, the school literary magazine published his first piece of fiction "The Lady Who Kept Things." In 1968, he wrote his first humor piece that was immediately picked up by *Field & Stream;* he was a columnist and associate editor of that magazine from 1976–1981. A distinguished academic career led to a professor of journalism and English position at Eastern Washington University from 1974–1983. Pat has ruled the humor roost on the back pages of *Outdoor Life* with his "Last Laugh" column from 1981 on. His columns have been collected in best-selling books, his rascally characters have been seen on stage, and his books have been popular choices in many book clubs. Pat's e-home address is www.mcmanusbooks.com.

John Meacham has been a hunter and fisherman for most of his 57 years. He grew up pursuing rabbits, squirrels, and pheasants, and angling for bluegills, catfish, carp, and bass in Central Illinois. After earning a degree in journalism from Southern Illinois University, he worked as a reporter, photographer, and editor on newspapers in Illinois, Missouri, North Carolina, and Tennessee. Meecham's first outdoor related humor story, about Dub "Lordnose" Nelson's mounted frog-gigging misadventure, was published in *Southern Illinois Outdoors* in 1990. Meacham later became editor of that magazine after it became *River Country Outdoors.* He is a regular columnist for *Adventure Sports Outdoors* and his stories and articles have also appeared in *Buckmaster's*

Whitetail, Buckmaster's Beards & Spurs, Petersen's Bowhunting, Petersen's Hunting, Turkey Call, and the Illinois and Missouri Game and Fish magazines. Meacham in the author of *Honey, He Shrunk My Head! And other Tall Huntin' and Fishin' Tales*, a collection of 21 stories. To order, send $16.50 to Lordnose Publishing, 4353 Chester Road, Chester, IL 62233, or visit www.chesterillinois.com/shrunk.htm.

Henry Miller is the outdoor writer at the *Statesman Journal*, a daily newspaper in Salem, Oregon. He best describes himself as old enough to know better, but still young enough to think he can get away with it. Miller was born in Missouri and raised in the earthy frontier hamlet of Santa Barbara, California, a resort town best described as being "for the newlywed and the nearly dead." Miller cut his outdoor teeth at the *Goleta Valley News*, most often described by readers as "publishing weakly," spent eight years cursing the heat at the *Shasta Sportsman* and *Redding Record Searchlight*, then moved to the more amenable climes of Salem, where he's earned a solid reputation among some of his friends as being "so twisted that he has to wear orthopedic hats."

Henry Morgan has been described "as a radio and TV personality possessed of an excruciatingly sarcastic wit." Born in New York City in 1915, died there in 1994, Morgan is best remembered as a panelist on *To Tell the Truth, I've Got A Secret, The Naked Mind* and was a popular guest on variety shows like *The Merv Griffin Show*.

Charles W. Morton (1899–1967) was a journalist, author, and editor, and wrote articles for several East Coast newspapers and magazines after 1928, including the *New Yorker*. Morton served in an editorial capacity for the *Atlantic Monthly* from 1941 to 1966 and was author or co-author of six books. His books include *A Slight Sense of Outrage; It has Its Charms, How to Protect Yourself against Women—And other Vicissitudes* and *Frankly George: A Letter to a Publisher from an Author whose First Book is About to Appear.*

Steven Mulak has been making up stories and selling them to magazines for thirty years, and they haven't caught on yet. He put in a career as a marine engineer, and since then has painted a few pictures, written some books, and managed to cash the checks before people found out about him. He has a house, a wife, two grown daughters, and a kennel full of bird dogs. At 57, he often wonders how it all happened, since he wasn't paying attention at the time. His parents are still waiting for him to get serious and do something useful with his life.

Bruce Nash "one of the barons of reality television" authored 80 books, 60 of them with former partner, Allan Zullo. Sports titles dominated, including a "Hall of Shame" series that catalogued funny and silly moments in baseball, football, and more.

Ted Nugent was born in Detroit in 1948, "middle finger first." The "Nuge" began bowhunting in 1953 and guitar playing in 1956; he recorded 29 albums from 1967–1997, selling over 30 million worldwide. Nugent is considered to be the number one guitar showman in the world. In addition to hosting a very popular morning show at WWWBR, Detroit, Nugent is editor/publisher of *Ted Nugent Adventure Outdoors* magazine, and an aggressive campaigner promoting individualism through outdoor sports and conservation to the youth of America. He has been honored on the floor of the U.S. Senate, in the Congressional Record and by many conservation, law enforcement, and sportsman groups. His dedication to and enthusiasm for the youth of America is easily demonstrated in his Kamp for Kids. His books (*God, Guns & Rock & Roll; Kill It & Grill It—A Guide to Preparing and Cooking Wild Game, Fish; Blood Trails: The Truth about Bowhunting*; and others) are best sellers. Visit Ted on line at www.tednugent.com

Patrick Jake (P.J.) O'Rourke has established himself as one of America's premier political satirists. His best-selling books include *Parliament of Whores, Give War A Chance, Eat the Rich* and *The CEO of the Sofa* have generated descriptions from both *Time* and the *Wall Street Journal* as "the funniest writer in America." P.J. was born in Toledo, Ohio, to a car salesman and a former tap and acrobatic dancer. He began life as a Republican, but in the late 1960s, he changed his politics to conform with the nation's youth. "At least, I was never a liberal. I went from Republican to Communist and right back to Republican." In the early 1970s P.J. joined the *National Lampoon* where he became editor-in-chief and created, with Doug Kenney, the now classic 1964 High School Yearbook Parody. In the 1980s, he decided the real world was funnier outside the magazine so he became a roving reporter covering crises and conflicts around the world. P. J. is known as a hard-bitten, cigar-smoking conservative yet bashes all political persuasions. As he says, "Giving money and power to government is like giving whiskey and car keys to teenage boys."

Jack Ohman is the award-winning political cartoonist of the *Oregonian* and one of the most widely syndicated cartoonists in the country. He has earned a number of professional awards, including the Overseas Press Club Award and the National Headliners Award from the Press Club of Maryland. Ohman is also the creator of the syndicated comic strip *Mixed Media*. He lives in Portland with his wife Dunham, a public relations executive, and their three children.

Buck Peterson makes his permanent home in Buck's Wilderness Lodge and Advanced Plucking Institute in Northernmost Minnesota (e-reservations at www.buckpeterson.com). For those driving, the lodge sits on Big Babe Lake, a much better walleye spearing lake than Lake Wobegon. His hunting, fishing, and roadkill cooking guidebooks and his Christmas CD quacked by Buck's Ducks are classics in the field. He is currently on assignment in the Pacific Northwest, scouring the shorelines for beached and/or harpooned gray whales on behalf of several well-known cat food manufacturers.

Lisa Price is a native of Schuylkill County, Pennsylvania. She enjoys writing about the humor of hunting failures, partly because her hunting success stories are a rarity. She lives with her three dogs, Sara, Alabama (rescued from the side of the road during a hunting trip to, where else, Alabama), and Josey Wales. She is a columnist for *Bow & Arrow Hunting* magazine.

Dr. Paul Quinnnett is a clinical psychologist and the president and CEO of the QPR Institute, an educational organization dedicated to preventing suicide. Author of seven books and an award-winning journalist, he is also Clinical Assistant Professor in the Department of Psychiatry and Behavioral Science at the University of Washington School of Medicine in Seattle and the past editor-in-chief of *Preventing Suicide: The National Journal*. Over 1,000 stories, articles, columns, and essays by Quinnett have appeared in *Sports Afield, The New York Times, Newsweek, Fly Rod and Reel*, among dozens of others. He is currently the fishing columnist for *Sporting Classics Magazine*. He has authored seven books for professional and lay readers, including the classic fishing trilogy, *Pavlov's Trout, Darwin's Bass*, and *Fishing Lessons*, the first books published on the psychology and philosophy of fishing in 300 years and now translated into Japanese, Chinese, and Korean. Paul is an avid angler, training consultant, and keynote speaker.

John W. Randolph was born in Crowley, Louisiana, the eldest son of a small newspaper publisher. He was an itinerant newspaperman, working on city dailies from Chicago to Baltimore to Washington, DC and New York City. His last 17 years were spent as copy editor and photo editor at *The New York Times;* he was named outdoor editor for the paper in 1956, to follow Roy Camp in that capacity. He died in 1961 of lung cancer. Personal observations from his son and daughter: "He was known as Jack Randolph by his friends and grew up in the country, which he loved, but spent his life working in the city, escaping to the country every weekend to hunt, fish, and party with family and friends. After he became a columnist, writing humor, he observed that his bosses had 'finally found something I could do.' He ate dessert before dinner; loathed pretense; loved a few operas, especially Rigolleto, could not balance a checkbook (and never tried); and suspected there was something under the hood of a car that made it run.

He once observed to a friend who bought a new home with a large lawn that 'there's too much lawn for one woman to mow.' He left the U. of Alabama after a year and a half having 'failed to learn how to shoot a good stick of pool.' He loved the game of poker but usually lost, good hunting dogs, proudly considered himself a duffer in the outdoors (it took 17 years of deer hunting before he shot one, he claimed, by mistake). He was amused by tackle and gear junkies but despised television pitchmen, referring to them as 'jolly boys.' His socks seldom matched though he did not know it. He was absent minded and lost things: if you gave him a hat, he'd leave it on a train the next day communing to work. He liked the bourbon drink 'old fashioneds,' smoking cigarettes, and was loved by all who knew him." His self-deprecating humor stands the test of time.

George Reiger is conservation editor emeritus of *Field & Stream* and active-duty conservation editor of *Salt Water Sportsman*. When he's not writing about conservation, he's teaching or lecturing about it, and has done so at universities as far-flung as Utah State, Mississippi State, Yale, and St. Francis Xaviar in Antigonish, Nova Scotia. Reiger's so mission-oriented, even his humor writing has subliminal conservation messages.

Mike Sawyers has been the outdoor editor of the *Cumberland (Maryland) Times-News* since 1979. His columns about hunting and fishing have won numerous awards from regional press associations as well as the Associated Press. Since 1971, his articles have appeared in most national hook and bullet publications, including *Sports Afield, Outdoor Life, American Hunter*, and *Petersen's Hunting*. He has been a regional editor for *Buckmaster* and *Outdoor Life*. A West Virginia native, Sawyers has degrees in fishery biology and journalism from Utah State University. Though he has had hundreds of how-to and where-to articles published, his favorite works are those that deal with life as it unfolds in the realm of the outdoors. Sawyers and his wife, Sandy, live in Rawlings, MD. They have three adult sons. Sawyer's book *Native Queen* can be purchased postpaid by sending $13 to him at P.O. Box 326, Rawlings, MD 2155

Jean Shepherd is perhaps best known as a radio personality yet his career included success in theater, film, and television. His radio program on New York's WOR-AM ran for twenty years. From 1958 to 1979, Shepherd built a huge following with his witty, unrehearsed stories about growing up in the Midwest. His book, *A Christmas Story*, Shepherd's own recollections of living with an oddball father, schoolyard bullies, and a Red Ryder BB gun in a Midwestern town, was released as a film, with his own voice over, in 1983. Shepherd, some speculated, was the prototype of the newscaster in the 1976 film *Network*. He died in 1999.

Max Shulman was a screenwriter, book, and play author, notable for creating the pop character, Dobie Gillis, who appeared in a popular 1950s TV sitcom and on the large screen. Other novels of Shulman's that went to screen include *The Tourist Trap* (1955) and *Rally Around the Flag Boys* (1958).

Walter W. (Red) Smith was born in Wisconsin and is a graduate of Notre Dame. His first job was with the *Milwaukee Sentinel*. In 1928 he went to the *St. Louis Star,* working at the copy desk and going on to writing about sports. In 1936 he went to the *Philadelphia Record,* writing a regular sports column, and in 1945 began his career with the *New York Herald Tribune*. Red Smith is an angler's writer, par excellence.

Jim Snook is a cartoonist living in Klamath Falls, Oregon. Jim has built his fan base the hard way—by carrying his mobile art gallery to state and county fairs, signing individual illustrations and self-published collections and calendars for an ever-expanding universe of fans. Jim's sporting interests are wide yet his images of hunters and fishermen are so informed that you know he's been there, done that. Enter his world at www.jimsnookstudio.com.

Russell Thornberry spent 18 years in Alberta, Canada, as a big game guide and outfitter for trophy whitetail deer, black bear, moose, and elk hunting. As he gained prominence for producing giant Alberta whitetails for his clients, he was also contributing to virtually every noteworthy hunting magazine in North America. Thornberry's books on outdoor topics include *Trophy Deer of Alberta; The Art and Science of Rattling Whitetail Deer; Bucks, Bulls, and Belly Laughs; Hunting the Canadian Giants; Buckmasters Whitetail Trophy Records*; and most currently, *Trophies of the Heart*. For the past 19 years, he has served as vice president and editor-in-chief of *Buckmaster's Whitetail Magazine*. Russell is an ordained minister and makes his home in Montgomery, Alabama, with his wife of 36 years, Sharleen.

Rich Tosches has spent more than 25 years as a journalist, including ten years as a staff writer for the *Los Angeles Times*. Prior to that, he was the West Coast sports editor for United Press International. He has covered the World Series, Super Bowls, and was also the national boxing writer for UPI, once being beaten senseless in the ring by then world middleweight champion Michael Nunn during a foolish George Plimpton-type adventure. Tosches was the humor columnist for the *Colorado Springs Gazette* for 10 years. He has been nominated twice for the Pulitzer Prize. In 2005, Tosches became the Western states roving reporter for the *Denver Post*, writing articles under the banner of the Rocky Mountain ranger. In addition to his book *Zipping My Fly*, he contributes a humor column to *Field & Stream*. Tosches has five children and lives in Colorado with his wife, Susie.

John Troy has been described as one of America's most gifted outdoor humorists. His latest cartoon collections include "Lunkers!" and "You Should Have Been Here Yesterday." His cartoon hunting retriever, Ben, is the Garfield of the sporting field and the Ben cartoon collections are classics.

James Thurber was one of the world's greatest humorists. Perhaps most famous for his classic story, "The Secret Life of Walter Mitty," Thurber was one of the mainstays of the *New Yorker* magazine where his short stories and essays were published for over 30 years. Self-described as "a wild-eyed son-of-a-bitch with a glass in his hand," Thurber's cartoons and illustrations were a parallel career. Thurber's first book was a team effort with E.B. White, a spoof of the sex manual genre entitled *Is Sex Necessary?* His collections include *The Owl in the Attic and Other Perplexities*; *My Life and Hard Times*; *The Middle-Aged Man on the Flying Trapeze*; and *My World—Welcome To It*. In his *Fables for Our Times*, a collection of Aesop parodies, Little Red Riding Hood shoots the wolf with a pistol, which is now a felony in Yellowstone Park. Thurber died in 1961. His good humor lives on.

Gene Trump is a part-time outdoor writer, photographer, and cartoonist making his living with his wife, Virginia, in Corvallis, Oregon. His award-winning humor articles and cartoons have appeared in *Fly Fisherman, Salmon Trout Steel Header, Northwest Flyfishing, Southwest Flyfishing, Field & Stream*, and other worldwide publications and websites.

Harold Umber starting working in the official magazine of North Dakota Game and Fish Department in 1979 and became editor of *North Dakota Outdoors Magazine* in 1986. Umber not only wrote for the magazine, his fine nature photography was used throughout the department, in books and related subject magazines. Umber retired from the magazine in 2003, which was real handy since he has a new bird dog.

Sam Venable is a humor columnist for the *Knoxville News Sentinel*. He assumed that position in 1985 after serving as the newspaper outdoor editor for 15 years. A native of Knoxville, Venable is a graduate of the University of Tennessee with a B.S. (the perfect collegiate degree for a newspaper columnist, he claims) in journalism and minor studies in forestry and wildlife management. Prior to joining the staff of the *News Sentinel*, he worked as a police reporter and feature writer for the

Knoxville Journal and the *Chattanooga Free Press*. Winner of more than three-dozen writing awards, Venable has been widely published outside the newspaper field. He sold his first magazine article as a senior in college and since has compiled more than 150 periodicals credits to his record. He also is the author of nine books: *An Island Unto Itself, A Handful of Thumbs and Two Left Feet, Two or Three Degrees off Plumb, One Size Fits All and Other Holiday Myths, I'd Rather Be Ugly Than Stupid, From Ridge Tops to River Bottoms: A Celebration of the Outdoor Life in Tennessee, Mountain Lands: A Portrait of Southern Appalachia, Rock-Elephant: A Story of Friendship and Fishing,* and *You Gotta Laugh to Keep from Crying: A Baby Boomer Contemplates Life Beyond Fifty.*

Charles F. Waterman has justifiably been called the dean of outdoor writers and was one of the first humorists to go afield. Not only did you know there was a gentleman behind the pen, but with the greatest of ease, employed all the sleights of hand of the humor trade. Charlie's casual asides and knowing quips shine with genuine warmth not often found in contemporary humor. Charlie passed away early in 2005 at age 92. Get to know this fine writer in his books. You can't go wrong with *Field Days: Irrepressible Tales of Fly Fishing, Wingshooting, and the Great Outdoors; Gun Dogs and Bird Guns;* and *A Charley Waterman Reader.*

Fred Webb was born in 1935 during the middle of the Great Depression to a family that made its living in the woods. By the time Fred started school in 1940, his dad had already been overseas for a year in the Canadian Army. At the time it was nothing out of the ordinary for boys of six or seven years old to be handling knives, guns, traps, and axes, all tools of the trade for making a living in the woods. Fred left school in the early 1950s and began a career guiding, cutting logs, and driving a truck. After a couple of years, he joined the Army, got married, and started a family—all this four years before he could vote or legally enter a beer joint. After the stint in the army, Fred eventually opened his own outfitting business. Since 1967, he has been a full-time guide and self-employed professional hunter, working with thousands of sports hunters and fishermen in New Brunswick, Newfoundland, Labrador, Quebec, and the Northwest Territories. Today he continues to run hunts in the NWT with his son and partner, Martin. Fred's books, *Home from the Hill* and *Campfire Lies of a Canadian Hunting Guide,* are available at www.safaripress.com.

Gene and Barry Wensel are double trouble bow-hunting twins from rural Iowa. Acknowledged by many to be the best whitetail deer hunters with a bow in the U.S., Gene and Barry have hunted with recurves and longbows for almost 50 years. As noted on their website, www.brothersofthebow.com, the Wensel brothers hunted deer with bows and arrows before non-military camo, compound bows, GPS units, and cell phones. Back then, muzzleloaders used round balls and loose black powder, and didn't have scopes. Gene's books, *Hunting Rutting Whitetails, One Man's Whitetail,* and *Come November,* and their videos, *Bowhunting October White-tails I & II* and *High Noon Bucks,* are classics in the field.

Bob Zahn is a noted sports cartoonist. His books include *Golfaholics, Love and Marriage and Divorce, The Difference between Cats and Dogs,* and *Sex is a Game.*

Don Zahner founded *Fly Fisherman* magazine in 1969, with its inaugural issue coming off the press in May of that year. The concept for *Fly Fisherman* was first introduced to an elite faction of the fly-fishing mafia—including Phil Wright, Ernie Schweibert, and Andy Puyans—in the back of a van on the banks of Montana's Madison River, where Zahner was egged on to disclose his flight of fancy by the van's other occupants, Jim Beam and Jack Daniels. In that blur, the mafia saw its new don. At once a celebration and demystification of a seemingly elite and distant sport, Zahner created in *Fly Fisherman* magazine a perfect balance of new equipment, instruction, destinations, and lore, what Schiebert called, "why we fish." The "idea whose time had come" found its champion and Zahner's unique view of the piscatorial world was on display in each issue's "Anglish Spoken Here" column. Zahner sold his successful magazine in 1978.

Ed Zern was born in West Virginia, caught his first trout there at the age of five, graduated from Penn State in 1932 without honors, went to Paris to write a novel (but got distracted), spent a year as a merchant seaman, got a job as a writer with a Philadelphia ad agency (1934–1943), and became vice president and director of a New York agency until 1965, when he escaped to devote himself full time to fishing, hunting, and writing. He's managed to hunt and/or fish in 34 countries on four continents, in 37 U.S. states and eight Canadian provinces. He sold his first story to *Field & Stream* in 1937, began writing his famous "Exit Laughing" column in 1958, and was fishing editor of that magazine from 1975 to 1982 (when, he says, cooler heads prevailed). Ed's varied career includes being past president of Theodore Gordon Flyfishers, the African Safari Club of New York, the Westchester Retriever Field Trial Club, the Advertising Sportsmen's Club of New York, director of the Atlantic Salmon Federation and the American Museum of Fly Fishing, a Fellow of the Explorers Club, a member of the Boone and Crockett Club, the Axolotl Society, and various conservation organizations. Ed passed away in 1994.